Items should be returned on or before the last date
shown below. Items not already requested by other
borrowers may be renewed in person, in writing or by
telephone. To renew, please quote the number on the
barcode label. To renew on line a PIN is required.
This can be requested at your local library.
Renew online @ www.dublincitypubliclibraries.ie
Fines charged for overdue items will include postage
incurred in recovery. Damage to or loss of items will be
charged to the borrower.

of historical
g historical
e period in
esar and on
ding of the
ertfordshire

The Falcon of Sparta

CONN IGGULDEN

MICHAEL JOSEPH
an imprint of
PENGUIN BOOKS

MICHAEL JOSEPH

UK | USA | Canada | Ireland | Australia
India | New Zealand | South Africa

Michael Joseph is part of the Penguin Random House group of companies
whose addresses can be found at global.penguinrandomhouse.com.

First published 2018
001

Copyright © Conn Iggulden, 2018

The moral right of the author has been asserted

Hardback back endpaper © Peter Horree/Alamy Stock Photo

Set in 13.5/16 pt Garamond MT Std
Typeset by Jouve (UK), Milton Keynes
Printed in Great Britain by Clays Ltd, St Ives plc

A CIP catalogue record for this book is available from the British Library

HARDBACK ISBN: 978–0–718–18146–8
OM PAPERBACK ISBN: 978–0–718–18147–5

To my son Cameron,
who came with me to Sparta.

In 401 BC, the Persian king ruled an empire from the Aegean to northern India. As many as fifty million people were his subjects – and his armies were vast.

Working together on land and sea, only Sparta and Athens ever turned them back.

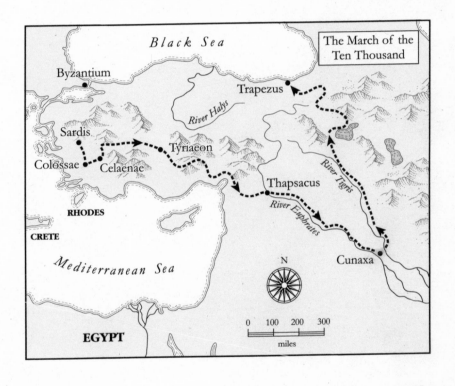

Prologue

In Babylon, starlings gaped in the heat, showing dark tongues. Beyond vast city walls, the sun leaned on those who laboured in the fields, pressing them down.

As he walked in the middle of the road, the Great King bore a sheen on his skin, of oil or sweat his son could not have said. His father's beard gleamed in tight black curls, as much a part of him as the odour of roses, or the long pan-elled coat he wore.

The air smelled of hot stone and cypress trees, like spear-heads against the sky. The streets all around had been emptied of those who lived there. Not a child, not an old woman, not a chicken had been left to scratch the earth as the imperial soldiers had cleared a way for the king to walk. The silence lay so heavy, the boy could hear birdsong.

The street of Ningal had been laid with soft palm branches, thick underfoot and still green. No foul odours would inter-rupt their conversation or distract the older man from this moment of instruction. His purpose was the very survival of his house, and he had allowed neither courtesans nor spies to stand close enough to hear. His captains thought it was a royal whim that had sent them out to clear the districts on either side, long before the sun rose that morning. The truth was that some words could not be overheard. The king knew there were many listeners in his court. There were just too many small satraps, too many kingdoms whose crowns he had crushed beneath his sandals. Ninety rulers paid their spies to listen, while a thousand courtiers jostled

I

for position. The simple pleasure of walking alone with his son, as any shepherd might have done, had become a luxury as great as rubies, as valuable as the thick gold coins they called 'archers' that bore the likeness of King Darius across the empire.

As they walked, the little boy stole sideways glances at his father, adoring and trusting him in all things. Young Artaxerxes matched his gait to the king's, though it meant he had to add half a pace every once in a while, skipping to keep up. Darius appeared not to notice, though Artaxerxes knew his father missed very little of anything. The secret of his long reign lay in his wisdom. If the little boy's opinion had ever been sought, he would have said his father had never been wrong.

On court days, the king sat in judgement on his most powerful lords, on men whose armies ran to tens of thousands, who ruled lands of jade and ivory about as far off as the moon. Darius would listen and run a hand down his beard, picking up a shine on his fingers. He would rub thumb and forefinger together, or take a grape from a golden bowl held by a slave kneeling at his feet. In such a way, Darius saw through to the heart of a problem while his advisers were still weighing and arguing. Artaxerxes wanted that extraordinary insight, so he listened, and learned well.

The city was as still as only thousands of soldiers holding knives to throats could make it still. The king's generals knew his wrath would fall on their heads if they disturbed him – and so father and son walked as if they were the only two alive in the world, with dust and warmth and the sun setting, bringing them ease after the heat of the day.

'Babylon was the heart of an empire once, a great one,' King Darius said. His voice was gentle, more that of a teacher than a warrior.

His son looked up, his eyes bright.

'Though Persia is greater,' Artaxerxes said.

His father smiled at his pride.

'Of course! In all ways. Persia is a dozen times larger than old Babylon's ambitions. The borders of my empire cannot be walked in a lifetime – or two, three. Yet it was not given to me, boy. When my father was killed, the crown fell to my brother. He took it before the tears had dried on his face – and ruled for just a month before he was murdered.'

'And you took vengeance on the one who killed him,' Artaxerxes said, wanting to please.

The king stopped and turned his face to the sun, closing his eyes the better to see the memories.

'I did. As the sun rose that day, there were three of us, three brothers. That evening, I was alone. I was spattered in blood – but I was king.'

Darius filled his chest, making the panels of his coat creak over the fine silks beneath. His son straightened in conscious mimicry. Artaxerxes did not know why his father had called him to his side that day, nor why even the famous Immortal guards were out of sight. His father trusted no one, so it was said, yet he walked alone with his oldest son and heir. At fourteen years of age, it made Artaxerxes light with pride and happiness.

'A king needs more than one son,' his father went on. 'Death comes all too quickly, as a desert wind can rise without warning. It can reach out as a horse stumbles or a knife slips. It can come from poison or treachery, from spoiled meat, from fevers and djinns of the air. In such a world, a king with just one son is a challenge to the gods, as well as all his enemies.'

Darius walked on, clasping his hands behind his back and making the boy scramble to keep up. As Artaxerxes drew abreast, his father continued.

'Yet if that first son, that most beloved boy, survives to become a man, a different game begins. If he has brothers then, so vital in the years gone by, they are the only ones in the world who can take it all from him.'

'Cyrus?' Artaxerxes said suddenly. Despite his caution, despite his awe for his father, the idea that his little brother could ever be his enemy made his eyes sparkle in amusement. 'Father, Cyrus would never hurt me.'

His father spun on the spot. The panels of his coat rose like the carapace of a beetle about to fly.

'You are my son and my heir. If you are taken, Cyrus will be king. That is his . . . purpose.' The king went down onto one knee and clasped the boy's hands in his. 'You will wear my crown, I promise you. But Cyrus . . . is a born warrior. He is only thirteen, but he rides as well as my own guard. You have seen how they look to him? Only last month, they carried him round the palace yard on their shoulders when he shot a bird in flight with his bow.' The king took a deep breath, wanting Artaxerxes to understand. 'My son, I love you both, but when I am on my last bed, when the empire is hushed and in mourning, on that final day, I will call him home – and you will have to kill him. Because if you leave him alive after that, he will surely kill you.'

Artaxerxes saw tears come into his father's eyes, sparkling there. It was the first time he had ever seen such a display of emotion, and it shook him.

'I think you are mistaken, Father, but I will remember what you have said.'

The king rose to his feet, his coat creaking. He had grown flushed, though whether it was anger or some other emotion was hard to say.

'Then remember this as well,' he snapped. 'If you say one word of this to Cyrus, anything at all of what I have gone to

4

such lengths to keep private, you will be cutting your own throat. Not today or this year, of course, while you laugh and play together. He will promise you his loyalty and I do not doubt he will mean it with all his heart. Then a day will come when you fall out, or when he sees he will never have the authority he wants, not as a mere prince. On that day, he will come to you and take the throne for himself. And if I am alive on that day, if he comes to me after, even if he has your blood on his hands . . . even then, I will have no other son and so I will embrace him. Do you understand, Artaxerxes?'

'I do,' his son said, his own anger swelling. 'Yet if you admire him so much, Father, why not just kill me here in the road and let Cyrus take the throne?' Before his father could reply, Artaxerxes went on: 'Because you have no other sons and you would risk the succession. You are truly so cold? It does not matter to you which of us is king?'

'If it did not matter to me, I would not have cleared half a city to walk in private with you. Do you see Cyrus here? You were the child we longed for, my brave boy. I do not doubt your intelligence, your wisdom, Artaxerxes. You have my blood in you and you will make a great king.'

Darius reached out and touched his son's cheek.

'I saw my father broken when he came home from Greece. King Xerxes had beaten the Spartans at Thermopylae, but then his armies were routed at Plataea. Just as his father's had been cut to pieces at Marathon ten years before. Well, no more! I vowed it when I became king. We have left enough of our blood in Greece, enough for a thousand years. Instead of war, my reign preserved peace – and brought us gardens and wine and gold and extraordinary learning. There are things made common today that would be sorcery in any other age. With you, we will go further – the greatest empire the world has ever known. If it is you. If the gods put Cyrus on that throne, he will wage war once again, I do not doubt. He is too much my father, too much *his* father.'

'I can fight, you know,' Artaxerxes said, stung. 'I know you don't think of me in that way, but I can.'

The king laughed and clapped him on the back. He loved his son too much to hurt him by disagreeing.

'Of course. Though any moneylender's guard can fight. You are a prince, Artaxerxes! You will be a king. So you need more than a quick smile and quicker sword. You need strength of a different kind. Beginning today. You are not too young for this.'

The king looked around them at the empty street. Not a face peered from a single window.

'Remember. On the day you are king, you must make an end. Until then, learn from your tutors, ride horses, enjoy the pleasures of women, boys and red wine. Do not speak of this day to anyone. Do you understand me?'

'I do, Father,' Artaxerxes said.

His serious face made the king smile, his entire bearing changing, so that he reached out and ruffled the hair of his son.

'I am a thousand times blessed.'

PART ONE

I

The mountain cradled the city like a mother with a child in her lap. Before climbing the steps to the great plateau, Cyrus decided to lead his personal guard to the river. The Spartans left their armour and weapons on the bank and charged into the water, gleefully washing away the dust and sweat of four hundred miles.

From the height of his warhorse, the prince smiled to see them splashing and running fingers through their hair and beards. The march east had made his men lean, like hunting dogs, darkening their skin and pulling taut the cords of their muscles. They had not faltered, though some of them had left prints of blood on the road.

'My lord, will you not change your mind?' Tissaphernes said softly.

Cyrus glanced over at his old friend and tutor. Tissaphernes sat a chestnut gelding that snorted and tossed its head, of a bloodline as fine as any in Persia. The nobleman kept his gaze on the Spartans, his expression sour.

'Should I climb the steps alone?' Cyrus replied. 'Should I come home like a beggar? Who am I, if not my father's son and a prince? These are my guards. They are the best.'

Tissaphernes worked his mouth as if a tooth bothered him. Prince Cyrus was in his twenties and no longer young and foolish. The tutor had made his reservations clear, and yet there they were on the banks of the river Pulvar, with men of Sparta washing like horses in the water, throwing up spray. The prince had brought an old enemy to the very eye of Persia. Tissaphernes frowned at the thought. He had seen Greek maps of the world that knew little of the great empire of the east. He had no desire to help Spartans fill in the location of Persepolis, still less the royal tombs along the river, just half a day's march away.

'Some might see it as an insult, Highness, to bring the very men who faced your ancestors, who denied them on land and sea. Spartans! By the deva spirits. Here, in the heart of the world! If your father was a younger man and well . . .'

'He would congratulate me, Tissaphernes,' Cyrus snapped, wearying of his voice. 'These men have run at my side. They did not falter or ask for rest. They are loyal to me.'

'They are loyal to gold and silver,' Tissaphernes muttered under his breath.

Cyrus clenched his jaw, so that the muscles stood out.

'They own nothing. Even their weapons come down from the hands of their fathers and uncles, or are given to them for acts of valour. Enough of this. No more now, old lion.'

Tissaphernes accepted the rebuke, bowing his head.

The Greeks had been brisk at their ablutions, coming out quickly to stand on the banks and dry in the evening sun. Local washerwomen hooted and called at the sight of so many naked men. One or two of the warriors smiled in return, while others loosened up with exercises. They were not made for laughter or light talk.

Irritated with his companion, Cyrus suddenly dismounted, stripping off his helmet, his tunic and armoured coat, his leggings and cloak, then removing his sandals, all with neat economy of movement. The prince was untroubled by nudity and strolled into the water with just a nod to the Spartan officer, Anaxis, who watched from the bank.

The washerwomen ceased their calls at the sight of a young man who wore his beard curled like a Persian and left a helmet marked with feathers of gold on his cloak. They may not have known his name, but they did not dare call out to him. Cyrus washed himself in the waters with slow care, almost as a ritual, a cleansing of more than sweat and the smell of horses. The Spartans on the bank were silent, showing respect. The prince had come home to mourn his father, after all.

The message had reached Cyrus fourteen days before and he had pushed the Spartans almost beyond endurance to be there in time. The prince had changed horses at crown taverns on the great Royal Road, or cut across country through tilled fields of wheat and barley, yet they had kept pace, loping along at his side day after day, as if it was nothing. They were extraordinary, and he was proud of their red cloaks and the reaction of others when they discovered who they were. The reputation had been earned, over and over again.

In that place, with the cool of evening upon them, Cyrus took heart. The city of Persepolis seemed subdued, but not in the public throes of grief. The streets were not lined with soldiers, nor draped in mourning cloths, with pots of sandalwood burning. Yet until he passed through the gates of the plateau above the city, he could not be sure the old man still lived. He turned at the thought, looking up at the mountain his father and grandfather had remade, to the imperial plain that was a line of green and grey at such a distance. Wild falcons circled lazily above it in the warm air, watching for fat pigeons in the fruit trees. That royal terrace contained palaces, barracks, theatres and libraries. His father's pavilion would lie at the centre of the lush garden they called a 'paradise', the secret green heart of an empire.

On the river banks, low bushes clung, their roots worn into smooth sculpture. White flowers of jasmine showed on trailing vines, filling the air with scent. The prince breathed deeply, standing waist-deep in the waters with his eyes closed. He was home.

The Spartans dried quickly as they patted themselves down with their cloaks and ran fingers through their hair, made cool despite the sun. The prince too was refreshed, dressing once more with care. He strapped on the armoured coat over his tunic, but also bronze Spartan greaves onto his shins, perfectly shaped to him so that the muscles and the curve of his kneecaps were marked in the polished metal. They were more use to those who stood with shields than those who rode, but Cyrus liked to honour his men in such a way. Tissaphernes thought it a foreign affectation and beneath him, of course.

If the young prince had not been coming home to his father's deathbed, Cyrus might have been amused at the way the people of the city gathered to watch the strangers. Traders from the fruit market had come wandering over, while those they paid to guard them looked on and glowered. The Greeks who wore red cloaks were famous even there, though entire nations and a stretch of open sea lay between Persepolis and the valley of Eurotas — three months and a world away. As well as the legendary cloaks, the Spartans wore their own bronze greaves, covering both legs from ankle to knee. They had come ready for war, even to escort a prince home.

They had stacked their shields in neat unguarded piles as they dived into the water, as if they could not imagine another man stealing from them. Each one was marked with its owner's name on the inside, while a single letter showed the enemy where Sparta lay in Greece — the lambda that was the first letter of the region of Lacedaemon. Each one was polished bright and cared for like a lover.

As he mounted up, Cyrus wondered if any of those staring

would ever know Sparta as he did. To the mothers pointing out the foreign warriors to their children, these were the very ones who had humbled Persian Immortals time and again, earning themselves a legend. Such men of Greece had smashed the army of Darius the Great at Marathon. It had been Spartans who led Greek soldiers against the Persian King Xerxes at Thermopylae and Plataea and Mycale. Persia had conquered almost thirty nations, but been turned back by Greece – and the warriors who wore red cloaks.

Those dark days were far in the past, though memories were long. Cyrus looked away as his men formed up in a perfect double rank, ready for his command. Spartans had come in the end to break Athens and rule all Greece, but they fought for him because he paid them – and because he understood their honour. The silver and gold he gave them went home to build temples and barracks and armouries. They earned nothing for themselves, and he admired them above all other men – except for his father and brother.

'Come on, old lion,' he said to Tissaphernes. 'I have delayed long enough. I must not wilt from this, though I can hardly believe it is not a mistake, even now. My father is too strong ever to die, is he not?'

He smiled, though his pain was clear. In response, Tissaphernes reached out and gripped his shoulder, giving comfort to a younger man.

'I was your father's servant thirty years ago, before you were born. He had the world in his hand then. But even kings have just a short time in the sun. It comes to us all, though your philosopher friends would question even that, I am sure.'

'I wish you had learned enough Greek to understand them.'

Tissaphernes made a scornful sound.

'It is the language of shepherds. What do I care for the speech of slaves? I am a Persian.'

He spoke in easy earshot of the Spartans, though they gave no sign they had heard. Cyrus looked at their officer, the one named Anaxis. Fluent in both languages, Anaxis missed nothing, though he had long ago dismissed Tissaphernes as a bag of Persian wind. For the briefest of moments, Anaxis met Cyrus' gaze and winked.

Tissaphernes saw the prince's expression lighten and jerked around in the saddle, trying to see what had caused the change of mood, who had dared to mock his dignity. He saw only that the Spartans were ready to march once more and shook his head, muttering about farmers and foreigners.

The Spartans wore their shields on their backs for long marches. Though they were in no danger, Cyrus passed the word for parade style. Marching through one of three capital cities of the Persian empire, they would carry the discs of golden bronze and wood on their left arms, with long spears ready in their right. They wore short swords on their hips, with the infamous kopis weapon ready at the small of their backs. Those heavy, bent blades were fearsome things, considered unsporting by their enemies. The Spartans laughed at that sort of complaint.

The bronze helmets they wore covered their beards as well as thick braids of hair that hung down to their shoulders. The helms hid both exhaustion and the weaknesses of men, leaving the cold aspect of statues. Having their features in shadow was just one of the things that made them so feared. Reputation meant something more. Carrying the weapons and shield of a father or grandfather meant more still.

As they left the river behind, Cyrus and Tissaphernes walked their mounts through the streets, the crowds clearing ahead, giving them room. An eerie silence fell, both among the people of the city and the men striding through it.

'I still think you should have left your mercenaries behind, Highness,' Tissaphernes murmured. 'What will your brother say when he sees Greeks chosen over Persians?'

'I am a prince and the commander of my father's armies. If my brother says anything at all, it will be that my dignity is the honour of our house. The Spartans are the best in the world. Who else could have kept pace with us these last weeks? Do you see any Immortals here? My servants? One of my slaves *died* on the road trying to stay with me. The rest have fallen behind. No, these men have earned their place at my side, by being at my side.'

Tissaphernes bowed his head as if to acquiesce, though he was angry. Cyrus treated the Spartans like true men and not the mad dogs they were. The Persian general knew without turning his head that some of them would be watching him as they marched. They trusted no one who stood close to their master, just as curs would threaten and growl. Still, it would not be much longer. The two horsemen led the Spartans uphill, following the road to the great steps that would take them higher, to the plateau of the Persian king.

The great steps had been cut wide and shallow to allow the king to remain on horseback as he returned from a hunt. Cyrus and Tissaphernes walked their mounts ahead and, in jingling ranks, the Spartans followed them up. Cyrus could feel the eyes of his father's Immortals on him as he approached the narrow gate of the outer wall. His father had spent the treasuries of nations on his plateau, both in deepening the cut across the face of the mountain and on all the luxuries that lay within. Though it was the garden of an empire, it was yet a fortress, with a permanent guard of two thousand men.

The final step ended at the door, so there was no place for an enemy to gather and attack. Cyrus felt the light change as Persian officers blocked the sun overhead, staring down at his party – and in particular at the Spartans on the steps behind, bristling with four weapons to a man. Cyrus showed a bland face as he looked up at the walls, lit gold by the setting sun.

'I am Prince Cyrus, son of King Darius, brother of Prince Artaxerxes, commander of the armies of Persia. In the name of my father, open this door that I may see him.'

They left him for a beat longer than he expected, so that Cyrus began to colour. His rising temper subsided as he heard chains and bars removed and the door swung open, revealing a long yard beyond. He swallowed, determined not to show fear. In that, he and his Spartans were well matched.

Without dismounting, Cyrus and Tissaphernes rode their horses through into the sunlit yard. The light was softer by the hour, shading gently into summer's evening. Cyrus knew that he was home at last, that he should relax and look ahead to seeing his father. He was not yet certain how the old man would react to him, nor he to the Great King. He felt unsure of himself in the face of that loss, rushing down upon him. Not all the strength of arms in the world could keep his father in it for one more day if it was his time. It was that helplessness that made Cyrus tremble – not the killing ground he entered.

The defences of the plateau were not just in the men on the outer walls, but also the funnels through which attackers would pass. If they somehow reached the steps and broke through the gates, each side of the fortress was separate from the other. Enemy forces could not rejoin until they had passed through two long and narrow yards, open to the sky.

Cyrus and Tissaphernes did not hesitate and rode through

to the end of the killing ground. Fifty ranks of six Spartans followed in perfect order, spear-butts resting on the dusty ground as they came to a halt before an even greater door ahead.

Behind them, the outer gate was shut and barred. More than one of the Spartans frowned at being held in a place where they could not manoeuvre. There were shelves of stone running all round that yard, the height of two men from the floor below. The purpose of them was not obvious and the Spartan officer Anaxis tightened his grip on his spear. He felt the hostile stares of Persian guards more used to looking fine in their polished panels than any actual fighting.

In the front, Cyrus and Tissaphernes glanced at one another and dismounted. Anaxis tried not to crane his neck to see who had come out to greet them, though the conversation was blocked from his view by the horses. He did not like that. It was his duty to protect Cyrus, and perhaps the fat, older one as well. Yet no orders had been given to remain alert or to watch for a threat. Anaxis knew he was in the citadel of an old enemy, but he was also the personal guard of one of their princes, a man he rather admired for his honesty and lack of affectation. Certainly, as Persians went, the prince was a good one. Cyrus had shown no fear, or anything other than concern for his father. Yet Anaxis found himself looking up to the stone shelves around them, almost like the long seats of an Athenian theatre. The Persians were half-decent bowmen, he knew. The Spartan did not like the thought of being overlooked, not in that place.

None of those thoughts showed in his face, which remained hidden in the shadow of his helmet. Anaxis stood like a statue in bronze while Cyrus and Tissaphernes spoke in low voices ahead. Yet Anaxis was pleased when one of the mounts moved, letting him see the prince.

17

Cyrus turned to the Spartans at his back, his face fixed and stern.

'My brother has given orders for me to enter the royal gardens without guards,' he said. Cyrus seemed about to speak again and shook his head. It was barely a signal at all, though Anaxis felt his heart sink.

'Perhaps your brother would not mind if I accompanied you,' Anaxis said.

Cyrus smiled at him.

'My friend, if there is treachery, one more man would make no difference.'

'I always make a difference,' Anaxis said, seriously.

'That is true, but I must trust in my brother's honour. He is the heir to the throne and I have given him no reason to doubt me.'

'We will wait here, until you return,' Anaxis said, dipping onto one knee. He spoke in the manner of an oath and Cyrus bowed his head before raising the man back to his feet.

'Thank you. You honour me with your service.'

Cyrus turned to find Tissaphernes watching with a scornful expression, gesturing to the gate that led deeper into the royal plateau. Beyond that long yard lay the first gardens, planted on soil brought up from the plains and tended by a thousand slaves. Trees had been set there, forming shaded avenues, with tiny monkeys chasing birds from branch to branch and the air thick with the odour of green boughs and jasmine.

Cyrus ignored the little seneschal who had come to meet him, not yet sure if the man's status was an insult or not. His brother Artaxerxes would be found at his father's side, of course. It meant nothing that he had sent a mere servant to accompany Cyrus through the gardens.

Tissaphernes seemed to shed the cares and strains of their

trek as he walked, breathing deeply of fragrances he knew well and seeming almost to grow as he stretched his back and stood taller. He had known Cyrus for all his life and been mentor and friend for most of it. Yet they shared a very different outlook. Cyrus loved people, there was no other way to describe it. They were his passion and he collected friends as other men will earn coins. In comparison to the prince, Tissaphernes could hardly hide his dislike of crowds and sweaty soldiers.

They walked for an hour through paths so twisting a stranger might have been lost a dozen times. Cyrus knew them all from his childhood and followed the seneschal with the barest concentration. His father's pavilion lay at the far side of the plateau, surrounded by palms and slaves, all waiting for his final breaths. Cyrus felt his throat tighten as he walked, listening for the wailing voices of his father's women.

Anaxis looked up at the first scrape of a sandal on the stone above. The Spartans had stood in silence for an hour or so, taking their cue from him. Anaxis cursed under his breath when he saw the troop of Persian soldiers walking out, filling the ledges on both sides. They wore ornate black armour and carried bows set with precious stones, like guards in a play or perhaps on the door of a whorehouse. To his eye, they looked like children who had run amok in a king's treasury.

The Persian officer wore plumes of black and white feathers that twitched in the wind, far grander than anything Anaxis had ever seen at home. The man's skin shone with oil and his hands with gems. He carried no bow, but only a short sword in a gold scabbard that had to be worth a small city all on its own. Anaxis raised his eyebrows at the thought. There was plunder and loot in that place. Such things were worth remembering.

'Ready shields,' Anaxis said clearly.

Many of the men had placed their shields on their backs or rested them against their legs. They took them up once more, grim with the same dislike. None of them were comfortable with archers standing in a superior position, while they were crammed into a killing ground below.

Anaxis looked at the stone walls with fresh eyes, seeing how smooth they were. Above his head, three rows of Persian archers halted to the left and right, perhaps as many men in all as watched them sullenly from below.

The plumed officer came down a narrow path at the corner, standing with his sandal half over the lip of the stone, so that Anaxis could see the studded underside of the sole. For a time, no one moved and the air grew still, with no breeze to give them relief. The shadows had crept some distance since the prince and Tissaphernes had gone, but the evening light seemed not to have changed. Though it was warm, Anaxis felt his scrotum tighten. The men looking down on the Spartans were smiling as they fingered their weapons. They had strung the bows, he noted. Though they wore the ceremonial armour of the royal court, they were arrayed for slaughter. He scratched his beard.

'How hard would it be to get onto that ledge, do you think?' he said to his friend Cinnis. In more normal times, Cinnis was a bulky man, rightly proud of his strength. Fourteen days of loping along on sand roads had made him leaner and more surly. He shrugged.

'If two men hold a shield flat, like this –' he held out his own by the edge – 'a third could be lifted up easily enough. You think they are going to attack?'

'I do, yes,' Anaxis said. He raised his voice to the rest, knowing it was unlikely anyone above them could understand a word of Greek. 'Someone has decided to strike us down, it seems. So. Shields ready to raise overhead. Stand in threes. Make no move unless we are attacked, but if we are, I want men flung up to them. I like this place. I think we should hold it until Prince Cyrus returns.'

'Or fight our way out to the river and away,' Cinnis murmured.

Anaxis shook his head, as his friend had known he would. Anaxis had given his word. He would not suffer the shame of Cyrus returning to find he had abandoned his post. Cinnis hunched his shoulders in rising anger when he saw the first bows bend.

Above their heads, the Persian officer drew in a great breath to give an order. Cinnis held out his shield, the far edge immediately gripped by another. Their eyes met in fury at the betrayal.

The plumed officer shrieked and the Persian bows bent fully, the noise like clattering wings as the first arrows plunged among them. As they struck, Anaxis stepped onto the shield with a dozen others along the length of the yard. Each of those men was thrown upwards, crashing into astonished archers. Anaxis arrived in their midst with his spear and the vicious kopis blade ready, laughing at their panic.

2

Cyrus paused on a wide path between lime trees. Tissaphernes went on a few steps before returning to his side.

'What is it?' the older man asked.

'I thought . . . Ah, I have been away from home a long time. It was the cry of birds, or the keening of slaves. The empire mourns, old lion. My heart weeps within me and I thought I heard its voice. My father has made the world around him. This place alone! It is a wonder to stand so high above the plain, to feel this breeze and know the shade of these trees, yet to recall this entire plateau was cut from the flanks of a mountain. Kings achieve more than other men, if they have vision.'

'Your father was always a man of will,' Tissaphernes said. 'Though he was not always right, he made a decision and then moved on it. Most men find such an act wearying, whereas your father grew stronger and more certain with every year that passed.'

'With fewer doubts.'

'Doubts are for children and the very old. We see too many choices at those times, so that reducing them all to a single act is harder. Yet as men in our prime, we cut away the weak choices and reach out for the sword, or the spade, or the woman.'

Cyrus glanced at the man he had known his entire life, seeing him lost in memory.

'You were there when he became king, of course,' Cyrus said, his voice dry.

Tissaphernes raised his eyes to the evening sky for a moment.

'You mock me. Yes, I have told it to you a dozen times, but I saw greatness in him even then. His brother was king – and your father accepted that and gave his oath of loyalty. He pressed himself to the floor and all men knew he would follow.'

'I know the tale,' Cyrus said, suddenly tired. Tissaphernes went on as if he had not heard.

'Yet another brother was not so great of spirit. No, Prince Sogdianus was not able to put honour before his own desire to rule. Just six weeks after that coronation, Sogdianus crept into the royal bedchamber with a copper knife. He stood before the court as the sun rose, though he was red and smeared with royal blood, though he left trails and loops behind him, as if he had sported in it. He told them all that he was king and not a voice was heard in complaint. It was then your father stepped out of the crowd.'

'I know, old lion. He was loyal to the first brother, but he took vengeance on the second. The court acclaimed his bravery and his right. He won the throne for himself.'

'He loved them both, but he was a man of iron loyalty,' Tissaphernes said, nodding.

'As am I.'

'As are you,' Tissaphernes agreed immediately. 'You have your father's heart, I think. Though he was never so tolerant of Greeks as you are.'

It was Cyrus' turn to raise his eyes and tut to himself.

'I have won their loyalty.'

'*Bought* their loyalty,' Tissaphernes said with a sniff.

'No. You don't know them. There is not enough gold in the world to buy the service of Spartans, if they choose not to give it.'

Tissaphernes made a hissing noise.

'Cyrus, my dear boy, there is enough gold in the world to buy anything.'

The younger man shook his head, but they had both seen a great pavilion between the trees. Guards watched them from the roadside and they fell silent at the prospect of meeting a dying king.

Cyrus felt some part of him unclench as his brother Artaxerxes came out to meet him. Older by a year, they were as different from one another as it is possible to be and yet share blood. Artaxerxes had always been the scholar. They had both trained under their father's stern eye, but it was Artaxerxes who had tripped himself with his own spear. Cyrus had been the one to dance with weapon masters, leaping like a salmon with great cries of joy. The younger brother had not understood the dark looks and bad temper that came his way at first. Even when Cyrus was old enough to understand his brother's resentment, it had not troubled him. Cyrus knew he had been born loyal, just as he knew he would never be king. All the skill he had earned for himself merely reflected glory to their father's throne. Even when the king had chosen Cyrus to command the armies and set him learning at the feet of their greatest generals, the young prince had known only that it would make him of more use, would increase his value to his father.

Artaxerxes had been spurred on by his brother's success and his own ambitions. He had continued his swordwork, that was clear from the wide frame and solid grip as he embraced his brother, kissing him on both cheeks and the lips. Artaxerxes held Cyrus' head in his hands and the glimmer of tears from the elder prince brought them forth from the younger. Fear overwhelmed Cyrus, so that he spoke as a dry whisper.

'Is he . . . ?' Cyrus could not go on. To ask if his father was alive was to suggest he might not be. He might as well ask if the mountains had fallen, if the rivers had run dry.

'No, though it cannot be far off now. He has been calling for you, Brother. I thought you would never come.'

'Stand aside, then. Let me see him,' Cyrus said, looking past his brother's shoulder.

'As you are? Your clothes are marked with sweat. Would you insult him?'

'Have new clothes brought if it troubles you! I have washed in the river and I am clean. Now, Brother, I would enter. Do not make me ask again.'

A note of iron had entered the voice of the younger prince. Artaxerxes hesitated, then stepped back, indicating the open doorway. Cyrus walked past without looking to see what Tissaphernes would do.

The pavilion was enormous, stretching hundreds of paces from the entrance in all directions. Inside were pools and gardens, feasting rooms and scores of his father's personal slaves to tend him. Silent young men in neat tunics offered to hold his cloak before Cyrus had taken a pace inside. Yet he did not stop. He was a boy again, running to his father.

Behind, standing at the door to the huge pavilion, Artaxerxes put out his hand as Tissaphernes approached. The older man went onto both knees and then lay flat in the presence of the prince. Raising him up, the heir to the empire bowed his head to whisper into Tissaphernes' ear.

'Has he spoken against the throne, against me?'

Tissaphernes shook his head as he came to his feet.

'Not a word, Highness. I swear it on the honour of my family.'

Artaxerxes became still as he thought.

'You were my father's friend. You have been loyal to the king of your youth. Will you be loyal to me?'

Tissaphernes chose to prostrate himself once more, pressing his forehead and lips to the ground. He waited there for Artaxerxes to touch him lightly on the cheek, giving him permission to rise. His skin was marked with small stones, sticking to his sweat.

'My loyalty is to your family, Highness,' Tissaphernes said, 'to the throne of Persia, to the line of Darius the Great, through Xerxes, to your father – and then to you. I am loyal to death and beyond. Call me in the afterworld and I will come to you.'

Artaxerxes nodded, pleased. He had never grown weary of the adulation he experienced. The capacity of men to give their honour into his care was only what he expected of them.

'And my brother? You have known him as well, all his life.'

For the first time, Tissaphernes hesitated.

'Cyrus is one to admire, Highness. I love him as I love my sons. Yet he will not inherit the empire that makes us great. That is what matters, more than my life or his.'

Artaxerxes relaxed a fraction, moved by what he had heard.

'Enter then, old friend. Bathe and change into clean silks. My father sleeps now for much of the day, but he will want to know that you came at the last. I thought you would be too late. I give thanks you were not.'

'Your brother . . . brought a guard of three hundred with him,' Tissaphernes said. 'Men of Sparta and exceptional warriors.'

Artaxerxes frowned, looking back along the path Tissaphernes had walked.

'He admires them, I know.'

'I have heard it said that their legend is much exaggerated,

Highness. I do not . . . believe that to be the case. They are skilful men. Your brother insisted on bringing them here, despite the trouble it might cause.' He paused, choosing his words and giving them a certain emphasis in his hesitation. 'Highness, I would not let them roam free in our lands.'

With a tight smile, Artaxerxes clapped him on the shoulder.

'They will not. I have made sure of it.'

Anaxis raced along the lowest step, killing as he went. The Spartan stayed low, crouched over, though his legs were strong and he moved in perfect balance. His eyes were savage at the betrayal, so that he went as an angel of death among the Persians, still sending their barbs as fast as they could. Anaxis shoved half a dozen men off the ledge in the first moments, knowing those below would kill them more quickly than he could. He lost his spear in the armpit of one, wrenched from his grip when he would not follow it down. The Spartan officer grinned at the next terrified Persian to face him, showing him the kopis blade at eye level, even as he swept it out at a man on the step above. Anaxis batted away a downward lunge, using it to foul the attack of another. He chopped a stranger's ankle when that man tried to send an arrow into the mad Spartan who had leaped through the air at them. There was no panic then in Anaxis, though a little regret. He knew he fought on his last day and he was very calm. The Persians had expected a slaughter – and they would get one, though they would not enjoy it as much as they'd thought.

On the yard below, the Greeks held their shields overhead, pinned down and unable to manoeuvre. Dozens of them had thrown their spears or used them to stab and hook the calves of the archers. Bodies in dark cloth lay thick on the ground and there were still a few Spartans among them. The Greeks stood in tight groups, overlapping their shields and peering out between the gaps, yet they were not cowering. In the glimpses Anaxis could steal, he saw Cinnis was keeping them in good order, calling out targets.

Anaxis found himself smiling as he feinted to unbalance the fellow in front of him, a snarling bowman of huge beard and breadth of shoulder. The man jerked aside to avoid a blow that never came, and in the moment of weakness, Anaxis tugged him sharply by his sleeve and pulled him over the edge to crash down on the Spartans below. They shouted in anger, calling for Anaxis to watch what he was doing. He chuckled in reply as he hacked and slashed, a dervish spattering blood and scales of Persian armour as he went.

So many archers had fallen into the long yard that some of the Greeks had taken up their bows and quivers. Most had shot hares as boys and they could hardly miss Persians who stood without shields, just the height of two men away. Six or eight of them began to return the long shafts. The Persians wavered at facing their own weapons, falling back in knots and clusters rather than continuing the slaughter.

Anaxis gathered three of his men to his side. Those below had thrown shields up and it was a relief to stand behind them as arrows hammered into golden bronze and wood. They were all wounded, Anaxis saw. Two of them wore the black stubs of arrows they had snapped off in their chests. They showed no sign of distress, though they struggled to breathe and blood dripped from them as their strength drained. A great strip of ribs showed white bone along one man's side. He shrugged when Anaxis pointed to it.

'I'll have it bound up after,' he said.

'I'll stitch it for you,' Anaxis said. 'Remember, now. Don't let Cinnis anywhere near it.'

'I'll remember,' the man said. They were old friends and they did not need to say more.

Anaxis grunted in pain as an arrow thumped between the shields into his side, piercing right through the ridged muscles there. He could see the feathers, but he dared not pull it out. The wound brought a wave of nausea, so that nothing felt right.

'I would like them to remember us,' Anaxis said. 'If you have rested, that is.'

'I thought *you* were resting,' one of the Spartans replied, indignantly.

Anaxis grinned. His kopis blade sawed quickly through the black shaft, making him grunt as something turned inside him.

By falling back in fear, the archers had left a space that suited them well. They were desperate not to let the few Spartans who had gained the steps get closer, nor any others to climb or leap up to join their companions-in-arms.

Anaxis and the others rushed them, holding up the shields. The Persians poured shots into that small group even as they howled and plunged amongst them once more. The shields became weapons at close quarters, the edge as useful as a spear to one who had been trained with it. There was panic in the Persian ranks as they fell back in tatters. Down in the yard, the Spartans who still lived began to sing the battle hymn of death, the paean.

Anaxis made it to the highest step before his kopis blade was finally dashed from his grasp. He saw lines of fresh Persian warriors coming out of doors on both sides, an endless stream of them, carrying bows or swords and spears. Spears were more suited to killing those who could not get out of the trap, he thought. That would have been his order, had he been the Persian officer. A slaughter with bows was an insult and there was no need for such pettiness between men. He felt his sight fading and offered up his soul to Hades and Hermes. It would be pleasant to meet King Leonidas, who had stood at Thermopylae. The man had known more than a little about Persian treachery. Anaxis hoped to raise a cup of good red wine with him that very evening, if he crossed the river in time.

In the yard, Cinnis saw those who had been thrown up to the steps cut down, one by one, taking the last hopes with them. The spears were gone, the quivers were all empty, though there were broken shafts everywhere amongst the dead.

The Persian archers no longer sneered. Scores of black-robed men lay dead in the yard and the blood of more stained the steps on both sides. Yet the Spartans had lost half their number and the best chance to break out had come to nothing. One or two still tried to lift colleagues up, but the archers knew it could be done by then. They concentrated their shots on any such attempt, so that the men fell back, spitted through by shafts.

Cinnis shouted orders to pick up the weapons of the dead and throw them. As arrows battered them to their knees, the Spartans did as they were told, with careful aim. The kopis blades whistled well in the air, as did the short swords. One or two shields were sent spinning after those and where they struck, men crashed backwards. A few of them fell into the pit and they were cut to pieces in instants, though the rain of arrows intensified.

Cinnis kept them together in smaller and smaller groups, using shields in clusters, so that they could shuffle across the field and collect fallen weapons, then send them spinning through the air to take a few more with them. On the steps, the Persian regiment kept coming out, fresh men aghast at the number of their own dead. They drew swords or strung bows and the last thing some of them saw was a kopis whirring at them.

The Spartans fought until the last four stood together. Each man was covered in blood and badly wounded, so weary they could barely hold the shields as arrows still thumped into them. The surfaces of beaten bronze resembled the plucked flesh of fowl by then, with pockmarks and broken quills so thick it made them hard to lift.

'Hold!' came an order from above.

Some of the Spartans knew Persian commands but ignored it. Yet the archers overhead all stopped and stood back, panting. The first Persian officer lay dead on the ground. His replacement came to the edge and peered down at them, shaking his head in amazement at the sheer savagery of the scene.

'I am Hazar Zaosha,' he said in halting Greek. 'An . . . officer of the Zhayadan. You understand me? The Immortals. You cannot win now. Will you surrender, men of Sparta? You are few and we are many. I wonder . . .'

Cinnis threw a sword at him and the man lurched aside from it. With a cry of horror, Zaosha stepped into space and dropped to the yard below. He looked up to see the four bloodied Spartans standing over him with bright interest.

'Kill them!' Zaosha roared. 'Kill . . .'

Cinnis cut him off with a chopping blow from a kopis, then fell across him with a grunt. Arrows stood out in his back. Cinnis breathed into the Persian officer's face as both of them died, though Cinnis smiled at him to hide his rage. It was bad enough that they had been betrayed by ancient enemies. It was worse that no one would carry the news to Sparta, to let the ephors know they had died well and without shame.

*

The pavilion was cooled by the breeze that came down the mountainside each evening, a wonder enjoyed by the king and the court, slave-born or royal alike. When the heat of summer was beyond endurance on the plains, there was nowhere like it. Cyrus felt the sweat dry on his face and breathed in, grief taking hold. He thought he could smell cinnamon on the air, though it was hard to be sure. He had not set eyes on his father for years. For him, the breeze was childhood and home.

He did not have to ask where his father lay. The number of slaves grew as he walked deeper into the pavilion. They clustered around his father's bed like bees, ready to answer his slightest whim. Huge guards stood unmoving at each compass point around the dying king, facing outward against all threats. Cyrus could see the man who lay propped up on bolsters, his brow mopped by a woman dipping a cloth in a bowl of water where petals floated. The odour of roses was sickly sweet as Cyrus dropped to one knee.

The Great King turned his head as one of the male slaves whispered to him. Darius looked for his son and Cyrus came forward, stopping as a servant held out a hand.

'Highness, your sword. Please.'

Cyrus unbuckled his belt and handed it over. The guards stood aside then and he came within arm's reach of the man who had controlled his life from the earliest years.

Cyrus smiled, though it was more in pain than pleasure. The old man had been eaten away by some scourge. Arms that had once held a royal sword were painfully thin, the skin stretched over bones, showing odd bruises and flecks of black.

'I am here, Father,' Cyrus said, sitting as a chair was brought to his side. 'I came as soon as I heard, as fast as I could.'

'I waited and waited for you, Cyrus,' his father said. The voice was a whisper and the prince leaned in to hear. 'I could not die until I knew you had come. At last.'

Cyrus saw a strange expression cross his father's face, something that might have been spite or triumph, he could not have said. The king's eyes drifted closed and the lines on his forehead eased. On impulse, Cyrus reached out and took the hand that had cuffed him a thousand times when he was a boy, feeling the warmth in his. He felt awkward as he searched for words.

'Thank you, Father, for everything. I wanted you to be proud of me.'

There was no reply and Cyrus placed the hand on the sheet, stroking the knuckles for a time before sitting back. The slave with the bowl of rose water leaned in and wiped his father's face once again. The breeze rolled through that part of the pavilion, though it seemed less gentle then, more like the scouring winds that came in autumn, that blew hot and unceasing and drove good men mad.

'Father?' Cyrus said more loudly. He stood up and watched helplessly as a stranger came in and listened to the king's breathing and heart, nodding.

'It will not be long, Highness. He may hear us. He may wake again – or not. He called for you many times. I am glad you came, in the end.'

There it was again, the barb – and from one who would not have dared in normal times. There was something like resentment in that pavilion for the king's son. Cyrus could sense it all around him.

In that instant, he'd had enough. He'd covered a dozen parasangs a day for fourteen days to reach the old man. Only the Spartans had matched his pace and they had been driven to injury and exhaustion. He told himself to take comfort in the fact that he had not been too late, but it was hard. Not a word of thanks or pleasure from the old man, just that strange note of bitterness, as if they had all been waiting for him.

Cyrus felt oddly deflated and at a loss as he stood back from the sickbed. He had feared he would be too late for days. In that impatience, he'd thought of his father's smile, of an embrace he had never known. It was all suddenly tin, the jewels of his imagination made glass. He had never made the man proud before. No matter what Cyrus had achieved, only Artaxerxes had ever mattered to his father.

Cyrus held out his hand for his sword to be returned to him. The servant who held it stared wide-eyed, clutching the jewelled scabbard and strap to his chest.

'Steward. Give me what is mine,' Cyrus said slowly.

He thought the day could not get any stranger, but then he heard his brother approach, with Tissaphernes. Both men looked relaxed and refreshed, Cyrus saw. Tissaphernes had changed his robes for flowing silks and had found time to bathe, his hair still wet. More surprising was the presence of armed guards with them, spreading out as they approached through the gardens. Their intent was unmistakable and Cyrus lowered his head, considering.

Before the steward could do more than yelp, the prince snatched the sword from his grasp and belted it on.

'There, that is better,' he said. 'Now, Brother. What threat brings swordsmen to this pavilion at such a time?'

'You,' Artaxerxes said. He smiled as the guards moved in and surrounded the younger prince. He saw Cyrus consider resisting them, but their father lay dying just a few paces away and events had overtaken him. Artaxerxes saw his brother's head dip and his teeth showed white.

'You are under arrest, Cyrus. On our father's order. To be held for execution.'

Cyrus had been about to attack. He had marked the man he would have to cut down to break the circle and he would have moved if not for those words. Instead, he turned round in astonishment. He saw his father was watching him, an expression of peace on his face. Even as Cyrus understood that the old man knew, the eyes closed once more.

His arms were held and his sword taken from him. His brother's personal guard marched him through the pavilion and back out into the paradise of gardens and paths. Artaxerxes and Tissaphernes walked behind him and Cyrus craned his neck to speak, though the guards prodded him along.

'Why do this, Brother? I have always been loyal. Not *once* have I given you reason to doubt me. Not once in a lifetime!'

He thought Artaxerxes pursed his mouth and set his jaw rather than answer. When Cyrus turned to Tissaphernes, the older man shook his head and looked at the stones of the path, unable to meet his gaze.

3

Cyrus sat on a soldier's cot. The door was locked, though it was merely the small room of an officer in his father's guard and a far cry from a prison cell. Whoever the previous occupant had been, the man had enjoyed a range of oils and powders, two pairs of Egyptian scissors, stiff brushes for nails and beard, as well as finely carved ivory probes for cleaning the nose and ears, all still arrayed by a washstand in the corner.

Cyrus could hear the noise of the barracks all around him, with shouted orders and barked laughter. He fixed his gaze on the door and waited. He did not yet understand what had happened, but he knew Artaxerxes too well to think he would be dragged out and beheaded without a chance to speak. His brother would want to gloat, or accuse – something. Cyrus knew it with the certainty of two lads who had grown up together. He knew Artaxerxes. He hoped so, anyway. He had been away from home a long time.

As the night wore on, the moon rose as a crescent in a clear sky, bright above the plateau. Cyrus thought he could not possibly sleep, but he turned to the wall and closed his eyes, his thoughts a whirl.

With no sense of time passing, he came suddenly awake. He was off the bed and standing in a heartbeat, blinking in confusion in the morning light. He had been exhausted, from days on the road as well as the strain of his arrest and grief for his father. To his embarrassment, he had slept like a child and woken refreshed and far more alert. With his life hanging in the balance! He ran a hand over his face, grimacing at the thick curls. He preferred to be smooth-shaven, but it took work and the finest blades. There was no razor on the officer's washstand. Presumably the man used scissors on his beard, or plaited it with threads.

Cyrus blinked as the bolts on the door were drawn and Tissaphernes entered, standing awkwardly so that between them the tiny room was almost full. Guards peered in from outside, but there was no way for them to join Tissaphernes, even to protect him. They merely glowered, while Cyrus waited for his friend to tell him what was happening.

The older man decided to sit on the cot, which creaked as he lowered himself. Cyrus remained against a wall and one of the guards loomed through the doorway to observe.

Cyrus merely raised his eyebrows when Tissaphernes looked to him. He felt he was the injured party and sensed he would give up his advantage if he spoke.

After an age, Tissaphernes sighed.

'Highness, I am sorry it came to this. I could have turned a blade aside from any other hand, of course. Not from your father.' Tissaphernes looked exhausted, as if he had not slept at all. 'Cyrus, I am to tell you the king's mortal aspect died in the night. I am sorry. Your brother is this morning the Great King, the god-emperor of Persia, may he be blessed by Mithras, Ahura Mazda and all good spirits. May he find welcome amongst his ancestors.'

Despite the shock of the news, Cyrus felt hope leap in his chest.

'If I am here at my father's order, however that came about, Artaxerxes will free me,' he said in relief. 'I thought a spirit or demon had taken hold of my father at the end, perhaps creeping in when he was at his weakest or raving with pain. At least now he is beyond their influence. I can . . .'

Tissaphernes shook his head.

'Highness, your brother confirmed the order last night. It grieves me, of course, but you are to be executed this very morning.' The man who had been his childhood mentor ran his hand down his beard, stroking the cone to the tip. Cyrus saw he was nervous. 'I am . . . to take you to the barracks square, without delay. There will be no ceremony or witnesses, beyond a few guards. Summon your dignity, my boy. Commend your soul to God and prepare for judgement.'

Cyrus stared. He did not ask about the Spartans he had brought to that place. The knowledge of their fate would be of no use, nor something he could affect. Yet he had learned from them how to be calm, at the only times it ever really mattered. He allowed his features to settle while he thought. He had no weapons, though he might wrench one from a guard. That would mean his life ended a few paces earlier than if he strolled to the square and knelt for the headsman. He saw no sign of support in Tissaphernes, but the old teacher was not his only ally.

'I would like to see my mother, before,' Cyrus said. 'To say goodbye.' He was watching Tissaphernes closely and hid a smile at the way the man frowned. 'Has she not been told? I am her son, after all.'

'I believe such things are the concern of the Great King,' Tissaphernes said primly.

They both raised their heads at a sudden clatter and alarm outside the cells. Different emotions flooded the two men as they heard a woman's voice snapping commands with the absolute certainty she would be obeyed.

Cyrus came off the wall, though his eyes glittered.

'I will not forget the part you played in this, Tissaphernes,' he said.

As if drawn up on strings, Tissaphernes rose from the bed.

'Highness, I have merely obeyed your father and your brother,' the man said, looking nervously for the first glimpse of Queen Parysatis.

'Get out of my way!' came a voice they all knew, a storm rushing down upon them. Tissaphernes winced in anticipation as the voice rang out once again. 'Bring my son out, from wherever you have hidden him! Cyrus? Where is my *son*?'

The guard in the doorway turned to face her. Cyrus considered strangling the man from behind, or perhaps breaking the neck of Tissaphernes as the older man tried to bow in that small space.

Queen Parysatis wore dark blue for mourning, though she had not rushed to the barracks before putting on a number of golden bangles that clashed and rang as she moved. Her hair was bound tight to her head and held with a golden net at the nape of her neck. She was still beautiful in her forties and moved as lithely as a young girl. Her scent came before her, bringing attar of roses to men who stood like stunned calves.

'Cyrus? Are you in there? Is that Tissaphernes with you? Come here to me, both of you. I will not enter some sweaty soldier's room! *Now*, Cyrus!'

The prince found he was chuckling in relief after the fear he had felt. Tissaphernes looked like thunder as he followed the guard out of the small doorway into the corridor beyond.

'Mistress, your son, King Artaxerxes, has given orders . . .' Tissaphernes began.

Queen Parysatis turned to the guard and laid a hand on the bare skin of his arm.

'If this man speaks to me again without first making obeisance, you may remove his head.'

The guard gave no sign he had heard, yet Tissaphernes chose caution rather than the chance of sudden death. He dropped to one knee stiffly, then the other, finally easing himself down until his forehead touched the floor. It was not particularly clean, Cyrus noted with some pleasure. Mouse droppings stuck to the man's forehead as he rose once more.

'Did I give you permission to rise?' Queen Parysatis said sweetly.

Tissaphernes went a darker shade in humiliation. Once more he chose not to test the authority of the lady in that place. He had lived enough years in the royal court to know that some problems were solved with blood – and only later, apologies. He pressed his forehead back to the floor and lay as if dead.

'Cyrus,' the queen said in greeting.

The prince took her hand and then knelt in turn.

'Mother,' he said in reply. 'I am grateful. Tissaphernes here seems to think my death was ordered.'

The queen waved her hand as if to brush away dust.

'I will have the truth of it, you may be sure. But not here, amongst these common men. We will not discuss *private* matters with servants and soldiers listening. Now, follow me. Your garments are soiled with sweat. They have kept you like an animal.'

Before Cyrus could reply, his mother reached out her leg and ground her shoe into Tissaphernes' back, making him grunt in pain.

'These men have reached too far,' she said, 'in their arrogance. But I will remedy it. I will make good. Come.'

She turned to leave and Cyrus glanced at the captain of the guards. The man's face was a good attempt at blank obedience, but his eyes were afraid. He knew his life was at stake if the new king came to ask why his prisoner had been allowed to walk out. Yet the queen would not be denied, indeed she acted as if the possibility had not even occurred to her. In the few instants the officer might have objected, Queen Parysatis swept by. Cyrus followed her, sensing the man's will flutter and fail. Even then, as Cyrus passed along the corridor and through the barracks, seeing his father's Immortals in various stages of undress and astonishment, he feared the shout that might go up to stop him.

His mother walked swiftly, though her dress prevented a full stride. Instead, she slinked along, her hips swaying ahead of her son. Many of the men who came out to see what was happening found their gaze drawn to the queen and were ensnared. Cyrus smiled to himself at the effect she could still have.

'I *will* not have my son held like a criminal,' his mother announced to the barracks. Her voice rang with indignation and some of those who came to doorways looked at their feet, as if they'd been caught doing something shameful.

If Parysatis had hesitated, or asked for permission, Cyrus thought the spell would have broken and one of them, perhaps one of the senior officers, would have halted his escape. Somehow, her authority held all the way to the door.

The barracks were some way from the edge of the plateau. Even with the queen at his side, Cyrus was tense with expectation of a shout, or a hand dropping onto his shoulder. He listened for the jingling sound of men running in armour and felt sweat trickle cold down his ribs. He had come like a lamb amongst wolves, and he knew he had not yet escaped. His time in the cell had allowed him to go over everything he had seen and heard. The conclusion was as inescapable as it was painful. There had been no mistake in the orders.

With his head down, he followed his mother through the guardhouse gate, rejoining a troop of slaves she had left outside. They lay stretched out on the ground and Cyrus guessed they had not moved since his mother's arrival. They leaped up as she stepped into her open litter, patting the cushions beside her. Cyrus got in, making the poles creak with his weight.

'Mother,' he began.

She shook her head.

'Not now, Cyrus. Your father was a stubborn man and I will have to have words with your brother before this ridiculous business is behind. Are we Egyptian, to be killing our own? Before Artaxerxes even has an heir? For that alone, your father was rash.'

Cyrus blinked slowly, accepting her assessment.

'I . . . did not think he would give an order to have me killed,' he said.

His mother raised her head and touched his knee as the slaves lurched into motion.

'Your father was a king, Cyrus. He put the empire before us all. I do not expect you to forgive him for the moment, while this is all raw, but in time you will see he was a man of great honour. He saw who you were – who you had become. He made a choice to remove you. In his way, it's quite a compliment.'

'He made an error,' Cyrus protested. 'I have always been loyal. I prize it in my men, I honour it in myself. I am a prince who will not be king. I have always known it. I was never a threat to Artaxerxes!'

'Dear boy, a king is one who removes a threat even before that threat is aware of itself. The empire brings peace and succour to millions. What is one life compared to that steady hand? I do not excuse your father, Cyrus. He will not take my beloved boy from me in his death spasm. I forbid it. You will come to forgive him in time.'

Cyrus felt like a sulky boy at her words. He resisted the urge to argue with the woman who had rescued him from death that morning. As the bearers made their way across the plateau, passing orchards watered by slaves and shaded in nets from the sun, he realised he would be dead at that moment if his mother had not come to the barracks. His blood would be soaking deep into the sand of the yard. It was a chilling thought. In a sense, that morning was the first of a new life, a new branch, a choice made. He was silent for a time, letting the motion of the litter soothe him.

'Where are my men, Mother?' he said after a time.

'All dead. Your brother had them killed.'

His mother watched her son closely, seeing the flash of anger that he could not hide.

'Can you blame him, Cyrus? You brought Spartans to the heart of your father's capital. Should he have meekly sent them home? Who knows how those savages think? No, in that, he was correct, despite the appalling cost. Your brother could not even manage that without . . . well, it does not matter now. Artaxerxes is king, though he has begun badly. He gives an order to have you killed and fails. He sends archers to kill your men and half a regiment is slaughtered in the act, with a royal cousin and two senior men.'

Cyrus smiled grimly, knowing the Spartans would want it known how they had died. Of all things, they considered the manner of death mattered as much as the manner of life. He whispered a brief prayer to their Greek gods for them, asking that they be welcomed into Hades. His mother turned to watch him.

'If I know your brother, he will be willing to set yesterday aside. It was one bad day – who can say it even happened, now? We live, that is what matters. I believe I can persuade him to undo the order for your execution, to restore you to your authority as commander of the armies. Artaxerxes needs you, Cyrus! Who else has been as loyal? Who else understands our armies half as well? Our enemies go in fear because of you. He would be a fool to lose you – and I will tell him so.'

Cyrus looked up from his thoughts and found the slaves had brought him to the outer barracks, where he had ridden his horse just the previous day. He turned to his mother with one eyebrow raised and she sighed.

'Let me speak for you, Cyrus. I don't want to make your brother back down on his first day as king. If I force him to swallow his pride over you, he will resent it and be angry for months. I don't doubt Tissaphernes has already whispered in his ear.'

'Tissaphernes will tell him I am loyal,' Cyrus said, though he realised he had no faith in the words even as he said them. His mother shook her head.

'Tissaphernes is his man, Cyrus. He always was. He is no friend of yours.'

Cyrus grimaced, feeling the betrayal like a muscle tearing. He was a royal prince. It was ridiculous to have thought he had friends at court, rather than men who schemed for influence and power. He missed his Spartans yet again. Anaxis had been a friend, along with Cinnis. It was hard to believe anyone had brought those two down, never mind the rest of them. He felt a savage joy that they had extracted such a high price. His Spartans walked with a legend on their shoulders. They would have wanted to add a few lines to it. More, they had understood loyalty. At times, it seemed no one else did.

He stepped down from the litter and held out his hand to his mother before the slaves could move. Parysatis took his fingers in hers and walked with her son to the gate. Cyrus knew he had left Anaxis and the Spartans in the yard beyond it. When light showed as a crack, he was not sure what to expect. His hand fell from his mother's as he looked on bloodstained walls, stretching sixty paces to the other side.

The bodies had gone, but the air was still thick with flies and the smell of death, stinging his eyes. Cyrus had visited slaughterhouses as a boy, with his father, to watch cattle bled and killed. He felt his stomach heave as something of the same mingling of blood and bowels returned to him.

'I won't go further with you, my son,' his mother said. 'Let me speak to Artaxerxes.'

She had paled at the stench that wafted out from that place. Cyrus saw how her gaze flitted from one brown smear to another, never settling as she tried not to imagine the violence that had roared through that place just hours before.

'Tell him I am loyal, Mother, that I have always been loyal. I have never given him reason to doubt me. Tell Tissaphernes as well.'

'I will, of course.' His mother raised her arms and drew him into an embrace. 'He knows your value, my son. I will remind him of all you have done. Go back to your work now and do not fear assassins. I will write to you when I am sure.'

Cyrus nodded, kissing her on the lips then striding out onto the sand, already hot under his sandals. He had entered with a guard of three hundred, with Tissaphernes at his side and his favourite horse under him. He would leave with nothing but his life.

He did not look back at his mother, or the men closing one gate behind and still others opening the one ahead. He could only hope her authority would protect him, though he feared a single arrow in his back for every step across that yard that reeked of blood. There were arrowheads glinting in the sand, with shards of spears and flakes of bronze that looked like gold coins. He mourned for those who had trusted in his word. Cyrus was certain of one thing as the last gate opened and he looked on the great staircase of rock leading to the plains below. He had been loyal – to his father, to his brother. In return, they had struck at him. And they had missed, though perhaps something had died in him after all.

He began to lope down steps he had climbed so easily on horseback. The city of Persepolis stretched out across the plain, but the entire world lay beyond. He was known throughout the empire as commander of all his father's armies. So he would leave his father's capital for a time – and visit far-flung regiments and the officers who led them – officers who had knelt to Cyrus to give their oaths.

He showed his teeth as he went faster and faster down the steps, leaving behind the stares of guards, the smell of blood and betrayal. He would come back. He would see Tissa-phernes and his dear brother again, he swore it to himself. If he had to raise an army, he would. The king's messenger had reached him at Susa, where the Royal Road began and headed west to Sardis. What had seemed an end could just as easily be a beginning. This was a new morning after all.

4

Cyrus staggered as he walked towards the fortress, set back from the track leading west. He was covered in dust and his eyes were red with wiping grit and sweat from his brow. He had been on the road for two days, with no food and only a small flask of water. He had learned endurance from the Spartans, how far sheer will could take a man if he were sufficiently determined – and if no one ever told him it was all right to lie down and die.

There were no rivers in that landscape of brown hills and dry ground. The fortress itself was made of baked mud around a well, the entire structure seeming to have grown out of the earth like an old bone. Cyrus thought it might have been one of those places where he had rested with the Spartans, but he could not be certain. He feared he would find it abandoned, the inner well gone dry, the soldiers vanished back to their hill tribes. He felt like weeping when he saw movement on the high wall by the gate, but he had no water and he could not weep.

'Open the gate,' he said. His voice was a whisper and he recalled he had kept a mouthful of water to wet his tongue, for this moment. He unwrapped the stopper and upended the bottle, but there was nothing. He had drunk even those last drops somewhere on the road.

He stood, looking up into the face of a soldier glowering at him.

'Get away, beggar,' the man said. 'If I come down there, I will beat you. Do not make me stir myself in this heat. Away!'

'Give me water,' Cyrus croaked up at him.

The soldier looked away, but all men knew the ache of thirst in that place – and the value of precious water where there was so little. The rivers were veins of life and all men lived between them. If they ran dry in a hot season, crops would be lost, entire villages made bones and dusty skin, silent in death. On the ramparts, the soldier swallowed and looked behind him. Without another word, he vanished from sight.

A smaller door set into the gate swung open moments later. The guard stepped out, his sword drawn and his eyes suspicious. He tossed Cyrus a half-full skin, as warm as blood, while he watched the hills around.

Cyrus gulped greedily, letting the blessed stuff fill him with life and purpose. He could feel his will returning and he thought of flowers he had seen watered that stretched up once more, before the very eyes. Water was life and he was desperately grateful.

'Thank you,' he said. 'I will reward you for your kindness to a stranger.'

'There is no need,' the man replied, reaching for his water-skin. It was hard for Cyrus to give it back, but he showed no sign of that struggle.

'I am Prince Cyrus of the house of Achaemenid, the son of King Darius. I say there is need. You saved my life. What is your name? Your role here?'

The man stood rooted in shock, his belief written in his face.

'I . . . I saw you before,' he said in wonder. 'When you came through with those men running like hunting dogs. I saw you!' He dropped to his knees and touched his head to the sandy ground. 'My lord and prince,' he said. 'Forgive me. I did not know you.'

'Rise up, giver of water,' Cyrus said. 'You have not yet told me your name.'

'Parviz, Highness. But what misfortune can have befallen you to stand here alone? Without even a sword? Was it bandits? We have only forty men here and the commander is often away in the town. Highness, have you come to relieve him from his duty? He is a lazy fool and it would not be a poor decision.'

Cyrus chuckled at how quickly the man had turned to advancing his causes.

'If you know who I am, you know you are at my command, Parviz.'

The man began to drop once again and Cyrus took him by the arm, so that he stood trembling.

'I do, of course, Highness.'

'Do you have horses?'

'Six fine mounts, my lord, though one is lame. I am sorry. If we had known you . . .'

'I will take the five that can be ridden. I must reach the city of Susa, where the Royal Road begins, Parviz. Your duty is to aid me, do you understand? Do you know Susa?'

The man shook his head and Cyrus suppressed a sigh. He was used to flying through the night on fast horses, but almost all his father's subjects would live and die within a day's walk of where they were born. Distant colonies like India, Egypt and Thrace were mere names to them.

'It lies to the west – over a dozen days from here on horseback. So gather and arm three of your best men. You will be the fourth and ride at my side. Find a sword and spear for me, Parviz.'

'My lord, we have nothing a prince would ever wish to carry. This is a poor place.'

'I need no jewels,' Cyrus said. 'Bring me a hunter's spear,

a soldier's blade. I feel the need to hunt, to ride fast and leave this dust behind me. I would see rivers and green woodland once again.'

'I obey, Highness,' Parviz said. He opened the small door and left it swinging as he raced away. Cyrus closed his eyes and raised his face to the sun.

In Susa, Cyrus left Parviz and his guards with the horses, while he stopped at a legion moneylender in the street of kings. Fountains and courtyards built for the glory of his father and grandfather lay around him, their images watching in white stone. Inside, he signed his name and pressed his royal signet to an order for one hundred gold archers, tossing the pouch to Parviz. His newest servant stood wide-eyed at the sight and could not resist peeking into the bag and fondling the coins. While Parviz changed half of them to silver, Cyrus took a day to bathe and have his muscles rubbed down. In a royal palace, tailors measured him for clothes and the local governor brought him the best mounts available. The prince ate well and saw his men to rooms near the city walls. When he had fulfilled his responsibilities to them, Cyrus rode over to the imperial barracks and training ground.

In silk and gold, he was immediately recognised by officers he had promoted and trained himself, rushing to do his bidding. The dusty beggar of the desert roads had vanished and he was thankful for it. Over the years, Cyrus had prided himself on rarely spending a second night in the same bed, so that he had visited every commander and officer in the western empire, from those who manned the city walls at Sardis, to remote mountain troops who guarded a single shrine. His face was known.

The barracks at Susa lay at the edge of the city, where once the land had been worthless. Persian gold had made an expanse of green grass and white buildings, watered and maintained by slaves, with a thousand men training at any given time. Cyrus had them stand to attention for him and he inspected them with Parviz at his side.

When he was alone with the regimental officers, he was given cool drinks and fanned in the shade. Every man there made light conversation at dinner, though they watched him and waited for his orders, wondering what had brought him to that place.

The prince kept his expression light as he mopped his mouth and leaned back. He turned to the polemarch, the senior commander.

'Polemarch Behrouz, I will need a personal guard, of course. Your men will do very well, from what I have seen. You are to be congratulated on their quality. Select . . . three hundred of the best to accompany me tomorrow.' He leaned in as the man nodded over his lamb chops. 'And, sir, some men might be tempted to send away the ones they dislike: the lazy, the complainers, the men of poor character. I will know if that has been done.'

'You will get only the best from me, Highness, I swear it. For your father's son, I cannot do less.'

Cyrus stared at the man, unsure if the news of his father's death had reached that place. It was unlikely, though it would be soaring out behind him. He had once heard an account of an eclipse, where the sun had been covered by a great shadow. The old man who had described it to the young princes had been an astrologer, brought hundreds of miles to instruct them. The detail that had stuck in Cyrus' mind was the man's awed memory of a shadow racing from the horizon towards him, faster than a galloping horse, covering the entire world. The news of his father's passing was like that shadow line. It could not be stopped or outraced. It would overtake them all and leave the empire changed in its wake.

Polemarch Behrouz of the royal barracks appeared uncomfortable with silence at table, so babbled on as Cyrus took a sip of red wine.

'In truth, Highness, I had thought you'd come about this business with the renegade Spartan. I swear we will run him out of the empire as soon as reinforcements arrive.'

Cyrus took a long drink before replying. His father had always preferred to negotiate over a meal, for the opportunities of distraction it allowed.

'Tell me what you think is true,' he said at last.

Behrouz blushed, but settled himself to report to a superior.

'The fellow commands some two thousand Greeks, my lord. I am told they were an army of Sparta, sent to protect Greek cities in Thrace to the north from some petty rebellion. This general sent home for those men and they marched out to meet him, accepting his command. But, Highness, this Spartan is a ruthless tyrant, as is well known. I have readied letters this very day, to ask for more men.'

'What is his name?' Cyrus asked.

'Clearchus, my lord. The people of Thrace sent their own letters to Greece, asking why this man, who had slaughtered a village without cause, why he has been given an army to do much worse.'

'I know of him,' Cyrus said.

Clearchus had been a famous governor of Byzantium, appointed while the Thirty ruled in Athens. When they had fallen, he too was cast out. It was true he was said to be a ruthless man, in the sense that he saw no room for mercy or compassion. Cyrus could have wished for a dozen of him at that moment. He felt a growing excitement in his chest and stomach, as if the wine had been stronger than he had realised.

'Where is he now, Behrouz, this tyrant of Sparta? Marching home?'

'Highness, I thought that was why you had come to us. He has camped in hills not three days' march from this city. We are ready to defend the walls if he comes, you may be certain.'

'And he has two thousand Spartans?' Cyrus asked.

'We captured one of his scouts, Highness, creeping about the walls of Susa. He said they had more than that, though the Greeks always lie.'

Cyrus found himself smiling.

'Yes. I have never known a people who delight in it the way they do. Does the scout still live?'

The officer nodded and Cyrus rose from his place, wiping his mouth with a cloth before throwing it down.

'Good. Show me to where you hold him – and find a fast horse.'

Cyrus took a deep breath and forced himself to calm, calling on the memories of Spartans he had known and asking in silence for their blessing and their aid. Anaxis would have chided him for the way his hands trembled, though it was lack of sleep and worry as much as anything else.

While he had waited for days in Susa for the Spartan general to ride in under truce, Cyrus had pulled layers of empire around himself. He had prayed in the temples and bathed twice a day, having his hair singed and perfumed. He had trained with sword and shield like a common soldier, though he'd found only a few men able to test him. The rest were too awed by his title, or too scornful of hard, physical work. The constant exercise and discipline he had known with the

Spartans had soured his indulgence for the soldiers of Susa. They seemed to spend a great deal of their time marching in fine uniforms, and very little in training with arms. In the evenings, Cyrus read in the palace library, but he could not relax. Sleep came fitfully or not at all. His father was dead; his brother ruled the empire. The world had changed. There were times when Cyrus thought he was the only one who even remembered how it had been.

Enough time had passed for the shadow line of his father's death to reach Susa. Cyrus had seen riders come in from the desert, so that the city began a period of mourning and all men averted their eyes from his. Perhaps his mother had prevailed on Artaxerxes; he had no way of knowing. Cyrus slept with a pearl knife-hilt in his hand in case she had not, though he doubted he would even hear an assassin before it was too late. The thought made his stomach surge with bitter acids, so that he belched. He felt uncomfortable that evening, less sure of himself than usual in the presence of the Spartan.

General Clearchus sat as if he might leap up for battle at any moment. Broad-chested and scarred along his arms, the man wore a red cloak over a bronze breastplate and leather kilt and greaves. His thighs were bare and thickly muscled, like those of a wrestler. He lounged like a cat resting in the sun, supremely confident in his own strength. Clearchus had not bargained for terms of a truce, but merely strode into Susa to meet the prince with only two companions, then left those men outside. They were not at war, after all.

Cyrus felt a nagging tension, perhaps because some part of his mind knew the general was a threat and would not close an eye in his presence. Yet in its way, the threat was honest. It was one thing Cyrus appreciated about the soldiers of that particular city. The Athenians would argue with anyone, absolutely for the sake of it. They seemed to enjoy tortuous knots and difficult moral choices. Persians were more similar than most of them cared to admit. With his own eyes, Cyrus had seen market traders ignore a queue of willing buyers to strike a bargain with the one customer who tried to argue the price.

In comparison, the Spartans wore their pride openly, though their enemies called it arrogance. They chose simplicity in all things, which meant they would not lie or deceive as a matter of personal honour, whether to spare the feelings of friends or to encourage the weak. If a man did not want an honest answer from a Spartan, it was best not to ask the question. Cyrus found himself smiling at the thought, though he knew his expression was being watched and judged.

'You ask a great deal,' Clearchus said. 'For a man who has already lost three hundred of my people.'

Cyrus felt anger spike in him at the words, at the implication that it was somehow his fault. Yet he leaned back in his chair, forcing himself to relax.

'I have explained that. I have also sent their salaries to the ephors of Sparta, dated to the day they were killed.'

'You saw Anaxis as a mercenary, then,' Clearchus said softly.

'He was a mercenary,' Cyrus replied. 'If he called me a friend, or I did, that was between us. I have fulfilled my responsibilities – and I remind you, Clearchus, that it was my father's support, my family's gold, that aided you in all your campaigns. Would Sparta have put your council of thirty to rule in Athens without me?'

'I do not speak for Sparta, especially this year, when I am called a tyrant by fools back home. No. Everything has a season,' Clearchus said. 'Even now, the Athenians are shouting again in their agora, claiming to have wrenched democracy from our unwilling hands. Loyal generals are murdered by slaves – and good men are left without honour, stripped of authority by those who never even knew command.' He sighed and rubbed the bridge of his nose. 'If Athenians rule once more in Athens, what did we fight to win? What has changed?'

'That is an argument to do nothing,' Cyrus said, suspecting the man was testing him. Very well, he would be as blunt. 'All lives are brief. Why then do anything at all but sleep in the sun? We all end up in the same place. Yet if we have pride, we fight to the last breath. I know you too well, Clearchus. As you know me. It matters that Spartan arms and Spartan laws ruled all Greece for a time. Let the small dogs bark now and tell themselves they are the victors. Some of us remember how it was. Thirty Spartans ruled in Athens, with three thousand Athenians to do your bidding. You gave them all a glimpse of greatness. They will not have forgotten that so easily.'

Clearchus chuckled, sitting back in his chair.

'I see you still like to argue. You are almost Greek in that.' He grinned at the prince's change of expression. 'Believe me, it was a compliment. Now, I do not seek to deny our debt of honour, Highness. You have been a friend to me, to Sparta – and to Greece. I merely sought to be certain you had not wasted the men who went with you. I knew Anaxis well. I grieve for his loss.'

'You will see him again,' Cyrus said.

The Spartan nodded.

'I will,' he said with absolute certainty, his eyes dark in his sunburned face. 'He will not go far from the river, no matter how long I make him wait. I will tell him you sent the news back to Sparta so that his name could be marked on the white wall – and his death pay, which will go to feed Spartan sons and daughters as they grow. And of course I will tell him you came to me seeking aid for your vengeance – and that I did not turn you away.'

'I will have to lie to many of those who come to stand with me,' Cyrus said seriously. 'Do you understand? I wanted you to know the truth of what I am about.'

'Your judgement was sound, then. I would not have forgiven a lie from you, Highness,' Clearchus replied. 'You buy my service and you earn my friendship. I will not fail you, but I will not lie for you either. If the other officers ask me why you are gathering a dozen small armies to march into the deserts of your Persian empire, I will tell them to ask you, that I am a simple soldier who stands where I am told to stand, and kills when I am told to kill.'

Cyrus blinked at the intensity of the man who sat before him. Clearchus was like a lion with his claws sheathed, who nonetheless knew he was still a lion.

'You should let me purchase a horse to carry you,' Cyrus said, giving himself time to gather his thoughts. 'It is not seemly for a general to walk alongside his men.'

'In Sparta, it is,' Clearchus said. 'I'll walk.' He shifted uncomfortably. 'In truth, I do not like horses. They peer at me.'

'You are afraid of horses?' Cyrus said in amazement, without thinking. The Spartan general became very still, as if time had stopped. Cyrus swallowed.

'I am *afraid* of nothing,' Clearchus said. 'I do not *like* horses. That is quite different.'

Cyrus found he had been holding his breath and he breathed out slowly.

'Yes, of course. They are not the same.'

Clearchus regarded him for a time. He seemed satisfied by what he saw.

'Perhaps we should discuss pay,' he said.

Cyrus looked up.

'You will serve me?'

'For one gold daric a month, per man, or twenty-six silver drachmas, yes. Raised to one and a half darics for battle or periods of unusually arduous service. I have two thousand Spartiate men, some eight hundred helot slaves and a few perioikoi – warriors of a lesser class. I suggest half pay for the perioikoi. The helots, of course, will need only food and equipment.'

'Of course,' Cyrus agreed. The terms were fair and no more than he had paid before, though he sensed the general considered it an irrelevance.

'I will put my seal to ten thousand darics, general. Will that be enough?'

The sum was vast and Clearchus did well not to choke on his wine. He wiped his chin.

'It is enough, Highness, yes. For so much, you will be honoured at home – and feared by your enemies.'

'You describe the only things of value in the world, general,' Cyrus said, probing the man. 'Is gold and silver so important, in comparison?'

To his surprise, Clearchus chuckled.

'There speaks one who has never put a child out in winter, when there was no food. Of course it is important. Your gold will pay for Spartans to be trained, for our people to survive and live in peace in the valley of Eurotas. No foreign army has entered our land of Hollow Lacedaemon since we discovered our way, not for six hundred years.' He paused, considering his audience. 'Though the Persians came closest.'

Cyrus inclined his head, accepting the compliment as it was intended.

'For yourself, though. That is what I meant. You serve for gold?'

Clearchus leaned forward, resting his forearms on his knees.

'Every one of my men is between twenty and sixty years of age. We march and fight for Lacedaemon for forty years, because it is . . . water spilled on a hot stone, our home. It must always be renewed, or it will vanish as if it had never been.'

'And when you go back there, when you have served, what then?'

'When we return, we will be fed and allowed to sit in peace, though the young boys mock old soldiers as they sleep. It was ever thus – all boys are fools.' He smiled and rubbed a hand over his face. 'I have not yet found a better way to spend a life than ours, Highness. Your gold buys my service, yes, but more, you will have the pleasure of seeing Spartans in battle. It is a rare gift and worth more than mere coins. After all, most men see it only once and never again.'

He leaned back and Cyrus smiled with him, the spell broken.

'Wine here,' Cyrus called to his servants. 'We must raise a cup to this rare gift.'

As he turned back to the Spartan, his expression became serious.

'Thank you, general. When I hear you speak, I miss Anaxis all the more.'

'Fight well and perhaps one day you will tell him that yourself,' Clearchus said.

'I am a Persian prince, though perhaps my status is uncertain this year.'

'There are princes in Hades, my lord. I have put one or two there myself.'

'Now you are amusing yourself at my expense,' Cyrus said.

'I am, Highness, yes.' The Spartan drank from his cup and smacked his lips in pleasure. 'I know this wine. It is from home.'

Cyrus smiled, pleased his gesture had not been wasted.

'Made by the sun and the soil and the vine.' He raised the cup and the Spartan copied the gesture. 'To those who have gone before. May we see them again,' Clearchus said.

Without another word, they clinked the cups together and drank them dry.

5

Xenophon opened the street door and stepped through, pressing his back to it as it closed. The young man was flushed and angry-looking, his chiton tunic and cloak bearing darker marks. As he breathed hard, something wet and foul slipped from the hem and landed on the stone floor.

The Athenian who owned the tiny house looked up from a table laid with a dozen kinds of green stems and leaves, as well as an array of mackerel he was deboning with a knife. The man was short and stocky, with white hair and a bald head as brown and freckled as old leather. Despite his age, he gave an impression of strength, with powerful arms and chest and slightly bowed legs showing bare under the table.

'Xenophon!' Socrates cried in delight, coming round the table and wiping his hands on an apron before holding them out in greeting. 'Have you come to join us for dinner? I have a Cretan recipe with bay leaves – and ripe figs after.'

Before the young man could reply, Socrates drew him into an embrace with great enthusiasm, almost lifting him from the ground. Despite himself, Xenophon found his mood beginning to improve.

'Xanthippe!' Socrates roared over his shoulder. 'Another for dinner!' He stood still for a moment, listening. 'Where *is* that girl? Is it too much to ask that she greets my guests? I am up to my elbows in fish. Your cloak is wet there. Is it raining? No, I would have heard. I would have felt it – the roof leaks again, for which I am also blamed. So, not rain. I see you smile now, as I seek your secrets, but you were not smiling before. It is those gangs of politicals, those children, of course.'

'They are not children, Socrates. They grow more bold and more cruel every time I am seen on the street. They live and breed like rats.'

'Better for them to throw fruit than stones, old friend.'

'It was both fruit and stones,' Xenophon said. He clenched his fist and flipped back the stained cloak to reveal a Spartan kopis on his hip. Socrates whistled softly.

'That is not a weapon for the streets of Athens. If you draw a Spartan blade in the shadow of the Acropolis, what will you do with it then?'

'They are a violent mob! They watch for me and pass word and gather wherever I go. I hear their steps clattering in the alleys, then they appear, roaring at me, showing me their red mouths! Spitting! You would have me walk through flying stones and screeching youths unarmed?' Xenophon demanded. He lowered his head. The humour had vanished in him, so that once more he looked mulish and flustered. 'When I was on the council, I had the right to bear arms. It has not been taken from me, with so much else. Would you have me defenceless?'

Without a word, Socrates took him by the arm and brought him further into the single room that was the heart of the house, with a set of rickety stairs to a single bedroom above. Xenophon ducked suddenly, barely avoiding a low beam he had struck many times before. He scowled and his friend chuckled.

'You see how it is better to be short?'

'I did not have this trouble in your old house,' Xenophon said. 'At least there, I could stand up straight.'

'But the rent! That old woman who owned it squeezed me like a plum.'

He picked up a couple of figs from the table and gestured with them, making Xenophon wince. Socrates sighed.

'When I was a mason, I ate and slept like a king. When I was a soldier, even. You never knew me then, when strength and skill with a sword was all I had. Three campaigns, Xenophon. Three times, I stepped onto the dance floor of Ares for my masters – and I saved the life of Alcibiades!'

'Really? You never said,' Xenophon replied drily.

Socrates clapped him on the shoulder, making him stagger.

'I have told the tale too many times, I know it, though a good story is a work of art, not unlike a statue. It is the polish that matters, as much as the stone.'

'The lies.'

'No, it is not the same. The polish. But let us return to your troubles, my friend. Each day, you endure these taunts and insults to your honour. You say they grow worse. You show me a Spartan kopis like you might use it, though your enemies are too young to attack in honour. Will you rush among them and kill children?'

'They are not children,' Xenophon replied.

'They are men, then? Bearded and trained? Armed for war?'

Xenophon shook his head, recalling the ragged gang members who had darted at him. He saw Socrates required him to answer out loud and he sighed.

'No, they were not men.'

Socrates nodded, holding a finger in the air to mark the point.

'To threaten with a blade you will not use feels like the

action of a weak man – and, my friend, you are not a weak man. Is that your intention, to wag a bit of sharp iron at them and have them cover their eyes and bow to you?'

'No,' Xenophon said reluctantly. 'Though I thought I might.'

'It is a good idea to think things through before you are arrested for injury or murder, I have always thought. Here, chop these for me, as fine as you can. Not the bay leaves, they are merely a herb. Ah, the greens – they are the stuff of life! The vigour of sorrel and nettle, amaranth and vetch and chicory and black nightshade.'

'Is that last not a poison?' Xenophon asked, as he took a knife and began to chop.

'The nightshade? Not if it is picked ripe and boiled, as I have done. Would I risk the lives of my boys? Of my noble guest? No. The whole world is a larder for a man with eyes to see, with hands to tease the good leaves from mere grass. Ask me how much this meal cost, Xenophon, this meal that will feed my wife, my sons, my guest and my own appetite, which is too often my master and never my slave?'

Xenophon eyed the array of mackerel, more than a dozen of the fish laid out on the worktop. He knew the philosopher too well, however.

'Not a single coin,' he said.

'Not a single coin!' Socrates echoed as he spoke. 'Ah, you are an oracle! Old Anatoli on the docks gave me the fish in return for my helping him mend his net. The knots are very interesting and I took away a new skill – worth more than a few fish. He thought he was paying me for my labour.' He leaned in close, his voice dropping to a conspiratorial murmur. 'In truth, I would have paid him. Eh?' He slapped the wooden table with a powerful hand in his delight, making the whole room shake.

Xenophon looked up at a clatter from overhead. He wished his old master would accept a gift or even a loan to live in a better quarter of Athens, but Socrates would not hear of it. A neighbour's argument began on the other side of the wall, quite audible as Socrates went on.

'But you distract me, Xenophon. With your talk of herbs and fishermen. Let us return to your problem. I do not like to see you angry. So . . . if you will not attack these unbearded youths, if you will not threaten them like an old woman, will you then gather them around and explain how they should not taunt and throw stones?'

'I do not think I will do that, no. My dignity will not survive it.'

'That is true. Boys can be rude, as I still remember. They would mock a gentle hand. And yet . . . you will not be harsh. Will you use a stick? Will you kick them? Better than a kopis knife, I think.'

'I might,' Xenophon said with satisfaction, imagining it. He chopped the wild greens as he spoke, his movements quick and sure as he added each handful to a huge bowl, ready for the family.

'Did you bring wine?' Socrates said. Xenophon shook his head, embarrassed. The philosopher shrugged, reaching beneath the table for an old wineskin and pulling out the plug. 'Never mind, there is a little here. Men of words cannot talk dry. Am I a wild ass or a goat to drink water? No, a man drinks wine, to warm his blood, to step outside himself and look back with another's judgement. That "ec-stasis", that stepping out, it is a secret of a good life, my friend. We cannot always be ourselves. It is too wearying.'

Xenophon found himself smiling as the older man set two rough cups before him and filled them both.

'My dear Xanthippe does not see the value in the wineskin,

not as I do. She . . .' Socrates thought better of whatever he was about to say as his wife came down the stairs. 'My dearest flower, Xenophon has consented to join us for our meal this evening. Did you not hear me call?'

'I heard,' Xanthippe said, curtly. She seemed irritated and Xenophon looked aside, allowing them their intimacies. 'The boys were out on the neighbour's roof again, did you know?'

'My beloved, we have a guest. And boys do climb. It is in their nature.'

'Hmm. When they are encouraged, perhaps. You are welcome in our home, councillor, such as it is,' Xanthippe said.

Xenophon bowed deeply to her and touched his cheeks to hers though his hands were full of green curls and threads.

'Thank you,' he said. 'Though, sadly, there is no council any longer. Your husband was helping me with a problem.'

'Oh yes, he's very good at solving the problems of others,' she said.

'My dear sweet fig, I have opened the last flask of the wine,' Socrates said. 'Would you fetch me another couple from old Delios in his little shop?'

'I will if you have the coin to pay for it,' she said.

'He is a friend, my love. Tell him I will pay him next week.'

'He said you must pay for last month before he'll give you any more.'

'Nonetheless,' Socrates insisted. 'Tell him I have an old friend for dinner. He will understand.'

Xenophon reached for his purse, but found his arm gripped by fingers that had worked mallet and chisel from their youngest years.

'You are my guest,' Socrates said softly. 'Do not reach for your coins in this house.'

'It is only what I should have remembered to bring.'

'We are where we are,' Socrates said with a shrug. 'Leave me my pride, my foolish vanity. Three new students came to join me last week.'

'You should teach them how to shape stone,' Xanthippe said. 'At least they would pay you for that. Or how to use a spear and shield. Not for all your questions. They pay nothing for what you give away so freely.'

'Will you fetch the wine, my pomegranate?' Socrates asked, his voice hardening.

Xanthippe decided she had pushed him far enough and went out to the street, shutting the door hard behind her.

'She is . . . a fiery woman,' Socrates said. He looked adoringly at the door. 'I do not deserve her.'

'Does philosophy truly earn so little?' Xenophon said. 'I can pay, as your student, if you would let me. I said so when you moved out of your last home.'

'I am a proud man,' Socrates said. 'As all Athenians are. I do not like to go with my hands outstretched, saying "feed me", "clothe me" to other men. No. I make my *own* way. I live on my wits. I feed the boys and my wife and if there are some debts and difficult months, what of it? We have such a brief time alive, Xenophon! Should I waste a day in worry? As I sleep tonight, pfft, I could be gone in a draught. My dear Xanthippe might find me cold tomorrow, my wife bereft and weeping, my sons forced to be slaves or to starve. Yet I could die in my sleep as a mason and the result would be the same. I could die on the battlefield and they would suffer just as much. Instead, I ask my questions, and sometimes men see truths they could not see before. It can be its own reward, Xenophon . . .'

'Ask me, then,' Xenophon said grimly.

'You know the truth already. It is my desire only to pluck it out, to make you hold it to your eye and truly see it. Some men cannot stand that light and grow strangely angry when they look in such a way. Critias was one of those – and his anger was his undoing in the end. May his soul find peace.'

Xenophon bowed his head in memory. Socrates nodded as if agreeing with himself.

'You are made of better stuff than him, I think. Very well.'

The two men faced each other across the table, the fish and chopped vegetables forgotten.

'Why do the young men of the street throw stones and rotten fruit at you?'

'Because they are allowed to run wild. Because this is not a wealthy part of the city. There is no order here.'

'Do they throw stones at all who pass along this street?'

There was silence until Xenophon shook his head.

'So, why you, my friend?'

'You know very well why.'

'Still, I wish to hear you say it.'

'They have seen me many times in this place. They know my name.'

'Do they hate your name, then? They surely must to throw stones at it.'

'They see me as a traitor,' Xenophon muttered, flushing.

'So not your name, then, but what you have done?'

'I have done nothing wrong. Nothing!'

'Why, then, would they believe you are a traitor?'

Xenophon threw up his hands.

'I came to you as a friend, not a student. I am not in the mood for this tonight. Why not pour the last of the wine, or let me buy more. We can talk of anything else. Let me leave this out on the street, in the gutters.'

Socrates piled the chopped vegetables and fish into the bowl with a slab of white cheese. He poured olive oil until everything shone, then crumbled thick pinches of salt between his fingers.

'Better to do this when my love is out of the house. She says I use too much salt and it is true, but what is life without it? And my friend, you have not come to me for a month, though all the city is in a ferment. You came today for answers, perhaps for advice. So, like the snail-sellers with their little bone picks, let us seek the meat within.'

The door came open again and the philosopher's wife returned. She glared at the huge bowl and the two men as she placed two clay amphorae of wine on the tabletop between them.

'Delios says he must be paid or there will be no more, that he is not a moneylender. He said you would drink him into poverty if he let you.'

'He is a dear friend, a hero amongst men,' Socrates said with satisfaction. He pulled out both stoppers of clay and leather, sniffing at them with pleasure.

'These are new and raw and young, my love. They are the first weeks of a marriage, new friends, new loves, new triumphs!'

His wife sniffed, though she did not resist when he gathered her into his arms. Xenophon had never liked her manner with Socrates. Xanthippe seemed to find her husband exasperating and embarrassing, but then they had raised three sons together. Though there was a thread of real bitterness in her manner, it was almost smothered by her love for the burly man who kissed her so soundly in that kitchen.

'Call the boys, my dearest,' Socrates said. 'The councillor was explaining his anger to me.'

'The council was disbanded,' Xenophon said warily. 'I have no position now.' He was familiar with the darting questions and still unwilling to explore further, though Socrates seemed to have forgotten his objection.

'Does a city not need a council, then? Are there no good men left in Athens to take on public works?'

Socrates passed him a cup of the new wine and Xenophon took a draught of it, seating himself at the table as Xanthippe roared for her sons and laid bowls, spoons and knives for them all. She lit an oil lamp and the room brightened to gold.

'Why must I say what you already know?' Xenophon said.

'Why must you resist? Do you see that you are?'

Xenophon set his jaw, his mood darkening as the room lightened.

'Very well. The council was disbanded when the Spartans were overthrown. Is that what you wanted to hear? The Thirty were captured and most of them were murdered in the street by the mob. Your own Spartan pupil, Critias, was hanged. That is why there is no council.'

'And you, my friend?' Socrates said softly. As he spoke, his three sons came clattering down the stairs from above, scuffed and laughing, though they took seats in silence when they saw their father and his guest.

'What about me?'

'How is it that you live? How did you survive the rebellion that tore down Spartan banners?'

'I was pardoned, with three thousand more.'

Xenophon clenched his fist as he spoke and Socrates reached out and patted the shaking hand resting on his table. The food was served and Xanthippe thanked the goddess Demeter and the nymphs of the sea for providing their food. Two of the boys were tall and slim as wands, while the last could have been a younger version of their father, with a thick mass of black hair. All three boys fell to eating like ravenous dogs, wiping every drop of oil with crusts of dry bread.

70

'If you were pardoned, why then do they cry out against you in the street?' Socrates asked. 'Why do they throw stones and fruit?'

Xenophon dipped his head.

'Some of them had fathers who died by order of the Thirty. They blame those of us who aided them in their work, though we wanted only order and the best way to live. What did democracy ever bring us, except destruction? How many men of Athens did we lose at Syracuse? How many more rotted in their cave prisons? Three times, Sparta came to us and said, "We are all Greek. Let us put an end to war between us." Three times, the democratic vote of Athens scorned that noble gesture. Even when we were losing, they came and offered us peace – and we rejected it.'

'And you were angry with them? You felt the Spartans were more noble?'

'I did, because they were. That is not an opinion. Athens gave a voice to the mob – and what does the mob ever want but to live without work, to lie in the sun, to be given what they will not earn! Of course I joined the Thirty in their labours. And I was right.'

'And now? The people of Athens have forgiven you?'

'No. They torment me. After all I did for them, they see me as an enemy! We held power for a single year in the long history of Athens, Socrates. And in that time, there was bread and the great plays were performed. There were no riots for months in the city. No criminal was allowed to choose the manner of his death! Those who threatened peace were killed – and there was peace as a result.'

'The violence stopped, then?' Socrates said, almost in a whisper. 'As these criminals were executed?'

Xenophon breathed out, his head sinking to his chest. Even the boys had stopped eating to hear.

71

'It grew worse. Day by day, month by month. We thought if we killed the leaders, the rest would settle and heed the law, but they kept springing up. First it was the sons and the uncles of the firebrands, then they seemed to grow like heads of the Hydra. On every street, men we did not know stood up to speak to the crowds. We told them to disperse – and we were not gentle. We enforced a curfew of the whole city at night and we hanged more and more of them.'

'But there was peace in the end?' Socrates said.

'No. They rose up, with torches and iron. In all the streets, killing the Thirty in their beds, murdering and looting and . . .' He shook himself, dragging clear of his memories.

'But they have forgiven you since then? It has been, what, almost another year? They must have put those dark days behind them? Surely they have rebuilt the walls torn down by the Spartans, to lay bare our submission for all Greece to see?'

Xenophon looked around him, at the stern-faced woman, the three sons watching him in fascination as they wiped a finger around the empty bowls, missing no morsel. He shook his head.

'The walls have been left as rubble, the stone taken for new houses. And no, they have not forgiven me. There are orators now who call for new punishments for those who aided the Thirty, for all the pardons to be set aside. They say they were too lenient before.'

No one interrupted the silence that followed until Xenophon spoke again.

'I don't know what to do. I cannot run, but if I stay, I think it will not end well.'

'You have no wife or children, Xenophon. Your life is your own. What are you, thirty?'

'Twenty-six!' he replied. Socrates chuckled.

'One day, we should talk about vanity, my friend. Until then, see your life now, as it is. What will you do? Go on as you have been? What change can you make?'

Xenophon straightened his back, accepting another cup of wine, though it made his senses swim. He tried to step outside himself and see his days as if he observed a stranger. The power of the wine was just what Socrates tried to do, so that great revelations came to those who had the nerve to answer honestly.

'I must leave Athens,' he said. 'Though it is my home, I must leave.'

He said the words almost in a daze. Socrates smiled at him and gripped his forearm across the table.

'Not for ever. Even Athenians forget and forgive in the end. You are a young man, Xenophon, marching in place with worry and fear on your shoulders. Throw such things aside! See the world. In time, you will return. They will have forgotten all these upheavals, I promise you. It is the way of men. Go far and thrive. Bring stories home to entertain my beloved wife.'

Xenophon stood and embraced the older man.

'All I have ever asked is to learn how best to live,' he said. 'You have always known what I can only glimpse. They should be led by you, Socrates. Athens would be great then.'

'Ah, lad, it is great now! I wish you could see it. If you trust my judgement so far, you might value the voice of the people just a little more. Critias was the same. I am teaching a young man tomorrow who tells me that man must have his guardians, as sheep must have shepherds. How is it that all my best students see no worth in our Athenian arguments, our questioning? The rest of the world is thick with tyrants and guardians of the people. Kings are like bees, they swarm in such numbers! Only in Athens do we give a voice to the young, the poor, the clever. To an ugly man like me, without wealth or patrons. My boy, what we have here is a flower under the midday sun, more fragile than glass.'

'The gods advise and rule us,' Xenophon said seriously. 'As a father instructs his sons. Kings and leaders are no more than the nature of man repeating that order. Or would you see authority in those who shout loudest? Would you let those with the most voices howl down the wise and the holy?'

'I have challenged the gods to strike me down before,' Socrates said. 'They . . .'

His wife reached across him to collect the bowls, so that she hid her husband from Xenophon's view. He heard the hissed words that passed between them, though he pretended not to. Some things were not for the ears of children, or the arbiters of public morality. Not everyone in Athens could appreciate Socrates' desire to argue and question everything, even to his own destruction. The thought was a strange one and Xenophon picked at it as the wine was poured once more, with a slat of cheeses laid down with bread and grapes. The boys asked permission to leave and rushed off as soon as it was given.

'You know, Socrates – you taught the Spartan Critias, who joined the Thirty and ruled in Athens before the mob came for him. How is it that I am chased through the streets and threatened for the part I played, while no one bothers you at all?'

'I am too well loved,' Socrates said. His wife snorted as she rubbed the bowls clean and he grinned at her. 'In truth, they know I love them. They do not see me hold myself higher than the common men. What madness it would be to do so! I am a man of Athens. I am a Greek. I am a mason and a soldier and a questioner. I walk barefoot among them

74

and they see the young lads gather to listen to me. I am no threat to them.'

'They call you the wisest man in Athens,' Xenophon said drily.

'What have I done that is worth as much as a cup of good red wine? When I cut stone, there it was, a new thing in the world. When I stood with my friends in a line and I knew pain and saw blood, I was feared. All I do now is ask questions in the marketplace.'

'Alcibiades said you made him understand his whole life was that of a slave,' Xenophon said softly. 'There are some who do not appreciate insights of that sort.'

'He is a great man. I am pleased I saved his life, even if he would not go to war again, after. As for the rest, I am almost seventy years old. When I walk through the markets, I wear a patched robe and carry a shepherd's staff. No one is afraid of me. But you, Xenophon. When you raise your eyebrow at them, when you assume the manner of your father, of those who think they know best, perhaps you do yourself no favours.'

Xenophon said nothing for a time, though they emptied the first amphora and began the second. In the end, the younger man nodded.

'I will think on what you have said. I will go to the market-place, to the recruiters there. While your wine is in my veins. And I will let the gods choose my path.'

'You are a fine man, son of Athens,' Socrates said. 'If I had my youth to spend again, I would come with you.' He looked behind him to where his wife was waiting. 'As my youth has gone and I am married, however, my time is not always my own. I wish you luck.'

They embraced once more and Xenophon slipped out of the door, a little unsteady, but with his gaze fixed far away.

When Socrates returned to his table, he found the pouch of silver coins Xenophon had left under an upturned bowl. He toyed with them for a time, deep in thought, then shrugged and sent for more wine to celebrate his unexpected good fortune.

6

The city of Sardis lay on the western edge of the empire, south of Byzantium. In Sardis, men believed distant Susa was the Persian capital. The city of Persepolis, where a mountain had been carved to a plateau, was not even a place of myth.

Wealthy Greeks walked with their guards in the markets in Sardis, selecting goods and spices for markets back home or their own pleasure. Blond slaves from Gaul or silk from China could be bought for vast sums in the city, though the true wealth was not for the vulgar gaze. High walls hid the estates of princes and kings, so that no one passing by knew that gardens as vast as any in the west could be found on the other side.

At the heart of the city, the imperial palace and grounds were kept in perfect readiness, though no member of the family had set foot there in a dozen years. An army of servants and slaves swept and painted and clipped hedges even so. They kept a good distance from the royal prince, so that he and his three companions appeared to walk through empty gardens. Like so much else, the privacy was merely illusion.

Cyrus wore light robes in the heat, with a curved blade at his hip, the handle set with rubies. A single gold ring adorned his left hand, the only other sign of wealth and power. The Spartan, Clearchus, padded along at his side, bare-legged and with a red cloak drifting back in the breeze as he listened.

'I thought I knew that part of Anatolia, my lord,' one of the men said.

General Proxenus would not call the royal prince a liar in that place, but doubt was written on his heavy features. All the Greek officers were fit and tanned, as their profession had made them. Somehow, Proxenus the Boeotian looked to be fashioned of bone. His forehead shaded his eyes and a great nose cut the air before him like a ship's prow. Clearchus liked him, but the Spartan understood he was witness to the game of kings, where honesty could get a man killed before he had ever become a threat.

'You cannot know every hill tribe, Proxenus, surely?' Cyrus said, clapping him on the back. 'All Anatolia is part of my brother's empire, even the rebellious south – and I command his armies. Perhaps I should march a few thousand eastern Persians into those hills, eh? Men who have never walked those lands before? No, I think I do need Greek soldiers for this work. Clearchus recommended you – and I have heard your name as a fine leader of men.'

'You flatter me, my lord,' Proxenus said, dipping to one knee before rising up.

'No more than is deserved. So are you willing, Proxenus? Can you find me two thousand hoplites of good quality? Trained and experienced men who will not run from savage tribes?'

'I believe I can, yes. I know a dozen captains and they will have kept records of the men they have trained. Some will be on campaign, of course, or retired. Two thousand is not too many.'

The Greek general looked at the prince and then across to Clearchus. There was something off, though Proxenus could not have said what it was. Greek soldiers were valued all over the world for their skill. They hired themselves as

mercenaries and commanded the highest prices. Still, Proxenus sensed something was not quite right. His instinct was
to refuse the commission, but on the other hand, the prince
had offered him a fortune.

'You want my men for just one year? To go into the hills
and clear out the tribes there?'

'As if they had never existed,' Cyrus said.

His eyes were large, Clearchus noted. The prince seemed
to be willing the man to accept his word. They watched as
Proxenus rubbed the bristles on his spade of a chin.

'I'll need to pay them part in advance to show good faith,
of course.'

'As you wish,' Cyrus said with a shrug. 'I will introduce
you to my aide, Parviz. He will arrange the first payment and
anything else you need. Hone your men, general. Bring them
to such an edge as to shave the hairs off my forearm and I
will thank you for it.'

'And then we will march against these Pisidians? In the
south?' Proxenus said.

'And then report to me that you are ready! I might wish to
see your men parade before I send them marching away for
a thousand miles.'

'I see. I am honoured, Highness, for your trust in me. And
that Clearchus spoke for me, though he has not seen me in
ten years. I will not let you down, either of you. From this
moment on, I serve the throne of Persia.'

'You serve Prince Cyrus,' Clearchus said.

The Greek general paused in the moment of dropping to
one knee.

'Are they not the same?' he asked.

Cyrus laughed, though he could have strangled the Spartan at that moment.

'My brother is the emperor!' he said. 'For eight years, I

have commanded the service and loyalty of every man under arms, from Sardis to India. Of course they are the same.'

He watched as the man dipped down, rising before Cyrus had given him permission. Cyrus frowned. The Greeks never made proper obeisance, stretched out on their bellies before him. He understood it was just their way, but for one raised in the palaces of Persia, it brought a prickle of discomfort in him.

When Proxenus had left, Cyrus turned to the other man, who had not said a word and merely watched while they walked through the gardens.

'I find I am weary,' Cyrus announced to the air.

Before he had finished speaking, a column of servants appeared, carrying table and chairs and setting it with fine blue glasses. Small dishes of food were added to ease the pangs of hunger, so that Cyrus reached for olives and roasted garlic as he sat, never noticing the servant who placed the chair under him.

Sophaenetus the Stymphalian could not help glancing behind to be sure a servant waited there for him as well. A glass was raised to his hand and he sipped at cool juices within.

'My lord, I am not used to such things,' Sophaenetus said.

'Perhaps you can become used to them, Netus, if you serve well,' Clearchus said before the prince could reply.

'General Netus, is it?' Cyrus asked.

The man bowed his head in reply, accepting the familiarity as if he had been given a choice.

'You heard what I said to Proxenus,' Cyrus went on. 'I imagine you know I have met with many such men over the past few weeks.'

'You must hate these Pisidians with a rare passion,' Netus said.

He looked into the distance as he sipped his wine, enjoying the breeze through the gardens. He imagined Clearchus was fretting at such a display of comfort. The Spartan would be looking for a patch of nettles or a thornbush to restore his usual misery, no doubt. Netus had never understood that outlook, not when the world was a place of gentle airs and hilltops, of fine flesh and flashing eyes. He watched both men closely, but the prince in particular. In the city, it was said Cyrus hardly slept for his labours, that he had summoned every soldier for a thousand stades in any direction. He certainly spent gold as a river, as if it meant nothing to him.

Netus waited for a reply, but neither man answered. He noticed the Spartan's expression had gone wooden, his eyes distant. He sighed.

'Your Highness, I have served alongside Spartans, Corinthians, Thebans and Athenians for twenty years. I worked my way to a position of authority and trust, so that men looked to me to give orders that would mean they lived or died that day. I have fought three major campaigns and I think a dozen small actions, surviving them all without a scratch or serious wound. On my fortieth birthday, a horse stepped onto my foot and broke half the bones in it. I could not work for six months and . . . well, funds are low. So I cannot say I do not care for coins, not at the rates you are offering. You buy my service – and my obedience. If you say, "Netus, I do not wish to discuss my true purpose," I will understand completely. I know some twelve hundred men who would jump up from their marriage beds to march away from Corinth for good pay. Your name commands respect – and men speak well of you. I can assemble twelve hundred who are the equal of any Spartan.'

Clearchus snorted and Netus turned a wry eye on him.

'Clearchus I have known for half my life. Well enough to say he is not a man for dissembling or half-truths, Highness. Nor, I believe, are you. I imagine you both have your purpose and I have no quarrel with it. Yet we are old hands, are we not? Let there be no more talk of dangerous hill tribes, not between us.' He chuckled and sipped his fruit juice. 'Clearchus has a couple of thousand Spartans at his command, as I heard it. For all he does not know good wine from vinegar, there is not a savage tribe in the world who could give him much trouble, no matter how they have bred, nor the height of their crags.'

Netus flashed a glance at the prince, to see how his words were being received. The Stymphalian blinked when he saw Cyrus was laughing, his eyes bright.

'I have amused you?' Netus said.

'Not at all, general,' Cyrus replied. 'Clearchus told me you would not accept the tale we agreed. As you say, I have other reasons to gather an army. If those reasons become the talk of the marketplace, it will not go well for me.' He sipped his own drink, assessing the man before him as General Netus inclined his head.

'I understand, of course. As I say, your gold buys my service. I am but a humble tool. The woodman's axe does not ask which tree it will cut down.'

Clearchus gave a bark of laughter, so that both men turned to him.

'Netus is not a humble man, Highness. However, I have never known him to gossip either.'

Netus smiled tightly.

'Perhaps such a humble axe might wonder if he will face horsemen or slingers. Or whether he will fight on sea or land. It is your choice, Highness, of course.'

The prince turned back and his expression was suddenly

serious. He looked around him, sensing the eyes and perhaps the ears of servants nearby. He gestured to the Stymphalian and General Netus leaned forward until the prince could breathe into his ear. Clearchus sat back so he could watch the man's expression change.

Netus did well, showing little as the prince leaned away once more.

'I see. The Pisidians it is, then. I admire a man who can keep his own counsel.'

They rose together and Clearchus clapped the Stymphalian general on his back as one friend to another. Servants came at a gesture to show the Greek to the gate and Cyrus and Clearchus were left alone.

'Did you tell him?' Clearchus asked, for once not sure of the answer.

'I did,' Cyrus said. 'I must have the best men with me, general, if I am to have any hope at all. If I have one talent, it is in finding those men.'

'You give me honour, at the same time as complimenting yourself, Highness,' Clearchus said.

'So I did.'

Xenophon winced as he heard his name called behind him in the busy street. Athens had been the richest city in Greece for centuries. Poor men had always come looking to make their fortune there, while others worked the warships of the Athenian fleet and spent their pay in taverns on the docks. Some preferred to steal, risking a public flogging or banishment. It disgusted Xenophon to see young men who could have joined any mercenary company lounging their lives away, drunk on cheap wine, sometimes even holding out their hands to those who passed by.

He had come to know a few of them as he and Socrates

walked the streets in conversation. The sight of the ugly man strolling barefoot in a robe as patched and grey as that of the poorest beggar had attracted attention, of course. Xenophon recalled the first time he had sat at the feet of the philosopher in the open agora marketplace, when Socrates had called a youth named Hephaestus to sit by him. The lad had been some sort of leader in a local gang. He'd swaggered up, with his friends calling out that the old goat would be using him like a woman. Xenophon had been annoyed, but Socrates had asked Hephaestus question after question, in a torrent. The old man had worked beneath the skin of the first jokes and crude replies, seeking the young man's true self. As he did, something came to life in the gang leader. One of his friends leaned in to make some jeering comment and Hephaestus had smacked his head for him, so hard the boy fell down and strode off in humiliation.

Xenophon had seen it a hundred times since. Yet Socrates denied knowing anything at all, saying that all he did was ask questions, until men understood what they really believed. For some, it was a revelation like the sun rising over the hills. For others, the knowledge was too much and they hated themselves – or more often, the man who had made them see who they truly were and what they believed.

Xenophon glanced behind and clenched his fists when he saw the shaved head of Hephaestus bobbing along in the mass of people. The young man was a thief as well as a bully and the crowds there were leaving the theatre of Dionysus. They walked and talked of what they had seen inside, lost in a kind of daze, while men like Hephaestus moved amongst them, cutting away gold chains and pouches of coin, whatever they could take. The gangs preyed on those too weak to defend themselves, and Xenophon detested them all.

Perhaps that dislike was what Hephaestus had sensed in him. Though the street rat followed Socrates like a bodyguard whenever he was out, Hephaestus had formed a rare dislike for Xenophon. Barely eighteen, he was more bone than flesh and not fool enough to challenge Xenophon directly. Instead, Hephaestus encouraged his skinny brethren to launch stones and eggs and fruit whenever they saw the Athenian nobleman.

Xenophon's rage had felt like armour at first, so that he had rushed at them when they came too close, or when some foul thing struck him on the face and neck. They'd hooted and screeched, scattering and calling insults. If he walked with Socrates, they merely watched and grinned at him, but on his own, they mocked the 'noble-man' or the 'horse-man' in their high voices.

On this day, they called his name merely out of habit – they had richer prey in the crowds. Xenophon had walked around the edge of the great city theatre, where thousands came each year for the festival of drama, to be drawn in to tragedies and comedy. Even Socrates had been mocked by the satires there, though the old man had roared so hard with laughter at the sight of the actor playing him that he'd rather spoiled the intended effect.

Xenophon found his feet had taken him away from the public stables where his horse awaited. His family estate was outside the city and he came in as rarely as he could manage in those days. He had no wife, no one who needed him. His parents had left him wealth enough never to seek work, but the years seemed to stretch ahead without much joy at the prospect. He looked at the row of recruiters arrayed before him, to the shaded awnings they had rigged with jugs of cool water or wine. They sensed his interest like hawks and turned bright gazes on him, seeing a tall young man at the peak of his strength.

He considered for a time, without responding to their entreaties, while the theatre crowd drifted away and Hephaestus and his grubby thieves went with them or on to some new vice. There was nothing in Athens for him, not that year. Xenophon had known power, as one of the administrators under the Thirty. The Thirty Tyrants, as they were called then, though Xenophon had known them as decent and ruthless men. They had certainly not allowed street gangs to flourish unchecked! Yet somehow the public executions had lit a fire under the city, until it spilled out in one great night of violence. His life had changed then and he could not see how to know peace again.

Xenophon walked to the first recruiter, a Spartan by his dress. The man took one look and nodded in satisfaction. He had seen that same expression many times before.

'Put your mark there, son,' he said. 'And in return, we'll make a man of you. Your own mother won't know you when you come home – and the girls will put flowers in their hair when they see you. They do love a soldier, son.'

'Very well,' Xenophon said. He sensed the man's surprise when he wrote his name on the slate rather than a letter or wax stamp.

'Any special skills, lad? Besides the writing?'

'Horses,' Xenophon said. He felt dazed somehow, as if it was happening to someone else. 'I know horses.'

The Spartan's eyebrows rose.

'A noble Athenian, is it? Running from her father, are you? Or debts?'

'I . . . I served the Thirty,' Xenophon said. 'I need a new start.'

The officer's face cleared, his eyes showing something like

sympathy. As a Spartan, he knew a little more than most about Athenian resentment.

'Ah,' he said. 'Then I should thank you for your service, son. They always forget we gave them three chances to make peace. They refused each time, so we pulled their walls down.'

'I've said the same,' Xenophon admitted. His thoughts were clearing and he found his old worries falling away as he considered his future.

'Where will I be sent?' he said.

'Most men ask about the pay first, but if you're a nobleman, I suppose you're not short. We're off to southern Anatolia, lad, to fight the Pisidians. Nasty, brutish bastards, with spears. We'll show them what Greek training means, bring back a few savage heads, have our way with their women and be back home by next spring. You'll have a couple of scars for the ladies and a few good stories for your sons. Honestly, when I think about it, you should almost be paying me.'

He handed Xenophon a stone token and pointed down the line to where a clerk sat at a table, half a dozen men standing around him.

'See that little fellow over there, the scribe? He'll take your name and details for you – and your pay starts from today, though we're not quite up to numbers yet.'

'How long before we ride out?' Xenophon said.

'That's the spirit, lad. Keen. Good. Won't be more than a day or two, I'd say. We'll take ship east and gather at Sardis. You've made the right choice, son. You'll go out a boy and come back a man, I guarantee it.'

Another potential recruit had come to listen and Xenophon saw the Spartan's attention switch to the newcomer. He could hardly believe what he had done, but it felt right.

He did know horses, and he knew men. Whatever else it took, he would surely pick it up on the march to Sardis. Yes. He felt lighter as he walked back into the city, towards where he had stabled his mount. It was the right decision. He only wondered if he should pay for a few lessons in swordplay before he left.

7

In the hall of kings in Persepolis, Tissaphernes prostrated himself on a black marble floor. He had learned not to rise before he was called – recent stripes on his back were testament to that. Artaxerxes forgave no slight, no insult. The young king sat on his throne and accepted the tribute of rulers and vassals alike, as if all men were slaves to him. Tissaphernes had seen the dark looks on noblemen as they'd left the royal presence, forced to leave their dignity behind them. The twenty-eight nations of the empire had all sent sons and senior lords to the funeral of Darius. For forty days, the empire had mourned his loss, with thousands of slaves chanting prayers to Ahura Mazda at every hour, to speed his soul to heaven. The great tomb was lined in gold that would not corrupt, with guards chosen for their beauty as much as their martial skill. Each had stood willingly to be killed with a single blow to the chest. The bodies were arranged on thrones of gold that faced the outer door, left to guard the realm of the dead. Their names would be recorded alongside that of the king, and their families raised a level in honour.

On that last day in the tomb, Tissaphernes remembered a sense of the mountains falling still all around them, with only the fluttering spit of torches on either side. Artaxerxes had gone beyond the outer door to commune with his father, weeping and murmuring secrets into the ear of the corpse. As they'd left, the wooden stairs used by the masons and labourers had been torn down. The tomb lay unreachable after that, high in the sheer face of the royal cliffs, like a window cut into stone.

Tissaphernes felt a muscle in his back stretch to discomfort as he waited for his old pupil to recognise his presence. He was more than sixty years old and the position was uncomfortable for him, for all he understood a young man's need to impress his authority on the court. The servants all went about in felt slippers, so it was said, aware that his disapproval would mean their heads spinning across the polished floor. A new king looked for laziness in those who served him – and punished the slightest transgression with great swiftness.

Tissaphernes looked up at a touch. He accepted the arm of the servant who helped him to his feet, then followed him down the length of the throne room. Guards lined an avenue as wide as a city street, with columns of polished granite that had been brought from Egypt by sea over a century before. The head and foot of each one was layered in gold, the wealth of an empire that drained back to the palaces and temples of its kings.

At the far end, Artaxerxes lounged, sipping at a golden bowl of something that had made his eyes wide and glassy. He tipped it up with a sharp motion, so that it left red marks at the edges of his mouth. As Tissaphernes approached and began to drop down once again, the king tossed it to a slave and rose. Two slave girls moved quickly to get out of his way as he stepped forward. Tissaphernes saw one of them pinch the other in a temper, though Artaxerxes did not notice. From beneath lowered brows, Tissaphernes looked them over with a connoisseur's appreciation. When two young women were chosen from multitudes and trained and fed to give pleasure to an emperor, their beauty was predictably arresting. The one who had pinched the other wore her black hair short, so that it left her neck uncovered. She caught his eye in particular, as her face had life and expression. The other was more like a doll for blank perfection.

'Old friend,' Artaxerxes said warmly. 'You may bow, I think. Perhaps I should grant you the right to bow always when you come at my command. As a mark of my respect for your age and experience.'

Tissaphernes was delighted at the idea, but custom dictated his answer.

'If I can give you honour, Majesty, my age is as nothing.'

Artaxerxes frowned in thought, then stepped back and let his outstretched hand fall.

'Very well, old friend. You may continue to prostrate yourself. Tradition holds us all in chains, I think. Even I am bound by it.'

'Of course, Majesty,' Tissaphernes said, dropping right down to the floor. At least it was clean.

He rose to find the sulky-looking slave watching him. Her lips were dark and full, he noticed. He knew it was more than his life was worth to be caught staring at her, so he looked away. When he came upright, he saw her attention had turned to a pendant she wore. He put her from his thoughts. Artaxerxes resumed his seat and seemed once more to be copying the stern glance of his father, with less authority.

'Majesty, I have reports of your brother Cyrus. I cannot explain them.'

Tissaphernes paused. He knew the king well enough to drop the lure in the waters and wait for the man to swallow it whole. Sure enough, the languid air disappeared at the name of Cyrus. Artaxerxes had not spoken of his brother since the humiliation of their mother's interference. For a time, it was as if Cyrus had never come home. The empire continued on and the reports came in from all the twenty-eight nations. To the west, to the edge of Greece, Cyrus' movements were reported as always, with no special emphasis. The surface of the lake seemed to have become still, but Tissaphernes knew the sons of Darius too well to believe that.

'What is it that concerns you?' Artaxerxes said. He glanced uncomfortably at the number of slaves and servants who would hear private family concerns, but then he was king, in the throne room of his capital city. He waved a hand to dismiss such petty thoughts.

'Majesty, you know I taught Cyrus when he was a boy. These hands have beaten him when he left a black cobra in my room.'

'And an ostrich,' Artaxerxes replied, chuckling. 'Yes, I remember.'

Tissaphernes did not share the king's amusement at the memory.

'I know him well, Majesty. Well enough to suspect he would not easily forgive the loss of his Spartan guards, nor how close he came to losing his head. If not for your mother's intercession . . .'

'Yes,' the king replied. 'Though his death would have left us weak. The nations look to us for stable rule, Tissaphernes. Cyrus knows our armies better than any man alive. Perhaps in time I will replace him, but as mother said, to do it so soon after our father's death would be to invite chaos.' The admission seemed to strangle his voice as he went on. 'Sparing my brother's life was a wise decision.'

Artaxerxes leaned forward. The slave girl had drawn her thigh up against his bare leg. Tissaphernes thought he could hear the whisper of her skin sliding over the king's. He dared not look down, not while Artaxerxes watched him as intently as the cobra both boys had placed in his room so many years before. Tissaphernes had always been terrified of snakes. He'd screamed like a woman then, only to hear two princes almost choking as they hung helplessly on each other, red-faced in their laughter.

'Unless you have new information, Tissaphernes ...? What do your spies report? Is my brother loyal?'

'Who can tell the secret heart, Majesty? Yet I have reports of huge sums being drawn on the royal treasury. Sixty, eighty thousand darics, more.'

'What of that? Perhaps he builds new barracks, or trains more men. The army is the strong right arm of the empire, Tissaphernes. You do not appreciate the costs involved. I think half my treasury goes to feed soldiers each year, perhaps more. The horses, the armour, the arrows alone! I remember my father's pride in the sheer number of men we could put in the field. Do you understand? My father did not complain of the cost, no; he took pleasure in it! Who else could afford such a host of hosts? If not my family? Tissaphernes, if that is all you have, you have disappointed me.'

Tissaphernes nodded. The king was listening intently, his slave girls forgotten. It was time to ease the hook back and hold him fast.

'Perhaps you are right, Majesty, though the amounts the prince demands are twice as great as the year before. I am concerned, though, at the number of Greek soldiers he has engaged.'

'As auxiliaries? We know his liking for those mercenaries, the Spartans above all others. What of it? A few thousand here and there to train and inspire our Immortals. Tissaphernes, my brother has administered the armies for years. As much as we may have ... disagreed on certain things, he would not endanger the empire, not for a million Spartans.'

'Majesty, I have reports of many thousands. He sends them north and east. He trains some in Thrace, some in Crete. Yet they are all in reach of him. A suspicious man might say it begins to resemble an army of conquest, Majesty. I do not know how many Greeks he has brought in, but he has raised thirty or forty *thousand* Persian soldiers under his direct command, all over the western cities. Perhaps more by now.'

Artaxerxes began to reply, but then thought better of it, becoming thoughtful. Tissaphernes did not interrupt him, but waited with his eyebrows raised. He had one last stone to place on the board.

'Majesty, you know I would not bring you wild accusations, mere wind and spite. Over the years, I have kept a few eyes watching, a few scribes writing, all over the empire. Some are men close to Cyrus. I have never heard a word of doubt about his motives. Not once.'

'And it is different now?' Artaxerxes said, his face growing hard.

'No, Majesty. Now, they say nothing at all. The birds no longer fly to me – and I wonder what could be happening over on our western border.'

Artaxerxes stroked the hair of the slave sitting by his knee, as he might have with a favourite hound. Tissaphernes risked a glance at her and found her smouldering resentfully up at him, her expression almost scornful. He flushed and looked away.

'Very well, Tissaphernes. I know you well enough to respect your instincts. If you say there's something in the wind, I would be a fool to ignore you. Go yourself, to the west. Take only a few men, but meet my brother. Judge if he is still loyal.'

Tissaphernes shifted uncomfortably, thinking of the months he would have to endure on the road.

'Majesty, the last time I saw your brother, it was to escort him to his execution. He will not look kindly on me, no matter his other loyalties. Perhaps I could . . .'

'Do as I have told you,' Artaxerxes said. 'I have allowed my brother to resume his old titles and authority. I have put aside orders I gave in grief at my father's death. If he kills you, I will know he is still angry. You see?' Artaxerxes smiled, showing white teeth. 'Even in death, you can be useful to me.'

Tissaphernes knew better than to argue further. He prostrated himself at the king's feet.

'You honour me, Majesty. I will go and return to you with the truth. Or I will die. Either way, I serve the empire.'

Xenophon stood in the sun and watched as a furious Greek sailor pitted his strength against a frightened horse. The man had seemed competent enough at sea, but as the rest of the recruits were lined up on the docks, Xenophon could only stare at the way he was trying to bully the whinnying animal. The whites of its eyes were showing and the sailor was swearing and lashing it with a strip of leather – as if the fury and pain would make the horse come to him! It had braced its legs on the walkway from the ship's deck to the dockside, with all its weight pulling back. With just one furious sailor pulling the other way, it looked as if the animal would remain there until nightfall.

Two hundred young men of the Greek cities were still trundling down a second gangplank to the docks, with no more than a few dozen on the soil of a foreign port, waiting for someone to tell them what to do. Xenophon clenched his jaw as he looked for the officers who should have been there.

They were not the same sort as the one he'd signed with, unfortunately. Xenophon had been disappointed not to see that man again. Instead, he'd been passed into the care of a couple of old soaks, with thirty years under their belts and maps of their travels in the veins of their cheeks and noses. As soon as the ship had been tied up at the dock, both of them had stepped down without a glance back, no doubt heading to their favourite drinking house. The young Greeks who had come to fight for Prince Cyrus had been left to their own devices.

The docks were busy with ships loading and unloading for as far as Xenophon could see. He reached under his new leather breastplate as he stood there, trying to scratch himself. He'd seen some of the other men rubbing stones against the inner layer and he understood better then, when the itching drove him to distraction. Experienced men knew where to spread a smear of oil, or how to smoke fleas from their coats, or just the importance of carrying a good flask of water. Xenophon knew none of the thousand little things that made the difference between misery and comfort. He was learning as fast as he could, but . . . He swore under his breath.

The sailor had lost his temper and was bawling at the mount, red-faced with embarrassment as a crowd began to form. Xenophon strode towards him and he was in time to see the horse give a great toss of its head, flinging the man back and forth as if he weighed nothing. As soon as the sailor found his footing, he raised his lash again.

Xenophon took it from him with a sudden jerk, throwing it aside.

'You are frightening an animal stronger than you. Do you want to see it break a leg on this dock?'

The man was so deep in his rage that he considered

striking the young man who stood before him. Xenophon could see it in his eyes, then saw the urge fade. The sailor had no idea who he was, but he knew well enough that there would be a terrible punishment for striking or offending one of the officers. It was enough to give him pause, while Xenophon took the reins from his unresisting hand.

'Let's get him calmed down, shall we?' Xenophon said more gently, as much for the benefit of the horse as the sailor.

The man muttered something foul under his breath that Xenophon ignored. In truth, the sailor was relieved to be able to stand clear, though he did not go far and remained with his arms folded and a sneer on his face. Xenophon understood the man would wait to judge his efforts, as he felt his own had been judged. The difference was that Xenophon did not care what the man thought of him.

The horse had watched the change of grip on its reins with bulging eyes. Xenophon had wondered many times how much the animals understood. He suspected horses were intelligent enough to be spiteful, or even to put on a show.

'There. Now, let's have a look at you, shall we?' he asked. 'What a fine coat.'

He kept a good grip on the reins, though he did not pull, or throw his weight against a stallion that could have dragged a man for miles. As he talked, he turned aside, as if he was just about to walk away.

The horse remained on the walkway as if rooted there. Xenophon saw the sailor grin out of the corner of his eye. The man leaned over to say something to the person next to him. Xenophon glanced at them and frowned when he recognised Hephaestus standing there.

The young man had joined on the same day he had, with the same recruiter. No doubt that Spartan had earned a bonus for himself. Xenophon had spotted Hephaestus on the docks in Athens as they'd gathered and he was still not sure what to make of him even being there. They were not friends, that much was certain. They hadn't exchanged a word on the crossing, though both men were aware of the other.

Xenophon still wondered if Socrates had persuaded Hephaestus to join up, rather than waste his life on the streets. The more troubling thought was that the old man might have put Xenophon up to it just to look after Hephaestus. The years Socrates had spent as a soldier had been relatively happy ones, so he always said. It would not have been beyond him to recommend a few seasons of marching and fighting to put the rest of their lives, the rest of their troubles, in some kind of perspective.

'Come on, Hippos,' Xenophon said, speaking to the horse. 'You don't want to be standing there all day, do you? There are others behind you, you know.'

Xenophon was intent on the horse when Hephaestus stepped up alongside him.

'Tell me what to do,' the young man said.

Xenophon raised his eyebrows in surprise, but then he nodded.

'All right. We'll speak calmly for a while, to let him know there's no danger here. I should think he's still a little uncomfortable from the crossing. Horses can't vomit, Hephaestus. They just get sick – and angry, sometimes. Go on and pat his neck, though be careful if he tries to bite you. He's still a little wild about the eye.'

Xenophon watched as the shaven-headed young man of Athens reached up and touched a horse for the first time in his life. The animal's neck trembled as if flies had landed, but the stallion did not snap at him. Hephaestus began to chuckle in sheer delight at the touch of the skin.

'I can see his veins,' he said in wonder. Xenophon smiled.

'Yes, though I think his great heart is slowing now. They respond to touch. Just keep stroking him. There, old fellow. I think you might come down off this old plank now, yes? It must have felt like madness for you to walk out on it while it shook and bounced? Yes, I imagine it did. Come on.'

Xenophon turned away once more and the horse followed him down, with barely a trace of the skittish fear it had shown before. He walked it up and down on the dock, with Hephaestus alongside the whole time, patting it or just keeping a hand on the mount's shoulder. Great ripples ran along the skin under his touch, but Xenophon saw the animal grow calmer, its head drooping.

'You have a feel for it,' he said.

Hephaestus looked at him in surprise, utterly vulnerable in that moment, before he looked away.

'Thank you,' he said. 'I wish I could ride. I've always wanted to learn.'

The watching sailor waved a hand at the two of them in disgust and went back up the gangplank to fetch another. Across the docks, the two officers were returning, refreshed and lubricated, ready to take command once more. They saw Xenophon and Hephaestus standing with the horse and called them over.

'You're the one who knows the mounts, then?' the older of the two said.

Xenophon nodded. He had no idea what had been marked against his name, but he knew horses could be frightening to those who had not grown up around them.

'I am. My father bred them.'

'Good. A couple of lads who know what they're doing might find themselves in demand out here, believe me. It's a hundred miles to Sardis – four or five days of marching in the heat. If you two look after all the horses, you might find better rations coming your way. There'll be proper cavalry in Sardis as well, in case you were wondering. Good ones, not like these bony old nags.'

Xenophon saw Hephaestus cover the ear of the horse he still held, as if to shield him from the comment. The action was so ludicrous it made Xenophon smile. Socrates had promised him new experiences. The old man who claimed to know nothing was wiser than he knew.

8

The wind was constant under the sun, though Cyrus hardly felt it as he trotted a fine stallion along the edge of a plain that stretched right to distant blue mountains. He had been observing the training since the sun rose, with Parviz at his side. The man who had been the first to give the prince water had become his loyal manservant and could hardly believe his good fortune or the rise in status. Parviz rarely left his presence. Cyrus found he enjoyed the man's brisk outlook and disdain for problems. All walls can be climbed, Parviz said, which was a strange motto for a fortress guard.

On the plain by Sardis, six hundred Corinthian hoplites marched and halted, split apart along lines Cyrus could not discern, then attacked one another in ritualised mayhem. It was war as theatre, perhaps. Cyrus had heard the Greeks enjoyed the spectacle of great tragedies played out before them, to weep or laugh and come away somehow refreshed. He had no interest in such things, though he wondered if they played a part in the training. When no enemy was present, he could see little difference between the forces of the Greek cities and the legions of home. Persians too could march and wheel and deploy in various formations.

Yet when the horns sounded, when the swords were drawn for blood and savagery, the Greeks went through Persian lines like a great iron sickle, sweeping them down. It was a mystery. Even regiments of Immortals did not fare well, especially against the Spartans. Cyrus knew it mattered to the Greeks that they held their father's shield, a brother's sword, an uncle's bronze helmet. They sometimes carried the honour of an entire family into battle. Though they could be killed, they could not be made to run, not with the souls of braver men watching.

General Netus the Stymphalian had been as good as his word, Cyrus noted. The man had trained new soldiers and salted older ones amongst them, making a fine force of twelve hundred in all. With the Spartans, they rose an hour before dawn and ran the hills around the plain for hours before returning to break their fast and begin weapon training. It was hard not to compare them with the Persian officers. Those men lived like the nobles they were, rising to be tended by slaves at a late hour and rarely breaking a sweat themselves. Netus, Clearchus, Proxenus and the rest all ran with their men, seeing no shame in it. There were lessons there.

From across the plain, he saw two riders galloping at dangerous speed. Cyrus winced at the sight. There was no need to risk their lives and he could see the horses were of fine stock even at that distance. Though the plain was flat, there could always be a loose stone, or a hole to trap a flying hoof. Both men had placed leopard skins over the horses' backs and sat high, perched with their knees gripping the shoulders as they plunged. One of them rode beautifully, as balanced as a tumbler, or a child running along a wall. The other was not skilled at all. He seemed rigid to the prince's eye, gripping the mane as if he thought he would surely fall.

Cyrus loved horses and the sight was a rare one, though insane. He saw the galloping animals were heading straight for the lines of marching hoplites. They too had spotted the approach and come to a halt, with orders roared at them. The men drew into solid lines, raising shields like a wall that gleamed gold in the sun. Spears stood as dark bars behind them. It was well done, but the two horsemen did not slow. They came at the lines like an arrow shot through the air.

While the hoplites looked on in astonishment, one of the riders whipped and jerked his horse to the front and then leaned out at such an angle it was clear he must fall. Cyrus watched as the young man lunged low down for reins that had been flapping loose. He understood in the instant that the lead horse had bolted and run mad, its rider utterly helpless, unable to reach the reins at all.

With the leather straps wound about his hand, the lead young man turned both horses neatly, bringing them to a halt. Cyrus trotted his own mount forward, wanting to exclaim on what he had seen. His presence did not go unnoticed, however. General Netus brought the entire force of six hundred to attention as if for inspection. They crashed a step together and stood shoulder to shoulder.

The young rider had dismounted to check the legs of both horses. He looked up when Netus called the men to order, but when his companion tried to lay a hand on his shoulder, Cyrus saw him shake it off in anger. Both of them turned as the prince drew up and leaped to the ground. Their expressions went from fury and shame to wide-eyed surprise as they recognised him. The man whose horse had bolted only bowed. The one who had caught him went down on one knee. It caught the prince's interest.

'What is your name?' he asked the kneeling man.

'Xenophon, Highness.'

'That was a brave act, Xenophon. You risked your life to save this man.'

'To save the horse, Highness. The horse is one of our best mounts. Hephaestus here should not have tried to ride him until he was more skilful.'

'I see. Please, rise. I have met many Greeks who only bow

to me, or make a show of dipping down as briefly as they can manage, as if the ground is too hot. You do not mind showing respect?'

Xenophon stood up straight and tall. He was sweating, his face flushed from the exertion. He shrugged.

'It does not diminish me to honour another man, Highness. If I give you honour, I lose none of my own. After all, I expect obedience from one like Hephaestus here. I expect him to respect my expertise and my status. He did not *do* that, of course, but I demand it from him even so.'

Cyrus blinked at the pair, seeing how the other man shook his head a fraction, resisting the description of him.

'You Greeks astonish me. You seem to think about everything. Do you never just act, without considering it first as a puzzle?'

'I signed up to fight Pisidians, Highness,' Xenophon replied. 'I imagined camaraderie and tests of courage. I wished to test myself, if you understand me. Instead, I am here, month after month, training others, being trained myself. Perhaps I should have given that decision more thought.'

Cyrus found himself amused at the younger man's visible bad temper, combined with a grim humour he could hear in the mocking tone.

'I imagine your way of talking wins few friends, Xenophon,' he said.

The Greek's jaw jutted forward as his stubbornness showed. He raised his head as if in challenge and Cyrus laughed, holding up his hands.

'Please. I do not wish to offend you, but to understand. In the cities of my father . . .' He hesitated and a shadow passed across him. 'In the cities of my brother, men know their place, exactly. They know it from their families and blood-line, from experience, from promotion, from their associates and relations – but they know to the last grain on the scale where they stand. We do not spend our lives in this fervour of possibility, this uncertainty. A man knows to prostrate himself to a prince and to demand subservence from those below him.'

'That sounds . . . restful,' Xenophon said. His honesty made him continue. 'Though in truth, it occurs to me . . .' He trailed off, unsure.

Cyrus gestured with an open hand.

'While you are in my service, I swear to you – nothing you can say here will cause me offence. I wish to hear the truth only.'

Xenophon allowed a small smile. He liked the prince of Persia who had brought half the world to Sardis to train.

'Highness, when you describe a system of masters and servants, I admire it – because I imagine myself the master, immediately. And a master would admire a system that benefits him, of course. Yet if I saw myself as one forced to labour in the sun, perhaps for a man I felt did not deserve to stand over me . . . then I would know resentment. If I kneel to you, it is because I give honour to tradition and because I feel men should know their station in life. Yet you have spoken kindly to me. Had you scorned me or abused me, I would have been less willing to bend the knee. Either way, I am a free Greek, Highness, an Athenian. I have sworn to serve you and taken your silver. My oath holds me, but when I stand before the gods, I will still be able to say the choice was mine.'

Cyrus chuckled, amused by the serious young man who thought nothing of disputing with him in such a way. He felt no answering prickle of anger, any more than he would have at a pup who nipped his fingers. It was a challenge without real teeth and it did not hurt him. He wondered, though, if he had been around the Greeks for too long.

Rather than argue the point, Cyrus stroked his hand down the leg of the great uncut stallion Xenophon had ridden.

'This is a fine beast,' he said. 'The equal of my own Pasacas, I believe.'

Xenophon cast a professional glance at the prince's mount, nodding acceptance.

'Your Pasacas is a hand taller, Highness, but yes, my father bred horses for forty years. He traded fortunes for Persian stock, I recall.'

'The best in the world,' Cyrus said lightly, knowing it was true. Xenophon smiled in reply. His flush had faded and Cyrus realised he should dismiss the pair of young men to their duties. He sought for a way to continue the conversation, knowing he would repeat it to the Spartan general that evening when they sat to dine.

'You are an Athenian who thinks like a Persian, Xenophon. I think sometimes I am a Persian who thinks like an Athenian.'

Xenophon chuckled, gathering the reins of both horses. He ignored the downcast Hephaestus, who waited without even bowing his head, looking from one to the other of them. Xenophon still wondered if Socrates was behind them joining on the same day. The thought lightened his spirits further.

'I only wish my friend Socrates could hear you, Highness,' he said. 'If you ever have the chance, you should seek him out in Athens and make these points to him. He will love you for it.'

Cyrus shook his head.

'I do not think I will go to Greece again, not for a time. My labours will take me east, far into the deserts.'

'I'm sorry to hear that. It has been an honour, Highness,' Xenophon said. He went down on one knee again, though he smiled as he did so. On impulse, Cyrus bowed to him, making them both grin as they remounted. Xenophon joined both horses on a long lead, while the disgraced Hephaestus trotted along in the dust behind.

Cyrus watched them go, his smile fading. It had been almost a year since his father's death. He had gone back to his life as commander of the Persian armies as if nothing had changed, although in fact everything had. He had brought Greeks into the field of war and then marched and trained them to sharpness under the best generals. He had perhaps twelve thousand hoplites in all, but it was not enough. His brother could put six hundred thousand men in the field – Cyrus knew the numbers better than anyone else alive. He knew he needed more Persian regiments. He could not win with only twelve thousand Greeks, not against so many! Yet the more he manoeuvred Persian forces into play, bringing them into range of Sardis, the more the danger increased. Some of the Greek generals had seen the flaw already. There were few enemies in the world who required such a host. As it grew, month by month, it would become obvious to all that there was actually only one.

Cyrus bit his lip, chewing a piece of broken skin there as the breeze washed over him. He had gathered an army, but the Persian part of it had come because he was a prince and commander of soldiers of the empire. He had chosen the officers carefully, men he had raised, men who trusted and admired him. Yet there would come a moment when those regiments realised where they were marching. If they mutinied then, he would be destroyed.

It would have been inconceivable against his father – an enterprise doomed from the very start. Against his brother, Artaxerxes, Cyrus hoped he had a chance. To the regiments of Persia, Cyrus was the prince they knew, the right hand of the new king. Perhaps they would stand with him. He had staked his life and the entire empire that when the moment came, they would.

He thought of the young Athenians who had ridden like the wind. The pair had clearly not been friends and yet one of them, Xenophon, had risked his life to save the other. It was hard not to admire such men. Cyrus had always known where he stood in the families and the court of Persia. Yet he saw then that it could also be a kind of death, a life unlived. Well, he had chosen to throw it all into the air. He would succeed or he would fail, but no man would be able to say he had known his place. He smiled to himself. It was a comforting thought.

9

Cyrus stood with Proxenus the Boeotian, the heavyset Greek general looking miserable in the rain. Clearchus had folded his arms and gathered his Spartan cloak around him, though he was soaked through. Cyrus had heard Proxenus sniffing and coughing all night in his tent. As might be expected, the general had said nothing to either of them. Cyrus had noticed how the other Greeks were careful not to complain when the Spartans were around. They accorded them a rare level of respect. Clearchus did not seem aware of it, of course, though the prince thought he must find it satisfying in private.

The mountains in the north of Phrygia were richly forested, so that entire armies could train in such a place, away from watching eyes, or their enemies. Six days' march north of Sardis gave privacy enough to bring a number of Persian and Greek regiments together for the first time. Clearchus had insisted on it. It was one of the ironies of Cyrus' position that his Persian officers did not yet know why such a vast host had been assembled, but the Spartan did – and at least some of the other Greek commanders had a suspicion they were not after hill tribes.

Clearchus had asked to see the quality of the Persian regiments he would command in battle. It was the merest common sense to agree to the request, but Cyrus was regretting it, after almost six weeks of mock warfare and fitness training. Just that morning, he had seen a Persian regiment routed by Corinthians bearing only staves and clubs, chasing them through the trees. The Persian polemarch waited by his horse a dozen paces away, craning his neck for some sign the prince would allow him to approach.

Cyrus seethed. It was bad enough to have Greek soldiers break Persian lines over and over again. Men like Proxenus and Clearchus seemed able to improvise new plans from nothing, then have their hoplites carry them out – quickly and easily. It left the Persian regiments looking clumsy and slow to react. More than once they'd found themselves continuing the advance from a previous order, when the designated Greek 'enemy' were off to one side, watching them and jeering. Those things could surely be remedied in time, Cyrus hoped, with the right officers. He glanced to his left and sighed at the sight of the bright-eyed Persian. Rather than delay further, Cyrus gestured. The man strode instantly through the outer guards, his chest filling like that of a bantam cock.

Clearchus and Proxenus looked on as the Persian lay full length on the muddy ground. In that at least, his manner was perfect. Cyrus might have appreciated the gesture more if Polemarch Eraz Tirazis had not overseen the complete rout of his men three times that morning.

'Highness, you do me great honour,' the officer said stiffly. 'I am not worthy to attend your presence. Grant only a moment of your day and I will be a thousand times blessed beyond my worth.'

Cyrus found he missed the blunt style of the Greeks.

'You asked for a word, polemarch. If my time is so valuable, perhaps you should use fewer of them, or speak more swiftly.'

'Of course, Highness. I wished only to say how disappointed I was this morning with the men.'

'With the men,' Cyrus echoed, raising an eyebrow.

'Your Highness must understand the regiments I was given to command are composed of peasants, most of them

Medes. They are not cultured fellows, if you understand me. They plod like cattle, forwards, backwards. They stop when they are told to stop, but merely stand then, without thought. I have had hundreds of them flogged for their insolence, but if anything they grow more sullen and more stupid each day.'

'What do you want, Polemarch Eraz? To return home? That can be arranged.'

'Highness, no!' The Persian seemed genuinely affronted. 'I ask only that I be given one of the Persian war groups. Perhaps my Medes would be happier with one who speaks their tongue a little better.'

'The Medes don't understand you?' Cyrus said faintly.

The Persian shook his head in remembered anger.

'They are fools and farmers, Highness. Peasants. I was trained in Persepolis, alongside imperial officers. My family can be traced back for forty-three generations. Am I a shepherd, to be tending such men?' He chuckled at his own wit. 'I think you understand, Highness.'

'I do,' Cyrus said. 'Though understanding a problem is not the same as knowing how to solve it. You I could have beaten. I could have your ears clipped, or your right hand branded as a mark of failure. I could have you sent home, or just give you a rope and an order to hang yourself. Yet I have hundreds of officers just like you, who see no reflection on themselves when their men are broken and sent running, time after time after *time*!'

Cyrus said the last as a roar, advancing on Eraz of Tirazis. In response, the man threw himself down once more and covered his head with his hands.

'Guards! Take this fool and strip him. Lash his back forty times in front of his men.'

The polemarch cried out in horror and confusion as he understood.

'Highness, how have I earned this punishment? Please! Let me hang myself, before enduring such a dishonour. What have I done? Please, I don't understand . . .' He was dragged away still complaining and beseeching.

Behind him, Cyrus raised his head to the rain that seemed to work cold fingers down his neck. Proxenus gave a great sneeze and Cyrus whirled on him, still furious with his own helplessness. The Greek general held up his hands in surrender, too miserable to do anything but blow his nose into a square of cloth.

The Spartan too cleared his throat, so that Cyrus looked over to him.

'You have something to add, Clearchus?'

'If I can do so without you ordering me to be lashed, I might, yes.'

Cyrus mastered himself with difficulty. He inclined his head, his mouth quirking up on one side.

'Please. I would not flog a Greek, even if you gave me cause. You know as well as I do – your service is not slavery. You have to understand my Persian officers expect such things from me. The others will see Eraz of Tirazis was flogged in front of his men and they will know he was at least in part responsible for the poor display this morning. He will spend a few days being tended by our doctors. If he has the sense to take the lash well, his men may even come to respect him more than they do at the moment. Perhaps I will send a tutor to teach him orders in the Median tongue while he recovers. Yes, that is worth doing.'

Clearchus nodded, though he saw the prince was clenching and unclenching his right fist as he spoke.

'I am glad you would not give such an order. It is a rare prince who knows his limits.'

Cyrus flickered a glance at the man who was telling him

he would not stand to be punished – a man who served him. The prince felt his temper surge and his face grow flushed. In turn, Clearchus watched the prince's attempt to control his anger with some interest.

'General,' Cyrus said, 'I am sorry for my manner. I see only problems today. Your men are . . . superb. I thought I knew the legend of the Spartans, but seeing you train in conditions even close to battle . . . the truth is extraordinary. Each Spartiate seems to think as a general, yet will take orders as a soldier. How is it done, Clearchus? If I had ten thousand such, I would not need all the rest. I could conquer the world with those alone.'

'We are raised to think for ourselves,' Clearchus said, 'but there is little point in freedom without judgement. Highness, all my men have trained and fought together for years, from their time in the boys' barracks at home. They follow orders, of course, but if they see a breach, or a weakness, they might choose to break formation and attack. No officer sees all the battle, no soldier either. It is why you sit a tall horse and why we send scouts ahead and to flanking positions. Yet no matter how well we prepare, there will come a moment when a hoplite soldier walks over two weaker men and finds himself ahead of the rest, perhaps in reach of a broken wall or an enemy general. If he waits for orders then, the moment will be lost. If he rushes forward without thought, his own lines might fail and be destroyed. It is a matter for very fine judgement indeed. When he makes the right choice, we raise those men up. We make them officers. We give them wreaths and houses, even. Yet if they bring destruction on their lines, all men spit when they hear of that day and no children are given a name that is allowed to wither on the vine for ever more.' The general shrugged. 'As I say, it is a balance.'

Clearchus looked off to the distance for a moment, considering his words. Cyrus saw and gestured for him to go on.

'That officer you sent to be whipped was, I think, too stupid to lead. He has no love of his men, no appreciation for their skills and their bravery. I have seen his Medes – they are solid men, not easy to break. Of course they do not want to march up and down hill with Spartans and Corinthians howling like wolves along their flanks! They are cold, wet, tired and sick of the life. To be harangued by such a man on top of all that – honestly, I am surprised they did not kill him. Their morale must be truly low.'

'What then would Spartans do with such a man?' Cyrus asked in despair. 'I have several dozen who are no better. And a few who are considerably worse.'

'We would start by having a quiet word with him,' Clearchus said. 'Five or six of us would explain what he had been doing wrong, in case he did not know. We would make sure he understood. When he was walking again, we would look to see if he had learned wisdom. Some men are broken by the experience. Others regard it as a rite of passage and become stronger. If not, I fear he would be left behind for the wolves. We allow no weakness, Prince Cyrus, but . . . our way is not for all. Indeed, our way would break one of your regiments. Much as beating a horse or a dog every day would make it timid or savage, but not better than before.'

Cyrus swore, smacking his fist against a panel of his coat so that the knuckles bled. Clearchus looked on calmly.

'If I may say so, Your Highness, you seem at times to be a man consumed with rage. Every army takes time to train. I have seen mobs and rabbles made into fine regiments before. Your Persians are no less fit, no more undisciplined than some others I've known. Yet you seem to wind yourself tighter and tighter, like a horsehair spring. Is this all there is, for you?'

Cyrus was bitter as he replied.

'Is my father's throne a mere bauble, then? Is it not worth the struggle to your eyes?'

'Not at all! I cannot think of a greater prize in the world than what you seek.' The Spartan general shifted uncomfortably, shooting a glance to Proxenus, who had come closer to listen. 'But . . . a life solely of war is not a happy one. When a man thinks of nothing else for months or years at a time, he loses something vital. I think vengeance is the same, if it is allowed to become a great furnace. A man can be destroyed by his own rage, Highness, I have seen it. His judgement can be drowned, if he is not overtaken by a great spasm, so that his heart bursts or his face sags like melted wax. I think if I did not have my wife at home, my sons and daughters, I would not work as hard. When I am home, I tend a little piece of land in peace. I grow olives and onions. I think of that small place when I am deaf and blind with the clash of metal and the smell of death.'

The general saw Proxenus watching in surprise and he flushed. Clearchus was not a man given to long speeches and yet he had reached out to the prince. Cyrus was an easy man to like, it seemed. Clearchus put the thought aside. Though he led ranks and files and armies, he was not immune from the desire that curled and whispered in all of them – to follow a worthy man. For the right prince, Clearchus knew his armies would walk into flames. He would himself.

'Highness, it is . . . sometimes difficult to keep the state of Sparta in my mind. I have given my life to her, my blood, my sweat and all my youth, but it is hard to keep her in my thoughts in the rain, when my straps chafe and I am weary. My Calandre is easier.'

'I have known a great love,' Cyrus admitted. 'Only one. But she married another.'

'Perhaps she will reconsider your suit if you are successful here,' Clearchus said.

Proxenus snorted and both men turned to see him chuckling into his cloth as he wiped a sore nose.

'I would go to a Spartan for advice on war, Highness. I would not go to one for advice on love. They choose their women from those who win races.'

'That is not true,' Clearchus said. Cyrus looked wide-eyed at him. He shrugged. 'Sometimes, that is true. Fast women make strong sons.'

'Fast women with fine, silken moustaches,' Proxenus said.

Clearchus looked calmly at him and Proxenus considered his words, looking at his feet. The Spartan barked a laugh then, clapping the sniffling general on the shoulder, hard enough to send him staggering.

'Prince Cyrus,' Clearchus said, 'you have gathered good men to you. If you give me a year, I will turn them into an army that can shake the world. I cannot make Spartans of your Persian regiments. Yet I might make Corinthians out of them, or Athenians. Possibly even Boeotians. That will be good enough.'

Proxenus took a swipe at him and Clearchus leaned away, chuckling. The rain increased its force, though their mood had lightened beneath the downpour. All three were at ease as they turned to see a messenger skidding on the muddy ground as he ran up the slope. The boy was Persian and he unrolled a mat then lay on it, holding out a scroll case of polished stone. Cyrus frowned at it as he broke the seal and tapped out a roll of parchment. The rain spattered against it like the skin of a drum, smearing the ink and making the letters run. His mouth tightened.

'I do not think we will get the year you need, general,' Cyrus said. 'It seems my brother has sent an old friend to inspect the armies of the west. Tissaphernes has arrived in Sardis and requests my immediate attendance on him.'

Cyrus rolled the message up, though it was too sodden to put back into the holder. He broke the tube over his knee and whistled for his horse to be brought, leaping up and throwing a leg over without a mounting block. As he gathered the reins, both Proxenus and Clearchus touched their left shoulders with their right hands and bowed their heads.

'General Clearchus, General Proxenus. I would value your counsel in Sardis. I would be interested to hear your impressions of this Persian lord. Shall I have horses saddled for you?'

Before the Spartan could refuse, Proxenus spoke over him.

'If you order it, Highness, of course. We took an oath of service, after all.'

Clearchus glared at the Boeotian, unable to say then that he would rather walk. Cyrus hardly hesitated, thinking ahead to a meeting with a man he would rather see killed than walking free.

'It would be faster, Clearchus.'

'You could ride behind me if you like, general,' Proxenus said.

'No, I won't be doing that,' Clearchus replied. He bowed his head and clapped his right hand against his left shoulder once more. 'As you command, Highness, of course.'

Tissaphernes had been in the palace at Sardis for a week by the time Cyrus rode in with just forty men. A personal guard of six hundred soldiers accompanied the Persian lord. Cyrus supposed it had taken some bravery even so, after what had passed between them on the plateau. As the prince rode into the open courtyard and jumped down, he found himself facing silent ranks of Immortal soldiers, their black uniforms unmarked. He could not help wondering if any of them had been there in Persepolis, when his life had hung in the balance.

The horsemen with Cyrus raised a cloud as they too jumped down and passed the reins to slave boys. Dust drifted over the armed forces of Tissaphernes, like a stain in the air.

Cyrus could feel his heart beating. He could not be certain his brother hadn't given an order to have him killed. He'd considered bringing thousands back with him, but more than anything else, such a display would have tipped his hand. He had to act as if all was forgiven between them, as if he did not consider Tissaphernes and Artaxerxes his enemies. Even if it meant his life, he had to act the part.

Accordingly, he strode forward and gave no sign of noticing the tension rise in the Immortal ranks. Cyrus smiled and held out both hands, embracing the older man and kissing him on his cheeks and lips in formal style. As he did so, the prince remembered an old Greek tale of a man who had found a viper frozen in the snow. The man took pity on the dying thing and pressed it to his breast to bring it warmth. As it revived, it sank its fangs into him and stole away his life. Cyrus had nursed a viper to his breast when he'd seen Tissaphernes as a friend. He would not make the same mistake again.

As well as Proxenus and Clearchus, General Netus the Stymphalian had accompanied the prince. He too came forward to greet the Persian, though Tissaphernes wrinkled his nose at the smell of sweat and horses coming off the men like heat as they gathered around to be introduced. His personal guard reached out to stop the Greek general coming too close and Netus gave the man's fingers a sharp twist that made him shriek in surprise. The look Tissaphernes turned on his officer then was pure poison.

'Perhaps you should go and see if the kitchens are ready for us, captain,' Tissaphernes said.

The man flushed in anger, his eyes glittering as he glared at the Stymphalian. Netus didn't appear to have noticed what he'd done, though Cyrus was delighted to have spoiled the display Tissaphernes had intended. It was bad enough to meet an enemy – but to be welcomed to a royal palace as if Cyrus were the guest and Tissaphernes the host was galling.

The prince smiled and rested his arm on Tissaphernes' shoulders, turning him. He knew the man's dislike of physical closeness rather better than most, so Cyrus hugged him tightly as they went inside.

'I am so pleased to see a familiar face in this place, old lion. I have missed you. I thought you were still angry with me, for . . .' he waved a hand in the air, 'all that went on before in Persepolis. Perhaps it was my imagination, but I thought it best to stay away, far to the west, at least for a few years while my brother settles in as Great King and god-emperor.'

'I see,' Tissaphernes said. He cast a doubtful glance at the three Greek generals walking behind them. He wondered if any of them spoke the royal tongue. 'Though I see you still consort with Greeks, Highness.'

To his surprise, Cyrus wagged a finger at him, as if to a naughty child.

'Well, you cost me my guard of Spartans, old lion. I had some apologies to make on my return to these parts. And the payments to their families! You cost me gold enough to outfit a regiment that day – and for what? I have always been loyal, you've said so yourself. I have served the throne and my father all my life – and I am willing to spend my life in service to my dear brother as well. You know me, old friend. I have put our unpleasantness behind us. I can only apologise and leave the past in the past. What else is there?'

Tissaphernes found himself relaxing under the torrent of words, all accompanied by the pressure of his old pupil's arm around his shoulders. He still could not resist playing the host as they went further into the palace corridors, leaving the heat of the sun outside.

In addition to his guards, Tissaphernes had brought a household of servants with him, including assassins, cooks, poisoners, saddlers, any sort he felt he might possibly need. Each of Cyrus' associates was taken in hand to be bathed and rubbed down before the meal Tissaphernes had prepared for them. He saw no sign of resentment in the prince, not even a flicker of it.

'Dinner will be served at sunset, Highness,' Tissaphernes said. 'My chef has been busy for days in preparation.'

Though he was reluctant to admit it, it looked as if he would report good news to King Artaxerxes. Tissaphernes had not wasted his week in the city. His best three spies had gone out to seek what information there was to be had. Each city had a royal network that reported back to imperial spymasters. It was only a matter of time before Tissaphernes would know every step Cyrus had made for the previous six months, each conversation, each action and decision. The spies were writing it all down as it came in, forming a picture he would read for himself. More importantly, he would dine with the prince and spend days observing him. Tissaphernes had known Cyrus from his earliest years and if there was deception in him, Tissaphernes would surely learn it. The old tutor felt his shoulders go back and his chest rise in pride at the trust in him. His judgement was literally a matter of life and death, with entire armies waiting on his word.

Tissaphernes gestured for two young slaves to accompany him. He loved to be bathed and he was feeling expansive, his mood light. He was, after all, the right hand of a Great King, the dagger of the royal house. The idea pleased him.

Dinner that evening was an intimate affair. Though Tissaphernes had brought men enough to stand on every corner and corridor of the palace, he allowed only six into the dining chamber to stand along the walls. The man himself was dressed in dark gold cloth, the loose robes keeping him cool, though he had put on powdered folds of fat since Cyrus had seen him last.

The windows were set high in the walls of that room, where King Darius had once entertained a satrap of India and hidden rubies in a bowl of plums to amuse the man, tossing them to his children like sweetmeats. A cool breeze blew through, funnelled down by the design of the tiled roof outside, a miracle of ingenuity from the original architect.

The table itself was topped with dark green marble so highly polished that it showed the beams of the ceiling above between the dishes, and the faces of the servers as they leaned over. Prince Cyrus sat at the head of the table, with Tissaphernes at his right hand. Clearchus sat on his left, with Proxenus and Netus the Stymphalian further away along the length.

Tissaphernes continued to play the host, recommending particular dishes. He watched to see if Cyrus would hesitate over any of them, but if the prince feared poison, he showed no sign. The lack of suspicion was promising, Tissaphernes could admit to himself. A man guilty of treachery might expect it in others. Yet Cyrus tore bread with his fingers and gulped red wine with every sign of relaxed enjoyment.

'These Greek fellows, Highness. Do they speak our tongue?' Tissaphernes asked.

To his surprise, both Proxenus and Clearchus the Spartan nodded, though Proxenus held up his hand and waggled it back and forth, as if to indicate less than perfect ability. General Netus watched the action with complete blankness, looking around him as if they barked like dogs to one another. Tissaphernes could see it was not an act, in that slight rudeness. The Greek did not see the sounds as real language, so treated them as the chatter of birds, a sound to be ignored, or even spoken over.

'As you see, old lion, Persian is the language of both trade and war, at least amongst those who make war their trade.' Cyrus spoke easily, as if they were friends still.

'I see. I will take care not to be indiscreet, Highness. Though your brother asked me to make a judgement on the readiness of our forces here. It is my task to inquire as to our strength – those under arms for us. Do you have those numbers?'

'Of course,' Cyrus said, spreading a ladleful of tiny white eggs across his bread and fish. 'I will have my seneschal make all those accounts available. You taught me calculations, Tissaphernes. I would be ashamed if you found fault with them now.'

Tissaphernes laughed as he emptied his wine and had it refilled. It brought a warm glow and he smiled at the prince. Perhaps the younger son of Darius was a greater and more forgiving soul than he had known.

'The food is very good,' Clearchus said in Greek.

Tissaphernes frowned at the man's bad manners, though Cyrus was quick to translate. Netus brightened at that, the first words he had understood.

'Ah. I brought my cook with me,' Tissaphernes replied. 'Honestly, I could not travel without him at my age. Nothing else agrees with me unless his hand has prepared it.' He patted his stomach ruefully. 'Beware the acids of old age, Cyrus.'

For just an instant, Cyrus found himself smiling as if they

actually were the old friends they had once been. He reminded himself that the man at table with him had been willing to see his head struck from his shoulders. There was neither friendship nor kindness in the fat old tutor chewing a paste of meat and oranges. It took no more than a glance at the guards along the walls to see they stood ready to defend their master. They watched Cyrus as an enemy, reminding him that he actually was one. Still, it was a fine meal and Proxenus groaned as they rose. They had sat through a dozen courses and wines, with Tissaphernes commenting eagerly on each one, singing the praises of his cook until Cyrus wanted to strangle him. The Greeks ate little, he noticed, though perhaps that was the example of Clearchus, who merely tasted each course as if he was checking it for poison. As of course he probably was.

In the twilight, after a long day, it was not hard to yawn. Cyrus leaned his head back and patted at his open mouth.

'Tomorrow, old lion, I will have some of our best regiments parade past for you. I have spent fortunes on them, but I think you will agree, it has not been wasted.'

'I hope not, Highness,' Tissaphernes replied, a note of warning in his voice.

Silence fell then and Tissaphernes saw the young prince raise an eyebrow. He realised Cyrus was expecting him to prostrate himself. It did not feel quite correct to do so, not to a man he had come to judge. Stiffly, Tissaphernes bowed from the waist. He flushed, and as he rose, he saw Cyrus staring.

Tissaphernes gave a weak chuckle.

'It is a new age, Highness . . .' To his surprise, he saw Cyrus' face harden.

'No, Tissaphernes. I am my father's son. I am brother to the Great King, Artaxerxes. Is it your intention to show disrespect to my family, the royal house?'

Perhaps it was petty, but then Cyrus had endured an evening with a man he detested, weighing every word said for what it might reveal of him. He seized on the moment and refused to let go, holding the older man's gaze until Tissaphernes blushed more deeply and lowered himself down, knee by knee, until he lay flat.

'It is important to remember which of us is the host, and which the guest,' Cyrus said softly. He made his voice change then, forcing lightness into it as he reached out and helped Tissaphernes to his feet.

'There. These Greeks don't seem to understand the importance of showing respect to a prince. It makes me homesick, Tissaphernes, to see you do it so very well.'

'Thank you, Highness. You honour me,' Tissaphernes said, though his voice had a strain to it that made Proxenus snort and then blow his nose to cover his amusement.

IO

The exact status of Tissaphernes as a guest could not be defined. Not a drop of noble blood ran in his veins, but he carried seals of state that lent him the authority to act in the king's name – and he clearly believed he had come to oversee the western part of the empire. His manner was far from that of a supplicant as he sat his mount on the parade ground in Sardis. The local governor had asked himself to the event, as well as every wealthy local family able to bargain, flatter or threaten for an invitation.

With the sun baking a vast, green training field, Tissaphernes watched regiments parade and wheel before him. He and Prince Cyrus were given relief from the heat by woven squares of bamboo and white linen, wafted by slaves. Cyrus tried to relax and enjoy the sight, but the thought that it would all be reported back to his brother soured the day for him.

In more innocent times, Cyrus would have enjoyed showing his best men and most difficult manoeuvres to his old teacher. He might have hoped then that news of his successes would find their way back to his father's ears in Persepolis. He could not do less that afternoon, not when he'd gathered vast numbers of men and trained them for months. Thousands of Greeks and as many Persian regiments marched across the field in complex patterns, demonstrating feints and small-group actions against one another. Cyrus had planned a climax of a staged attack to impress Tissaphernes, as he might easily have done before. Now he thought it was all too much. He sweated as he smiled and called for cool drinks.

The prince and Tissaphernes were the only two mounted on that vast field, with all the other guests and visitors arrayed on white curved benches around them, as if they were the crowd at a Greek theatre. The mood was light as the merchants and nobles enjoyed the sun. More than a few had brought unmarried daughters and they tried to catch the eye of a royal prince who seemed to scorn parties and balls and was rarely seen in public.

Cyrus wondered if there was any morsel of gossip that would fail to find its way to the ears of Tissaphernes and through him to his brother. He doubted it. Until Artaxerxes produced an heir, Cyrus was in the direct line to inherit the throne. His love affairs, or lack of them, were very much the concern of the crown. He cursed himself for not putting up a better front in the months he had been given. He'd thrown himself into the labour of gathering a vast host, regiment by regiment. It had not occurred to him that his brother might send a man to ask in seeming innocence whether the prince had visited the theatres, or courted any women of high families. His two Greek mistresses did not count.

Cyrus felt a bead of sweat trickling down his cheek and knew he was winding himself in knots. He hated to lie, and the strain of dissembling was wearing at him. He remembered his mother telling him of a holy man who was famed both for his temper and the control he exercised over it, so that no one ever saw him angry. On his death, there was a suspicion of poison and his body was opened to learn the cause of his passing. His muscles were found to be knotted and twisted together, after years and years of clenching his anger to himself and not letting anyone see.

Cyrus felt like that holy hermit whenever Tissaphernes turned and exclaimed on some aspect of the display that pleased him. All he could do was incline his head and smile in the sun, while his fears only grew. His father had maintained spies over the entire empire, everyone knew that – not even the spies were aware of the extent of his network. Cyrus had tried to act as if he was observed, as if every word said aloud could be overheard by his worst enemy. That had to be the safest course when he didn't know whom to trust. Yet it was easy to forget caution on warm nights, with good food, good wine and friends. It was possible to throw a whole life away in a few words.

The crowd sat up when four hundred Spartans entered the field through a gate, coming in at a fast lope that would have them intercept a Persian regiment standing to attention on the other side. The women fanned themselves as they watched those men trot in perfect ranks, their red cloaks flickering. There were different schools of thought amongst the Spartans themselves when it came to the cloaks. Some commanders ordered them removed before battle, considering them fit garments for a winter's night or a display, but far too easy for an enemy to grab and yank in a fight. Others such as Clearchus could use them to trap an opponent's blade, or blind him with a sweep of the cloth, then plunge the sword through it. It was a matter of personal choice for the men whose lives depended on their martial skill, but Cyrus had to admit, they did look good on the parade ground. The mock battle he and Clearchus had planned would please the Persians watching, if not the Greeks. The Spartans themselves had only shrugged when they'd practised the manoeuvre in rehearsal. They knew they were the best, regardless of what some Persian prince wished to show to his old tutor.

Not forty paces from where Tissaphernes and Cyrus sat their mounts, the Spartans drew their shields from their backs and settled the grips against their forearms. At the same time, they brought the long spear-points slowly down, so that they held them like weapons and not staffs. They were ready to attack in heartbeats and Cyrus found himself swallowing at the thought of facing such men on the field. All the other ranks had come to a halt to observe this last action. Even the birds and the watching crowd became still.

Cyrus began to pray in silence that the Persian regiment would not break and run on the parade field. He had arranged eight hundred archers in their number, taking care that they carried only shafts without heads. Yet he had not been able to do the same for the Spartan spears, not without making them useless. Clearchus had refused to destroy the weapons of their fathers just for a demonstration. They would endure the rain of arrows and refrain from cutting the Persians apart in return.

The two forces came together at what seemed a slow trot. Cyrus found himself clenching his fist as the Persian ranks halted at two hundred paces. The archers drew and loosed smoothly, the clatter like the wings of pigeons. First came the rattle of bowstrings and the shouts from the archers, with orders roared on the Spartan side. Shields were brought up and overlapped, forming a great gold dome of bronze, wood and leather, then the hammering sound rang out as thousands upon thousands of shafts struck. Each of the eight hundred archers had a quiver with twelve shafts – so they sent almost ten thousand arrows into the shields. It was a fine display at a distance, with the hours on practice targets showing in the grouping. Few shots went wild and Cyrus saw the interest in Tissaphernes. The older man clapped his hand against the smooth leather flank of his saddle, applauding the attack.

On the field, the Spartans rose slowly from their crouch. Where laughter and pleased comment had arisen in the crowd watching, silence fell once more. The spectators felt the baleful glare the Spartans gave the Persian regiment. The bronze helmets turned slowly and remained fixed on laughing Persian archers. Cyrus saw Spartans reach to snap arrows from their shields. He swallowed as he understood the tips must have pierced the bronze sheet, that some of the shafts had not been made safe. The prince did not know if it had been the sort of simple error that bedevilled his regiments, or the result of spite from one of the Persian officers, perhaps hoping to leave a few dead Greeks upon the training field. Cyrus saw the Spartans discussing the attack amongst themselves. He could only stare and hope they would not consider a reprisal. The men in red cloaks stood in challenging attitudes, taunting the enemy, leaning forward like leashed hounds. They seemed not to have taken wounds. Yet each shadowed gaze was fixed on the archers. Cyrus remembered the reported words of King Leonidas, at Thermopylae. When the Persians of his day had told him they would blot out the sun with arrows if he did not surrender, he had shrugged and told them he would fight in the shade.

Tissaphernes chuckled at whatever he thought he saw, as Spartan officers brought sullen men back to attention. The long spear-points came up and the shields were strapped behind them in marching order once more. Facing them across the field, the Persian archers were still clapping one another on the back and standing in loose formation, as if they were at a wedding or a festival. Cyrus seethed to see them. If it would not have shamed him in front of Tissaphernes, he might even have wished to witness the Spartans charge in that moment, to teach his men never to drop their guard. It would be like setting foxes loose amongst chickens, he realised. Even as a lesson, there would be blood.

Tissaphernes did not seem to have noticed the foolishness of the Persian archers. As the displays were at an end, he and Cyrus dismounted together, passing their horses into the care of servants. Tissaphernes stretched and yawned, smiling slyly at the prince. The older man flicked his fingers to summon another iced drink, his fourth, though each one cost a month's salary – an entire gold daric. The ice was brought down in vast blocks from the mountain lakes, then stored deep underground for the summer months. It was, in a single blue glass cup, the very essence of both wealth and civilisation. Tissaphernes was addicted to the sweet juices piled high with fine ice shards. More, he was addicted to the wealth and authority that brought it to his hand.

'That was a grand display,' he said, sipping and sighing in pleasure. 'It does these foreign men good to know defeat, especially against Persian soldiers. I would not like to report to your brother that your Greeks have been getting ideas above their station.' He peered at the standing lines, frowning. 'I see no striped backs amongst the Spartans. I wonder if you are stern enough with them.'

He left the last as a question and Cyrus was forced to bite down on his first response. The prince was commander-in-chief of all the armies of Persia. Tissaphernes surely knew Cyrus was vastly more experienced than he in such matters. More, the older man seemed determined to needle him and hint at a higher status than their last meeting, as if he carried the approval and trust of King Artaxerxes. It was impossible to know the truth of it. Cyrus could hardly ask him outright, or send a messenger to his brother. As a result, he had to endure waspish taunts and veiled threats without showing a flicker of resentment. For all he knew, Tissaphernes had been told to test him, exactly as he was doing.

'I leave the Spartan discipline to their own officers, on the whole,' Cyrus said. 'If one of their number is lazy, for example, or eats too much, they will punish him with astonishing cruelty, saying that he endangers all their lives. They take such matters very seriously, as an assault on their honour – and the honour and reputation of their home city.'

'Such pretensions,' Tissaphernes sniffed. 'As if men such as those can have true honour, or even understand the idea. I'm sure your brother would not like to hear your admiration for them. Or do you deny it?'

Cyrus found his anger surging again, so that it was hard to reply evenly and without heat.

'I will not deny it, old lion. Any more than I would deny the sky is blue. I admire good soldiers. The Spartans have no equal.'

'They are better than our Immortals, then?' Tissaphernes pressed.

'Thermopylae tells us they are. Plataea tells us they are. If I am to keep my brother's borders strong, I must have the best, to train our regiments.'

Tissaphernes grew colder somehow, though he spent a moment fussing with his drink before he replied.

'Some men might choose not to mention Plataea, Highness, where Spartans routed our infantry and then slaughtered those left in camp. That was a dark day. Yet here you are, praising the sons and grandsons of those very same savages and scoundrels. See them there, the way they stare! If you were a good master, you would have one of their officers lashed for the insolence of his men. I must say, I wonder what your brother . . .'

'Artaxerxes will know the empire is at peace,' Cyrus interrupted, 'and he will know that peace is won with strong borders – and trained armies ready to march at any hour. I have gathered the best, to improve our Persian regiments. To be the whetstone that keeps them sharp. That is all that matters to him.' Cyrus bit his lip rather than let even more anger seep into his replies. He could not tell if Tissaphernes was genuinely outraged by the arrogance of the Spartans, or whether he sought to prick him into a revelation that might destroy him. 'Either way, it is my concern.'

Tissaphernes turned to one of the officers he had brought with him.

'Polemarch Behkas, do you see that Spartan officer? The one who wears a leopard skin on his shoulders. Yes, the plumed helmet, there. Summon him to me.'

Cyrus felt his mouth open in surprise. He did not try to countermand the order, knowing his own dignity would not survive it. Tissaphernes had brought the officer. No doubt the man was loyal to only one master.

'You think to give orders in my barracks?' Cyrus said instead, his thoughts racing.

Tissaphernes half-turned, watching him. To his astonishment, Cyrus saw the man's hand rested very near the dagger that lay beneath his sash, as if he considered drawing it. The day had gone wrong suddenly, the man's spite revealed. Cyrus found himself floundering as General Clearchus came trotting back to the two horsemen, halting and removing his helmet in a swift motion. The Spartan stood with his legs at shoulder width, appearing relaxed. If anything, he looked as if he expected praise. He raised his eyebrows when Tissaphernes gestured angrily in his direction.

'The arrogance of this man displeases me,' Tissaphernes announced to the air. 'As the representative and royal plenipotentiary of King Artaxerxes, blessed be his name and long his life, I desire this fellow to be lashed, as an example to the rest. Polemarch Behkas, detail one of your stronger men to wield a flail. Strip this Spartan to the waist and lay on. I shall count aloud.'

'You will *not*,' Cyrus snapped, his astonishment giving way to anger. 'You have no such authority here.' He gestured sharply at the officer moving even so to take hold of General Clearchus. 'Stand away from that man. Prostrate yourself immediately!'

He said the last as a roar and the polemarch obeyed. To Cyrus' shock, Tissaphernes remained on his feet, though he paled and stood trembling.

'Highness,' Tissaphernes said, his voice strained, 'your brother, the king, wished there to be no confusion. I speak with his voice, which is the authority of the rose throne itself, at least in this rat hole, so far from the real world. If you will have my bags brought to me, I have within his personal seal – his holy word set in gold. I am sure you would not wish to disobey a direct order from the throne itself.'

'You are not the throne – and you do not give orders here, Tissaphernes,' Cyrus said with scorn dripping in his voice. 'I command the armies of the empire. Alone. What do you know of warfare? Do you see those Spartans there on the field, with spears and short swords and their kopis knives in the small of their backs? If you lay hands on their general, they will not sit idly by. If you tear his skin, I will not be able to save you from their wrath, nor any of your men.'

'I see,' Tissaphernes said. His lips had whitened as the tension grew and he dropped his air of amused patience. 'They frighten you, then, with their savagery! How interesting. I wonder truly who is the master here, if your wild dogs can so easily slip your leash.'

'If I may,' Clearchus said, surprising them both. 'If you will forgive me, His Highness, Prince Cyrus, is not correct in his observation. My Spartans will not interfere, not if I give the order.'

The man spoke fluently and precisely, his court Persian excellent, with an accent of Susa. Tissaphernes looked at him in irritation, but the Spartan ignored him, bowing to Prince Cyrus.

'Highness, if my men have displeased your brother's representative, I will endure the lash, of course. There is no question. Nor will my men draw iron in reply. We understand discipline – and indeed justice. I believe it will be an excellent lesson for them.'

Clearchus waited then, looking unblinking at Cyrus as the prince considered. With Tissaphernes watching, both men had to guess the other's intentions without giving the slightest signal of cooperation to the one watching them.

After a long silence, Cyrus nodded.

'Very well. It is true Tissaphernes here found something to dislike in the manner of your men. If you would remove your breastplate and cloak, you will be lashed as an example.'

Cyrus breathed out as the Spartan went down onto one knee and bowed his head before rising and stripping off his garments. He knew the man preferred to bow rather than graze his knee in the dirt. It was a signal that he had made the right choice. Cyrus tried not to show his relief. It was only days since Clearchus had told him he did not have the authority to order him whipped, yet there they were.

When Clearchus wore only a leather kilt and sandals, he seemed, impossibly, to have grown larger. The man could have been carved from great slabs of dark wood. The muscles hammered into the metal of his breastplate were actually less impressive than the set within.

On the field, the Spartan helmets still hid their features, so that they looked coldly on but did not move. Everyone there had seen Clearchus strip to the waist. He gave no sign he even knew they were watching as he strolled to the visitor benches and rested both hands on a white-painted post, one on top of the other. Tissaphernes looked sourly at the display of Spartan muscle, but he set his mouth and signalled once more for his man to fetch a flail, determined to see it through. He felt somehow that he had lost the climax he had intended to provoke, but he still wanted to see the Greek cry out. The thought of making a Spartan shriek or weep would be compensation for an otherwise uninspiring day.

As the officer uncoiled the strands, Cyrus watched the Spartans stand to attention. Clearchus looked up at the sky and muttered something Cyrus was not close enough to hear. He did hear the cords hum as they cut the air, each one tipped with a bead of lead. The first stroke cracked across old scars, leaving red lines that dripped watery blood as the officer drew back.

'One,' Tissaphernes said, his smile quirking up at a corner. He found his own back was aching at being forced to stand. As the lash whipped across a second time, Tissaphernes whispered to a servant and accepted the chair that was brought for him with a grateful sigh.

'Two,' he called. 'Or was it three? Should we begin again?'

'It was two,' Cyrus said. 'I will keep the count to forty. Please, do enjoy another iced juice.'

He managed to make the last suggestion sound like an insult, so that Tissaphernes flushed. Cyrus wondered how he had missed the spite in the man before. Had it always been there, or been brought forth somehow by the change of occupant on the rose throne? Cyrus had called him a friend for a dozen years, but perhaps that was when Cyrus had been a prince and Tissaphernes a poor army officer and teacher. As one rose and the other fell, it seemed to have revealed a bitterness in the older man, or a weakness that may always have been there.

Cyrus watched as Clearchus endured stroke after stroke. There were perhaps a dozen cords in the lash. Each blow cut his skin into patterns that criss-crossed in peeling diamonds, revealing whiter flesh beneath. The Spartan rested his hands on the post and Cyrus saw the moment when Clearchus noticed he was gripping it very tightly. The man breathed out and loosened his hold, standing with his legs slightly bent.

It was hard to judge the rhythm of the flogging. If the lash struck as Clearchus breathed in, it knocked the air out of him. Cyrus saw he tried to time it so that the blows came between breaths, but the Persian wielding the lash was not an expert and his timing was irregular. More than once, the man paused for an age to run his fingers through the cords, separating them.

As the count reached thirty, Cyrus saw the Spartan was sweating, his muscles shining along his sides. His blood had been flung by strands of the whip, so that he was surrounded by a halo of red spots. More than one of the fascinated families had felt the touch of droplets on their skin. A young woman held up a bead of it on her finger in delighted horror.

Twice more, Clearchus had to make an effort to unclench his hands from the post, each time visibly harder than the last. He made no sound of pain, beyond the grunt when the air was driven out of him. By the time the fortieth stroke fell on his torn flesh, the crowd watched in awe. They had learned something of Sparta that day, and Cyrus could see from Tissaphernes' scowl that it had not been to the man's liking.

Clearchus turned to the prince with a slight smile on his face.

'I hope my blood repays the dishonour, Highness. Thank you for your trust in me – and in my men. You honour us.'

'It is forgotten,' Cyrus said, though they both knew it was not. 'Please return to your men. Tell them your courage impressed me.'

The Spartan general went down on one knee. Clearchus moved stiffly, accepting his garments and helmet from the wide-eyed Persian officer who held them. He returned to his men and they marched back across the field without a word.

Tissaphernes watched them go, his expression sour.

'I wonder if such as they are worth the river of gold you have spent on them,' he said.

'I believe they are,' Cyrus replied, shaking his head in disbelief at what he had witnessed.

'Hmm. I find I am weary after so long in the sun. I have new trade concerns in the city here, gifts from your brother's hand in reward for my years of service. I will visit them tomorrow, before I return to his side.'

'Like an old family hound,' Cyrus said. 'Toothless and blind and creaking in the joints, but still, somehow, alive.'

'Oh, not blind, Highness,' Tissaphernes said, flushing. 'Not blind at all.'

With elaborate courtesy, the older man prostrated himself fully on the ground, waiting in stillness until Cyrus bade him rise. Neither man seemed happy with the exchange as they parted and the gossiping crowds began to drift away.

11

As the sun rose into an empty blue sky, Tissaphernes and his retinue rode into the centre of the city. The Persian was accompanied by so many horns, drums and flying pennants, it looked almost like a royal visit. Entire districts of Sardis ground to a halt to see the great lord of the east who had deigned to come amongst them.

Cyrus came onto the high balcony of his palace rooms in response to the cheering. In the distance, he caught a glimpse of Tissaphernes before he passed out of sight. The Persian rode a grey horse and had slaves tossing silver pieces to the crowd, while Immortal soldiers marched in uniforms unmarked by anything like fighting or hard labour. Cyrus clenched his jaw, hearing his teeth creak as he rested his hands on stone and breathed in the cool air. He had no doubt by then that spies were watching him, but with his manservant Parviz he went down to the stables, where the sound of the city and its rapturous welcome were more muted. When Cyrus had mounted up and settled himself, it pleased him to turn left out of the stable gates, heading away from Tissaphernes to the barracks on the other side of the city.

There was a very different mood in that quarter of Sardis. The guards at the gate stood back for him with bowed heads and Cyrus rode into a near silent compound. Just a few young warriors could be seen. They stopped their exercises in the yard to watch him dismount. Parviz sensed the threat in the air, but he had vowed to protect Cyrus and the little man glared like a bantam cock, though any one of them could have taken his sword from him.

Cyrus held his head high under their hostile scrutiny. If they challenged him with their stances and glares, he reminded himself of what Clearchus had said, that all young men are fools. Perhaps if they were lucky, they would live into their forties or fifties, to wish they could exchange all their wisdom and experience for just one day of that glorious, reckless youth once again.

Passing into the gloom of the interior, Cyrus paused, letting his eyes adjust. The walls had been washed in lime, so that the barracks had a light feel. It was clean and smelled of straw and some of the rubbing ointments Cyrus knew the Greeks used on bruises and wounds. He heard a groan in the room ahead and nodded to two Spartans who sat at a stone table. Each of them carried a small cup and he saw dice strewn across the surface, as well as piles of copper coins. Neither man moved to rise in his presence. They merely watched. Cyrus felt his right fist close. Some impulse made him stop and face them, leaning over the table.

'Do you not give honour to your officers any longer? What would General Clearchus say if he saw such insolence?'

The two men exchanged a quick glance and stood, the game forgotten. Cyrus brushed past as they began to dip down.

He stopped at the threshold of the room beyond, seeing a young woman drawing a thread through the general's back so that the skin wrinkled like cloth. She had already stitched a dozen neat black lines, like worms across the flesh.

Clearchus turned to see him. The movement caused him to hiss through his teeth.

'I thought Spartans don't feel pain,' Cyrus said as he came further in.

Clearchus groaned and scratched the stubble on his cheek.

'Who told you that? Are we made of stone? Of course we feel pain! We do not *show* we feel it. Not in front of enemies, at least.'

Cyrus found himself pleased he was not considered an enemy. He smiled and Clearchus chuckled, though he closed his eyes as he did so, looking tired.

'Paniea here has been working all night on my patchwork. I hope your friend was satisfied.'

'Tissaphernes is not my friend,' Cyrus said seriously. 'I doubt he ever was. Look, I came to thank you. I don't know if he simply wanted to hurt me, or to show me his new degree of status. He used to be a mere teacher of princes. Now he is a trusted companion of the Great King. At the same time, I am cast down, allowed to keep my life and my work, but nothing else. Tissaphernes wished me to understand the scales had swung against me. If you had refused . . .'

Cyrus glanced at the young woman, seeing her silent concentration. Clearchus saw the look and shook his head.

'Paniea is deaf, Highness. She cannot hear you. She does, however, have great skill with needle and thread.'

'I think I will cut her throat even so,' Cyrus said, drawing his knife.

The young woman did not react and he put it away again. Clearchus raised his eyebrows and the prince sighed and went to close the door behind him, pulling up a chair.

'You bought me a few days, general. Yet I do not think we have that year you wanted, truly. Tissaphernes leaves tomorrow – and what he will report, I cannot say.'

'Have him fall from his balcony,' Clearchus said.

'He has already sent reports with birds he brought from Persepolis. At such a distance, no one can be sure they will reach their destination. Equally, I cannot be sure they will not. Either way, I cannot know how my brother will act until Tissaphernes reaches his side. For personal reasons, I would love to see that old fool fall from a great height, but I need even the three months or so it will take him to return to . . .' He caught himself in an old habit. The heart of the empire was not known in the west and it took an effort to name his brother's capital in front of an outsider. 'To Persepolis. I should be thankful he is not a young man. He will move slowly along the Royal Road.'

The woman patted Clearchus on the shoulder and indicated by mime that he should lie on his stomach. As Cyrus watched, she poured red wine over her stitching, cleaning the dried blood from her handiwork. She took a square of cloth and pressed it over the black lines, patting the general like a favourite dog. Clearchus smiled at her and Cyrus wondered if they were lovers. He knew the Spartans were open about such things, recognising half a dozen kinds of love. In that way, they were very different from Persians, with all the taboos Cyrus had drawn in with his mother's milk.

Clearchus looked once more a general of Sparta as he rose to his feet and tested the range of movement in his arms, finally nodding to Paniea and passing her a gold daric.

'Very good,' the Spartan said to her.

She seemed delighted and bowed deeply. Both Cyrus and Clearchus took the opportunity to look at her breasts as they were revealed by the motion.

When they were alone, Cyrus too came to his feet.

'Tissaphernes is my enemy,' he said. 'If I was not certain before, I am now. No matter what he believes I am doing here, even if he suspects nothing of my plan, I think he will still whisper into my brother's ear that I should be replaced, perhaps by himself, or one of his favourites.'

'Then you have a simple choice to make,' Clearchus said. 'You could give up this enterprise and accept a simpler life, in Athens or Crete, say, or somewhere else far from Persian influence. Or you summon the regiments you have already gathered and go early. If you are right about Tissaphernes, and if you wish to see it through, you will have to push the men hard. Your brother commands vast forces, Cyrus. It is my belief we can beat them, but I would prefer them not to know we are coming. Surprise is worth ten thousand men.'

Cyrus fell silent for a time in thought. When he looked up, it was with a wild look in his eye. Clearchus hardly had to ask which way he had chosen to jump.

'My father was not the oldest son, have I ever told you?'

'I believe you mentioned it, yes. Three times that I can remember.'

'He was not even the second son. That second son murdered the first – and then my father stepped out of the crowd with a bronze sword in his hand, seeking vengeance. That is all I ask, general. Justice and vengeance. And the throne. I do not think it is too much.'

'Very well, Highness. I will have every archer and falconer we have in rings around Sardis, ready to bring down any message birds Tissaphernes may have left behind for his spies to report. I'll have every room in the city searched to seek out their cages. And all the while we will bring in the armies we have gathered in your name. Greek and Persian both, from all the cities of Greece, from Lydia and Egypt, they'll take ship to join you.'

The general stopped then, a shadow passing over his face.

'What is it?' Cyrus asked him.

Clearchus shook his head.

'I believe you when you say they trust you, these men, that they know you of old. I have seen enough of you to be sure you are correct. They will lay down their lives for you because you ask them to – but also because of who you are. You command, in part because you are a prince of Persia, a trusted son of your family.' He paused and took a deep breath. 'When you ask such men to stand against the throne itself, some of them will mutiny. Be in no doubt about that. I can work to prepare for that moment. I can salt regiments with officers I trust, who have taken personal oaths to you. I can even spread the story of how your father took the throne from an older brother. But there will come a day when they understand there *are* no Pisidians, no hill tribes, or at least not that we care about – that the enemy is the rose throne and King Artaxerxes himself, commander of a great host of their own people. We could lose it all before a single arrow is shot, before one sword is drawn. Those are the stakes, Highness. Perhaps you should give a little more thought to retiring to some fine estate to raise horses and sons. As I say it aloud, it does not sound like such a terrible dream. Many men would not think twice about accepting a path that leads them to peace.'

Cyrus smiled, a little sadly. The white-walled room had seemed cool at first, but with the door closed, it had grown stifling.

'I am not many men, general. I am a prince of the house of Achaemenid. Most importantly, I have judged my treacherous scholar brother as unfit to sit on that throne. I was loyal to him my whole life. No longer. I will bring him down. I am the rightful king. That is my decision.'

'Very well, Highness,' Clearchus said. 'Then I shall gather your armies.'

Tissaphernes sat comfortably in the private office of the richest moneylender in Sardis. Two enormous imperial soldiers flanked him as he tugged the robes at his knee, settling them along a crease.

The man who faced him was a distant cousin through marriage to the royal house. Tissaphernes had never met Jamshid before, though he believed he knew the type. The man had used his relationship to the throne to build a trading empire that spanned all the way from India to Egypt. Trusted by the crown, Jamshid had amassed a vast fortune, merely from the fees for government contracts. From ships to grain to gold coins themselves, some part of every deal stuck to his fingers. Entering his sixties, it was rare enough for Jamshid even to conduct business on his own behalf. He usually left it to one of six sons and nephews, but news of Tissaphernes' arrival in the offices had reached him and he'd hurried across the city to accommodate a man who spoke with the king's tongue.

The royal seal lay on the table between them, drawing the eye and the light so that it seemed to glow. The symbol was a combination of a mounted nobleman and the eagle of the royal house. If there was any doubt, the presence of Immortal soldiers from Persepolis was proof enough of royal favour. Jamshid could hardly restrain his excitement at the thought of what deal might require his personal presence. He had to wait as his servants brought wine for Tissaphernes and a steaming glass cup for himself, redolent with a fragrance that filled the office.

Tissaphernes accepted a full goblet of the red wine, then

passed it back to be sipped by one of his companions. The merchant pretended not to notice, though he felt the insult as a sting. He knew very well that this was the man who had ordered a Spartan general whipped – the whole city was alive with the news. It seemed the Persian was a wasp, of sorts.

To cover his discomfort, Jamshid indicated his own, steaming cup.

'Herbs for my digestion, which has been very poor recently. A brick of medicinal leaves came from the Yunnan province of China, along with forty bolts of red silk, fit for the emperor himself.'

'That is very generous, Jamshid,' Tissaphernes said smoothly. He smiled as the merchant failed to hide his dismay at the slip. 'His Majesty, King Artaxerxes, will be delighted at such a gift.'

'Of course,' Jamshid replied. A wasp indeed, to have such a sting! The merchant sipped at his cup and hissed to himself as he discovered it was still too hot. He watched as Tissaphernes drained the wine and had it refilled from the same jug. Both men sat back and smiled, watching each other closely.

'The gossip of the markets is that you will return east tomorrow,' Jamshid said.

Tissaphernes inclined his head.

'The wisdom of the market is . . . rarely wrong.'

'I hoped you would grace my establishment before today, Lord Tissaphernes. May I say it has been a delight dealing with the factors of King Artaxerxes. The accounts are correct to the last coin, the debts and interest are all paid with exact perfection. The world is set aright after the tragedy of his beloved father's passing, may he reign in heaven for a thousand years.'

'These debts . . .' Tissaphernes said, rubbing the fold of flesh under his chin with one finger. 'I imagine you have issued gold and silver to Prince Cyrus over the past few months? It is hard to find a merchant house or a money-lender who has not.'

Tissaphernes watched the blood drain from the merchant's face, along with his sly confidence. Such a man did not need more than a hint to go running for the hills, with all his slaves and money bags around him.

'My lord, if you have news I should hear, I beg you, please, speak clearly,' Jamshid said, his words tumbling over themselves. 'F-from my personal wealth, I have handed over ninety thousand daric archers to His Highness, Prince Cyrus. For anyone else, it would have been impossible, but the prince is commander-in-chief of the Persian army. There has never been a limit on his credit. All his papers have been honoured in the past, all of them! Please, have you heard something? You will earn the gratitude of my house and all the moneylenders of Sardis.'

Tissaphernes leaned back and sipped at his wine.

'The house of Achaemenid honours its historic debts, of course,' he said. 'Yet seasons change and come to an end. The careers of men, perhaps even of princes, rise and fall. It is nothing more than nature, as the days lengthen, or the young grow old.'

He saw the confusion in the face of Jamshid and sighed elaborately.

'If I must be blunt, there are some who believe Prince Cyrus relies too much on Greek mercenaries, at the expense of our own Persian soldiers. The king will no longer pay such riches straight to the coffers of Greek cities. Are they our slaves, our client states? No. Why then should we fill their mouths with gold? My advice to you, Jamshid, indeed to your brothers in trade, is that you should not reach beyond your grasp. There. I have said too much.'

The merchant blinked at him. Slowly, Jamshid rose to his feet and bowed over the table, pressing his forehead to the polished wood. Tissaphernes saw he was trembling.

'Thank you, my lord Tissaphernes. You are a friend to this house to have come with such a warning. A thousand thanks.'

'You have been a loyal supporter of the crown, Jamshid,' Tissaphernes replied, sweeping up the royal seal. 'In return for your service – and your silence – you may construct a copy of this seal in plaster and raise it over your door. All men will know you have a patron in King Artaxerxes and the blessing of his royal house.'

Tissaphernes left the man and his staff prostrated, weeping and slapping the floor in delight. He visited one other moneylender in the city, one whom it was said Jamshid would not have warned, as they hated each other. Every other moneylender and merchant would hear the news before the sun set. Tissaphernes only regretted he would not be there to see the first demands for payment, the first wagons of food refusing to leave their yards. Mercenaries had to be paid. It would not be long before Prince Cyrus would be forced to send his Greeks away.

Tissaphernes chuckled to himself as he was helped to mount, the servant grunting beneath him as he took the weight of a haunch. His solution to the problem of Prince Cyrus had been a master stroke. It signalled disapproval, without open conflict. Once Cyrus learned there would be no more gold flowing from the Persian treasury, he would have to return to his brother's court to hear his new status. There would be no more arrogant displays and sneering comments from a younger son. Tissaphernes beamed as he sat his mount and watched the imperial guards form up around him. He looked them over carefully. They represented the throne, as he did.

'Take me home,' he called, shaking his head in pleasure as he imagined recounting the events of his trip to the king. There was more than one way to bring a dog to heel.

On the evening after Tissaphernes had left, Cyrus entered the jade dining hall in the palace to find a glum group waiting for him. He knew Proxenus well, and General Netus the Stymphalian. Clearchus was there, along with Cyrus' man-servant Parviz, who clutched a leather wrap to his chest and rocked back and forth on his chair. Menon the Thessalian was one of those Cyrus had recruited over the previous months, a man who seemed content to ask few questions. However, Menon had brought a thousand Greek hoplites and, just as welcome, eighty peltast spearmen. With no armour beyond a small shield, the javelin throwers were all young and fit, and lightning-quick on their feet. Cyrus was delighted, knowing a good unit of peltasts could ruin an armed charge.

As far as Cyrus knew, neither Menon nor Sosis the Syracusan who sat at his side had any idea of his true purpose. They had gathered and trained men for his silver and gold. He thought he had every general and senior officer in Greece under his command that year.

His gaze fell on the two Persians sitting at that table, both men visibly uncomfortable with a conversation that had almost certainly been in Greek before the prince arrived. Orontas was the most senior general of the Persian faction Cyrus had brought to fitness over the previous months. Though he was darker than the rest and more slender of frame, if numbers meant anything, Orontas should have been the most senior in authority – as he commanded many more men than the Greeks. The reality was somewhat different, however, Cyrus noted. Orontas sat slightly apart from the rest, so that it was the Spartan, Clearchus, who subtly commanded the table.

The other Persian, Ariaeus, was an arresting figure. Cyrus knew him first by a reputation for horsemanship, in which he was said to excel. The second in command of the Persian forces was a general in his own right. Cyrus might have wished to deal with Ariaeus rather than the dour Orontas. Ariaeus wore his hair to his shoulders and was physically the match for any of the Spartans, with wide shoulders and powerful legs. He was said to enjoy the company of young men and wrote ghazal poems to their beauty in the evenings. The Greeks preferred him to Orontas, without a doubt. Yet at thirty, he was both younger and his family a degree beneath that of Orontas. Whatever the prince might have preferred, Orontas was the senior Persian officer.

As Cyrus entered, they all rose. The Greeks bowed. Ariaeus copied them as if there was nothing strange in it. Orontas caught his colleague's movement out of the corner of his eye as he braced one hand on the table in preparation for prostrating himself on the floor. Cyrus watched in resignation as Orontas hesitated and stuttered through a deeper bow than the rest, coming back to attention as the prince gestured for them all to sit. Greek manners spread like a sickness through the Persian ranks. On the other hand, if it brought the same courage, Cyrus thought it would be a fair exchange.

Food arrived as a series of steaming dishes, a line of servants appearing at the edges of the room. They were all hungry, but Cyrus could see they were exchanging glances as each one considered how best to tell him something he would not want to hear. His servant Parviz looked practically in tears.

'Enough of this silence, these guarded glances!' Cyrus ordered. 'What is it? Someone say something!'

'It seems Lord Tissaphernes left a parting gift, Highness,' Clearchus said. 'Your line of credit has been disavowed. At this moment, we cannot lay claim to a single silver drachma in Sardis. You will not need me to tell you that you have twelve thousand mercenaries who must be paid on the first day of each month – which is eight days from now.'

'We don't have enough food for the rest,' Parviz said, holding up his leather packet as if Cyrus could see the columns of figures from across the table. 'We have funds to go on as we are for perhaps another week, but without payment, the mercenary contracts are void; without food, the men starve. General Orontas has presented the tally of grain and meat needed for eighty thousand active men in training. It is . . . impossible. Highness, we cannot meet the bills. The word has gone round and there is not a cattle farmer or fruit seller in Sardis who will extend our credit for a single day.'

Cyrus had taken up a knife to spear morsels as they appeared on his plate. He tossed it onto the table and rose to his feet.

'Tissaphernes left this morning. Perhaps the moneylenders of Sardis have closed up shop, but how fast can the news travel? Can I get ahead of it? There is gold in Byzantium, four days' hard ride to the north. My name and my seal will still be honoured there. How much do we need?'

The men at the table gaped at him. It was his own officer, Orontas, who spoke first.

'Highness, if you incur new debts to the crown, they will *not* be honoured. Not only will you beggar the moneylenders in Byzantium, you will damage the reputation of the royal house! Please! There must be another way.'

Cyrus narrowed his eyes as he listened. He shook his head, reminded that Orontas did not know his true purpose and had no understanding of the threats he faced. Even so, it was hard to be civil to the man.

'General Orontas, Tissaphernes has gone beyond the trust placed in him by my brother, King Artaxerxes. Whatever the rights and wrongs of my choice, I must have gold to pay the men. The greater dishonour would be in releasing an army of mercenaries to carry the news that Persia cannot pay its debts! No. I need . . .' he paused to think, 'another ninety thousand daric archers for what I have in mind. Twice that many if I can get them. Such an amount will give me breathing room, time enough to appeal to my brother and see this matter resolved. Do you understand?'

The Persian thought better of his previous decision to bow and came away from the table to throw himself at Cyrus' feet. His colleague, Ariaeus, watched him with a glimmer of amusement.

'I did not see, master, I'm sorry. I understand and serve you.'

'For which I am grateful,' Cyrus said wryly, aware of the Greeks watching. 'Clearchus? I will need an official guard. I cannot walk into a merchant's home in Byzantium on my own. With your back, I cannot ask . . .'

'It will heal as I ride, Your Highness,' Clearchus said clearly. 'I would not miss it.'

'Good. Bring a dozen of your men. Parviz? You too. Run to the palace stables and get the horses ready. If there is a message on the road ahead of us, we must overtake it, or lose everything.'

'Highness? May I accompany you?' Orontas said, his voice muffled.

Cyrus looked down and shook his head.

'No. I will take General Ariaeus. Make your men ready to march, as soon as I return.'

Ariaeus beamed at the decision. He cast a look of pity at Orontas that Cyrus saw. He let it pass, but he was weary of his own officers in that moment. Some of them were more concerned with petty rivalries than their own service to him.

12

Four days of hard riding had taken its toll on them all, but none more so than Clearchus. Despite the legendary endurance of the Spartans, his stitches had begun seeping after just a few miles of jolting around on an animal he disliked and hardly knew how to control. Each day ended with Cyrus ordering the horses and men into a road inn, then waiting for Clearchus to catch up in the small hours. As a matter of pride and personal responsibility, Cyrus would not leave the roadside until Clearchus reached him. It seemed to take longer and longer each day as the Spartan grew pale and his back bled through its wrappings, but he made no complaint, even in the mornings, when the pain was at its worst.

The small party had not been troubled by road thieves or the city guards in Byzantium. Cyrus was chafing at every lost hour by then and would have gone straight to the richest moneylender of the city. It had surprised them when a trembling Parviz reached out and took hold of his master's rein inside the walls, drawing the animal to a halt. As the prince looked at him in astonishment, Parviz dropped the rein and bowed so deeply in the saddle that he was in danger of being pitched onto the road. Even so, the man spoke.

'Highness, you are covered in dust and sweat. Forgive me, but . . . you wear your desperation in the open, where anyone can see. I apologise for my rudeness, but you have come so far. I would not see you throw it away with recklessness now. Please, master. Your father keeps . . . kept a fine estate in the city here. You can bathe and dress in clothes more fitting to your titles and family.'

'And if the news from Sardis passes me by while I bathe?' Cyrus murmured. 'This wild ride will have been wasted.'

His manservant could only bow his head and Cyrus gathered up the reins, rubbing his thumb along the ornate stitching.

'I apologise, Parviz. You are, of course, correct. Still, make haste.'

It was barely two hours later when the prince leaped lightly to the ground by the merchant Shaster's city home, dressed in a fine panelled coat and a silk tunic, with the road dust washed from his skin. While he had made himself presentable, Cyrus had sent Parviz ahead to announce his presence, so that the gates opened before him. The prince was quietly pleased he had taken the time to change. He walked with a straight back and carried a jewelled scabbard on his hip that in itself would have fetched five thousand darics. Such a display was important.

He had not met Shaster before, though Cyrus had heard the name a dozen times over the years. Of all the merchants and moneylenders in Byzantium, Shaster was the one most able to survive the loss he would take – when the crown failed to honour the loan. The man was said to be as rich as Croesus, the old king of Lydia.

Cyrus beamed and extended his arms as he sighted the master of the house, coming forward to interrupt the fellow's attempt to prostrate himself before more than one knee had touched the tiles.

'Please, Master Shaster, I am a guest. On urgent business of the rose throne. I am only grateful that you were present in the city as I passed by. Byzantium is the jewel of the west. I would not have wanted to take my business on to Sardis.'

Cyrus watched closely as he said the name. He and General Clearchus had agreed the line, in order to observe the man's reaction. Yet the merchant only kissed his hand, pressing his lips against the prince's knuckles. Cyrus doubted the beard had ever been cut since it first grew. It covered Shaster's face entirely beyond his nose, forehead and eyes. The great length of it was constrained in charms and precious gems that rattled with every movement.

'It is an honour, Highness. I had hoped to meet you for many, many years. My wife will be delighted when I tell her you came to me, to us, over all others.'

Cyrus felt a pang of guilt as he recalled the words of Orontas. It was hard to look a man in the eye and ruin him, but he forced his smile wider. His cause was just. When he was king, he would make all things right. Cyrus clung to that, to help him still the small voice of guilt that groaned in his heart.

'I am only sorry I cannot stay to see your family, but I have had news of a great rebellion in Thrace. I have twelve thousand mercenaries under my command – the best in Greece. Such men must be paid. My brother, King Artaxerxes, will honour the debts, of course. I will put my ring to it. Do you have ninety thousand here? I have brought men to carry the chests.'

To his alarm, the merchant Shaster wound a coil of his beard through his hands, visibly distressed. He would have dropped to the floor if Cyrus hadn't reached out to hold his arm.

'Highness, I am sorry, but such a sum! I have thirty thousand in gold in my personal vault here. If you can give me just two days, I will have the rest brought to your lodgings, or even escorted to your forces as they march. Master, I am sorry. With just a little warning, I could have had it ready for you.'

Cyrus tried not to show his frustration. He patted the old man on the shoulder.

'Never mind. Thirty thousand will do. Bring me wax and a stylus. I will mark your ledger for the record.'

'Yes, Highness, of course. I am so sorry . . .'

'I cannot delay here,' Cyrus reminded him.

The merchant left the room as if he was on fire, all unknowing that he had saved himself from bankruptcy.

Thirty thousand coins required two carts that left the city as the moon rose, surrounded by Spartans on horseback. Four more were left in the road, unneeded. The small group took their mood from Cyrus, who seethed to himself. He was not certain if it was because he had been forced to lie or to incur a bad debt – or because he had won only a third of what he needed by doing so.

As the sun rose the next morning, a rider came trotting along the road from the direction of Sardis. That part of the empire was peaceful and yet the man was cautious at the sight of such a well-armed party. He saw them from a long way back and gave them a wide berth. In turn, Clearchus and the Spartans eyed the man's leather satchel and wondered what message it might contain.

'Do you want us to take him?' Clearchus said to the prince.

'No. Let him go,' Cyrus said over his shoulder. 'Whatever news he carries, it does not matter now. My course is set.'

Over the days that followed, the armies began to gather in Sardis, Persian and Greek alike. The plains around the city were marked by latrine ditches, tents and campfires by the thousand. Fields of green wheat and barley were trampled down, the crops lost for the year. Greek hoplites arrived on massive oared vessels at the coast, while fresh Persian infantry marched in from desert posts, their commanders greeting Cyrus in awe and pleasure. Their delight at seeing the commander and first soldier of the empire rarely lasted long as they joined the gathering host. Cyrus had kept his inner circle as small as possible, but as Clearchus had warned him, there was no hiding the purpose of such a sea of armed ranks. Anyone with eyes would know there were no hill tribes in the world that could trouble that army. Nations were won or lost by smaller forces than the one that grew around Sardis.

Cyrus slept a few hours each night, when sheer exhaustion drove him to collapse on a cot pallet, only to rise again when Parviz touched his shoulder. In the evenings, the prince entertained his Persian officers in groups of a dozen, summoning them to test the waters. Clearchus, Proxenus and Netus the Stymphalian were all in attendance at those times, watching their Persian colleagues with disconcerting focus. There were questions that could not be avoided and Cyrus grew less patient each time one was asked. No, they would not be invading the free Greek cities. No, he would not name the enemy they would face, not until the moment was right.

Clearchus had healed of his wounds, applying goose grease and damp bread to one part on his shoulder that festered, until the poison was drained from it. He offered to show the scars to some of the Persians, but they demurred, made uncomfortable by the frankness of the strange Greek generals. It was Clearchus who remained behind each evening at the last, when all the other guests had excused themselves. If they were the sort who would not leave until the hosts had retired for the evening, Cyrus would reconvene his most trusted few in a secondary room as soon as the palace was quiet and the servants asleep.

'With us, or not?' Cyrus asked each night.

If the Greeks were flattered to have their judgement taken seriously, they did not show it, looking glumly at each other before they replied.

'That fellow tonight would not meet your eye at all,' Clearchus said. 'Nor mine, when I tried to engage him in conversation. I assume he was not one of your appointments?'

'You are correct,' Cyrus said. 'He dates from before my time, raised to the post by my father. Unfortunately, he is a competent officer and I need him. Proxenus? Your judgement?'

'I didn't like him – and I trust my instincts. So I would not trust him further than I could spit.' The heavy-boned Greek accompanied his words with a shrug that was like mountains moving. 'Not like that cheerful little one, last night. You are a hero to many of your people, Highness, but not all. It's my belief tonight's polemarch, this Arras, or Araz, whatever his name was – he should be left behind, or sent away on some errand. I do not think he will be loyal.'

'I can't send away every man who looks sullen or disloyal,' Cyrus said tightly. 'If I am to succeed, I need to know I can depend on them, on their expertise and experience.' He shook his head like a twitch as anger overwhelmed him. 'I cannot succeed without trusting my officers, but every one of them will come only because I speak for the king. So tell me, how can I bring them to battle against my brother? Is it impossible?'

The prince looked around at the men gathered in his name. The truth was that he trusted the Greeks he paid by the month a great deal more than the Persians who came to him as professional soldiers of the empire. The Greeks wanted to win and that mattered. More, they seemed to have taken a personal dislike to Tissaphernes and all he represented. They brought an almost unprofessional enthusiasm to their work after that particular Persian had one of their number whipped, no matter how well Clearchus had borne the humiliation.

Netus the Stymphalian cleared his throat. At that late stage, Cyrus had accepted that the Greeks had to know the plan. It may have galled the prince to keep his own people in the dark, but at least he could discuss the problems with his most trusted mercenaries without having to play games or lie to them. He looked to Netus, remembering how they had walked together in the gardens of Sardis, discussing the terrible threat posed by Pisidians. The man had not believed it for an instant, which at least suggested his judgement was sound.

'Highness, I have been thinking about the problem for some time now. It occurs to me that you have no right to sit on that throne instead of your brother.'

'Careful, Netus,' Clearchus rumbled without looking up.

'I meant that your Persian regiments will not want to stand against the true king – and would not – for anyone else in the world but you. You are the heir to the throne, after all. If we bring King Artaxerxes to battle and he falls – if his horse stumbles and he breaks his neck, am I right in saying that you will be king the moment he is dead?'

'That is true,' Cyrus said.

Netus nodded.

'Then perhaps you have a right of challenge. Instead of taking an army to invade and destroy, you are bringing a personal reprisal against your brother, for the wrongs he has done to you. Your army is merely to force him to accept that challenge and keep you safe while you take the justice that was denied to you before. It is my understanding that your personal guard was murdered, that you were put in a cell and held for execution. You are the wronged son, Highness. If your Persians resist, if they dare to threaten mutiny, I would tell them that.'

There was a long silence in the room as the Stymphalian

fell silent. Clearchus had raised his eyebrows to the point where they threatened to disappear into his hairline.

'You old fox, Netus,' Proxenus said. 'That is exactly how to play it. Your commanders will understand a personal matter, Highness. A matter of family honour and recompense. It could work.'

'Some will still resist, Highness, I am sure,' Netus went on. 'But we can face that when and if it comes. Perhaps we can cut out a few of the worst whiners and complainers before we meet in the field.' The wiry Greek grinned at the thought and chuckled when Clearchus thumped him on the back.

'Very well,' Cyrus said. 'It is my intention not to wait for the few who have not yet arrived. We've lost weeks already gathering the army here. Tissaphernes will still be on the road ahead of us, but we must leave soon, if we are to have any chance at all.' He looked around, seeing the generals exchange glances. 'What else?'

'There is the matter of paying the men, Highness,' Clearchus said. 'The thirty thousand darics we took in Byzantium is down to nothing. It went on stores and carts, enough to feed the army for a month on the road, six weeks on two-thirds rations. It will . . . not be enough.'

To their surprise, Cyrus waved a hand, showing them the sort of breezy confidence they had not seen for the best part of a year.

'I have given that matter some thought of my own, gentlemen – and I've sent messages to one or two of my oldest and richest allies. By the time we are marching on wheat dust and spring water, I think I will have whatever we need. I cannot say there will not be hardship, but what campaign could ever promise such a thing? There are few certainties but one. My promise is that if you make me king over the body of my brother, you will never want again. Is that enough for you? I swear it on my honour and I will take the hand of each of you in my oath, if you are willing.'

One by one, the Greeks came forward and took his hand, gripping hard enough for the knuckles to show white as they tested his resolve. There was no doubt in the prince's eyes. Clearchus was not certain if that was a good or a bad thing, given what they faced.

Summer was well advanced by the time the great column formed to march at Sardis. The Greek contingent might have been lost in the host of Persian infantry if Clearchus hadn't insisted on his Spartans being the vanguard. The general said it was because they would surely go faster if his men set the pace, although the other Greeks complained he was setting himself above them all once again.

The Persian contingent came to just over a hundred thousand infantry when the last of them had come in. They were short of both archers and slingers, having only a few thousand of the former. There were also very few cavalry, though Cyrus had seen that the Athenian, Xenophon, was tending the animals they had, keeping them in good order. The young Greek had found himself a role as master of horse and seemed content when Cyrus cantered past him. In all, it was not quite the army Cyrus had intended to take against his brother and the vast resources of the Persian empire. He could not escape the sense that the entire enterprise had been rushed. Assembling a host with the slightest chance of overcoming the Persian king had been a near impossibility from the beginning. The men had not been trained as well as he'd wanted, though Clearchus promised to continue the work as they marched – and their fitness would certainly improve day by day. One hundred and twelve thousand soldiers would march south-east into the deserts – far away from the Royal Road and watching eyes. Cyrus found he was desperately, painfully proud of them all.

The first scouts and peltast skirmishers set out a day ahead of the main force, with groups of a dozen trotting away every six hours after that. It would become a game for the main column to try and run down the lightly armed men. The officers knew it raised spirits on the long trudges through featureless lands and did not forbid it. The prospect of catching sight of a group of scouts kept them all more alert and was the source of a brisk trade in betting tokens amongst the regiments and of course the scouts themselves.

Cyrus had not given them a destination as he made a final inspection, but he had passed the word that they would not dawdle. Though they would cut a trail through wilder lands than Tissaphernes travelled, their destination was wherever he could force Artaxerxes to take the field. The thought of such distances was daunting, not least because they had to carry with them all they would need.

Cyrus found himself clenching his jaw in irritation at the sheer number of camp followers. He had made Sardis his base for almost eight months, paying his mercenaries in gold, while the Persians took pay in silver from the regimental quartermasters. For all that time, the city of Sardis had been host to tens of thousands of soldiers with money to spend. Trade had flourished, from smiths and theatres and leather-workers, to high-quality weapon-makers, armourers and, of course, both male and female bed partners, who had appeared in large numbers, making a living from lonely men waiting to go to war. Some of those hangers-on had grown close to individuals of Greece or Persia. Others preferred more temporary arrangements or took what they could get. The result was another twelve thousand or so who would play no part in any battles they faced, but still had to be fed and clothed and guarded on the trail.

The prince gripped the bridge of his nose between finger and thumb and cursed the name of Tissaphernes in a muttered whisper. He had not expected to have to move at all that summer, when the heat could kill active men. Worse, taking away his ability to pay had been a serious blow, for all he thought it had been done out of petty vindictiveness rather than because the man doubted his loyalty. In all his life, Cyrus had never had to think about the difficulties of mounting a campaign without the limitless wealth of the royal treasury behind him. It was like looking for an ocean and finding it gone – as if the world had been tipped over. He had to learn to bargain with suppliers for the first time, bringing a sharpness borne in anger to the negotiations that surprised him as much as them. He'd found he enjoyed forcing the price down. It was an exercise in power he had never understood before, a form of conflict without bloodshed. The thought was a strange one, for a royal prince. Cyrus knew the army shuffling into column was more his than it would ever have been without that pressure of time and coin. He was proud of them, even the whores, even the men he thought would betray him at the last.

They had come at his call, whether their reasons were noble or not. The assembly of his people and the Greeks had made its own ocean on the bare ground, a column that would stretch for so many miles that those at the front would be an entire day ahead of the rear. The very idea made his thoughts spin and a dull pain threaten to begin behind his eyes.

When they were ready, hundreds of pentekoster officers roared their fifties to silence all along the vast squares, waiting to fall in behind one another. Cyrus rode with Clearchus to the head of the column, where two white bulls had been tied to iron posts hammered into the earth. The Spartan had agreed to wait behind for the last groups of hoplites who were coming over from Crete. Clearchus had refused the offer of a horse, saying the last time had been enough. Even so, he had sworn a solemn oath to bring those men to Cyrus' side.

Cyrus breathed deeply, smelling lemon and mint on the air, along with the drifting scent of charcoal. His soothsayers were ready to observe and interpret the spatter of blood and all his officers knew there would be a thick slice of beef sent to their fires that night, so that they looked on the straining animals with anticipation. Cyrus raised his hand and the silence was complete for a moment, with just the breeze making cloth flap like wings.

As he dropped his hands, the soothsayers sawed at the muscular throats of the bulls, spilling a vast slick of blood. They would all march through the pools that followed, leaving red prints for a mile or more. It did not matter. Blood was why they were there. No one assembled such a host for peace.

Horns sounded, blaring across the morning. Banners rose all along the column and the waiting squares, fluttering wildly in the wind. Regimental drummers who walked with their instrument strapped across a shoulder began a rhythmic beat to set the marching pace.

Cyrus sent a prayer into the blue sky, asking for good fortune and a crown of gold to fall to his hand. The river Meander was three days away through the green lands of Lydia, the city of Colossae a day's march further on. He would wait there for Clearchus to bring in the stragglers.

The Persian prince watched from the side of the road as the Spartans set off in silence, arms swinging. Those first days would reveal weaknesses, he had no doubt: the mistakes in their planning, the myriad of things that had been forgotten, left behind. Yet it would show them what they faced as well – and those who reached the resting place at Colossae in good order would have learned they were equal to the task. Cyrus knew he would take a rabble from a dozen sources and hone it to a single blade, step by step. So he smiled as he turned his horse on a tight rein and dug in his heels. Only the Spartan general and a dozen guards remained behind. Cyrus saw Clearchus shade his eyes and thought he could feel the man's gaze. He dipped his head to acknowledge it and saw Clearchus do the same. The way was open ahead, wherever it would lead them.

13

The great column reached the river Meander at a good pace. It had been a little chaotic at first, with men who were not used to staying in ranks for six or seven hours tripping themselves up and fouling the lines behind. Yet so early in the long march, the men had not suffered unduly. There were new blisters to wrap each night, though most of those who suffered accepted the advice of the Spartans, that it was better to let the skin harden in the open air rather than risk damp and rotting flesh.

They crossed the river on a makeshift pontoon of seven fishing boats lashed together, causing much laughter amongst the men. Very few of the Persians could swim and they gripped each hull with white fingers, prising themselves free to clamber onto the next one. The Spartans were at home in the water and some of them splashed or fished while they waited, keeping cool in the sun.

By the time they had marched another long day, the men were beginning to show some sign of hardening. It was true there had been half a dozen sprains and injuries – it was impossible to move men and weapons across country without wrenched knees or dropped swords causing astonishing wounds. Yet they had shared experiences together. Cyrus hoped to build his army around that common history, so that when his Persian regiments saw the enemy, they would choose the prince and commander of the armed forces over an unknown, scholar king. A man they knew, who had faced trials and ridden at their side for months, over a mere stranger.

It could not have been a gentler start. Cyrus rested the men for seven days at Colossae, while he hunted in the royal parks. He saw no sign of Clearchus, though Menon the Thessalian reached him with another four hundred and news that Clearchus would catch up by Celaenae and not to wait. Cyrus took a dozen racehorses from the imperial stables for his own use, handing them to Xenophon. It was still too few, though the prince could not conjure trained cavalry out of thin air and had not the funds to consider buying more. Aside from his own mounted guard of six hundred, he knew the benefit of fast messengers. He would have mounted all the scouts ranging ahead of them if he'd had the horses to do it. Without them, he could not help seeing the huge army as a slow and plodding thing, vulnerable to a sudden strike or an ambush.

By the time they left Colossae, blisters had healed and strained muscles had grown stronger. They set off once more with a spring to their step, horn blasts making the horses whinny as they galloped along the edges. His guards made a fine display, the riders separated from the animal by the skin of a leopard or a gazelle.

Cyrus found he enjoyed the hours riding alongside the men each day. When they came across a road or a track, they followed it. Yet most days were spent moving over fields and valleys towards distant landmarks, keeping them in view no matter what lay in their path.

He felt his fitness increase, though he worried when even their vast column was dwarfed by the mountains they approached, or swallowed up in a pine forest. He sent men back down the road then to look for Clearchus, but there was still no sign of him. Away from Sardis, the prince realised how much he had come to trust and depend upon the Spartan. Without that solid presence, that certainty, it all seemed suddenly hollow, as if he only played at wearing a crown.

Of all the men there, Cyrus knew his brother's armies of the east better than anyone – even better than Artaxerxes. If his brother considered Cyrus a true threat and summoned every regiment under his command, he could put more than half a million men into the field. It was a number to make Cyrus start from sleep in the middle of the night. Worse still was that his brother would have the wealth of twenty-eight subject nations and the royal treasury to back him. The Great King would not suffer shortages of food or firewood and be unable to replace them. Artaxerxes would drink wine instead of water each night, as he marched with soldiers the equal of all the stars in the sky.

The citadel of Celaenae lay just three days' march from Colossae, on the river Marsyas. Cyrus waited there for Clearchus to bring the last of them, regretting that he had ever agreed to leave the general behind. As each evening ended, the prince could see the puzzled glances amongst the others, particularly the Persians. They saw no special need to wait for a single Spartan, no matter his rank. Yet the prince did nothing and the days dragged on, despite all the urgency before. The sense of excitement at the beginning faded slowly as the men settled into life in camp, seeking their entertainment in the local town. Cyrus did not hear of the ones who had to be hanged, nor the massed brawl between the Stymphalian contingent and a regiment of Imperials. Such things were kept from him while he waited.

On the fourteenth day, Clearchus arrived, calm as a spring breeze. He brought eight hundred hoplites of various cities, two hundred peltasts with their javelins and forty Cretan archers. Cyrus forgave him his lateness at the sight, though Clearchus apologised even so and went down on one knee to him in front of the newcomers.

'That is the last of them, Highness – and they were lucky

to survive when their ship foundered on the way over from Crete. They have a thousand tales to tell and I don't doubt you'll hear them all as we move on. From here, we are on our own. No one lies behind us.' The Spartan looked into the distance like a hunting dog scenting prey, his nostrils flaring.

'I thought you were not coming, for a time,' Cyrus said.

Clearchus looked at him, his eyes steady.

'I gave you my word, Highness. They'll have to kill me to drag me from your side.' As the prince smiled, Clearchus went on: 'Of course, that could very well happen.'

There was a renewed sense almost of holiday amongst the men as the regiments set off. For a time, they passed through a satrapy where the roads had been well laid. The men enjoyed marching on flat stones and if battle lay in their future, it was so far ahead that it became a problem they could ignore.

Their commanders did not share the general good mood. Clearchus found himself snapping at light-hearted comments. He took his trade seriously and he at least felt the tension of the trials ahead slowly growing. Cyrus too withdrew to his own company, spending whole days in silence as they marched or rode down the veins of the empire. He could not help thinking of Tissaphernes on the Royal Road, wondering if they had overtaken the old man, or if he still rode ahead. Those same stones had carried the first King Darius to invade Greece. That great road had taken his son Xerxes to the west, never knowing that he would see his army slaughtered and his fleet scattered to the four winds. Yet Cyrus had been forced to take a route to the south of it, far away from royal messengers who would race home at the first sight of his men.

Such thoughts seemed to bear Cyrus down as he spent long hours sweating under the sun. He lost the sense of his men as a lean fighting force when he realised it took half a day just to feed them a single meal. They were a city on the move, and at the noon halt, what seemed an entire town would trundle up on carts. Cooking pots clattered and firewood was gathered. The mood of a summer festival would take hold, even to the point of setting tents where men queued to spend their money on fumblings within. It all took an age and Cyrus could only fret and watch the sun, shading his eyes against its glare.

Like locusts, they descended on taverns whenever they encountered them, no matter how small or run-down. On the Royal Road, Cyrus knew such establishments were built to the same design, decreed by imperial order. All the pleasures of civilisation waited for weary travellers like beads on a chain, all the way to Susa.

Denied those luxuries, Cyrus' army stripped villages bare of everything they could not hide from hungry soldiers. The army would have starved without those extra rations, but Cyrus was only too aware of his last daric coins disappearing, seeming to vanish even as he counted them. When he could hold the last of his funds in one hand, he took the column sixty miles across country to the city of Tyriaeon, in the small kingdom of Cilicia. He rested there in an estate he had known well as a child.

After two days, as Cyrus had expected, it was Clearchus the others elected to speak to him. None of the Greek or Persian regiments had been paid and he had nothing left to fill the coffers. The prince sat at a table on a terrace in the evening sun, enjoying dates and soft cheese from the region.

'Ah, general, I thought they would send you. Please sit and eat. These are the finest you will ever taste.'

Clearchus looked exactly as he had on their first meeting, as if time could have no hold on him. In turn he saw a young man made weary by too much responsibility.

'Thank you, Highness,' he said. He took a sweet date and chewed it, spitting the sharp stone into his palm. 'Very good.'

Silence fell between them and Cyrus waited, amused to be able to test his resolve against that of a Spartan. They finished the plate of dates and a servant brought a platter of thinly sliced meat and roasted garlic cloves, sitting on the board like tiny white eggs. Clearchus loved garlic and took a handful, crunching them.

'Highness . . .' he said after an age.

Cyrus chuckled, interrupting him.

'You are a good man, Clearchus. As much as you detest this sort of thing, you volunteered to be the one to ask me about paying the men. I told you before that I had sent messengers, did I not? That is why I took us so far out of our way. I have a friend in Cilicia who will help us.'

'You know the king?' Clearchus said, belching into his fist. He raised his wine cup to the gods and took a long draught of it to clear his mouth of garlic. As he did so, he noticed Cyrus' expression darken.

'He and I . . . are not friends. I knew him when we were both very young, but we fell out and it has not been right between us since then.'

'Did he take her from you, or did you take her from him?' Clearchus said.

Cyrus snorted into his wine, spilling some of it on the tabletop.

'Must you always be so . . . Spartan, general? So blunt?'

Clearchus shrugged.

'I find such things are usually simpler than we make them out to be.'

172

'Well, in this case, yes, we both loved a woman. And she loved me, but married him! How is that for simple? No wondrous tale of young lovers here, Spartan! She chose the wrong man.' The prince sighed in memory, his eyes dark in the evening sun. 'I miss her still.'

Clearchus sat up straighter in his chair, though he emptied his wine again and hardly noticed as a servant drifted in to refill it.

'Some men can be petty and small, even in their victory. Yet you have brought an army into his territory – an army I assume he could not possibly match. Is it for conquest, then? Will you kill him?'

Cyrus looked at the general for a long time, considering. He rubbed one hand over the palm of the other, feeling the calluses that had formed under the reins each day.

'If I could have him fall from his horse and die, I would,' he said slowly. 'But she loves him and she has borne two children for him. I know she loves me, but she *chose* him. You cannot go back, Clearchus. Never.'

'Women,' Clearchus replied, raising his wine. 'They are a source of wonder to us all.'

They clinked the cups together and drained them. Both men were feeling the effects by then.

'I love her,' Cyrus said. 'I have always loved her.' He blew air out, emptying himself. 'We are at the edge of Cilicia, barely on the border. I have sent messages to say I am here – and she has replied. I do not know whether she will help me, general, but there is no one else.'

'Will she come to you? Or shall I have horses brought up?'

'She'll come to us, so the messenger said. Tomorrow. In the afternoon.'

'And did she mention her husband . . . even in passing?' Clearchus said.

Cyrus shook his head and the general raised his eyebrows.

'Well, that sounds promising.'

'No. She loved us both, but she chose him,' Cyrus said miserably, drinking once more. His teeth had taken on a crimson stain from the wine and his eyes were glassy. Clearchus slapped the table suddenly, startling the prince from a reverie.

'Then we'll show her what she gave up, Highness! I'll have the men put on a fine display. Let her see the dashing young prince, the war leader. Is her husband a tyrant? Cruel, old, ugly, short?'

'No,' Cyrus said with a wave of his hand. 'He is merely a man, like any other. I cannot see his virtues, but as I said, she . . .'

'Chose him, yes,' Clearchus finished. 'Leave it with me, Highness. And do not drink any more, or you will be no good to us tomorrow. With your permission, I will return to the men.'

Cyrus waved him away and leaned back, raising his cup to have it refilled once more, though his eyes remained closed. Clearchus chuckled, wondering if he'd ever had such a poor head for drink. He decided he had not. The general strode away into the darkness, beginning to jog when he thought of all that had to be done.

Cyrus woke at dawn and vomited great streams of yellow acid. There was a lake on the grounds of the estate and he swam in that, then ate eggs and cheese to settle his stomach. By the time he had managed to get dressed and his servants had helped him mount from a block, it was late in the morning and the sun had risen into an empty blue bowl, with heat that built and caused his headache to thump. He found some comfort in keeping his left eye closed as he approached the camp and was challenged. The guards stepped respectfully back when they completed the ritual, though they all knew him on sight by then. He heard one of them mutter a coarse remark about hangovers, but had neither the will nor the stomach for a reprimand.

As he became more aware of the bustle around him, Cyrus assumed the Spartan general had not slept at all. Each regiment was busy with polish and brushes, with lampblack and oil, making themselves as unnaturally shiny and neat as it was possible to be. Cyrus sat his mount in a state of confusion. Had he ordered a presentation parade? He could not recall. Some details of the evening were lost to him, or returned in flashes to make him cringe in embarrassment, his eyes widening. He had talked of his love to a Spartan general! Cyrus covered his face with a hand.

'Highness?' came a voice.

Cyrus looked down to see the young master of horse. The Athenian. As the prince stared blearily at him, Xenophon went on, looking disgustingly healthy and cheerful. 'Highness, if you would dismount for a time, I could brush Pasacas here and plait his mane and tail, ready for the inspection.'

'The inspection?' Cyrus said slowly. He felt a thread of memory come to him and sweat trickled down his back. He looked up at the sun and swallowed as he saw how late it was. He'd spent the morning being so ill he could hardly do more than sweat and groan. It came back to him then and he felt his chin and cursed softly at the feel of bristles.

'Xenophon, I need Parviz, my manservant.' He dismounted, sliding off his horse as if he'd lost the use of his legs and staggering into the Athenian. 'I need to be shaved and I need fresh clothes. Parviz, sir. At your fastest pace.'

Xenophon jogged away with the reins looping behind him, forcing the warhorse to follow. Cyrus squinted at the sun. He would never drink again, he swore it. The cost was just too great.

'Highness, there you are!' came the voice of Parviz.

The man who had once kept watch on a desert fortress had grown into his new role with both pride and energy. Cyrus saw Parviz was carrying a folding chair and he sank into it gratefully. Servants gathered around him, with bowls and cloth and oil. Parviz began stropping a razor on a piece of leather, then a piece of rough cloth and finally the wind itself, turning the razor into the breeze. He would allow no one else to shave the prince and it had become something of a ritual for them both. Cyrus closed his eyes.

'Shade here!' Parviz yelled in his ear. 'Fetch a shade for the prince. And fresh clothes. Privacy here – is this a market? Bring those panels and place them around His Highness.'

It was a relief to let Parviz take over and Cyrus opened his eyes at the press of a cup into his hand. When he saw it was only dear, sweet milk, he smiled in relief.

'Thank you. More of this, please, Parviz. Bring the entire cow if you have to.'

As the sun began the long slow drift through the afternoon, the regiments remained in squares, their ranks perfectly measured. Each man stood with his feet slightly apart, waiting for the inspection of a queen. Stretcher-bearers had come in from the camp followers, knowing that men who stand in the sun can suddenly faint. There were always a few and because they fell like trees without putting out their hands, the injuries were sometimes appalling. The rest of the camp had been made to march three miles further back, so the queen would not have her view spoiled by whores and urchins.

Cyrus found he could not keep still. He walked his horse Pasacas up and down the front ranks as he waited for her to appear. He had not laid eyes on Epyaxa for six years. He had become a man in that time, where he'd been almost a boy before, certain that she would choose him, too certain of himself. His stomach had settled and his headache had dwindled almost to nothing, for which he thanked God.

'There she is! She comes!' Parviz said at his side.

Cyrus looked up to see a chariot drawn by a pair of black horses and surrounded by running soldiers in dark breastplates and leather kilts. There must have been eighty men jogging alongside their mistress and he was reminded once again that she was another man's wife and queen. He rested his hands on the saddle pommel and waited as the chariot approached, wondering if she would look the same and what she would see when she laid eyes on him.

Horns sounded along the lines, though they were heralds blowing welcome rather than the battle blast. The chariot aimed for the prince sitting a warhorse ahead of them all, turning in a great circle so that it almost faced the way they had come.

Queen Epyaxa of Cilicia extended her hand to her charioteer and stepped out. Cyrus felt a pain in his chest that had nothing to do with the amount of wine he had drunk the night before. Her dark hair had been bound into a rope that moved like a cat's tail down her back. It swayed as she stepped to the ground and she was the same, undiminished by time. The prince dismounted and watched as she dipped a knee to him. As he looked down on the nape of her neck, he found himself wondering if the Greeks understood the significance of her gesture. There were twenty-eight nations in the empire – and the kings and queens of those states would bow or drop a knee to a member of the imperial family. When the Greeks did the same, rather than a proper prostration, they were assuming the airs of royal houses themselves.

Cyrus blinked, realising that he had not given permission for her to rise. He could see a flush had appeared on her neck, a subtle stain of colour. She thought he was angry with her still.

'Please rise, Epyaxa. I was struck by how little you have changed. It is as if I stood here then, a younger man.' He took her arm as he spoke, though his hand dropped as her charioteer shifted uncomfortably. Her guards were not used to seeing their mistress touched by anyone.

'Ah,' she said to them, smiling. 'Prince Cyrus is an old friend. I am in no danger here. Captain Raoush, you have delivered me safely and you may leave. I will send a messenger to you when I am ready.'

The captain prostrated himself on the dust immediately, choosing an angle that honoured his mistress a touch over Cyrus, though included them both. The charioteer clambered back to the ledge-seat and took up the reins. Cyrus looked at the vehicle in envy, and spoke before the man could unfurl his long whip.

'My lady, I have arranged for you to inspect these few men of mine. If you order your charioteer to return with the rest, I would be honoured to take his place.'

The queen inclined her head and the charioteer set down his whip and reins without a word of protest, though he glared as he watched Cyrus take them up. Epyaxa opened a small door to reach the padded bench at the back. She leaned against it then rather than sitting down. The sun was too warm and the breeze too good on the skin for anything else.

With a grin, Cyrus snapped the reins and the chariot lurched forward, scattering the queen's guardsmen before they could be run down.

'Sorry, just getting used to it . . .' Cyrus called over his shoulder.

His passenger thought correctly that he had done it on purpose. Cyrus snapped the reins again and both horses surged into a gallop. She heard the prince cheer them on, faster and faster as they looped out, far away from the army he had gathered to impress her. The speed was terrifying and exhilarating at the same time, bringing back memories of Cyrus and his friend racing one another along the banks of a great river. He still had the touch, she thought. As they went, relying on his skill and strength, Epyaxa watched his back and his balance, remembering the way the muscles of his arms had moved when he held her. She felt tears come to her eyes and could not have said if it was in memory of youth lost, or love lost, or just the wind and dust.

14

After he had agreed to bring her back from that first wild loop across open ground, Cyrus drove the chariot at a more sedate speed along the waiting regiments. He even stopped at intervals for the young queen to step down and speak to his senior officers. Epyaxa seemed to enjoy herself in the presence of Greek and Persian alike. Cyrus watched Clearchus become almost fatherly, the Spartan's wide chest expanding even further as he answered questions from the young queen. General Orontas blushed as deeply as a young boy when she took his hand. Epyaxa patted them and smiled and put both men at their ease. At her side, the prince stood as if he had invented her, delighted by a day that had begun so badly and somehow ended so well. He could not help thinking how his life might have been different if she had come to him that last time, while he waited in a cypress grove. It had been the longest night of his life and when the dawn came, he'd mounted his horse and ridden away.

They were under the sun without shade for what seemed an age. Some of the men did faint and were discreetly collected and laid down out of sight to recover. Both Cyrus and the queen found themselves strangely weary by the time they returned to a pavilion Parviz had erected for the evening meal. The regiments themselves were dismissed, to march the three miles back to camp. There, they would eat and rest after a day spent under the sun. The men were all hot and sweating, but they smiled at the prince's obvious adoration of the young woman at his side. Many of them made crude signs with their hands as they passed, but not when an officer was watching who might have had those hands struck off.

Orontas, Ariaeus and Clearchus joined the other generals at a long table that had been assembled with bolts and beams that very day. Cyrus and Epyaxa sat at either end, beyond arm's reach. Clearchus noted that the prince laid his right hand on the cloth between courses, palm up as if in entreaty. Clearchus could not have said if Epyaxa responded deliberately, but she laid her left forearm on the table. She might have been reaching to him, and the Spartan smiled to himself.

Orontas attended to the food with visible interest. Cyrus had laid on the very best for his guest and the Persians in particular sighed at dishes suffused with saffron, cardamom and rose petals – herbs far too expensive to flavour the ordinary meat and bread given to the regiments.

Around the table, the other Greek generals had been allowed to attend the prince and his guest. Proxenus was there, guarding a wine jug he seemed to consider his own, though servants flitted in and out like hummingbirds. Netus the Stymphalian laughed uproariously with the Thessalian, Menon, then looked startled as they found themselves the centre of attention. Wine flowed and the aches and sunburn of the day faded, though half the men there could feel heat coming off their skin, as if they held some part of the light within themselves. They were all experienced men and Clearchus was not the only one to note the casual placement of hands on that table. As a result, they made light conversation for the form of it, but ate swiftly and refused extra helpings. One by one, each of the officers drained his cup for good manners and cleaned his knife on a tablecloth, then stood, bowing to Prince Cyrus and the queen in turn.

The prince had drunk no wine that night, claiming his stomach would not allow a second attempt to ruin it. As the last of his generals left, musicians entered on padded slippers to fill the air with a gentle song and the notes of a lyre. On impulse, Cyrus stood suddenly, making his way down the table to sit next to Epyaxa.

'There,' he said. 'I don't think I could hear you over the music. Thank you for coming to me. This has been a perfect day – a jewel in a time of hardship. You saw the army, the men. They are rough company at times. This, though – it makes me miss the conversations we used to have. Do you remember?'

'Of course,' she said.

He took the hand she laid on the cloth in his. He found she was trembling. It was a sudden intimacy and it allowed him to speak of other things, that mattered more.

'I waited all night, before I was sure you were not coming. For the longest time, I told myself it was still dark, until I could see the whole grove around me and the green hills beyond.'

'I should have sent someone to you,' she said softly. 'I am sorry.'

'No, you made your choice. It was better for me to leave and go on with my life.'

'You did not marry,' she said, leaning in closer.

He shrugged, though her words were like a knife in him. He forced a laugh.

'I could not find another . . . who was your equal. Isn't that ridiculous?'

'No,' she said. 'I have wondered many times . . .'

He saw her hesitate.

'What did you wonder? We are private here, Epyaxa.'

'I wondered what my life would have been if I had gone to you that night.' She turned her hand in his, so that it rotated in his palm like a bird making a nest. Yet she did not pull away from him. 'Syennesis is a cold man. You would hardly recognise him. He does not say one word to me for days or weeks at a time. Yet if I had not gone to him instead of you, I would not have my sons. It is confusing. If not for them, I think . . .'

She shook her head and closed her eyes, so that a tear spilled from under kohl-dark lashes, staining her cheek. Slowly, he drew her hand to his lips and kissed it, feeling the shiver that ran through her.

'I have thought of you each evening, as the sun sets,' he said.

'Please. No more talk. Send the servants away,' she whispered.

In the morning, Clearchus walked the three miles from the camp to the pavilion to find Cyrus and Epyaxa enjoying a breakfast outside in the early sun. The day was cool and there was dew on the ground, though it would burn off.

'General! I hope you will join us,' Cyrus called.

Clearchus bowed to them both and greeted the queen courteously as he sat down and was served slices of melon, figs and a light cheese. In such company, Clearchus would certainly not mention the empty coffers, or anything he suspected was going on between them. He ate in silence for a time and watched the way the pair looked at one another.

'If you will take me home, Cyrus, I'll have the chariot and carts sent out to you later this morning,' Epyaxa said. 'As we . . . discussed.'

The prince reached out and touched her hand, as if there was nothing more natural in the world to him. Epyaxa blushed in the company of the Spartan, though Clearchus found his plate fascinating in that moment.

Cyrus rose and extended his hand to her. His eyes were

dark with all the conversations Clearchus had not heard the night before.

'Come, my love. I will take you back, to your husband and your sons.'

Her eyes glittered with what might have been tears as she stood up. Clearchus watched them both go, chewing a piece of melon rind thoughtfully. He hoped it meant the queen would deliver the coins they needed. He liked Cyrus, but a leader had to pay his mercenaries, or go without them. A month or two might be allowed to pass without sign of silver, but beyond that, all contracts were broken and they would desert. The Greeks knew their own value and the Persians were too used to being paid on time every month. Cyrus was responsible for them all. Clearchus thought of what he'd had to do to get it, though the prince seemed happy enough. Certainly, more relaxed than the Spartan could remember seeing him before. It was interesting to consider the two mistresses Cyrus had brought with him, travelling east with the camp. As far as Clearchus recalled, one of them looked a great deal like the queen of Cilicia.

Clearchus thought of his own wife and sons. It had not been a marriage of love for him, at least at first, though he felt great affection for his Calandre. All Spartans were required to father children before they could walk the mercenary path. It was only common sense, considering the perils of their trade. He sighed to himself. He had known love once or twice in the years of campaigning. It did not seem quite as important as it once had. Yet he could remember how it had been and he envied the young pair, though grief and loss shone in their eyes.

When Cyrus returned, he was accompanied by half a dozen carts and the same charioteer as the day before. Clearchus and Proxenus raced Orontas to peer into the chests within. The three senior men ran their hands through gold and silver coins, laughing in relief. It was surely enough. Of the three of them, Orontas may not have known their destination, but the Persian was not a fool. He understood very well that something important must have gone wrong for the prince to be denied the network of moneylenders. The coins were food and repairs and armour, but also months in the field they would not otherwise have had. The coins were warfare – the time to use the vast force the prince had assembled.

For Clearchus and Proxenus, the chests were the chance to raise a prince to be a king. A good part of it would be handed over to bankers in Persian cities along the Royal Road. For their chits, passed west by bonded messenger, funds could be drawn at the edge of the empire, by Greeks. Those coins would keep Sparta safe and strong, would allow Athens to build ships, write plays and argue in the council. Whatever the noble cause, reality was always bought with gold and silver.

As the vast column moved off two days later, Cyrus seemed glum. They headed away from the border with Cilicia, marching east. The prince spent hours simply watching the marching ranks pass him, as if the tide of men might not take him away with them. They walked with straight backs and took pride in their appearance while he was there, but his gaze was afar, his thoughts in the arms of a woman who had given him only one night. It had not been enough. If she had asked him, Cyrus would have marched his army to rescue her. He would have hanged her husband from his own walls and ridden away without looking back. Yet she had not asked. He thought Epyaxa loved her sons and perhaps also the man she had married. The heart of a woman was a complex thing, he thought. She had given him a night, but it had not felt like an ending.

'I will return here,' he muttered to himself. 'When I have fulfilled my promises. I will see you again.'

The prince's army marched sixty-six miles over the next three days. The going was easy and the days remained clear, but Clearchus insisted on filling every water barrel and flask whenever they came to a river. It meant entire afternoons were lost when they came to a bridge over running water, but the summer heat was a constant threat and the soldiers drank constantly as they perspired. Cyrus bought salt whenever they reached a market or a city. Men's sweat dried white and the experienced soldiers knew they would grow weak and dazed without it, unable to keep up.

It was a relief to have the chests Epyaxa had given him. Cyrus had not asked whether her husband would mind her taking a fortune from their treasury and giving it to an old suitor. The prince told himself he would pay all his debts when he had met and faced his brother. Justice would wait on vengeance.

As Cyrus rode alongside Clearchus and Proxenus, or with Orontas and Ariaeus to give them honour in turn, he bent his head whenever he caught a scent of jasmine, as if Epyaxa travelled with him. She had been a distant, half-forgotten ache before he'd stopped in Cilicia. Though he left her far behind, once more in his memories, the pain was sharper and harder to put aside.

In Persepolis, Tissaphernes had bathed and been massaged by imperial slaves before the sun rose. Lit by lamps, he had enjoyed the benefits of civilisation that so much of the world lacked. By the time he rode up the horse steps to the gate-house of the plateau, he was cool and refreshed. The sun rose on the other side of the walls, so that he stood in shadow, while the world behind was lit gold. Tissaphernes turned in the saddle as he reached the top. He recalled standing on that final step with three hundred Spartans and a young prince at his side, with Darius on his deathbed in the paradise within. The dawn breeze washed over him and he smiled at how things had changed. As he had climbed the steps, he had risen in other ways, in status and influence. He sat on the right hand of the Great King. Even Prince Cyrus had sensed his new authority and been abashed by it.

The gate was opened by soldiers who prostrated themselves to him. Tissaphernes appreciated the gesture, though his formal status was uncertain. His own servants and slaves referred to him as 'Lord Tissaphernes', of course, but a man could choose any name in his own household. Tissaphernes knew only too well that he was merely a trusted member of the court, a companion. The lack of official title irked him like a thorn caught under the skin and he hoped Artaxerxes would put it right when he made his report. He had been away from court and comfort for six months. Such a trial surely deserved a reward.

The gardens were perfect as they had always been, with slaves to gather every falling leaf and trim each bush to such perfect lines that they appeared made, rather than grown. Tissaphernes wore loose robes of silk and open sandals. He followed a seneschal along the shaded pathways, though they did not turn their steps towards the pavilion where the old king had died. That had been taken down and a new lawn grown and watered from seed to replace it. Even the stones of the path had been relaid, he saw. Such things gave him more than satisfaction. The sense of perfection was so exquisite, it was almost pain. So much of the world spent lifetimes grubbing in the dirt for enough food to survive. It was joyous to see what could be done with freedom and unlimited wealth. Tissaphernes could not imagine anything better in existence than the Persian court. The royal family were like gods to ordinary men. He realised that made him a companion to gods, which pleased him.

Ahead, King Artaxerxes stood at the edge of a field, carrying a black horn bow in his hands. Tipped in gold, it looked a deadly, baleful thing. Tissaphernes eyed it as he approached. He laid a mat down rather than ruin clean silks, prostrating himself on it and raising his hands to his head in obeisance. Artaxerxes could have interrupted him at any part of the process, but the king merely peered down the shaft of an arrow until it was done. The son had also been raised by his father's death. Artaxerxes still demanded the rituals of obedience, though no doubt he continued to claim it was for the dignity of the throne and not his own pleasure.

When Tissaphernes came to his feet once again, the king had placed his arrow on the string and was looking across the field at six female slaves, walking up and down with Spartan shields held overhead. Tissaphernes saw the young women were beautiful, dressed in tunics that left their legs bare to the upper thigh. He raised his eyes at that, but the king was a young man and had not yet tired of that particular hunt. There were tales of girls brought to him from all over the empire, chosen for their beauty. Some he kept for himself, while others were handed over to his guards as a reward.

Tissaphernes recalled it was those who were falling out of favour who were given the task of carrying shields for the king's archery. It was not exactly a punishment, but certainly a mark of displeasure, or a warning. Tissaphernes sighed. His master was hard on women, but he would grow gentler in time, as all men did.

'Watch this, Tissaphernes,' the king said over his shoulder.

He drew and released smoothly, sending the arrow arcing out to the furthest shield. It struck with a thump that knocked the young woman carrying it to the ground in a tumble of kicking legs. The king grunted in satisfaction. He held out his hand without looking and a slave passed another perfect shaft across his palm. He said nothing more for three shots, all of which struck home. No one else fell, though they staggered at the impacts.

'That is a fine bow, Your Majesty. Your skills have only improved. Truly you are a master of the weapon.'

Tissaphernes knew it was obvious flattery, but Artaxerxes had practised every day and he deserved the praise. Most men thought of him still as the less martial of the two princes. The truth was that he had made himself strong, all unknown to the world. Tissaphernes knew better than most that the king could acquit himself with honour with the sword and war spear, as well as the bow. Some were born to be warriors. All men knew that. They saw that some were more daring, faster and more lithe. They had skills that were like magic to the untrained. Yet there was another way, though it was slower and less flashy. A man could simply work, every day. Artaxerxes was the proof. If a man had discipline, his bones would grow harder, his muscles like ropes, his fitness extraordinary. His body could be trained to react at incredible speed. Artaxerxes spent each morning pouring sweat from his labours. As well as his slaves, he brought sword masters to the court to train him. Prince Cyrus had been born a warrior, so it was said. Artaxerxes had made himself one. Tissaphernes could see it in the way the king moved. The man who had been a scholar had become a leopard in a panelled coat.

After another dozen shots, the king rubbed one forearm with the other, feeling the muscles move and wincing to himself. He handed the murderous-looking bow to a slave and faced Tissaphernes.

'Very well, Tissaphernes. Report to me. Tell me how my dear brother licks his wounds in the west.'

The king began walking as he spoke, so that Tissaphernes had to hurry to remain at his side. They left the slaves behind and walked across the green field, to where the edge of the plateau cut the sky from the land ahead. Artaxerxes waved his hand at the shield-maidens and they trooped back, heads down so as not to disturb the king. Tissaphernes could not help looking at one or two of them as they passed him, golden shields resting on their shoulders, long tanned legs flashing in the sun. He was sixty-two years old, after all, not eighty.

Artaxerxes walked to the very edge of the plateau, placing his right foot so that half of it lay over a sheer drop and emptiness. Birds flew in lazy circles lower down the mountain, so that Tissaphernes and the king were above them. The first capital city lay spread out at the feet of Artaxerxes in a labyrinth of roads and green gardens, like strands of silver web at such a height. Smoke from cooking fires and bakeries rose in thin streams, forming a haze. Tissaphernes found himself both afraid and enthralled by the scene. It was a long way to fall, so far the mind could not properly understand it. Some part of him knew the danger of such a height and made his stomach try to crawl up his throat.

'Your Majesty, I met Prince Cyrus on the western edge of the empire, where he still keeps company with Greeks and other mercenaries. I stayed twelve days in Sardis and had many opportunities to observe him and those around him.'

'And what did you see, Tissaphernes? I sent you because you know him best of all. Is he loyal, still?'

Tissaphernes took a deep breath. He had read his own notes and the reports that had come to his hand many times on the road. He had wrestled with the answer to that exact question over each stage of the endless journey home. The months of travel that separated the west and the heart of empire meant that many things would have changed even as he reported. Yet he had seen much.

'Your Majesty, I do not believe he is,' Tissaphernes said.

Artaxerxes jerked round to face him, the view forgotten as his face hardened to a hawklike gaze that reminded the older man of his father.

'You are certain? Speak carefully now, Tissaphernes. War follows your words.'

Tissaphernes swallowed and went on.

'Majesty, I spoke to three spies in Sardis. All of them told me the prince has gathered vast numbers of soldiers. Unusual numbers, my lord. In itself, that is not so surprising – there is much talk of some hill tribes and rebellions.'

'Yet you believe he has turned against me, against his house?'

Tissaphernes bowed his head slowly.

'He has gathered a dozen Greek generals and more of our own. The Greeks are the key to this, Majesty, to my conclusion. The Persians parade in great squares, but the Greeks are scattered all over the west. I have reports from Crete, from Athens, from Lydia and Cyprus. They train in those places, but they answer to your brother and they take Persian gold.'

'How many are there?' Artaxerxes said. He did not seem disconcerted by the news. As far as Tissaphernes could tell, he was pleased.

'No one can be certain, my lord. I spoke to one man who said thirty thousand Greeks, another who said only eight thousand. That is the heart of my suspicion. If your brother commands the forces of the crown, why keep them apart?'

'Your conclusion then, Tissaphernes?'

'I believe he is gathering an army to come here. To take the imperial throne and the empire for himself.'

To the older man's surprise, Artaxerxes threw his head back and laughed, wiping his eyes.

'I wish . . . oh, I wish my father could stand with me to hear you. He predicted it, did I ever say? I will enjoy telling my mother what her misplaced mercy has brought about, what a worm she kept alive and so endangered us all.' His voice hardened as he spoke, the humour vanishing.

'Very well, Tissaphernes. I thank you for your labour. You have proved yourself to me and I am grateful. You may have saved my life, so I bestow the title of "Pir" on you. You are a wise elder and all men lower in station will address you as "My lord", or "Pir Tissaphernes". My seneschal will alter the records and give you a copy.'

Tissaphernes threw himself full length without unrolling his mat. The dusty ground brought tears to his eyes, which he thought no bad thing in the circumstances.

'Majesty, I am overwhelmed. You do me too great an honour.'

'Not at all, Tissaphernes. Should I not reward good news?'

'Good news, my lord?'

'Of course! It is my task to bring the imperial army to the field, like kings of old. You will accompany me, Tissaphernes. You have always talked so bravely and well of your time in the army. I will enjoy seeing you remember those golden years of your youth.'

Tissaphernes could only mouth his eternal delight at such a prospect, though the thought of months more on horseback made him want to weep in frustration.

The king stared down at the capital city dreaming beneath them both.

'If my brother wishes to face me in battle, perhaps I will surprise him, eh?' Slowly, Artaxerxes closed a fist as if he made an oath, raising it to the sun. 'My father will watch us both, I do not doubt. If two princes come to a battlefield, Lord Tissaphernes, only one can remain at the end. The other will feed the kites and crows. It is just the way of things.'

15

Cyrus halted the men at Thapsacus, after driving them hard for days. The city was both wealthy and ancient, and he longed for a bath and the privacy of wealth and power. A great white arch loomed above the city and the river Euphrates ran close to the walls. Thapsacus had formed around a great bed in that ancient river, beginning as a place just to water animals and exchange trade goods. Over countless generations, the city had grown to one of the great hubs of the region. Spice and slave markets vied for space and there was wealth enough to support streets and parks and a governor's palace. It was the last of the west, the final taste of civilisation before the gasping heat of deserts and mountains beyond.

Cyrus took his column into the city, billeting as many men as possible there. The market traders sold news as well as saffron and sugar, ivory and iron nails. Within an hour, Cyrus knew Tissaphernes had reached Susa a month before, resting for just a day before going out. The column had gained on the Persian, reducing his lead. It was a good thought.

By early evening, every stable in the city was filled with men, every basement and storehouse, every home. Cyrus packed the royal park with them, allowing his regiments to rest in gardens designed by his grandfather. They were still too many.

Outside the walls, camp labourers put up tents and carts in rings, assembling forges and workshops, cookshops, tents and latrines. There was little need for shelter in the summer months. Though dust could be raised on scouring winds, most of the column slept out under stars, content with a thin blanket or cloak.

As the sun smeared reds and lilacs across the horizon, his most senior men came through the grounds of the small royal palace to Prince Cyrus, subdued by the grandeur all around them. Oil fluttered in golden bowls and thick tallow candles sat in every alcove. The light itself was a symbol of wealth and power, giving the evening a sense of private revelry, or secret ritual.

In the feast hall, Cyrus stood to one side rather than face every man coming in. He seemed to talk idly to Clearchus while they gathered, but in truth he watched and judged the arrivals. The hall was one of the few places in Thapsacus where he could address all his generals. There were no theatres in Persian cities, though he thought he would have them built when he was finished with his brother. If a king could remake a mountain, his son could surely remake an empire.

Over the sixty days he had spent on the road, Cyrus had learned the names of every officer under him and scores of those in lesser ranks. Those two months had become a restful dream when he looked back – a journey together without any great urgency, with few distractions and little danger. He could not add to their number once they'd begun the long march east. Neither could he force the pace beyond reasonable briskness. They were on their way like an arrow shot from a bow: they could not be called back.

As Clearchus had promised, basic training had continued on rest days and evenings, but in the main they had simply walked and walked. It was hard for a man to remain a stranger after sixty days alongside another. Cyrus felt bonds that had formed almost as hoops of iron around him. He had come to know which of his officers he preferred to deal with and which to avoid. As he watched men like Proxenus and Netus the Stymphalian enter, he welcomed them as friends and colleagues. He felt a more tenuous bond among his own, for all they shared a language and a culture that the Greeks could never know. Men like Orontas and Ariaeus seemed to be of the past, of the world he wished to overthrow. Cyrus felt a spike of dislike in him as both men entered. Even so, he smiled at them. Some men believed loyalty could not be forced, but Clearchus had a theory Cyrus thought rang true. No matter what a commander actually felt about his men, it took very little to give them a golden memory that would last for the rest of their lives. A royal prince was so exalted over even his generals, that just a word could reach their hearts like a blade between the ribs. They would work themselves to death for him after that, if he did it well. That had been the advice of the Spartan and Cyrus had not been too proud to try.

The prince forced himself to nod to Orontas and Ariaeus, watching as both men prostrated themselves as a matched pair, looked upon curiously by the Greeks. Ariaeus hailed some of the others as he was released, taking up a great goblet of wine and greeting those he knew and liked. Orontas lacked that ease and only sipped a fruit juice. From the beginning, Cyrus had seen only cool obedience from that particular man. There was no new hoop of iron he could see in Orontas, no discovery of brotherhood. Besides Ariaeus, there were half a dozen Persian officers who looked to Cyrus as if blinded by the sun. He sighed to himself. Yet his most senior man was a very cold fish. If Orontas broke his neck falling off the city wall that night, Cyrus knew he would bear the loss with great dignity. Unfortunately, the man didn't drink wine. Orontas was the very model of an abstemious Persian. After the meal, he would probably spend the evening praying in a temple to Ahura Mazda. Cyrus shook his head as he sipped from his cup. Some men were born without a sense of greatness in them, that was simply the truth of it. Orontas was competent and thoughtful, but there was no golden thread, no deep well there. Or if there was, he chose not to share it with his prince.

Menon the Thessalian entered, looking up at the vaulted ceilings in awe, with Sosis of Syracuse at his side. Cyrus smiled to those two as well, though it was in part the recollection of a young Spartan who had trouble pronouncing his 's' sound. Clearchus had lent him to Sosis as an aide for a day, forced to announce the senior officer wherever the Syracusan general went. It had left Sosis weeping with laughter, hanging on the young Spartan as the man grew colder and less amused by the hour.

As each one came in, they were shown to a place at table by waiting servants, with their cloaks or coats made to vanish. Some remained standing, chatting in groups of friends. Others took their seats immediately and laid out their eating knife alongside the ones already placed for them. Cyrus saw one of the Greeks eyeing a strangely shaped melon blade with a curious expression, then testing the edge with a thumb. The prince was amused at that, though his admiration for the Greeks had only deepened. They valued plays over poetry, discipline over obedience, words over music. He had learned all he could of them over the years – and then the months on the road, a closer relationship than he had known before. Living cheek by jowl with soldiers gives a rare insight, he had discovered. He knew by then how much of their success in war was bound up in personal pride, in the absolute certainty they were the best in the world – and that Greece had no equals in the fields of war or the arts. Cyrus found himself wincing when he recalled the evening of

Persian music he had put on for his generals. There had been a great deal of laughter, all the worse because of their efforts to control it.

Cyrus thought Orontas was probably the least personally aggressive of all his generals, but the man had been reduced to spluttering rage by their comments. He'd had to be dissuaded from challenging Proxenus to a duel of honour, though the Greek would probably have eaten him alive.

In some ways, his Greeks were all barbarians, Cyrus acknowledged in private. Yet they fought like Ahriman's demons – and they would not yield. It was the key to their success, he had decided. No matter how a battle turned, with disaster and death staring them in the face, they did not run. Every Persian army he had ever seen accepted that there were times, when the battle was clearly lost, when the officers were dead and the enemy were roaring in, that it was only the merest common sense to run for the hills. It was entrenched in the imperial culture. Pride in success, loyalty to one's officers – but if they failed, the script changed. If your side was crushed and overwhelmed, the day could not be won back. Failure was the end.

Cyrus whispered a blessing to Ahura Mazda as he drank and walked to his place at the head of the table. They came to order then, standing by their places or rising to their feet. The prince looked down the length of the hall, seeing how the generals had arranged themselves without prompting. He shook his head, suddenly irritated with them all.

In Greek, Cyrus began to speak, then repeated it once more in Persian. Language lessons too had been a part of their long march. The progress there had been a great deal slower than he'd hoped.

'Gentlemen, do you see how one side of my table is Greek, the other Persian? Please, you are not enemies. I have seen you eat together and train together for months now. Yes, please rise, once more. Seek out your opposite and change places.'

There was a great deal of laughter as they did so. It was not quite the success he'd hoped for, as too many simply ended up on opposite sides once again, but it had lightened the mood and he was pleased for that.

'Thank you,' he said. Cyrus gave the signal to the royal seneschal and all the servants trooped out, leaving the seated men to pour wine from jugs at table. Cyrus watched as a number of them immediately did so.

'When I see you sit as friends,' he said, 'it gives me hope for our people – and for the future. We use different coins, but all men value gold and silver, however they have been pressed. The metal is what matters most. Those at this table may speak different tongues, but we are all warriors, all soldiers. We understand injustice. We understand dishonour.'

The smiles withered as his voice hardened, all eyes on the prince. Cyrus spoke quietly, but there was no other sound in that hall and they heard every word in both languages.

Cyrus glanced at Clearchus and saw the Spartan dip his head, just a fraction. This was the moment they had planned and prepared. Though Cyrus felt his heart beating like a bird's, he had agreed it could not wait until they sighted the imperial army of Persia in the field. He had to trust his men with their true purpose, or risk losing them at the worst possible moment.

'Gentlemen, I have ridden and walked with you all the way from Sardis. No matter what else happens, you have marched with me through the lands of Babylon. You have seen the great Euphrates, the artery of the empire. Having you here fills my heart with pride. Yet for some of you, perhaps the journey will end tonight.' He breathed in deeply, as the simplest action seemed to become something that required thought and conscious control. Slowly, Cyrus rose to his feet and leaned down on his knuckles as he glared out at them.

'My intention is not and never has been to seek out Pisidian hill tribes in the mountains. I could not reveal all my plans while other ears listened in Sardis. I hope you can forgive me these necessary deceptions. Even tonight, there will be spies to listen and report. Yet I have brought you here even so.'

He paused to drink a gulp of wine. Clearchus stared at the table in front of him, willing the younger man to find the right words.

'My father, King Darius, was not the oldest son. He took the throne from his brother when he judged that brother unfit. He took the crown when it was wet with blood and put it on his own head. Gentlemen . . .'

He leaned further forward and in that moment, they seemed not to breathe, as if he stared at a painting. The thought made him smile.

'Gentlemen, I judge my brother Artaxerxes unfit for the rose throne. I have gathered you and trained you and brought you to this place, not as an ending, but as the beginning of a new reign.'

The Persian generals turned to one another and hissed and murmured, their shock evident. The Greeks had to feign surprise. It was poorly done and Cyrus wondered if there was anyone left among their number who actually did not know the purpose of bringing such an army into the east.

'I am commander-in-chief of the armies of Persia,' Cyrus pressed on. 'I am my father's son, in the direct bloodline of the house of Achaemenid. I am the heir to the throne at this moment. If Artaxerxes suffers a fever in his sleep and dies tonight, I am king tomorrow! Understand me, then. I am no usurper, no traitor to the throne. I *am* the throne, the king in waiting. Like my father before me, I challenge my brother on the field, as is my ancient right.'

Clearchus nodded and growled in the back of this throat, as did many of the other Greek generals. They rapped their knuckles on the tabletop, supporting him, aiding him with their voices and their manner, swaying those they sat amongst. Cyrus saw General Ariaeus doing the same, rumbling for them to hear the prince as he refilled his cup. That was not a great surprise, somehow. It would be hard to resist the tides in that room, he thought. He prayed it would.

The prince dared not look at Orontas as he spoke, though every sinew in him strained to turn just a little and see how his words were going across. Orontas could carry all the other Persians with him, as the most senior man. In the same way, if he refused, he could sow a seed that might become a vine to strangle them all.

'Will you deny me that right of challenge?' Cyrus demanded from them.

The Greeks who spoke both languages shouted twice that they would not, lending their voices to a chorus of support. More of the Persians were joining in, Cyrus could see. He allowed himself at last to glance at Orontas and saw how many others were watching the Persian general in turn, waiting for him to respond before they decided themselves how to jump. Though slight of frame and no firebrand, in that moment Cyrus understood Orontas was a true leader of men. They looked to him as they looked to Clearchus, and no one could have said what those two had in common beyond that simple truth.

Orontas was watching him, wide-eyed, his mouth slightly open. He, it seemed, had not suspected the full truth of the great trek. Cyrus felt his excitement drain away as he saw he had not won the table, not while this man resisted him. Yet the prince was not a coward and he responded with a direct assault, crying the man's name over the noise.

'General Orontas! My father's hand raised you to your rank. You took an oath to him – and to me, as commander of the army.'

'And to your brother,' Orontas said.

The words were almost lost in the chatter, but Cyrus picked them from the air. His brows drew together and he felt his face darken and flush. Clearchus and Proxenus had discussed what had to be done with anyone who refused his order.

Cyrus did not want to see Orontas left in his own blood, but he clenched his jaw and vowed he would see it done, if he was forced. There was no going back then. He would make all things right when he was king. If he had to, he would pay a death price to the man's family. It would be just one more debt against his name, one more wrong to put right.

'Will you deny me my right of challenge, general?' Cyrus asked softly.

Some of the noise died away and Cyrus saw Orontas judge those around him before he shook his head, his eyes dark with sorrow rather than jubilation.

'Highness, I would not,' he said.

The table erupted in cheering, so that Cyrus was buffeted by men leaping to their feet on either side of him. Through it all, he saw Orontas wipe a hand across his brow, bright with perspiration. Orontas sat looking down at the table, his wine cup still untasted. The man had not refused his prince. Cyrus rather wished he had, so that it could have been clean, the sword wound sharp and quickly done. Instead, the Persian would leave his table alive and yet without the prince's full trust. It was a sour note to weigh against the jubilation in the others. With a pained smile, Cyrus raised his cup, saluting the men he had brought to that place on that night. Orontas took a cup of water and together they toasted the royal house of Achaemenid and the challenge of a royal prince. He had them. By wine or by water, by God, he had them all.

King Artaxerxes rode his horse along the face of regiments stretching into the distance, further than he could see in the haze. He felt his chest swell with pride at the thought of deploying so many men at his word, as a hawk flies from the gauntlet. He spoke, and they would destroy. It was the only real power in the world and he found himself giddy with it, as if he had drunk sweetened wine, too long in the skin.

The army that had come at the king's summons was in four parts, each the size of a city. More than a march of regiments, it was a migration of nations. Artaxerxes had sent messengers north and south and east, but not to the west. He had not wanted to alert his brother before it was time. Instead, the royal house of Achaemenid had gathered a host equal to the grains of sand in the deserts. They scoured the land of food as they drifted across the face of the empire, growing all the time as more and more came in.

The king saw Tissaphernes approach on horseback. The man hovered like a biting fly, prevented from a closer approach by impassive ranks of imperial guardsmen. Artaxerxes regretted giving the man a title and the authority that went with it. It had been a moment of petty pleasure for him. He'd known his old tutor preferred the soft life at court to that of a campaign. It had amused the king to send him out once more, so that the man had to feign joy. Yet Tissaphernes had taken to the role with an enthusiasm that quite surprised the king. Tissaphernes commanded his flank of the army with a stern eye, pointing out errors of placement and structure until half a dozen men had complained. Artaxerxes had those officers flogged and three of them had died, so the complaints had ceased abruptly.

Artaxerxes found he was already weary of the organisation involved in keeping so many soldiers fed, watered and supplied, never mind the cattle and horses and forges and chariots and tents . . . He closed his eyes. If nothing else, his brother had already cost him unimaginable sums in gold. Yet none of that should be his concern. He was the falconer. They were the bird leaning into the wind.

'Majesty?' Tissaphernes called, leaning aside from the shoulders blocking his view of the king. 'One of my messengers came in this morning. A bird, Majesty.'

Artaxerxes ignored him, wishing only for silence. There was a certain turbulence at the heart of his old tutor. The king wondered why he had not seen it before. Some men have a placid soul, so that they give peace to those around them. Tissaphernes achieved the opposite, leaving ripples and anger in his wake. The king knew he could have the man killed with just a word to one of the guards. They would take his tongue or his head without a moment's hesitation. Yet that was a power Artaxerxes thought he should resist. He was not a child to lash out on a whim. No, his answers would be measured, and all the more terrible for that.

'Majesty . . . the bird brought news of your brother,' Tissaphernes persisted.

The king looked over at last, seeing the fat man was flushed and sweating in the sun. Artaxerxes gestured impatiently and Tissaphernes was allowed to approach, tugging his robes to hide the patches where he had sweated through.

The king waited while servants helped the older man to dismount and prostrate himself, pushing him firmly down as he tried to prevent the sandy ground from touching.

'Report then, Lord Tissaphernes. Tell me of Cyrus.'

'Majesty, the crown maintains aviaries at Susa, Larisa and Mespila. Your father was both fortunate and far-sighted to have done so. His wisdom protects us still, Highness. Of course, the birds had their crofts in Persepolis, so when they returned, the message had to be carried out here to the deserts. What good judgement it proved . . .'

'Tissaphernes? Tell me of my brother. I wish to rest and bathe, not listen to you.'

'Of course, Majesty. Only one of the birds came through, but it mentions a great army led by Prince Cyrus, just as I predicted, Majesty. Coming from the west, from Sardis.'

'What else?' Artaxerxes said.

The man bowed his head to reply.

'Majesty, there is nothing more. The scrolls attached to the birds are tiny, or they cannot fly at all. It is a miracle one of the pigeons got through to Persepolis, through falconry and storms and the strange magics in the deserts.' The man saw the king's glance sharpen and finished quickly, realising he was babbling once again. 'There is no more, Majesty.'

'Very well. It is enough. We know where he was, what, a few weeks back?'

Tissaphernes nodded.

'Good. I have gathered an ocean, Tissaphernes. I may never do so again and for that I am thankful. This one time, I have called the entire armed force of Persia – except for those of the west.'

Artaxerxes looked along the regiments marching through the desert bowl, their eyes narrowed against the dust and the breeze.

'I should thank my brother for allowing me to have this experience. I try to fix it in my mind, Tissaphernes, so that I will be able to recall it for ever after, when my spirits are low. It is . . . a glorious sight, a royal view.'

Tissaphernes raised his head to see the array of marching lines. He did not share the same romantic streak that seemed to have been inherited by both of Darius' sons, but he appreciated the raw power of that army. There was not another so many and various in the world. He rode with the rightful king to destroy traitors. It was hard to imagine anything finer or more satisfying.

16

Sixty miles out from Thapsacus, the terrain turned to desert over a single day, going from scrub lichen and grasses to wider and wider expanses of open sand, until true dunes stretched ahead, shimmering in the heat. No river was allowed to pass without them refilling every cask and skin and bottle they had. The maps they carried showed the river courses like dark threads, but the accuracy was not as great as Cyrus would have liked, not when survival depended on it. It was late summer in Babylon and the heat was a living thing, a tongue of flame that flickered and pressed among the marching men.

Clearchus had sensed the mood deteriorating in the ranks ever since they'd passed through Thapsacus. It had been there in muttering soldiers and sly glances at Cyrus. The news was out at last. None of those men, neither Greek nor Persian, had signed on and taken pay to face the limitless armies of the Great King.

The sense of brotherhood they had developed over months of training and marching together seemed to fray like rotted cloth. Fights had always broken out in the evening camps, of course. The combination of men, coin, wine and weapons was a dangerous one. It was far less usual for a brawl to begin on the march, especially when it turned into a riot between hundreds that left two Persians and four Greeks dead on the ground. Worse, the men refused to say what it was that had started the fracas. Clearchus was not even sure they knew. They were angry and growing angrier by the day, that was the heart of it. He warned his officers again about the heat, about what it could do to tempers. He lectured regiment after sullen regiment about the need to wash away old sweat or suffer blisters and boils of the skin. He gave a thousand orders and focused their resentment on him, rather than each other. Yet the mood only darkened.

Another six days passed as they travelled south and east into the deserts, leaving the last trappings of trade and civilisation behind them. On the seventh day, the entire contingent of Greeks stopped dead at the foot of a hill and let the Persian regiments tramp on without them. Their officers rode up and down the lines, bawling astonished orders. In response, they stood like mules, digging heels into the sand and clenching their jaws. The Persians looked over their shoulders as they went on, until they too were halted while their officers worked out what to do. The column stood under a midday sun that was like a lash across bare skin. Regiment after regiment of the Greeks ignored commands or threats shouted at them. Instead, they sat down, though the sand blistered whatever it touched.

Cyrus came riding back from the front, where the scouts still ranged ahead. He called Ariaeus over to him. In comparison to Orontas, the Persian general was known to be well liked in the ranks. Ariaeus was usually accompanied by young men chosen from among the rest for physical beauty. Such a fellow accompanied him then, running alongside as Ariaeus reined in and leaped down to prostrate himself. Cyrus halted the action with a gesture.

'What's the word, Ariaeus? Why have we stopped? I gave no orders.'

Ariaeus knelt on the sand to reply, though it stung his skin. Cyrus found his patience vanishing.

'Answer me! Stand up straight and speak.'

The Persian gaped as he came up once more.

'Highness, I wished not to offend. Our regiments have stopped only because the Greeks stopped first. I understand they have not taken the news well. About our ... destination.'

'What? They are mutinying?' Cyrus demanded in shock.

The word carried with it the most severe punishments. Entire regiments had been butchered like cattle in the empire before, after just one man refused an order. As a result, that term was rarely even spoken aloud, for fear it would be its own spark. Both Ariaeus and his companion paled. It was with relief that they registered the approach of others on that scorched white plain. All three turned and shaded their eyes against the sun to see Orontas cantering a horse towards the prince, with Clearchus running behind him, the Spartan's hand gripping the horse's tail.

'Dismount and bow to me, general,' Cyrus shot to the Persian before he could say a word. 'Is it a mutiny?'

He registered the grimace that crossed the Spartan's face at the word, but Clearchus shook his head in immediate denial as he replied.

'Let me talk to them before we give it any sort of name, Highness. There has been some unrest, of course. It is no more than we expected . . .' The Spartan sensed the gaze of the two Persians on him and rephrased. 'It is not more than you told me we might expect. They feel they were lied to and they are afraid of what is to come, of facing the royal forces.'

'Highness,' Ariaeus said. 'Give the word and I will have them all flogged, then one in ten castrated before the rest. There will be no more refusing to march after that, you may be certain. These foreign soldiers merely need to be reminded that you are the heir to the throne, of the house of Achaemenid. You have every right to challenge your brother, Highness.'

The man spoke as if his mouth dripped with oil, Cyrus thought. Though Ariaeus had put his own arguments as succinctly as he might have hoped, it was still somehow rather distasteful.

'If General Ariaeus tries such a thing with my Spartans, they will destroy this army around them, Highness,' Clearchus said.

'Destroy?' Cyrus replied, challenging him.

Clearchus gazed back in silence, still outraged at the Persian's threat. It was Cyrus who looked away first. He turned to the Persian general.

'I need to get them moving, Ariaeus. Not to waste good men. Let the heat work on them for a time. They chose to stop at midday where there is no shade! Wait a few hours and offer them the chance to move on to the valley that lies ahead on the maps. I will send cool water to them then – and a calm advocate, when they are ready to hear me.'

Clearchus raised an eyebrow in question and Cyrus nodded to him as he turned away. Ariaeus was a superb horseman, but a calm advocate he was not. Cyrus thought if he sent Ariaeus, even if he forbade the threat of castration, there would surely be another riot.

Menon the Thessalian came trotting up from the ranks. He had taken a recent blow to the face and his right eye was swollen and already darkening. Proxenus was not far behind him and that great bony Greek was furnace-red, though whether it was the sun or embarrassment was hard to say. Both men bowed and Menon spoke as the prince turned to him.

'Highness, I would like to address my men before any punishment is considered. We knew there could be . . . reluctance. They signed up to fight hill tribes not imperials, after all. Yet they are innocents, Highness, most of them. I suspect the

Spartans are leading them in this. My regiment is merely watching for a chance to join you here, I'm certain. If you will allow me to speak to my officers, I know I can bring my lads out from the rest.'

'Your face . . . what happened?' Cyrus asked.

'Ah, that, er, was a personal disagreement with another man, Highness. A gambling debt.'

It was so obviously a lie that Cyrus didn't bother replying to it. Instead, Clearchus spoke.

'It looks like you've been punched in the face, Menon. Don't you think I could call my Spartans out of line? They are not just lads I paid and trained, but men I have known my whole life! I have four cousins and two nephews in their ranks!'

'What of it? If you were sure, I think you would already have tried,' Menon snapped, surprising them all. 'Yet your beloved Spartans don't stand apart, do they? They refuse to go on, just like the others. I do not see them marching away, do you? So perhaps this is not the time for Spartan boasting, Clearchus. Just for once, you know, while we sort this out.'

The silence that followed was more than a little awkward.

'I have no doubt you could both bring your men out of the column,' Cyrus said. 'Yet if I allow you to approach with that intention, when the others see what you are about, they will surely kill you. Even if you are correct, they will not have come of their own accord. I cannot have mercenaries who feel they are slaves!'

His voice had grown loud as he spoke and both generals let his anger break into their own silent struggle.

Clearchus looked up at the prince. He went to one knee, a gesture which had Menon rolling his eyes and was not lost on the others.

'I have dealt with such things before, Highness. Let me

speak to them all first. If I fail, Menon can try to call out his group. It might even work, or they will argue and it will be the spark for violence. Either way, grant me a chance first, alone.'

'They are in awe of Spartans,' Cyrus said. 'All my people know you – and all the men of Greece look to you. So is it all just a myth? Or is there something more than discipline and skill with a sword?'

Clearchus smiled.

'We build no monuments in Sparta, no statues and no city walls. We are the walls, Highness. We are the monuments. I am a Spartan and all Spartans know me, because I am of them.' He shrugged at the blank stares of those around him. 'Some are born to lead, Highness. Some are just born. In Lacedaemon, we train the mind as well as the body.' He smiled for a moment, as if in memory. 'It may be that the mind is just as important. So let me try first. Let me discuss the problem. Before calling them out, before castration or flogging. Please. Ride on with your Persians and the camp followers to where we would have stopped this evening. I will come to you there. I give you my word, sworn on Ares. Unless I am killed, I will come.'

'Very well,' Cyrus said.

The greatest honour he could give Clearchus in that moment was to ride away as if he considered the matter settled. The thousands of men and women in the camp had caught up while they had been talking, looking in confusion at the seated ranks already arguing and gesticulating. Some of the women called out to men they knew as they passed, but were ignored or met with shrugs.

Cyrus saw a few dozen horses being brought up along the flanks. He recognised the young man Xenophon, and his companion Hephaestus, riding the edges of them. They were keeping the animals and a dozen urchin boys in good order as they halted and exchanged news with the seated Greeks. It was such an ordinary scene, but at the same time it was new and terrible. His mercenaries had refused him. A hollow seemed to have opened in his chest, beneath his coat, a sense of sickness. He shook his head, dug in his heels and urged his mount forward.

'Sunset, general,' Cyrus called over his shoulder. 'I will have wine.'

Clearchus looked at the generals who had come to that place with him. He inclined his head after the prince.

'You heard the prince, lads. Go on.'

Menon began to say something, but Proxenus bumped his shoulder hard as he passed and the moment was lost. In a variety of moods, from anger to grim acceptance, they left the Spartan tyrant to face the Greeks alone.

Clearchus stood before the regiments. At first, some of them threw stones to drive him off, but his own Spartans put a stop to that with angry words and gestures. It was Clearchus who had to intervene to stop fighting breaking out between them on the burning sands. Under the lash of the sun, all the men were already growing parched, gasping like hounds.

'Gentlemen,' he said, settling them. 'Gather close and hear me, but do not shed blood in this place of no life. Nothing grows here but bones. Would you wish to be left on such a plain for all eternity? No. Why then are you shouting and threatening men who were your brothers only yesterday?'

A barrage of sound came back from them, but Clearchus was pleased to see them shuffle forward. He had a good, strong voice and he knew he could reach thousands and be heard, but only if they gathered round as if to listen to a play.

He waited as they came closer, signalling with both hands

for them to approach while he thought. The prince was out of sight, with both Orontas and Ariaeus. The other generals had gone with them, leaving the Spartan to soothe the betrayal these men felt. As Clearchus stood there, he wondered how he was going to do that.

At first there was a constant clatter of talk and movement amongst the regiments. Some were already appalled at what they had begun, while others felt only more justified with every moment, their fears realised. They argued and shouted and threatened one another, but around Clearchus a ring of silence began to spread, until all men turned. The Spartan was standing before them, tears spilling down his face. As they fell silent, he wiped at his eyes with his forearm, almost in anger.

'Well? What, did you think a Spartan could not weep? Prince Cyrus became my friend when I was in exile from my own land and treated as an outcast. However, since you are unwilling to march with him, I am forced to make a choice. I am your general; I am his friend. I must either break that friendship and go with you, or betray my loyalty to you and go with him. You have put me in an impossible position.'

They leaned in, settling themselves as whispered arguments broke out.

'I know I must choose you,' he said. 'Yes! I will not have it be said that I led Greeks to a desert and abandoned them for native soldiers. Since you will not obey me, I will walk alongside you. I will endure whatever happens to you, at your side. I can do no less. I brought you to this place. I trained you and ran with you. You are my nation – my friends and my allies. I will not abandon you now.'

Some of them cheered him, while others looked troubled. Clearchus was not surprised when half a dozen men stood up, wanting to answer him as if they stood in the agora in

Athens. Greeks could not hear the sky was blue without discussing it and coming to a conclusion on their own. He loved them for it, though sometimes he thought it was a kind of madness.

The Thessalians crowded around him. Clearchus saw some of the angriest were from Menon's contingent, though he did not know if that was because of Menon's poor leadership or just that they had a few firebrands among them. They had certainly not expected to find the Spartan on their side and they beamed at him and offered him a few gulps of warm water. Clearchus listened patiently to three speakers from among the Greek regiments, though they merely repeated their sense of betrayal. One young man seemed to think it all needed saying again and repeated that the prince had asked them to fight hill tribes, not the Persian king. Clearchus nodded along to each point, though he privately thought the fellow was a fool.

'However we reached this point,' Clearchus said at last, when it seemed the young Greek would never come to a halt on his own, 'we are here now. We cannot go back, or make better decisions in the past. We stand here, in this place without shade, this day. Our greatest concern should be the lack of supplies, perhaps. We have no more food or water for tonight if we break contract with the prince. I do not imagine he will give us a last feast to see us on our way! No, gentlemen. The prince has been a friend to me, as I have said – and a great ally to Greece. His gold will raise sons and daughters at home for a generation. Yet if he is to be my enemy, I would rather be far away from him. He outnumbers us ten to one and I do not think he will let us go with everything we need to cross the desert.'

New men leaped to their feet to speak. Clearchus nodded as they called for a return to Greece or to buy provisions from the camp market. He only hoped there were more sensible men listening to the debate. In his experience, it was often the ones who said nothing who mattered most, the ones who thought it through, who had a better understanding than those he privately referred to as 'the sailors' – the men of wind. He was pleased to see no Spartans among the speakers, though they watched him and waited. Menon had not been wrong in one sense. The Spartans could lead the rest in the right circumstances. Yet one wrong word would inflame old passions, especially among the men of Athens. The history of Greece was one of almost constant warfare, and old rivalries ran deep.

Clearchus let them talk their throats dry in the afternoon heat, adding his own thoughts whenever they ran out of arguments and grand gestures. Little by little, he hoped to show how poor their choices were. They had not planned their little rebellion, but simply allowed resentment to spill into sudden action, like a child kicking a door in a temper. The truth was that they could not possibly leave without being seen – and if they were seen, there was a good chance they would be attacked by the same men they had walked alongside for months. The prospect was not an attractive one. More, if they left, they would have neither food nor water, nor the means to carry either. That too was a dark prospect. Point by point, Clearchus made sure they understood, all the time saying he was on their side. The only moment he demurred was when the most rash wanted to attack the prince's army, to loot the camp for supplies. Clearchus shook his great head at that, saying he could not be involved in such a betrayal, but if they insisted, he would help them elect another to lead them. The point did not pass and the discussion moved on.

'Gentlemen and friends,' Clearchus said at last, when the

sun was hovering above the horizon and the terrible heat was beginning to fade. Flies had found them by then, drinking salt from their skin and eyes. They were all burned red from sitting in the sun for so long. 'Gentlemen, you always knew that the life of a mercenary would involve risk, even death. That is our trade – though we prefer to deal it out to the other fellow.' He waited for a chuckle to ripple through the crowd. 'Perhaps you did not expect to face the prince's brother, or the Persian Immortals we broke once at Plataea and Marathon. For perilous service, it is more usual to be paid half as much again, is it not? One and a half darics per month. You were not even offered such a fine reward, though, were you?'

They agreed that no one had suggested as much gold as that. A number of men looked thoughtful at the sum. No skilled labourer could earn even a fifth as much. For most of them it would be like taking three or four years' pay over a single campaign. Clearchus had only to wait a few moments before one of the Corinthians stood up.

'What if we sent men to the prince and demanded he pay the rate for perilous service? One and a half darics per man per month? Would he agree to that?'

Hundreds of heads turned to Clearchus to hear how he would answer.

'I am certain of it,' the Spartan said after a time. 'But he will not forgive you if you take perilous pay in gold and then refuse to march for him. If you agree to this, it must be the end. We will win through, I swear it. I will *bring* you through. We are Greeks, gentlemen. We are well paid because we have no equal. Mind you, it might be an idea not to mention the size of that payment to the Persians.'

That idea brought a roar of laughter and he smiled at them. In that moment, the crisis passed. Regiment after regiment came to their feet and brushed sand from their skin. It had not been about gold, but they'd aired their resentments and Clearchus had listened. When he called his Spartans to the front, they came quickly into ranks. At first, they would not look him in the eye, though they stood ready to move.

'Spartans, to order,' Clearchus said. 'Raise your heads, now.' He waited until they were watching him and met their gaze with confidence.

'We will fight for Prince Cyrus as he challenges his older brother on the field of war. Is there any one among you who would prefer to go home?'

There was silence, as the evening breeze swirled sand around their ankles, a blessed touch of coolness. The Spartans stood in lines with the companions of their youth. They could no more run than they could fly away like birds. Clearchus dipped his head, almost as if he bowed to them. He had called them to the front for that reason – and because he thought Spartans should always lead. There would be no more talk of betrayal among them after that.

'Walk with me to camp,' he said. 'I will see the prince on your behalf. I will arrange perilous pay for every man here. Do not fear reprisal for the events of today. I will forbid it.'

Somehow, it did not seem such a grand claim, coming from him. Clearchus had stood alone before an angry mob. He marched out once more across the sands, with the Greeks following in perfect ranks.

Cyrus had found he could not just wait in the camp with a bowl of soup and some stale bread, not while the future of his wild gamble was being decided. Instead, he asked his manservant Parviz to bring him a fresh steed, letting Pasacas rest. Xenophon and Hephaestus had brought a fine gelding trotting on a long rein between their own mounts. Cyrus noticed the younger one was sitting more competently in the saddle, so that he moved with the horse.

'You are a better rider than when I saw you first,' the prince said.

The man blushed and nodded. He dismounted and bowed at an angle that suggested he was at least a royal prince, if not the king of a small realm. Cyrus sighed to himself and mounted up.

'One of the scouts spotted a herd of ostrich, east of here. I will take spears and hunt while I wait for General Clearchus to return to camp. If he comes in, send someone out to me immediately.'

The prince stared at the horizon, looking for some sign of the huge, running birds who roamed like deer and could cover astonishing distances. For all he knew they'd already left the area, but he wanted to ride. He'd expected his Persians to cause him trouble when they heard they would face his brother. Seeing the Greeks refuse his order had shocked him and thrown all his plans into disarray.

General Ariaeus came riding up through the camp then. He ignored the young Athenians, tossing his reins to Xenophon without truly looking at him. Cyrus waited while the general prostrated himself on the ground.

'Highness, I sent a few men back to observe the Greeks,' Ariaeus said. 'One of them has just come in. He says they are on their way in good order once again.'

The general glanced at the pair watching. Hephaestus stared at him as if he was talking gibberish, but the other seemed to be concentrating on his words. Ariaeus turned his shoulder slightly, ostentatiously excluding the Greeks.

'Highness, could they be hostile?' he went on. 'Should I rouse the camp against them? What if they have come to take our water and supplies?'

'Is General Clearchus their prisoner?' Cyrus asked.

'I do not believe so, Highness. The boy said he was walking alongside the other men.'

'Then, no, they are to be welcomed as before. Fetch wine to my tent, general. I told the Spartan I would broach a skin for him when he came in. I can hunt ostrich tomorrow.'

17

In the morning, Cyrus woke in some pain, turning aside from the bucket that had been placed by his head with a sound of disgust. He had spent much of the night drinking himself to insensibility with Clearchus. He remembered declaiming a poem in court Persian and moaned in horror. The Spartan would not sing, he recalled. Clearchus said his people only sang when a new king was raised up, or when they believed they were going to die. The general had not been as drunk as he was, Cyrus realised, wincing as flashes came back to him. Had he really given his childhood impression of a donkey, braying at the older man and falling over laughing? He prayed that part was just a fevered dream.

Flipping back a rug, Cyrus urinated into the sand in a corner of the tent, his eyes tight shut. The air was hot and foetid there, with slow flies knocking against him as they looped past. For a moment, he thought he might vomit again and cursed himself for a fool. He knew he would not feel fully right until the evening. A whole day ruined by his excesses of the night before. He needed to eat and drink water and then ride hard for a few hours to settle his stomach. There was no shelter in the desert and he didn't want to have his tent assembled each time he needed a little hole dug in the sand. Loose bowels were an embarrassing feature of a long march, one that was not often mentioned in training. Cyrus prayed he would not humiliate himself. His father had told him once that the men would forgive all but two things in those who led them. The other was cowardice.

He stood in a wide bucket to be washed down by his servants, then allowed himself to be wrapped in cool cloth while he was shaved and his hair brushed and tied back. He lay down on a folding table to be massaged, then sat naked on a bench while his undergarments and armour were brought. He waved away fat dates and white cheese. The sun was some way above the horizon by the time he emerged from his tent. As he'd finished dressing, he'd heard voices calling the camp to order, urging the men along. The uproar was growing, so that Cyrus put aside his own distress as he came out, squinting into the distance.

The deserts stretched as far as the eye could see ahead of them, but the hills and dunes hid valleys, rock spires, rivers with green banks and even villages. For all they seemed alone, the horizon told a different story.

Thin black threads rose into the sky ahead. Cyrus had been taking the men east, always east, heading for his father's capital. He'd known no hostile army could approach Persepolis without being seen, and had accepted their presence would eventually be reported back to Artaxerxes. Yet the imperial forces were vast, too large to assemble in just a day or even a month. Cyrus bit his lip as he wondered. Each quarter of the imperial army was larger than the forces he had brought to that place. His plan had depended upon never having to face more than the elite core around his brother.

He thought he knew what the smoke meant, but he was not surprised when Orontas came to his tent as it was being taken down for the day's march. The general dismounted from a black stallion, handed his sword to a servant, then lay face down on the sand until the prince commanded him to rise and report.

'Highness, I have word from the scouts ahead. Those furthest away are reporting burned crops and deserted villages.

If we march all day, we will come upon the first of them by this evening.'

Cyrus was silent, staring at the slowly twisting lines of smoke, thin as hairs at that distance.

'Tissaphernes,' he said after a time. 'It seems my old friend saw more than I'd hoped.'

He glanced at Orontas, but the Persian was careful not to show any expression in the presence of his prince. Cyrus might have known his ultimate intentions as far back as Sardis, but his Persian officers certainly had not.

'Highness, I wonder . . .' Orontas said. He stammered slightly and his voice faded.

'What? Speak freely.'

'If your brother, King Artaxerxes, is in the field, he is not yet nearby. I think we would have seen the imperial ranks by now if they were close.'

'Go on,' Cyrus said.

Orontas seemed to grow in confidence as the words spilled out of him.

'Villages and crops are burned ahead of an invading army – it is in the manual for officers, Highness. But it is done to starve a strong enemy to weakness. I wonder if it suggests your brother does not have the forces he needs in this area, at least at the moment.'

'Perhaps. Though if you are right, I do not see how that benefits me. Without replenishing our supplies as we go, we have food for, what, a week? Nine or ten days? If you know the manual, general, you will know there are one or two suggestions for defence against the tactic. If the land is burned ahead of our route of march . . . ?'

'Take a different route,' Orontas finished for him. 'Though my point stands, Highness. If King Artaxerxes and the royal army are not yet in place, we may be facing a much smaller force. There could be just a few hundred burners ranging ahead of our scouts, looking to weaken us and do as much damage as possible. If we can overtake them, we can put a stop to it, or at the very least, slow them down and limit the damage they can do.'

'The scouts?' Cyrus said. 'They would be slaughtered if I gave that order. Most of them are boys.'

Orontas chose that moment to kneel and prostrate himself once more.

'Highness, let me take a hundred of your guard, to scour these burners from our path. Just a hundred, like a thrown spear. I will ride further than our scouts and catch them by surprise while they ruin and pillage. It takes time to destroy stores, Highness. I can catch them, I am certain of it.'

Cyrus had never seen the level of fervour in Orontas he saw in that moment. The man actually trembled as he stared into the distance.

'Rise up, general,' he replied, his eyes glimmering. If only Clearchus had been there to see it. 'Very well. Ride far and fast and bring me the heads of those who burn villages in my father's lands.'

Orontas came back to his feet, though he bowed over the prince's hand and held it briefly to his own forehead.

'You honour me, Highness,' he said.

Cyrus turned as his horse was brought to him, as well as a mounting block. He still felt a little bilious and full of acid, so he was pleased to see the steps. With a grunt, he swung up and over, settling himself and taking the reins.

'You say my brother cannot be close, general, but he cannot be too many days away either. I will bring the army on at our best pace. Send a rider to me this evening with what news you have learned. Until then, may Ahriman be blind to you. Good fortune in your wake, old friend.'

The column had formed as he and Orontas had spoken, waiting for the prince to give the order to march. Cyrus rode to the head, where Clearchus looked rested and fit. The Spartan had watched the exchange and his gaze followed Orontas as the man mounted up and cantered along the flank of the column, signalling to the officers of Cyrus' personal guard. Clearchus was not strictly responsible for those men, though he considered they came under his general authority. Even so, he narrowed his eyes as he saw Orontas assemble a force of horsemen and make ready to ride.

The Spartan could not help wandering over to the two Athenian lads he had come to know. The older, Xenophon, was in the middle of some angry speech, spitting insults and rolled oats as he gesticulated after the Persian horsemen. Clearchus could not remember the name of the other one.

'That Persian general, Orontas . . . I see he has taken your spare mounts,' Clearchus said. 'What does he need them for?'

Xenophon almost choked as he recognised the speaker. He bowed and cleared his throat, then cuffed Hephaestus on the back of the head when the younger man just stared.

'General Clearchus, it is a great honour,' Xenophon said. 'Your reputation precedes you.'

'Is there anything in that reputation about being patient with those who do not answer my questions?' Clearchus asked.

Xenophon shook his head.

'No. General Orontas wishes to ride ahead of the main force – to seek out the raiders who scorch the earth ahead of us.'

'Why then are you angry?'

'He . . . the general did not wish me to accompany him. He said he would not take a Greek, that we were not to be trusted.'

'I see,' Clearchus said. He rubbed his chin as he thought.

Orontas was not the sort of officer given to rushing off on wild assaults. If he'd been asked to name one more likely, it would have been Ariaeus. There was something wrong.

'How many horses do we have left now?' he said.

Xenophon blew air out as his irritation rekindled.

'Including the two mounts Prince Cyrus rides, forty-six. That is why I was angry, general. I am the master of horse – and what did he leave me?'

Clearchus nodded, his eyes distant. He decided to ask Prince Cyrus, though he had a terrible feeling it was already too late.

Cyrus was shading his eyes from the sun when a Persian officer rode up to him, tossed the reins to a marching serv-ant and approached the king's personal guard, not daring to come closer than arm's reach.

'I crave a word with you, Highness – about my cousin, Orontas.'

Cyrus turned at that.

'He is about to leave. What of him?' he demanded. Seeing the man was panting with some exertion, the prince ges-tured him in.

The Persian had a slight resemblance to Orontas about the nose, Cyrus thought. He waited while the man dipped down, holding out a folded parchment marked with a seal Cyrus knew. Orontas carried a carved sapphire that bore the symbol of his house, an ear of wheat and a wild horse. Pressed into a clay disc, it stood out clearly. Cyrus saw the parchment had been slit along its edge and he scowled at the implica-tions, his mind leaping ahead.

'What is so important that you have brought it to me?' he said, dreading the answer.

'Highness, my cousin charged me with taking this to King Artaxerxes. It says he will bring a force of horsemen out of your army – and begs the Great King not to strike him down when he comes. He is my blood, Highness. Yet if I could, I would cut away all that we share in my shame.'

Cyrus felt cold. He sensed the gaze of the captain of his guard on him and nodded sharply. The man understood well enough what had to be done. In turn, Cyrus gestured to others and gave the order to halt all preparations to move off.

In the distance, General Orontas turned to stare at the disturbance. Though he was far away, Cyrus thought he could see some part of the dread and fear that Orontas must have felt, perhaps in the way the man sat his horse.

There might have been a moment when the Persian general could have galloped away from the rest, though he would not have made it far on loose sands. The captain of the guards had already edged men out to intercept Orontas if he ran, while Cyrus watched, looking for the moment when his general understood he would not ride to freedom.

The general's head drooped suddenly, so that he stared at his saddlehorn, with his hands gripping the reins. Cyrus continued to watch as Orontas was made to dismount and had his hands bound. General Ariaeus approached him then to tie on a long rope, securing the other end to his own saddle. Cyrus was too far away to hear what passed between them, though he told himself he would learn every word that evening. The column lurched into movement at last, with many heads turning to see the general staggering along, his expression tight with humiliation.

Prince Cyrus sat his horse at the side of the column as thousands passed him, waiting for the moment when Ariaeus would draw alongside with his new slave. At first, the prince had been going to let the moment pass in silent condemnation, but he felt his ire grow. With the merest gesture of his fingers, he drew Ariaeus to him.

Clearchus had come close enough to observe, with Proxenus and Netus. Menon the Thessalian had also approached, though he and Clearchus had fallen out on the march and he kept his distance. Still, they were all fascinated to see what Orontas had done and what Cyrus would do in turn.

Ariaeus jumped down from his grey mare with a flourish, well aware of their eyes on him. He could have let Orontas keep his pride, but instead gave a great tug on the rope and sent the man sprawling onto his belly in front of the prince. In an instant, Ariaeus stood astride his countryman. As Orontas struggled to rise, the Persian general touched a warm knife blade to his throat, so that he became very still, understanding that his life was measured on a single word from a prince he hated – and perhaps the outrage of a flashy warrior he had never liked. Orontas found he could be calm. He had seen it many times in those who stared at their own death. There was no struggle at the end. He breathed slowly out, pleased he could meet the prospect of eternity with something like dignity.

'No protests, Orontas?' Cyrus said suddenly. 'No arguments?'

The general who had commanded regiments for the imperial family looked aside, to where his cousin stood with eyes downcast.

'It seems I trusted the wrong man, Highness.'

'Something we share, then,' Cyrus snapped.

Orontas shrugged, looking away to the east.

'Highness . . . No, it does not matter,' he said.

Cyrus stared coldly at him.

'Have I injured you in any way, general?'

Wordless, Orontas shook his head.

'Why then this betrayal? Am I not my father's son? Are you not sworn to serve my family?'

'No, Highness,' Orontas said. He spoke in reproof, his voice growing louder. 'I am sworn to serve the crown. I thought to do that by joining your brother, the king. I . . . am sorry. I considered my actions for a long time. I did not want to stand against you, my prince. You have been nothing but kind to me. The men sing your praises. Yet . . . I did not feel I could go on.' He raised his head, though tears glittered in his eyes. 'I have made my choice, Highness. I accept the consequences.'

Cyrus did not reply for a long time. He knew he had but to give the order and the man's life was at an end. All those who watched expected it from him. Still, he sought a way to keep Orontas alive. For all the petty irritation he felt around him, Orontas was a fine soldier and respected in the regiments. If there was a command or a single word that could have won Cyrus his loyalty, the prince would have spoken it aloud in an instant. He looked to Clearchus for something he could not have named, anything. His appeal was met by silence and Cyrus sighed.

'Take this fallen man from my sight,' he said to his guards. 'Make his ending quick, a single blow – and treat him with honour as he prepares himself.'

He turned back to the prisoner watching him. Cyrus took a knife and cut the ropes that bound the man's wrists, so that Orontas rubbed them, watching the prince he could not follow.

'May I write to my family, Highness, before your sentence is carried out?'

Cyrus repressed a surge of anger that would have seen Orontas dead at his feet. Yet he was a prince and his father's son. He mastered himself.

'Of course,' he said, turning away from the man for the last time.

They all heard Orontas sigh, his resignation to his fate. In that moment, Orontas knelt and prostrated himself before a prince of the house Achaemenid, though his own death lay heavy on him.

'General Ariaeus?' Cyrus called.

The man was ready for his orders and was kissing sand before Cyrus could say another word. The prince nodded to him as he rose.

'You are in command of the Persian forces, general. Take this gentleman who is cousin to Orontas as your second in command. Give orders to all but the Greeks – and take the orders of Clearchus. Is that understood? Will you serve me loyally on those terms?'

'I will. I will take this honour to my grave, Highness,' Ariaeus said. 'I will make you proud.'

'Just do better than the last poor bastard,' Cyrus said.

He turned his mount, in time to witness Clearchus bowing his head to Orontas before he dug in his heels. Proxenus and Netus rode with the prince back to the column, leaving Menon to follow in their wake. The Greeks were serious in their manner, as befitted the loss of a colleague, but not one of them disagreed with the prince's decision. The column would march deeper into the deserts by that evening. They would leave the body of Orontas behind them, for the sun to wither, for the birds of prey to tear and snag.

In camp that evening, Prince Cyrus came to the fires of the Spartan section to share their food. He regretted not bringing his own when he saw how little they would consume, with cold water as the only refreshment. Even so, they made him welcome and he sat cross-legged with them on the hard ground, raising his head to Clearchus as both men accepted a thin slop of grain and curdled milk, with a piece of goat's cheese and an ancient fig.

'What brings you to us, Highness?' Clearchus said when they had all finished and wiped out the bowls.

'Orontas intended to ride to my brother,' Cyrus said, staring into the flames as they burned low. He thought to ask for the fire to be built up before he recalled they had to carry every stick of wood with them in those barren wastes. Life struggled in such a place, without water, without warmth in the dark. The night was already growing chill, so that his teeth chattered as he went on, clenching his jaw.

'He believed the royal forces to be close. He told me he would ride out ahead to hamstring those who burn crops and poison wells. It was a good idea then – and it is now.'

'Leave it with me, Highness,' Clearchus said. 'I will put some of my lads in command. Or that Athenian, perhaps, who was so put out at having his horses taken from him.'

'Yes . . .' Cyrus said. 'We need eyes far ahead of us, to know where my brother pitches his tent. But . . . I do not know about the men Orontas chose. Can some of my own guard be traitors? It seems hard to believe. How can I trust them now?'

Clearchus reached to a pack by his side and produced a flask. It looked like yellow ivory in the firelight, with figures carved on the surface. Peering through the shadows, Cyrus thought they might have been involved in sports, though it was not likely.

'The last of my supply, Highness. Perhaps it is the night for it.'

The prince accepted the flask and drank deeply, his eyes widening as it burned him.

'Is that made from grapes?' he said hoarsely.

'The skins, I believe,' Clearchus said, chuckling. He raised the bottle and smacked his lips.

'Highness, Orontas was a leader of men. I know he had some connection with one of your noble families, but he rose because he was sharp and strong – and he had that quality that other men will follow.'

'Is that why you bowed your head to him?' Cyrus said.

'Ah, you saw that, did you? No, Highness. That was to give him honour for the manner of his death. He took the news like a Spartan. That is a rare thing. I have seen grown men complain to the ephors because they were bitten by another man's dog. Like children! We are soldiers, Highness. We understand tomorrow could be the last day. Or the day after. A soldier has so little control over the time or manner of his ending. He can always choose how he faces it.'

They were silent for a time, passing the flask back and forth until it was empty. Cyrus found the burn eased and became almost pleasant.

'The others?'

'The others thought they were carrying out your orders, Highness. I would not think more of it than that. Some men learn to lead – I do not believe it is born in us. Most are willing to be led. They ask little from life beyond wine and food and warmth – and later, children and a home. They do not want to decide which way, whenever the road forks. They do not want others to come clamouring to them, crying "east or west?", "live or die?" That is left to hard and lonely men like you, Highness.'

'And like you,' Cyrus replied.

'Ah, well, I'm a son of Lacedaemon. I have a silver skull and molten bronze in my veins. I have walked the streets of Sparta and tasted the water of the Eurotas river that runs in a dry land. I have stood on the acropolis of Sparta and called out my adult name.'

He smiled as he spoke, but the words sounded like a ritual and sent a shiver through the prince.

Clearchus yawned suddenly and stretched like a child. He looked up at the stars and shook his head.

'The night is old, Highness. I will send my lads out with horses tomorrow. We'll find these raiders and hang them. Or we'll find your brother's army and cut them to pieces. That's what we came for, after all. Orontas should have waited a little longer.'

The prince came to his feet, his spirits lifted by whatever he had drunk and the Spartan's words. He inclined his head just as Clearchus had done to Orontas, then staggered away through the dunes to where he had left his own blanket and pack under the stars.

Clearchus rose to stretch, looking after the prince until he had vanished. The Spartan liked the younger man, for all his insecurities and need to be reassured. He would make a fine king, if he ever got the chance.

18

Alarm horns blew in the darkness. Bearded soldiers stumbled from their blankets and tents, rolling out bleary-eyed, swords and shields ready to hand. The noise of galloping horses could be heard, followed by the roars of polemarchs and pentekosters summoning their men to the line. It took time to strap on greaves and breastplates, though their breath came fast and sharp. They sat in clusters, wrenching at knots and belts. No immediate attack sprang at them. Officers stalked amongst the seated groups, urging them to speed, reminding the men to lace their boots and push the helmets right down. The growling tones were almost soothing in the ritual, words they'd all heard a thousand times before. There was chaos somewhere, no doubt, but not in those lines. Or it was just another drill, no doubt ordered by that Spartan general who seemed to delight in such practices, while good men should have been deep in slumber.

They came into squares without panic, each regiment forming with shouts in the darkness.

'Line here, on Demetrios of Athens!' or 'First four assemble on the horn banner!' Regimental officers called out their men by name and rank, summoning them to the positions they had learned over months. It took a long time, though it seemed just moments. With gruff calls of farewell and good fortune, the camp followers drifted back, leaving lovers and friends and masters. The warriors of Greece and Persia waited alone in a great curved line drawn in the sands. The alarm horns died away, the work done. They stood without speaking, though never in silence. The creak of leather, a gauntlet tapping nervously on a shield, the screech of ungreased armour, dried by sand and heat – all of it made a noise like metal in the desert, as if a great dark creature of scale and bronze had woken and was stirring itself to fight.

The more experienced of the men had not drawn their weapons, though their hands opened and closed for the comfort of them. If there was to be killing that day, they would need every trick to keep their strength when the sun rose. They feared its heat by then. They were all darker than they had been back in Sardis or Greece, though some still peeled in great patches, where the sun had burned them almost to the bone. The rest were lean from small rations, their skin made leather by sand and the bites of flies and lice.

They had come a long way in the footsteps of the prince. Though many were nervous, they took comfort from those around them, waiting for whatever had caused the horns to sound. Hundreds made peace with the gods, touching amulets or keepsakes from home, raising them to their lips and murmuring brief prayers. Then such things were put away. They pissed into the sand where they stood, so that steam drifted up.

Banners rose high above the regiments, unrolled by boys from the camp who carried the poles with great pride. The Pegasus, the bull, the owl and the Spartan lambda stood above the ranks of the Greeks, while Persian regiments stood under lion, falcon, griffin and sun. Boys brought water to anyone who called for it, or went scurrying back for some forgotten item, noticed by the soldiers only as they came to a halt. The boys shouted and called at first, though their high voices fell to whispers as they passed between the standing ranks of men, awed by the presence of that dark army under the starlight.

A pale band appeared in the east, bringing with it the first faint breeze of the day, as if the night would be scoured away in a layer of sand. It revealed the barest outlines of the army of Prince Cyrus. They faced the direction of travel, looking east as all men will, to the source of the light, to the rising sun that burned away all childish fears. They faced that grey band and waited for the first warmth on their faces, instead of the terror of being blind and afraid, each man alone amongst his fellows.

The horizon had been a dark blade, separating land from sky. As the paleness grew across its length, those with sharpest sight cried out in warning, while the rest still stared and asked what was happening. In among the Greeks and Persians, there were thousands of men whose far sight had become little more than a blur, though they could fight well enough in sword's range. Those men grabbed boys from the camp, turning them to the light and demanding to know what was out there over those dark hills.

The boys strained their eyes, seeing the horizon ripple as if the land itself moved. They pointed and shouted when the first light caught the tips of banners there. All those who had come with Cyrus heard the rumble that came to them, though it sounded more like the fall of stone in distant mountains, a long growl that went on and on. Far away, they saw a line that seemed to be the earth itself, resolving into black shields and the dust of horses. The army of Persia was in the field to face them. They marched as a host of hosts, darkening the earth.

Some of the regiments roared their defiance, howling at the imperials, rousing one another to a battle fervour. The sound increased at first, then caught and failed, dwindling until once more they stood in awestruck silence. The lines ahead of them had continued to grow until they could fill the entire world. No man there had ever seen so many soldiers in one place, an uncountable sea.

Cyrus had brought a hundred thousand Persians and twelve thousand Greeks. Thousands more stood in horror behind his regiments as the camp pulled back step by step. They had walked lightly into the green hills of Babylon and on, into the desert, taking confidence from the strength of numbers. All that dwindled in the face of so many, come to destroy them, without ceasing, without chance of mercy. Those who had walked from Sardis with the prince felt their scrotums tighten, their stomachs and bladders ache, while sweat trickled cold along their ribs. They despaired.

Cyrus threw his helmet to one of his personal guard then dug in his heels, understanding as an instinct of leadership that his men needed to see him. He rode out with his hair unbound, with banners flying, his servant Parviz and six hundred horsemen riding with him over sandy ground. He did not turn his head to his brother's army, preferring instead to look across the ranks of those who had come so far in his name. They were his, in a way that was difficult to describe. Their lives had been wagered on his word. It was a bond as deep as any family, with the stakes as high as they could possibly be.

Clearchus and the Greeks settled the right wing close to the river Euphrates so that they could not be flanked or encircled. Cyrus came to a halt in the centre, raising his personal banner, a falcon on a huge square of silk, set with jewels. He looked left and right, taking pride in the hundreds of regimental symbols, the life's blood and traditions of the army held on spears for anyone to read.

On his left, the Persian regiments stretched away under Ariaeus. Cyrus held the centre because it was where his men expected him to stand. Yet as the sun rose and he watched his brother's army come closer and closer, he looked for the royal eagle of Achaemenid in the centre of the line ahead – and could not see it.

A runner came pelting through the ranks to him, already shining with sweat as the man darted around horses and dipped down close enough almost to vanish under the hooves of the prince's mount.

'General Clearchus asks for final orders, Your Highness. He wishes you to know that all the leaves of the forest cannot overcome a sword.'

Cyrus felt one side of his mouth quirk. The Spartan could not resist trying to raise his spirits. Clearchus was a father figure to them all, at times.

Before the prince could answer, he saw his personal guard pointing over to the left and shading their eyes against the rising sun. Out of the furnace, they called the name of his brother. Cyrus peered east and swallowed as he understood. His brother was in the centre after all. Yet his army was of such a size that the centre of it was past the furthest edge of the prince's forces. For the first time, Cyrus felt himself tremble, the breath stop in his throat. His brother, or perhaps Tissaphernes, had anticipated him.

He looked over his right shoulder then, past the young Greek who waited for orders, to the entire wing under Clearchus, Proxenus and Netus. Menon the Thessalian was there too, though his men made the buffer into the Persians, so were the leftmost section of the Greek force – and least honoured, as Cyrus understood it. The Greeks bickered and fought amongst themselves, falling out on the march and in camp. Yet they were the advantage his brother did not have. The one force the Great King could not match and could not answer. Cyrus sent a prayer to Ahura Mazda, closing his eyes into the rising sun.

'On your feet, boy,' he called to the messenger. 'Here is my order. General Clearchus is to advance the entire right wing at speed – away from the river, across the face of our army, before the enemy is in range. They are to strike at the centre of the royal lines, where they see eagle banners – on the left of where I stand. Repeat that to me.'

The messenger's Persian was perfect as he said the words without a mistake, though his eyes were huge. In the end, he bowed and half-knelt before racing away, his skin already bright with sweat.

Cyrus watched his brother's lines come closer with a sick fascination, as a man standing under an avalanche might watch the mountain fall, yet remain rooted to the spot.

Clearchus noted the messenger racing back to him. The lines were silent on the right wing as they waited for the enemy to come within range of stone and spear. The mood was serious, though the mercenaries of Greece were confident enough. They had seen the standard of Persian soldiers in those who had trained with them. The prospect of facing similar men in battle did not trouble them unduly. Yet sheer numbers had smothered laughter and talk. Watching an army tramp towards them like a tide coming in across a bay was a sobering experience.

'I . . . have orders . . . from the prince,' the young man said.

'Shouldn't you be fitter?' Clearchus replied. 'You might have to do this all day, son.'

'Sorry, general,' the man panted. 'The prince says to advance your forces against the enemy centre, over there, sir.'

The messenger pointed, though Clearchus did not bother to look. Proxenus was not far away, the man happier in the saddle than Clearchus had ever been. Clearchus signalled for the messenger to wait as Proxenus came close enough to raise his eyebrows in question.

'Prince Cyrus would have us push ahead of his Persians, to attack the king's guard in the centre. Apparently, it's over to our left. I can't even see it from here.'

'Leave the river?' Proxenus said immediately. 'That is . . . a rash move.' He peered into the distance and shook his head. 'The enemy are . . . very *close* to be trying something like that, Clearchus. I don't know if I can even get my men moving before they're on us.'

In the presence of listening soldiers around them and the messenger who would report back, the two generals stared at one another in silence. The order was a desperate throw of the dice that would probably get them all killed – or the single strike that could win the battle before it had even begun. Proxenus was clearly unwilling, but Clearchus knew the general would fall in line if he confirmed the order. The other Greeks might advise, but discipline was the very heart of them. They understood a general or a prince must sometimes send men to die, to hold a hill or a line. Their task was to follow the orders and sell themselves dearly, to allow a victory. It required trust – and faith in those who led them. More, it required men who understood their leaders could be wrong, that they could be sent to destruction in error or pride – and yet would go anyway.

Even so, Clearchus said nothing for a time. He could see Menon the Thessalian angling over to see what was happening, but that made him decide all the faster. The man had said some foolish things about Sparta, with its single theatre and one river in a dry valley. If they had not been allies, Clearchus would have taken him to task for it. He thought he still might if the man survived the battle. He had sent Menon to the leftmost point of the Greek wing as a demotion, though the spiky little man did not seem to understand that.

'Return to Prince Cyrus,' Clearchus said. 'Tell him we will advance as he has ordered.'

The messenger bowed and raced away once more. Proxenus turned from where he had been staring at the enemy lines. He looked at Clearchus once again.

'If you cut across the field, they will encircle us, my friend. The king's army overlaps on our left. If we draw in the right as well, he will fold in the wings and that . . . will be that.'

'Yes,' Clearchus said. 'Before we can break the centre, we have to rout the wing ahead. If we can do that quickly, we can turn in then towards the king. I will not let Prince Cyrus say we did not come, but we will have to go through them all first.'

Proxenus chuckled.

'I do like you, Spartan.'

'I don't care,' Clearchus said. It was not clear whether he was joking or not, and Proxenus let his smile slip. 'Go back to your men. Tell them to keep up.'

Clearchus looked back to two of his men standing with long silver horns.

'Blow the signal to advance,' he said.

He checked his sword was free in the scabbard as well as the kopis knife in the small of his back. His shield felt like a good weight, an old friend on his left arm. He held out a hand and a spear was handed over to him. He hefted it and when he smiled, his expression was terrible.

The horns sounded, over and over. The Spartans set off, leading the entire Greek wing alone against the Persian army. They marched with the river on their right flanks and their red cloaks flying. Ahead of them lay a shifting mosaic of white-coated horsemen and archers. Chariots made lines ahead of the rest, dragged through the soft sand by labouring horses. They bore scythe blades at the height of a man, and on hard ground they would make a frightening foe. In command of that part of the Persian army was the new-made Lord Tissaphernes, resplendent in white coat and seated on a grey mare.

Cyrus saw the Greeks advance and blessed them. He watched them detach from the standing lines behind him, but then clenched his jaw when he saw no deviation from the path they had chosen. His brother's position was still far over on the left, but they went forward as if Clearchus had not understood his order. The prince ran his hands over the shaft of a javelin, his horse snorting and pawing at the sand as it sensed his frustration.

The river glittered over on his right as the rising sun struck the waters. He understood Clearchus had not wanted to be encircled by such a vast number of the enemy, but Cyrus was the heir to the throne. If his brother fell, he would command the entire field in an instant.

He watched as the Greeks put daylight between the rest of the army and themselves, marching into the face of the imperial host as if they were the aggressors. It looked like one boy with a stick choosing to rush an entire regiment. Cyrus swallowed the lump in his throat. They had not refused or run when he had commanded them. He could not stand and watch them destroyed.

'Sound the advance! General advance. Steady now! Advance against the enemy!'

Horns blared all down the lines and the prince's Persian regiments lurched into movement, black squares looking small against all those they faced. Still, they too had found their courage. Cyrus took his place in the front ranks of the centre, though he knew his brother would find no one to oppose him when the forces met, so great was the difference in their numbers. Cyrus' only chance was to turn the field, or sweep through with his strongest right flank against the weakest left wing of the enemy. He peered ahead to see banners becoming clearer with every step. They were barely eight hundred paces apart by then, so that archers and peltasts were limbering up their arms and shoulders, ready to attack, while every other man who would have to endure it readied shields and prayed they would not be struck down.

Cyrus caught his breath when he saw the ranks around his brother. King Artaxerxes was hidden from view by a shifting screen of soldiers and chariots. His banners were there in a cluster on the prince's left, the golden eagle of Achaemenid. Cyrus has brought his falcon banners to challenge. One of them would fall.

Clearchus loped along with eight ranks of Spartans and four more of their helot slaves, each two hundred and forty men wide. Behind came the forces of Proxenus and Netus, with Menon grumbling in their wake. Clearchus glowered at the sight of chariots ahead, knowing they would be fearsome to those who had never seen them before.

'See how those old carts struggle in the sand,' he called along the line. 'Tell the men to jump those blades. We leap higher than that in the gymnasium, boys.'

His Spartans chuckled as they remembered, and he decided suddenly not to give the Persians the respect they sought.

'Men of Greece!' he roared as he marched along. 'Who are these people who dare to stand before us? No one, despite their vanity. We are warriors, the best the world has ever seen. *Homaemon* – we share the same blood. *Homotropa* – the same customs. *Homoglosson* – the language we speak.' His voice had built to a crescendo, huge in volume and impact. 'And *Homothriskon* – the same temples and gods. That is why we win. We are one people, indivisible. For today we are not Spartans, or Thessalians, or Athenians. We are Hellenes. We are men of Greece. Shall we show them what that means?'

His Spartans gave a great growl and the rest responded, showing teeth as they walked with him. Little by little, the pace was increasing. They knew they were heading into range of arrow and slingstone. It was time.

Each of the men who rode horses leaped down and slapped the mounts away from them. Boys who had run alongside took the reins and turned them back to the camp, now some miles behind. They cheered the soldiers on in high voices.

'Double your pace,' Clearchus roared, the sound carrying.

He heard the order repeated further along the line and the army made a sound together that was more than just an explosion of breath. It was a challenge to those they faced. Thousands began to sing the paean, the song of death.

'Ready shields and spears!' Clearchus called.

The Persian line was suddenly coming up fast and the air above filled with thousands of arrows, like blades of grass or dark hairs against the sun.

'Shields up! Steady your pace!' Clearchus roared again. He was not out of breath. He ran every day in training and he was barely winded. 'Engage the enemy! Keep formation! Keep discipline. For Prince Cyrus. For Greece. For Athens. By the gods, for Sparta!'

He kept up a stream of orders as his men advanced like a swung blade for the last hundred paces. The paean ended with a note of sadness rather than a roar, but it struck terror into the enemy even so. Arrows rattled against their shields, but most of them passed overhead, shot from archers who had not understood their pace. Held to the last, the barrage of Greek javelins battered lines down. Helots launched from ranks further back with grunts of effort. The Spartans kept hold of their spears and advanced with them held out low, a wall of thorns.

The Persians under Tissaphernes broke before the Greeks reached them. The front ranks fell back in chaos as the men there tried to turn from red-cloaked Spartans with death in their hands. Chariots turned over as the wheels caught in the sand or were dragged sideways by the horses.

Clearchus exulted as the way cleared before him. His Spartans drove the enemy like goats or cattle, killing anyone too slow to get out of the way, but holding discipline. He shouted the warning anyway, the constant fear of any general, that his men might become drunk on anger and break formation. He had seen armies made mobs before. Destruction always followed.

His Spartans were the edge of the shield, so that none of those behind could run mad without passing their own allies. They advanced steadily, with shields ready and spears stabbing out. Some of the ranks behind had drawn knives to see to wounded enemies, chopping down as they stepped across so that no one could leap up and cause chaos once the main lines had passed.

The entire Persian wing collapsed and the slaughter that followed was terrible, until every man of the Greeks was covered in the blood of strangers. Only the fact that so many of that wing had been mounted saved them at all. Tissaphernes withdrew some thousands out of range of thrown spears or slingstones, saving his own life in the process. Clearchus and Proxenus could see the man sitting his horse amidst white banners, but he had fallen back behind the main lines and Clearchus could not walk him down. The Spartan saw the Athenian horsemen were gathering themselves to ride out, but Clearchus ordered them to hold position. Amateurs and young men charged superior forces. Professionals rested themselves and climbed the mountain step by step. They had few enough horses anyway. Keeping a dozen or so back would not change the outcome of the battle.

Clearchus had to roar at his men to halt them as they began to push on, breaking through the main forces and glimpsing the curving river and open plains beyond. He needed the eyes of Argus to see all he needed to, in that place. They had done well, but the king's army was barely bleeding and still so vast as to appear unmarked. The dead were left where they fell. Those they faced were fresh, though their eyes were already wide with fear.

'Wheel left now! Break through them to the centre!' Clearchus said.

He and his Greeks would roll the front edge of the Persian snake like a carpet, from one end to the other. It would bring them into contact with the Great King's position, exactly as Cyrus had ordered. Clearchus shrugged off weariness as the first excitement faded. This was work, the hardest work he had ever known. The sun's heat was growing and he felt his tongue had grown dry. There were no water boys to be seen and so he shrugged and cleaned his sword in the moments of respite.

As he turned, he sent Proxenus to the flank with a line of Cretan bowmen, in case Tissaphernes tried a charge or rallied some Persian archers. To that point, Clearchus knew he had lost very few men and he wanted that to continue. He had seen one fellow caught by a chariot scythe, his own fear holding him in place when any other man would have dived and lived. That was the lesson. They had to keep moving. If they stopped, they would be overwhelmed, as a hawk can be brought down by crows.

19

Cyrus felt fear clutch at him, making him want to race his mount from the field. He had never known anything like it, as if he had been taken by the throat and shaken. He could breathe only shallowly and he felt his heart thumping, surely loud enough for those around to hear and know he was afraid. He saw his own death in the vast lines and the metal shimmer of the Euphrates river.

'I am a prince,' he whispered to himself, 'of the house of Achaemenid. I am a son of King Darius, a grandson of Xerxes. I will not run from this. I *will* stand.'

Ahead, he watched Clearchus lead out the Greeks, looking like men racing under a wave before it crashed down on them. Persians poured around them and they were swallowed up before his eyes, driving on and on into the enemy.

On his left, Cyrus saw his brother's imperials would overlap his flank with entire regiments. He did not have the numbers to stop them encircling him. Nothing ruined fighting strength faster than men knowing their retreat had been cut off, that they could not run, that there were enemies behind as well as before them. It was the simplest tactic of the Achaemenids – to bring so many to the battle that they overwhelmed whoever stood against them. The entire point of war was to bring ruin and destruction, as fast and as brutally as possible. Cyrus swallowed, his throat suddenly dry. His brother's army would curl around his own like a claw – and it would be over.

Cyrus felt the fear pass as soon as he had faced the worst. If his brother fell, he would be king. That was all that mattered. If Artaxerxes had brought the entire world to that plain by the great river, still only two lives would decide the outcome. The prince felt calm settle on him, like dust in the air. He breathed more deeply. It was not too hard. It was not too complex. One blow would end it all.

Six hundred horsemen rode with the prince as his personal guard, all fiercely loyal. Those who would have gone with Orontas still felt the sting of shame and the suspicion of their colleagues. They were desperate to prove themselves.

When Cyrus saw his brother's lines would overlap, the prince knew he had only one choice left. He would gamble his life on a single hour. He would be the spear-point, but once thrown, it could not be called back.

'Parviz!' he bellowed.

The man looked up, pleased to be needed for anything. Parviz rode an old mare well enough, but he was no kind of warrior, not like the prince's guards.

'Fall back now,' Cyrus called to him. 'This is no place for you.'

The prince saw the man's face crumple in dismay, but at least he would live. Cyrus was already shouting to another.

'Captain Hadid!' he called.

The captain came forward and bowed his head to receive orders, but there was no time, not really. The space between the armies was closing like the last arrow of evening. When they clashed, there would be no room to ride out.

'My guards, with me!' Cyrus dug in his heels, trusting them to follow.

For a moment, his horse lunged ahead of all the rest, rearing as he kicked it into motion. With a howl, his men converged on the prince as he darted north across the field.

He was the swallow coming home beneath the clouds, a royal falcon in the storm.

Cyrus found himself grinning as the air became a gale and the rhythm of his gallop beat like a drum under him. He braced a knee under the saddlehorn and sat high, leaning over the horse's shoulders as they worked together. He carried a javelin in one hand and his sword rested behind him, ready to be drawn.

His brother's banners beckoned, calling him on. Cyrus caught glimpses of his guards galloping alongside, forming a wedge. It was madness, but he found himself calling the challenge to the lines ahead. His voice was lost in the roar of hooves and men, but there were no words to it, just a wild shout and a promise of vengeance. Cyrus felt tears come to his eyes, stung by grit.

The enemy knew who he was, of course. From the first moment the prince had come out of his regiments, they had known him. No one else could have gathered six hundred horsemen but the royal prince of Achaemenid. Those ahead jerked back and forth as the prince bore down on them at full gallop, though whether it was fear of the massed charge or fear of him, Cyrus could not tell. They had been close as he sprang out; he was on them in moments, before new orders could change their formation.

Some of them gave way rather than stand against those spears and horsemen travelling as a blur. Dozens fell back or threw themselves down in fear. Those who were braver or too slow to jump aside were smacked down suddenly, broken as if they had fallen from a cliff. Cyrus felt the impacts sting his legs. He saw men knocked aside by the plunging shoulders of his horse, driven under flashing hooves. He heard their screams as thin wails vanishing behind as his guards drove a spike into the screen of the Persian king.

The two royal brothers saw each other in the same moment, almost in a beat of stillness. Cyrus forgot he was galloping through moving men and saw only the astonished eyes of Artaxerxes, the ornate helm turning to face him. His brother's mouth was open and red. His hand was reaching for a sword, but Cyrus was too fast, too solid, too much the vengeance he had promised. He had lost his javelin in the chest of a stranger. His sword was in his hand. He raised the blade high and struck at his brother's neck, hammering him back, so that the king flailed and cried out in horror. The blade struck metal, turning in Cyrus' hand as it caught the edge of the breastplate. Yet he had seen blood. It was a moment of perfect clarity, the air sweet and cold. Cyrus breathed out in something like joy.

Clearchus had no time for satisfaction. The Greek square drove hard into the imperial forces, denying them any opportunity to rally. The Persians could not react fast enough. By the time their officers even understood what was happening, the Spartans were through and hacking into a new regiment. They created a rolling rout ahead as men turned and ran rather than face that red-cloaked edge and the bloody swords that flickered in their hands.

Clearchus fought with shield and spear alongside men he had known for years. On that day, they were all united on the field of Cunaxa, by the river Euphrates, the great life serpent that made the desert green.

'What do you think you're *doing* there? Keep a proper distance between those ranks!' Clearchus roared at the men of Proxenus, marching behind his own. Chastened, they shuffled back, his outrage strangely calming in the face of the enemy. If Clearchus could find the time to notice poor form, perhaps it was not quite as hopeless as some of them believed.

Not one of them had seen so many people in one place before, not in the theatre of Dionysus in Athens, not in the crowds in the sacred groves of Delphi. It was a glimpse of an empire greater than anything they had imagined, and they could only blink and gape and press on.

The Greeks maintained the flattened square, with two hundred and forty Spartans and their helots as the leading edge and forty ranks marching behind. They fought like the professionals they were, in calm ferocity. No one broke rank to pursue a fleeing enemy. They marched forward as if they followed a narrow path – and anyone in that path was cut down. Those to either side were ignored unless they attacked. The Greeks went forward with shields already studded with broken arrows and dented by stones. The enemy saw only helmets they could not pierce, round shields and greaves beneath. The Spartans were men of bronze, with no weaknesses. Greek spears darted in and out from their ranks like the tongues of snakes, coming back bloody.

Clearchus saw one of his men stagger. Something had flown over the crowded lines and rung his helmet like a bell. It caught the general's attention and made him look at the men with fresh eyes. The front ranks were slowing as they tired.

'Proxenus, will you let my men take all the glory?' he called.

The other general raised his eyes to heaven.

'Let me past and I will show you what glory is,' Proxenus replied. 'Why must you always be first, Spartan? Were you bullied as a child?'

'Truly, you have no idea,' Clearchus said, though he grinned and shook his head as he spoke. Before his tenth birthday, he had won three boxing matches with Spartan boys taller and stronger than him. He had won the last with his right hand broken. He rubbed the knuckles in memory.

'Spartans, ease the front ranks. Ease back! You've shown them how to do it. Now let Proxenus show what he has learned! Tell Menon to advance on our left, in ranks sixty wide. And to keep up!'

The expressions of the Spartans were hidden by the cold gaze of the helmets, but Clearchus knew they were weary. His men were superbly fit, but they needed to rest. Nothing tired a man more than fighting, though chopping wood came surprisingly close. Clearchus peered along the lines, watching for the slightest weakness or broken formation. For all he had kept his manner light, rotating three thousand men in the heat of battle was murderously hard. Men died in the process, through inattention or a surge from an enemy when they thought a line was giving way and pressed forward. Yet if it was not done, the best soldiers in the world would fall. Everyone they met and killed was fresh. Only gods could fight all day without respite.

Clearchus watched the Spartans slow their brutal pace. The Persians ahead gave a howl as they saw hated enemies appearing to falter. Clearchus found himself snarling under his breath, wanting to cut the high-pitched excitement right out of them. He saw black-coated Immortals had made some sort of stand, but it would be Proxenus and Menon who would face them.

'I am in place, Clearchus,' Proxenus called over his shoulder. 'You go and rest those weary old legs of yours.'

'I'll stay. I've been wanting to watch Menon in an actual fight. He talks like a hero, after all.'

Menon the Thessalian turned and shouted, 'The enemy is in *front*, you Spartan bag of wind,' making Clearchus chuckle. He really did not like the man, but there was some truth in what he had said. If Menon fought as well as he complained and bickered, he would be a hero indeed – and Clearchus would forgive him the rest. He would not like him, but he would still take his hand and fill his cup of wine.

Across the field, Clearchus could hear the clash of arms, the sound of distant killing like a tremor in the air. There was death in that place, a sour taint in every breath. A battlefield was a place of constant fear, he knew. A good commander had to focus on the task before him and not lose his mind worrying about the rest of the battle. His men were capable of great feats, but they had to be hoarded and spent like a miser with his coins. Prince Cyrus had brought barely twelve thousand Greeks to Babylon. A great deal of the battle would be between Persian and Persian.

Cyrus saw his brother fall from his horse and exulted. Every undermining fear and weakness faded away. His personal guard still crashed horses into the maddened warriors around the Great King, but those actions went on almost outside his notice. Cyrus felt clear-minded and calm as his brother lay on his back and spat blood. Artaxerxes had been caught by surprise and struck at full gallop, his own horse barely in motion. A finger's width higher and Cyrus would have crushed his brother's throat and sent the crown of Achaemenid rolling in the dust.

The prince saw his brother's men turn their gaze to their master, though Artaxerxes was clearly dazed and unable to give orders. Cyrus looked up to see faces he knew, who recognised him in that moment. He became their focus, the man who had dared to strike the king. They lunged at him and, to his astonishment, he saw Parviz ride across to keep him safe. His manservant had disobeyed him to accompany his master. As Cyrus watched, Parviz used his old mare to block three imperial guards.

Cyrus did not see the javelin thrown. Someone in the

king's force had witnessed the attack on Artaxerxes and flung the spiked rod in rage. The weapon came arcing over and as Cyrus sensed it and looked up, it struck him in the cheek, breaking bones and wrenching him sideways. He could not understand what had happened. He knew he had triumphed, and yet the world spun around him and the sun jerked crazily across the sky as he fell, hitting hard. He heard another snap and began to struggle up. Blood poured from his own mouth then, from a cheek that was gashed and open. He could feel shards moving on his tongue, like slivers of broken pottery. He shook his head, but the motion only made it worse, so that the figures of advancing Immortals swam and wavered. He saw Parviz standing over him, refusing to step aside from those who rushed down upon them. Cyrus watched as the little man killed an imperial guard with the neat strokes of a fortress soldier. A moment later, Parviz was hacked apart, falling to stare across the sandy ground.

Cyrus put out his arm to raise himself up, then cried out when it would not take his weight. He stared at his right hand, unable to comprehend how it could hang limp and not grip the sword that lay before him on the sand and earth.

His hearing returned, though he had not realised he had been deafened for a time until it did. The light seemed too bright and he heard a great ringing of metal on metal. His guards had dismounted to protect him on the ground, hemming him in with their mounts all around him. His brother's Immortals roared like thunder in the hills. They came surging in and Cyrus saw men cut down, falling almost across him. He felt his senses returning, his sense of who and where he was. He needed just a moment to catch his breath, to find the strength to face his brother once more.

Cyrus saw Artaxerxes rise up and accept a sword from another. His brother's chin was red with blood he had spat out and he walked holding his side with his left hand, bowed over broken ribs. Cyrus struggled to rise again, but there was nothing in him. He saw his brother meet one of his guards head on, knocking the man's sword aside and hacking him down with three savage blows. Artaxerxes was the scholar! It made no sense for him to stalk so across the field. His brother had oiled his beard black and full over a panelled coat that Cyrus remembered their father having worn.

His brother came to stand over him and Cyrus drew a dagger from his belt, unseen. He tried to speak, but his mouth was too torn and full of blood. He began to move, but the king put a boot on his chest and pressed him down.

'Thank you, Brother,' Artaxerxes said, raising his sword. 'I do not think I was truly king before you stood against me. Can you understand? You have given me today . . . a great gift.'

On the last word, Cyrus moved, but he was too slow. Artaxerxes struck down. The king's sword chopped into Cyrus' throat and cut almost through.

Beyond that first pain, Cyrus knew nothing more as his brother hacked at him again and again, then wrenched his head free and raised it to show those who stood in horror all around. The eyes turned and the mouth moved as if in prayer, but Cyrus was blind and dumb.

Artaxerxes turned his brother's head to look at it, staring in wonder for a time before kissing the lips almost tenderly. The battle was still being fought, but he was not concerned. The only life that had mattered was that of Cyrus. Artaxerxes had taken it, exactly as he had promised his father he would, so many years before. The king found he had tears of pride and memory in his eyes. Even his mother could not deny he had acted within his rights as king. Artaxerxes had been challenged and he had gone out himself, in armour, to meet that threat. Truly, Cyrus had made him a king on that day, as mere blood and inheritance never could. On impulse, Artaxerxes knelt to pray, holding a closed fist up to his mouth as he bowed his head. In that moment, he had never been more convinced of the favour of God. Then he rose and tossed his younger brother's head to the captain of his Immortals.

'Put that on a spear and carry it high. Let them see! Call for the surrender of all those who came here with Cyrus. Advance on their camp. The battle is over. Give thanks to God! We are delivered! Victory is ours.'

The cry went up around him, swelling into a great roar that deafened as it delighted. The king wrenched suddenly at his breastplate, where it had buckled and pressed him. It came away in two pieces, a crack running from his neck to his waist. Artaxerxes had to enlist two of his men to help him back to the saddle. His brother had struck him a terrible blow and he knew ribs were broken. Blood still pooled in his mouth, though he thought it was from biting his tongue in the fall rather than some internal wound. He hoped so. It would not do to collapse at that point, with his brother's head on a spear at his side. It eased his ribs to be able to hunch over in the saddle and he closed his eyes in relief as the horns sounded. If his father could see, Artaxerxes knew he would be proud.

Clearchus was ready to bring the Spartans to the front of the Greek square once more. Menon had done well enough as the sun rose to noon, though it was the regiments with Proxenus who had fought more like Spartans, at least while the real ones stood behind. Clearchus had congratulated them on their form. They had advanced some sixteen hundred paces since the Spartans had fallen back to rest, not one step of it uncontested. Clearchus tried not to think of the numbers of intact regiments ahead of them. Prince Cyrus and the Persians under Ariaeus had their own battles to fight. Clearchus could only hope it would undermine imperial morale to know they were being attacked from the flank, from within. There had not been time for the Greek square to reach the king himself before the armies clashed, but Clearchus knew they had torn through thousands and surely ruined the advance. Even so, there was no clear path out.

Imperials in white or black coats pushed in on all sides. Those ahead fell back, with every attempt to hold and rally quickly overwhelmed. Cyrus had said the Persians practised marching drills, but only rarely worked with the weapons they carried. That lack of skill showed as his men broke through over and over, soldiers against farmers with blades, terror spreading ahead as line after line decided they would not be the ones to stop the Greek advance.

Clearchus assumed it could not last. There had to be one officer or one regiment who would choose to stand and fight to the death. As soon as the Greek advance was blocked, he knew others would coalesce around them. He had seen a wasp smothered once, rolled into a ball by a thousand bees. Not one individual bee could match the invader, not even a dozen of them – but by sheer weight and savagery, they tore the wasp to pieces even so. He watched for that moment as he brought his Spartans to the front once again, refreshed.

Ahead of them, Imperials paled at the sight of red cloaks and bronze shields coming to the fore. They braced themselves and began to die. The pace suddenly increased and Clearchus began to grin as he marched forward with the rest. Despite the sheer insanity of their position, against every rule of battle he had ever learned, some sort of victory was in their grasp. He could feel it. As far as he could tell, they had not lost a hundred men since the battle began, but had killed and broken thousands. If the Persians could not do better against their armour and their skills, the day could still be won, even against the largest army he had ever seen. He felt hope bloom in him and he wiped sweat from his eyes when it stung. Somewhere across the field, horns began to sound and voices were raised. Clearchus cupped his ear to listen, hoping they called victory.

King Artaxerxes rode the lines with his brother's head held high. The aftermath of a battle was chaotic and his brother's men would fear his vengeance. They were right to, he vowed to himself. He would oversee the mass execution of regiments who had dared to stand against the crown, at least when they had surrendered and been properly disarmed and bound. He felt his heart swell with pride. His ribs ached worse than he could believe, but his mood soared and was light. Horns blew and there was no mistaking the Immortal regiments in black or the cavalry in white all calling for the forces of Cyrus to surrender. The head on a spear worked wonders, though not one in a thousand could have told the swollen, battered thing had ever belonged to a royal prince.

The battlefield had widened in the manoeuvres, so that the far edges were hours apart. Yet the news spread as the Great King arced around the regiments like a comet, safe from their javelins and stones as he rode in the midst of hundreds of victorious horsemen, all yelling in triumph or pointing their swords at regiments who had betrayed the royal house, promising retribution to horrified soldiers. Many of Cyrus' men had not even come to blows, but they stood condemned and trembling as Artaxerxes himself cantered across the field, with royal banners streaming beside him.

*

General Ariaeus had been in the thick of fighting from the first clash of ranks. His hair was wet with sweat under his helmet, though he dared not take a moment to feel the air, not with so many archers and slingers hoping for just such a prize as he.

Ariaeus had put aside all thought of the size and strength of the enemy. His loyalty and his life were pledged to Prince Cyrus. The only oath he had ever broken had been the one to the man's brother. He still wrestled with that and he could only redeem it if Cyrus became king and forgave him. The world was as simple as Ariaeus could make it, far simpler than Orontas had believed.

The battle had not gone well, not from the first moments. Ariaeus had watched in mounting concern as the Greeks had raced off against the swarm of horsemen and infantry under Tissaphernes. The general had seen orders go back and forth, so he hoped it was not some personal vendetta. Before Ariaeus could adjust his own formation in response to having his right flank left naked, the prince himself had galloped across the face of his Persian regiments, his royal guard barely keeping up.

Ariaeus knew well that a leader could change his plans on sight of the enemy, even had to, if the conditions were different or the terrain revealed some advantage he had not known before. Warfare was not for plodding men but for those with sharp wits, who could see a risk and take it while the enemy were still asleep. Yet he had seen an entire battleplan torn up and thrown on the fire in the first few hours of daylight. Instead of being part of fast manoeuvres and sudden strikes, he found himself in sole command of the Persian centre – a hundred thousand men who looked to him to keep them alive. He'd sat his mount with a dark expression as the Imperials marched closer, but he had kept the formations and filled the gaps, edging his new flank towards the river, though it thinned his ranks further. Damn Clearchus, for leaving them so exposed! There was every chance the royal Persian army would fold around both flanks that day – and that would be the end, without a doubt.

The fighting began in savage violence, and for an age Ariaeus was able to watch a struggle of leviathans, the populations of entire cities hacking and spearing one another along a line that stretched into the distance like the shore of a dark sea. Dust rose in vast clouds, kicked up from the sandy ground. The sky blackened in spasms as arrows and javelins flew back and forth between the heaving armies. The sound was immense, the breathing of a beast as they pushed forward and were driven back. The killing went on and on and Ariaeus looked up to see the royal eagle banners on the move.

In an expanse between struggling regiments of Persians too mixed by then to know friend from enemy, onto the sandy ground rode Artaxerxes. At the king's side, a guard looked up at the spear he held, his white teeth visible at a distance as the fellow laughed and cheered.

Ariaeus grew cold as he understood what he was seeing. They carried the head of Cyrus, high above the ranks. A sense of sick horror washed through him, but then he stared with new eyes at the dusty battlefield. With Cyrus killed, the forces Ariaeus commanded suddenly looked smaller. The Greeks were already lost, as far beyond sight and recall as if they had never been.

Ariaeus closed his eyes for a moment, wishing Orontas was still in command, though the silent plea diminished him. It broke his heart to open his eyes and see the destruction still going on. Cyrus was dead and nothing was good in the world.

'Sound retreat!' he called suddenly. 'Pull back in good

order to the west and south. The prince is dead. There is no honour now on this field.'

'Yes, general,' his messengers said, appalled.

As they began to turn, he snapped at them once more.

'Tell the men not to run! The king will kill us all if we do not withdraw now. Get out in good order and we may live to see another day. Run and we will all be lost. Be sure they understand.'

The messengers raced away, darting through lines of soldiers. Ariaeus continued to watch the imperial army breaking his regiments into blood and bone. It was over. All they could do was try to survive.

With his back deliberately straight, Ariaeus turned his horse away from the fighting.

'Slowly now, lads. March with me – with your heads high. Our cause is lost, but we are not.'

The closest ranks were relieved not to have to take another step towards that victorious enemy, already howling their delight as more and more heard the news.

PART TWO

'What age am I waiting to reach? I will not get any
older, if tomorrow I hand myself over to the enemy.'

Xenophon

20

On the plain of Cunaxa, by the river Euphrates, dust lay fine in the air. It had been raised by the feet of hundreds of thousands marching, kicking and bleeding into the sandy ground. Clearchus halted the Greek square when he found himself unopposed for a time. At first, he thought it was because his men had crashed through another Persian regiment and reached open ground, but he could hear cheering somewhere off to the left, a thin and distant sound that could have come from either side.

For the first time that day, he lost his sense of the battleground. For the first time in his life, he wished he had a horse to help him see further than his men, already looking to him for orders in the lull. Fighting was still going on around them. Horns were being blown over on their right, which made no sense. Yet no one advanced on the Greeks. Imperial regiments marched past at the edges of their vision, but did not swing towards them. Behind the Greeks was a great plume of dust and annihilation: all the dead and dying who had already crossed their path. There would be no second challenge from those.

Clearchus rubbed his jaw, staring in all directions and hoping for something to become clear before he had to tell his men he had no idea what was going on. He had broken the Persian left wing, though he had no doubt some of the cavalry still licked their wounds nearby. He'd turned across the face of the imperial army to lunge for the king's position, but then he and his men had found themselves lost in an ocean of men, so that they had to defend on all sides. The Greeks had trudged and fought for hours – and killed countless numbers. In a flickering glance, Clearchus thought he had ten thousand still, despite the dead. His Spartans had held the leading edge for longest, but they'd lost the smallest number. He felt his chest swell at that. Each man was known to him, so that each one left behind on the field was like losing a brother or a son. They did not overvalue themselves, he thought in pride. Clearchus reminded himself to mention it to Menon. The Thessalian still trudged along further back, glowering away like the sour old goat he was.

'Orders, general?' Proxenus called on his right hand.

Clearchus almost barked a reply, as he might have done if they were still under attack. Yet ahead and to the sides, great squares moved away from them, the moment they were close enough to recognise banners or the red cloaks of the front ranks. The dust had grown thick in places, so that Clearchus felt a stab of panic almost. To lose a sense of the battlefield was a common experience for men fighting for their lives, even for the generals trying to keep them in formation. To do so in the middle of the largest enemy force in the entire world was an error that could mean their destruction.

Clearchus saw Menon pointing at something over on their flank. The Spartan set his jaw and squinted, but he could see nothing out there where the dust was thickest. He had the sudden sense that only chaos swirled around them. With a grunt, he knew he had to stop and get his bearings once more.

'Ares protect us here!' he growled, then raised his voice to the parade-ground bellow the men expected from him. 'In *three* . . . paces! Square to halt! Hellenes . . . ! Halt!'

The Spartans crashed to a stop on a left pace and brought their right legs down hard alongside. All ranks stood to attention, with sandy air spiralling around them. A breeze came from the north then, bringing the pale dust against their faces so that they had to blink. Panting men found grit in their mouths and cursed softly. The land itself seemed against them in that moment.

Clearchus tensed at the sound of horses, but he knew the men approaching, at least by sight. He struggled to remember their names but could not bring them to mind. Both had been part of the fighting, that much was obvious. They were marked with blood, though it did not seem to be their own. The nobleman had a grim look, Clearchus noted, an expression the Spartan knew very well. The other was shaking his head in beaming delight, quite unable to believe what he had seen and done that day. Clearchus also knew that reaction, and was hard-pressed not to grin at a young man who had discovered he enjoyed war.

'I won't hang on your foot as if I'm begging for alms,' he called to the two mounted Greeks. 'Dismount. Tell me what's happening. Forgive me, I cannot recall your names.'

'Xenophon of Athens, general,' the first one said as he swung down and took a grip on the reins. 'My smiling companion is Hephaestus.'

'What of the battle? The prince? In all this dust, my messengers have not reached me for an age.'

Clearchus glanced at the sun, which was growing red as it crept to the horizon. They had been riding and fighting all day and were exhausted. Only the prospect of another attack at any moment was keeping them awake.

'Prince Cyrus fell, general,' Xenophon said. He turned away rather than see the other man's hopes crumble. 'His brother took his head. I saw that much before I caught up with you. After that, the fighting . . . well, you know.'

Clearchus gave no sign of the grief and shame that rushed

over him. The entire Greek force needed steady leadership in that moment. The news was already spreading through them and so he pressed his own reaction aside and smiled, though he looked older in that moment by ten years.

'I do, son, yes. You've done well today. That matters.'

'Does it, general?' Xenophon asked. His voice was bitter, and in reply Clearchus smiled at him.

'It means you're alive to fight again tomorrow. Which matters to me, as I have only a few horses.'

The general looked around them, seeing once more the dark shapes of marching regiments in the distance, like pieces moving on a board where he no longer understood the rules. He felt his stomach contract at the thought. His Greeks were far from home, surrounded by the greatest military force the world could assemble – led by a god-emperor with every reason to want them cut into small pieces. Clearchus chuckled to himself.

'The gods do like to test us, don't they?' he said.

Xenophon looked warily at him, clearly wondering if he'd lost his mind.

'Mount up, lads,' Clearchus went on. 'We are on a hostile plain, with enemies all around. All we can do at this moment is march back to our camp. I have a little folding desk there that I do not want to see gracing a Persian tent tomorrow. Now, the setting sun is directly behind us, so we have been turned to face east again. The order is to turn about – and march fast and hard to the camp. If anyone gets in our way, charge and kill them.'

Across the Greek forces, captains and pentekosters echoed the order, turning the square in place.

'Spartans to the front!' Clearchus bellowed.

Menon called something in angry reply, but it was almost a ritual between them by then. Clearchus made a note to punch him in the face if they both survived – or buy him a drink, one or the other. Some of Menon's men hooted as the Spartans came through to take up the lead once more. No, Clearchus decided. He would knock the bastard right out.

The Greeks were weary by then. It showed in stumbling steps, in the way spears dragged on the ground or were leaned upon as shepherds used a staff. Only the Spartans held theirs alongside, ready to attack. It was why Clearchus had put them to the front, though they'd borne the brunt of fighting all day. They were fitter by far than the others, in his estimation. That mattered most at the end of a battle, when men felt their limbs grow heavy and their feet become slow, so that they shuffled along where once they had walked like leopards.

In tight square formation, they marched across the battle-field, heading west. Dust clouds still roiled and spread, hiding the enemy from view. At times, the Greeks seemed to walk alone through a vast and empty landscape.

Clearchus and Proxenus looked for the Persian regiments that had come to that plain with Cyrus. They expected to encounter General Ariaeus at any moment as they crossed to where he had stood earlier that day. Yet the field lay empty before them.

Clearchus kept a count of paces in his head on the way back, though he knew such tallies were notoriously unreli-able in a running battle. He still couldn't work out where he'd ended up as he turned towards the camp. More than ten thou-sand were still there, unprotected, waiting for them. Many of his men had friends and lovers amongst them, but Clearchus had the responsibility. He could not leave them to be slaugh-tered, raped or taken as slaves, though he had considered it. That was the fate of those who lost battles, and Prince Cyrus had certainly lost, if the news was true. Clearchus clenched his jaw, refusing to examine the swing from triumph to disaster while it was still so fresh. His Greeks had gone through the enemy. He had been untouchable, the dream of every officer who had ever trained men – to achieve such a superiority of arms that you were unstoppable in the field. To have victory snatched away in the moment of that joy was utterly brutal. He could not think of it, for all a small voice within told him it was his task to do so. For once, he refused the greater vision and concentrated on one thing, like a junior officer. He would march to the camp. He would save the camp followers – and only after that would he consider their awful position, thousands of miles from home, surrounded by the enemy.

No one came to block their path in an hour or so of marching. The dust was beginning to settle around them, though the sun was setting as well, threatening to leave them blind. The two Athenian horsemen had rounded up half a dozen mounted scouts. All the riders of the prince's personal guard had vanished and, apart from those few, the entire Greek force was on foot.

Clearchus almost called a charge when he caught sight of shields and armour ahead, but it was the battle line from that morning, or the remnants of it. Men who had gone to the plain of Cunaxa with pride and courage and the sun before them lay sightless in the dust, their skin already yellow and cold. Gingerly, with winces and shaking heads, the Greeks had to step over lines of the dead. That point was where the Persian regiments of Cyrus had first crashed together with those of King Artaxerxes. The dead were indistinguishable, though they'd carried other banners and come to that field to serve different brothers. They lay together, so tangled in death that no man could have told them apart.

One or two still moaned, their voices hoarse or reduced to a whisper. They called for water, though the Greeks had none and would not have offered the precious resource if they had. One man called for them to kill him and his prayer was answered by a Corinthian, with a slash across his throat. None of them would forget that silent part of the march, barely a mile, but over an earth strewn with strips and hills and hollows of the dead. They saw fingers lying on the sand. One of the Greeks picked up a hand on impulse, but his companions cried out in disgust and told him to throw it back. He did so with the utmost reluctance. Many more gathered fallen knives or helmets, especially if they had lost their own. Trophies were a part of war and Clearchus had to threaten them with execution on the spot when he saw some dip down to wrestle rings off dead men.

One of the few moments of satisfaction was when they came across a group of Persian scavengers engaged in the same stripping of the dead. The men looked up in horror as they realised the forces marching towards them were not their own, but the Greek enemy coming back out of the dust. Clearchus did not have to give an order. His Spartan front rank rolled right over them, leaving them with those they had tried to rob. Yet he feared the same would be happening at the camp and he pushed the men faster.

Twilight was upon them by the time they saw carts and tents. The camp lay some miles behind the battlefield and he and his men had marched right through their first steps of the day, an age and a tragedy before.

Their position had not gone unremarked, though no new challenge had come. The Persians were not short of horses and Clearchus had seen them riding close, counting numbers, gauging what strength remained. They'd vanished then for a time, no doubt to report the presence of the Greeks still on the field to their master. He'd set his jaw. There was nothing he could do about that. More horsemen had appeared after a while, cantering along the edges at a distance of a couple of hundred paces. They did not seem to fear archers or slingers. Clearchus would have loved to charge them, but with his men on foot, it would have been an exercise in exhaustion. They needed to reach the camp for water and food – and anyone alive they could protect. The rest had to wait.

The Spartan swallowed a lump in his throat when he saw the camp growing ahead of them. Ten thousand men, women and children – a town in the wilderness, all waiting for news of a great victory and a new king. It was not to be.

The air was clearer there, with the fighting all behind them, though the light was fading. Clearchus felt a vast sense of relief as he marched towards fires and tents. He could not let himself think about the prince, not then. The pain was too recent and the loss too great.

His head came up suddenly at the sound of horns. Over the hills ahead of his marching forces came a dark line of Persian horsemen, with exactly the idea he'd had. They didn't know the prince's gold was all gone. They imagined the camp contained the wealth of a royal house. Others would take the young and the comely as slaves. The slaughter would be terrible for the rest.

The Spartans stretched aching legs in the gloom and took a firmer grip on their swords. The enemy cavalry would reach the camp before them and yet they could not fly, nor sprint to waste their strength and arrive too weak to fight. All they could do was lope on at the best speed possible, while screams rang out ahead.

Clearchus saw the two young Athenians lead the scouts out, drawing swords as they galloped through a narrow stream and in amongst the tents of the camp.

'Good lads,' Clearchus muttered, feeling his chest ache and his legs grow heavy. He had marched and fought all day. He shrugged as he went. It didn't matter. Only death would stop him and that came for everyone.

'Ready spears! Ready shields!' he called to his Spartans.

Sweat ran in rivers from him, making him shine, as heat burned in his lungs. The Greeks answered with a great coughing roar as they reached the outskirts of the camp, filling each lane between the tents and sighting the enemy.

The Persian horsemen had been enjoying the best sport they could have hoped to see. A camp without defenders, in the middle of flat, dry ground. They'd galloped in as hunters and whooped to one another. Then they saw the red-cloaks coming at them between the tents and found they could not ride clear. Wherever they turned, there were more soldiers, hacking swords into their legs, throwing spears that snatched companions away. It was indeed a slaughter, but not the one they had expected.

Clearchus heard Persian officers roar new orders, calling their men back from what they now believed was an ambush. Both forces had approached the camp from opposite sides; the Persian horsemen withdrew the way they had come. They'd found no gold, but they drove small groups of shrieking women and children as they went, trying to shepherd them back to a greater force. For their part, the prisoners darted away whenever they saw a gap in the chaos. They called for help at the tops of their voices and Clearchus drove his Greeks on through the camp, forcing them to keep moving. He had no idea how many enemy there were. For all he knew, a hundred thousand horsemen lay over the hills around them.

Only the shock of attack kept his momentum. He drove hard against Persians still trying to capture slaves, breaking up the small groups. Many of the women were speared by those who laid hands on them, rather than be allowed to escape back to their rescuers. It was a bloody business and the darkness was swallowing them all and making each moment harder than the last.

Clearchus found himself walking alongside Proxenus, perhaps because they were of a similar age, while younger men raced ahead. They were both panting like bellows, each as red-faced as the other. They exchanged a look that was part pain, part amusement. They could barely stand – and yet they could not stop, so they went on.

Ahead, Proxenus saw two young women of surpassing beauty dragged out of a tent by a trio of black-clad soldiers. One of the Imperials was festooned with gold cups and jewellery he had found. He took one look at the two Greeks advancing and mounted up, digging in his heels.

Half a dozen Persian horsemen rushed past in the next lane. Clearchus groaned as he heard them shouting out what they had seen. They would swing back for such a glimpse of wealth. Before they could be reinforced, he attacked, batting aside the sword of the Persian who lunged at him. The soldier was forced to release his grip on a woman's hair when Clearchus hacked through his forearm. The man screamed then, the sound quickly cut off.

The other woman ran away into the darkness, but the dark-haired one stood, panting wildly, her eyes showing the whites as she rubbed her wrists in a nervous gesture.

'Prince Cyrus will reward you for saving me,' she said.

Clearchus sighed, feeling the wave of grief and anger rise once more, threatening to drown him.

'No he won't,' he replied.

He saw the woman's eyes widen and her breathing grow shallow. She took a step away from him and he reached out to her automatically.

'Tell me your name, girl. Mine is Clearchus.'

'Pallakis,' she said. She half-turned from him, checking the way was clear. He knew she would bolt.

'There are Persians back there, Pallakis. They will not treat you well if you run to them. Do you understand me? I came back for the camp followers. You can come with us.'

He watched as she struggled with the desire to run from bloody knives and horrors all around her. He remembered seeing her before, wearing filmy gauzes that revealed as much as they hid her form. With Cyrus away from the camp, Pallakis wore a simple dress of white and gold that ended at her thighs, belted at the waist. She wore strap sandals but no jewellery, nor paint beyond a dark line around her eyes. Clearchus preferred the look of her day off, perhaps because it reminded him of the women at home.

The men of Proxenus and Menon still tore into every tent, killing any Persian who had thought to shelter there until they had passed. It was savage work, with muffled screams and the sounds of struggle always close around them. Clearchus saw the young woman shudder as she looked at him, her gaze suddenly fixed.

'Can you save me, Clearchus?' she said.

The Spartan knew very well that she was a woman used to manipulation. It was a simple appeal, without obvious artifice or flirtation. Perhaps that was why she had been a mistress to a royal prince, Clearchus thought. It did not make the appeal any less powerful.

'I will try, Lady Pallakis,' he said.

'I am not a noblewoman,' she replied immediately. 'I am a companion to . . .' She broke off, unable to finish.

Menon came trotting back through the lines of tents, the general failing to hide his appreciation of the beautiful woman, or his irritation when he turned to Clearchus.

275

'I am sorry to interrupt you, general. Some of us are busy securing the camp, if you remember.'

'Pallakis, this is General Menon,' Clearchus said. 'He is from Thessaly, a northern part of Greece. They are said to favour their goats there, if you understand me.'

Menon closed his mouth on a reply as two of his men came rushing up to report. They too noticed the young woman, and Clearchus saw how Pallakis put a hand up and across, as if she wished to cover herself. Her thin white dress gave very little protection. He raised his eyes for a moment and undid the clasp that held his cloak. With a swirl, he draped the red cloth around her. Pallakis looked suspiciously at him, though she clutched it close.

'I think perhaps the price is too high, Spartan,' she said softly.

Clearchus saw despair in her as she contemplated her fate. As a companion to Cyrus she had been treated gently, given anything she wanted. That had been snatched away in an instant. On all sides, there were men who would happily spend an hour with her. Clearchus wondered if she would choose one to keep her safe from the rest. He thought of his daughters and sighed, noticing anew the way Menon was looking at her. The man seemed to sense his disapproval.

'Why should *you* be claiming her, anyway?' Menon said. 'You think being the leader gives you the right to take her for yourself, just like that?'

Clearchus had to repress a spasm of anger. He found Menon's bitterness either amusing or irritating, but they had lost the day and he was weary. Sometimes, his choices were simple.

Without a word, Clearchus advanced on Menon, surprising the man as he was about to speak again. Though he said nothing, Clearchus drove the general back a step with his chest, knocking into him.

'You can challenge me if you like, Thessalian,' Clearchus growled. 'Until then, go about your work. Gather the camp followers and ready your men to move. I will not wait here to be discovered by any more of the enemy. Do you understand my order, general? Can you carry it out? If the answer is no, tell me the name of your second in command and have him brought here. I want him to see what happens to you. I will not *waste* a lesson!'

He said the last in growing anger, letting Menon see just a whisper of the fury Clearchus felt at the way the day had gone. The wave would crash down on them all when it was quiet, but the day had not ended, not then.

Menon stalked away without another word, though he glared at Pallakis as if he might say something. She watched the Spartan snap orders to half a dozen others, and around them something like calm returned. The Persian cavalry had been driven off, so that at least the screaming had stopped. In its place came noises she knew rather well – the sounds of a camp being made ready to move. Each of the lanes between tents filled with running men and women, urged on by Greek soldiers. Tents became bales of cloth and spars of wood in just moments. Carts were loaded, but after a time Proxenus gave orders to leave the bulk of them. They had no idea when the next force of Persian cavalry would appear. Wailing began as men and women were prodded and ordered into movement, leaving their treasures behind. There was no justice to it. Some families kept all they had, while others went empty-handed and tearful.

Clearchus seemed almost to have forgotten her, though she stood at his shoulder and wore his cloak. Pallakis prayed silently for the soul of Cyrus, already gone on its way. He had been a decent man, the third love of her life. She thought of the jewels he had given her and whether she would be allowed to keep them.

'Am I under your protection, Clearchus?' she asked.

The Spartan turned to her, seeing her fear.

'Yes, you are,' he said without hesitation. 'If Menon or anyone else gives you trouble, tell them you served the prince, that you were his woman. I will stand for his honour when he can't. He was my friend.'

'So . . . am I to be . . . yours?' she said in a small voice.

Clearchus had already turned away after speaking. He sighed.

'Pallakis, we are barely ten thousand men. There are perhaps a similar number in the camp. Around us on the plain and the hills are hundreds of thousands – too many to count. They are all loyal to a Persian king who is our avowed enemy, do you understand? A man who knows very well by now that we came all the way from Sardis to take his head.'

'You think we are going to die?' she asked him.

'I think . . .' He saw her fear and changed tack. 'Oh, the Great King is not a fool. He knows we are mercenaries. Perhaps he will buy our service, eh? No, I meant . . . your worries are misplaced. I have two daughters, Pallakis, both close to your age. That changes a man, if you understand me. From a young fool into a wise fellow, beloved of all he meets. Except for Menon, as you might have seen. That man is eaten up by his own anger. I cannot like him.'

'May I go to my tent, Clearchus, to see if my jewels are still there?'

The general summoned a passing Spartan with a low whistle.

'Go quickly with Lady Pallakis. Protect her with your life,' he said. She did not object to the title a second time, accepting it as it was meant.

Clearchus watched her go. Prince Cyrus had always had good taste, he thought. The woman was exquisite. Why did she have to be Greek? That dark hair and fine skin was . . . He caught himself, making a growling sound as he struggled to control his thoughts. He had been taken from his parents' home to the training ground at the age of seven. By twelve, he had been a wolf to other boys. One cloak a year was all they had been given. As his old tunic had rotted away, he'd often gone naked beneath and hardly bathed for months at a time. He missed the weight of the cloak from around his shoulders, though he felt lighter, as if she had taken some of the day's pain with her.

Proxenus appeared once more from some way off, jingling along to where Clearchus stood in thought. The Spartan watched him come, each of them assessing the strength that remained in the other. There was no humour then. Darkness had come and its embrace had saved them. The morning would reveal an enemy still intent on their deaths.

'Some of those Persian riders got clear,' Proxenus said. 'Our archers have no shafts any longer and no way to get more. I couldn't get slingers out in time.'

'So the Great King will know we are at the camp. He will know exactly where we are before the sun rises. I think there is a chance tomorrow is our last day, Proxenus.'

'Is that Clearchus, or Menon's voice I hear?' Proxenus said, his eyebrows rising. 'I thought Spartans could not be broken?'

Clearchus chuckled.

'You are right, of course. We should move out tonight. They will expect us to head back on our own path. The west will be blocked, I think. It is what I would do. North, then, is where we will go.'

'Good,' Proxenus replied. 'Your orders are to move the men north. For the camp followers to accompany us, with whatever water and food they can carry.' He relaxed a fraction. 'Menon still wants to leave them. He says they will slow us down.'

'And he is right,' Clearchus said. 'They will. My friend, I cannot see a way out of this.'

To his surprise, Proxenus gripped his shoulder, a gesture unusual between them.

'This was a bad day. When you have slept, you'll be restored. The problems will be the same, but you will be better able to face them. I will speak to that general Clearchus tomorrow. He will be full of ideas, I have no doubt.'

Clearchus smiled.

'You are a good man,' he said.

21

The night had not been without alarms. Twice, the rumble of horsemen had seemed so close they'd braced for an attack before it dwindled once again. Vast forces were either out hunting them or surrounding them in the desert. It was hard not to imagine an encircling noose, tightening slowly as the moon crept across the sky.

Away from the old camp, Clearchus had been reminded that the men, women and children who had come out with the army could not march like one. As he tried to put distance between where he knew they had been seen and where they would eventually spend the night, a great tail began to stretch behind the square of his soldiers. Many of the camp followers were still stunned by the reverse in their fortunes. They staggered and stumbled along, women carrying children on their hips, men burdened by items they had snatched up, even if there were no longer carts to carry them. It was a mess, a wrenching away from all they had known.

For the first hour, Clearchus had contented himself sending men back to that comet's tail of people to urge them to greater pace. When that only resulted in angry voices raised and a woman shrieking at one of his Spartans, trying to make him carry her young son, Clearchus halted the entire group. In the darkness, he gave new orders. His men understood the stakes and they did not complain. It was Menon who reminded anyone who would listen that he had advised them not to bring so many. They did not need slaves, he said. To have any chance at all, they needed to get as far away from the Persian army as possible.

Clearchus sent a thousand Spartans and a thousand Corinthians to the rear. The people of the camp had to march then with Greeks breathing down their necks behind, ready to force them on. Some at the back were more than willing to use spears as staves, striking at anyone fool enough to complain. They marched in that way for hours, until the camp followers were made bold by misery, calling out that they had to rest or die, that the children could not go on.

Clearchus gave the order and they sank down where they stood. He bit his lip as he struggled against weariness, selecting guards from among the youngest. He tried to spare his Spartans from remaining awake, as they would be more use to him fresh, when the sun rose. The general yawned and started when he found Pallakis at his shoulder, holding his cloak out to him.

'My lady?' he said.

She bowed her head.

'It is yours, general. I found a blanket when I went to my tent.'

He accepted it from her hand, with private gratitude. A man missed his best cloak when it was gone.

'I hope a blanket is all you took. I will be stripping the camp tomorrow, my lady. Half the followers are too burdened to march a full day. I saw one man trotting along with a saddle on his shoulder! How far do they think they will get with their worldly goods on their backs?'

'You left half the carts behind, Clearchus. They are desperate and afraid,' she said. 'Some of them have lost everything. Can you blame them?'

'For getting themselves killed trying to carry a favourite chair into the desert? Yes, I can,' he said.

She moved behind him and he spun on her, taking her wrist in his hand.

'What are you doing?'

'I thought . . . Cyrus used to want me to rub his neck. You are tired, Clearchus. We need you to be sharp, more than anyone.'

He cleared his throat, embarrassed to have snapped at her.

'Right. Yes, that would be good. Thank you.'

He put his cloak on the sandy ground and lay on his elbows, slightly raised. Pallakis knelt beside him, working her hands into the muscles of his neck and shoulders. He was surprised at how painful it was. He'd assumed a woman who had been mistress to Cyrus would have been expert at such things, or perhaps it was that the muscles there were just as sore as the rest of him. He had fought all day and marched for hours . . . The Spartan was asleep before he knew what was happening, snoring gently as Pallakis looked down on him, her hands tracing old scars with a lighter touch. He was a handsome man, she thought. His age was hard to tell, though she would have guessed at fifty or there-abouts. If he had been twenty years younger, she might have thought about blowing those ashes back to life.

He began to snore more loudly as she returned to her blanket. Most of the camp followers lay in family groups, or centred around a cart. They clung to one another in their fear and she could see eyes following her progress as she crossed the camp. She had no family, of course. Everything Pallakis had known had been lost in a single day. She curled up on sandy ground and put an arm across her face, so that they would not hear her weep.

In the morning, Pallakis woke with a start of fear, but the gruff voices she heard were those of Greeks rousing them all to work. She yawned and stretched, coming to her feet to see hoplite soldiers loping along the edges of the camp in groups of fifty, each one led by a pentekoster. Some of them were heading off into the hills, seeking higher ground. Many more were among the men and women of the camp, directing them to a particular flank to empty their bladders and bowels. Pallakis saw many people urinating where they woke, so that the air became thick with the odour – or perhaps it was the smell of fear. She could see nervous strain on every pinched face, and hear it in the wails of sobbing children. A few had lost their fathers in the fighting the day before, but for the most part, they were just reacting to the grim faces and anger in those around them.

They had no spades to dig a toilet trench, so thousands left little piles of excrement where they stood. It was not a pleasant sight and the smell was such that Pallakis was only pleased they would be leaving the spot behind when they moved on. For a time, they would be nomads, until the king's army crashed down on them or they died of thirst. Water seemed more scarce than meat, as the herd of goats, rams and asses had been driven with them. Some of the remaining carts were being broken up for firewood as she stared across the camp. They would eat, but her mouth was sore and dry.

It was not long before the soldiers shouted for them to move or be left behind. Pallakis had to smile when she saw one young man walking bowed over by a huge pack of tools more suited to a mule. The man's wife was unburdened, but still found time to frown at the prince's mistress when she passed by and smiled at her children. That was an expression Pallakis was beginning to see more often. It seemed that the prince's death allowed a few in the camp to show how they despised the woman who had warmed his bed. In reply,

Pallakis only set her jaw and showed them nothing of her loneliness.

Clearchus knew his business, that was obvious. As Pallakis strode along, lost in the midst of thousands who were strangers to her, she saw Greek soldiers making a solid rank behind, driving them like cattle as they had done before. The people of the camp had not been told a destination. Each hour that passed sharpened their needs, so that voices were raised in complaint. The sun rose, pitiless, drying their throats further. Even those who suffered most could not do much more than croak for water.

They reached a river before noon. Pallakis had no bowl or jug, but in a daze, she clambered down to where the waters had cut a cleft in the land. Kneeling on the edges, she drank from cupped hands, over and over, as if she could never be full again. Yet as soon as she moved away, she felt the first whisper of thirst return. Sweat glistened on her skin and her hands were stained with orange mud. She could no longer run fingers through her hair and just tied it back into a great sheaf, more like straw than the glossy fall she usually knew.

Still the sun beat at them, but they did not go on. Some sort of discussion was taking place on one edge of the group. Pallakis moved with a drift of people, heading together to hear and see what was happening. She was not surprised to see Clearchus there, with the other officers in a group around him. They looked to the Spartan to save them, trusting in the legend. She prayed to the gods he could bring them through. As she stood there watching, she saw Clearchus look straight at her. He raised his hand in greeting, so that some turned to see who had caught his attention. Pallakis did not look round when she heard whispered comments at her back. She had no protector in that place.

One of the younger men stood to listen to Clearchus with

reins wrapped around his arm. A fine horse draped its head over his shoulder, looking for a treat in his closed fist. No doubt the animal was as hungry as any of them, Pallakis thought. She saw the young man notice her and she smiled at him. She liked horses. They were freedom of a sort. Certainly more freedom than she had ever known on foot. The young man smiled back and Pallakis made herself look away, realising she had to be careful.

'Water we have, food we have,' Clearchus said to those around him. 'We'll find villages as we go further, I do not doubt. It is true this is a hard landscape, but we can walk out of it. Shelter – no, there's not much of that. Though I see no sign of a storm coming. I think I would welcome one if I did, just to feel clean once more.'

'We cannot defend so many,' Menon said, not caring if he was overheard by the crowd. 'Alone, we could have force-marched beyond the range of the Persian king in a week. With ten thousand camp followers, you have killed us all.'

Clearchus took a step towards the Thessalian.

'In time of war,' Clearchus said, 'how would you have me respond to a man who weakens morale?'

'You were the chosen leader of Prince Cyrus, who lies headless on the plain behind us. Did the gods say you should lead us always, Clearchus? Is it because you are a Spartan, their favourite? I say we should elect a new leader. I put myself forward – and I will take only the fittest and fastest of the camp followers. Do not grumble at me!' He snapped the last to the men around him, growling in dissent. 'Clearchus has given us a choice between leaving some behind – or the death of every man, woman and child here.'

'You underestimate us,' Clearchus said. 'But if you wish, we should hold a vote. If you are unhappy with my leadership.'

Menon glanced quickly around him, seeing immediately

how that vote would go in the angry expressions of the generals.

'No,' he replied. 'You are not ready to listen, not yet. I will not be the one to complain in time of war, as you say. Play the hero, Spartan. Show the wisdom and judgement that brought us to follow a dead prince, to this desert, surrounded by enemies. I tell you, you will get us *all* killed.'

Proxenus laid a massive arm over Menon's shoulder and began to rumble something in his ear. Menon shook it off with a curse. He stalked away from the rest of the group, taking out a baked leather water bottle to refill it in the river. The crowd parted before him, exchanging glances.

Clearchus watched him go, then turned to the rest as if Menon had not said a word.

'According to the last map I saw, the river Zapatas is to the north of here, two or three days of marching. The hills you can see in the distance are green and there should be animals and birds to hunt where there is water. We'll eat the draught animals and leave the last of the carts behind us. I imagine our lads can bring desert bustards down easily enough. A few fit archers merely have to follow the birds. They cannot fly far and they tire more easily than we do. It will be a feast every day!' He smiled, though his eyes remained cold. 'More importantly, the river is said to be fast-flowing. I would like to put at least one fast-coursing river behind me. I do not think the Persian king will simply allow us to leave, not without a fight.'

'How far until we are out of his territory?' Netus asked. He had taken a wound in the fighting and had strapped his left arm close to his chest. Of all of them, he looked the least able to march and Clearchus suppressed a wince at the thought.

'If they let us go, some two thousand miles – seven

hundred parasangs or so. We might try to reach the Royal Road.'

'Where King Artaxerxes can run us down all the more easily,' Netus murmured, not quite willing to argue the point.

Clearchus glanced at him before going on.

'If we head north, we should pass out of Persian lands in a month or so, crossing into uncontested territory. I do not fear hill tribes and savages, gentlemen. Not compared to the entire Persian army. The desert doesn't last for ever and there are rivers. If you would have me lead, I'll take us all north, at the best pace we can make. We'll be thin by the end of it, but I believe we'll get through.'

'A month or so may be the pace for soldiers,' Proxenus said. 'But there are old women and children in the camp. How fast can we go with them?'

'You are agreeing with Menon?' Clearchus replied angrily. 'You'd leave Greeks to be raped and slaughtered by shrieking Persians? Have you ever seen the rout of an army, Proxenus? Netus? Any of you? I have. I have seen a city sacked and put to the torch. I have given the order to do so.'

He closed his mouth firmly and stood, breathing hard. Slowly, he unclenched his right fist and forced a smile.

'Well, we cannot change the past. All we can do is protect these people who trusted us to keep them alive. We can send our few horsemen out to keep an eye on the enemy, and we'll refuse battle as long as we can. If they see we are intent on leaving their territory, they might let us go.'

'You don't believe that,' Netus said wearily.

Clearchus shook his head.

'No, I think we'll have to fight, at least once. The king has too many brash young generals – and one old, fat one – who want to nail our skins to a wall. Yet I have seen the quality of the men who stand with us, generals. They found no equal yesterday, not in the Persian lines. Our square marched right over their vaunted Immortals, their noble legions. We gutted them. They will be wary of us now. By all the gods, they are right to be.'

Every man there heard the tumult beginning at the same time, so that they turned towards the sound like a pack of hunting dogs catching a scent. In the crowd, Pallakis felt her heart thump in fear as Clearchus began to give orders in a completely different voice. No longer was he the gruff but kindly leader of men. His tone allowed no disagreement and he sent the others away at a sprint, scurrying to their positions, drawing swords as they went. She stood on her toes to see what was happening, but so did everyone else around her and she was not especially tall, so that she could see only the backs of others. She did feel the hand of a husband who had been frowning at her just before, as it came to rest on her upper thigh. Pallakis slapped it hard and moved away into the crowd, not looking back. Such a man would never have dared to touch her the day before. His arrogance showed how her star had fallen and made her afraid. She decided she would have to get a knife. Perhaps Clearchus would lend her a kopis blade.

Pushing through the crowd, she half-feared a sudden rush of panic as they came under attack. Instead, she saw three men on horseback approaching the neat ranks of Greek hoplites taking post ahead of them. Pallakis was too far off to hear what they were saying, but she saw they held open palms out, as if intent on showing they carried no weapons. A truce, then. She dared not hope, after the terrors back at the camp. The Persians could be kind to those they loved. They were unbelievably cruel to those they considered slaves or an enemy. All foreigners fell outside their castes, so that the lowliest beggar in Persepolis would consider himself her master, or the equal of any of the Greeks. She wondered if Clearchus understood that was how they thought.

Her old status still held with some, so that the crowded Greeks let her through to the front. Clearchus had strolled over to that part of the square, smiling up at the horsemen as if they were not mortal enemies fresh from a battle. Pallakis felt her heart constrict in her chest at the sight. How could her prince be dead? How could Cyrus not be there, in all his youth and greatness, with his visions of Persia reborn? He had inspired her a dozen times with his dreaming and now, somehow, it was at an end and she was alone. She felt tears come and ignored the stares of those who saw it and whispered to one another.

Clearchus looked up at Tissaphernes, the Persian sitting a fine white mount and smiling wryly, as if they had not been trying to murder each other just a day before.

'You won't believe me, Spartan, but I am glad to see you survived,' Tissaphernes said. 'Have your scars healed from the lash? I imagine they must have done by now.'

'Why would you seek to annoy me, Tissaphernes?' Clearchus replied. 'I might enjoy killing you, as few other men in my lifetime. You are not a fool. Do you want me to strike you?'

Tissaphernes dropped the act and sneered down at him, pleased to be sitting so high above the Greeks.

'You speak the king's tongue with a savage accent, Spartan, did you know that? You sound like a herdsman, or a servant. I can only imagine you were taught by one. And it is Lord Tissaphernes. King Artaxerxes rewarded me for what I told him about your plans. Had you realised that yet? I am the one who persuaded the Great King to raise the armies, to be ready in the field for traitors from the west. It was my warning that saved the throne for its rightful owner. I imagine he will reward me with a palace, now it has turned out in our favour.'

Clearchus rubbed his chin, feeling the bristles there. He would have to grow a beard, he realised. There would be no queue to be shaved in the mornings, not for a while.

'Tissaphernes,' he began. 'You came here calling for a truce. Yet you seem determined to taunt me into anger. If there are games being played, I think you are the one playing them. Now, why don't you simply say what you were told to say. Leave the decisions of war to those who understand them.'

Tissaphernes coloured and shifted in his saddle.

'Very well, Spartan. I would rather have seen this ended today. I could have brought a hundred thousand men to surround you, to send arrows down your throats . . .'

'Were you given some kind of message, perhaps? By the king?' Clearchus interrupted, wearying of the man's spite. He would happily have watched Tissaphernes swallow his own tongue and choke to death, but if the man was reluctant to speak, perhaps there was something worth hearing.

Tissaphernes stared coldly in silence for a time, then spoke as if he was reciting something that left an unpleasant taste as it passed his lips.

'King Artaxerxes holds no grudge against those his brother paid. He understands the fault lay with the traitor, Prince Cyrus. The king witnessed great bravery on the field from the Greeks. He invites the generals to discuss how best to send them home without further bloodshed or fighting.'

'There,' Clearchus said faintly, his thoughts spinning. 'That is more like it. Where is the king camped, Lord Tissaphernes?'

The use of the title was not lost on the man, but he still shook his head.

'The army is all around you, Spartan. Yet I will not say where my king resides, not yet. Tell me your answer and I will bear it to him. I will return this evening to guide you to the king.'

'I accept,' Clearchus replied.

'The invitation is to all Greek generals,' Tissaphernes said, looking over Clearchus to the lines of soldiers and the crowd straining to hear them.

'I have one or two I would prefer to leave behind,' Clearchus said, thinking of Menon and the damage he might do if he ever stood before the Persian king.

'General Clearchus, do you think I am some Persian farmer? Some innocent? We have questioned men who came with you from Sardis. With fire and iron, until they sang out all their secrets. We know how Cyrus damaged the king's reputation in Byzantium, drawing funds that would not be repaid. We know to the last cup of grain how much you spent, how much you owe, how many you seek so foolishly to protect. The Great King has asked to see the Greek officers who did so much damage to his imperials yesterday.' The Persian smiled, his features shining. 'Now, I would rather see you slaughtered where you stand, but I obey the king's orders. So unless you wish to offend His Majesty, you will be accompanied by Netus the Stymphalian, Menon of Thessaly, Proxenus, Xenias the Arcadian, Sosis of Syracuse, Pasion the Megarian . . .'

Clearchus raised his hand.

'Very well, Tissaphernes. I will come. As for the others, we'll discuss it.'

'Who knows,' Tissaphernes said. 'Perhaps you will refuse. Perhaps you will yet decide to offend my master one *last* time. I look forward to hearing your answer. Until tonight, Clearchus.'

The three horsemen turned away together, leaving Clearchus to watch them dwindle to specks on the horizon. The Spartan swore under his breath and Proxenus chuckled to hear it.

'You think it is a trap?' Proxenus asked.

'I have no way of knowing,' Clearchus admitted. 'It could be. Brother, I am at a loss. I would not give Menon the satisfaction of agreeing with him on anything, but the truth is, I don't see how we can protect these people in this place. Perhaps I should have marched straight out and left them all.'

'No,' Proxenus said firmly. 'I would not have followed that order. I would not hear the cries of these children in my last moments. You would not have left them behind.'

'Menon would have,' Clearchus muttered, looking over the crowd. He saw Pallakis there again, somehow snagging his gaze as it drifted across the faces of strangers.

'You are not Menon,' Proxenus replied. 'You are a better man. I will come with you tonight. If they mean to betray us, I'll take that fat fool down.'

'It is a risk,' Clearchus said. He made his decision and the terrible tension left him. 'Very well, Proxenus. I will stand with you, however it turns out.'

'Or we could just run. I am open to that idea as well.'

Both men looked over a crowd that included small children, old men and women, the lame, the slow. The camp had trundled along on carts since Sardis. If they ran, they would not last a day.

'Will they have wine at a truce discussion, do you think?' Proxenus asked.

Clearchus brightened considerably.

'I imagine so.'

22

Clearchus rubbed a finger down his cheek, where a line of sweat itched him. He missed the rituals and routines of the camp proper. With Persian horsemen appearing out of the gloom, it had seemed only sense to abandon everything that could not be made to roll or run in instants. As it was, the remaining oxen plodded along at a pace so feeble they could be caught by a small child on a mule, never mind imperial cavalry. He would have ordered them slaughtered and jointed if there was an easy way to carry the meat. Still, he missed the simple order of the cooking lines. He missed the tents and servants who made his comfort their priority. They seemed to have vanished, either killed or enslaved. He hoped it was not the last. The Persians used slaves poorly, so that they rarely lived long. He preferred the Spartan style, where a man's slaves were prized and kept fed. Clearchus had four helots of his own in the ranks. They considered him a father, almost, he thought. He suspected they cursed his name when he made them exercise or sent them off on a long run around the hills, but they had to be fit. Carrying his kit and watching his back required both stamina and patience.

He did not run that day, with the weight of decision on him. Some of those who had abandoned the camp had brought a little food with them. Others went out hunting ostrich and bustard, three of them coming back with a fine buck deer like conquering heroes. It was more trouble to find firewood enough to cook the meat. One of the families had to be held back as they watched their only cart broken up to be burned. Clearchus looked at the old fellow who still cursed and gestured crudely in his rage. The gods were capricious, though it hardly seemed the time to remind him. The Spartan wondered if the man's indignation said something wondrous about the Greeks, that they could raise their fists to Fate and the gods themselves, or whether it simply meant some of them were fools.

The thought did not improve his mood, though a thick slice of venison was being browned for the generals who would go to meet a king that evening. His stomach creaked at the thought.

The news had spread quickly through the camp, so that all twelve senior men had come in to discuss it or give him advice. No doubt the smell of venison played its part in that as well, but Clearchus greeted each one warmly.

Menon was the last to come in, looking sour and nettled. The sun was beginning to set by then and as far as Clearchus knew, the man had eaten nothing all day. Menon approached him with obvious reluctance, his mood confirmed by the first words from his mouth.

'You'd have us all approach you on bended knee, I suppose. I can see why you got on so well with the Persian prince, Spartan. You have the same arrogance. Shall I throw myself to the ground for you? Would that please Your Highness?'

'I think you should stay behind, Menon,' Clearchus replied, ignoring the taunts. He found Menon petty and bad-tempered, but his men had fought well. Apart from his resentment of other classes of Greek, Menon actually did know his trade.

Menon looked at Clearchus, then the faces of the others. He knew Proxenus and Netus were as thick as thieves with the Spartan. One or two of the others had agreed with him in private that they found the man arrogant, but still they faced him as a group, as if Menon were the outsider.

'I am a general of twenty years of service,' Menon said. 'The last I heard, you had been disavowed by your own ephors in Sparta. You found a prince willing to pour gold down your throat, but that does not make you the leader here, no matter what these fools think. What, because Cyrus said you were? Perhaps we should hear from the prince now, then? Raise your hand, Prince Cyrus, if you think Clearchus should rule us. No? Nothing? Then I will decide my own fate, Spartan – and the fate of my men, who look to me.'

'You are a poisonous little bastard, aren't you?' Proxenus said. 'Clearchus is giving you a pass, Menon. In case there is treachery tonight. Don't you understand?'

'Your friend is a thinker,' Menon replied. 'As far as that goes. As much as that is worth. I wonder what the Persians offered him this morning, when they came to speak for the Great King. I can't help wondering if General Clearchus has shared all they said. Keep your peace, Proxenus. I wouldn't trust you further than I can throw you.'

'Very well!' Clearchus snapped. 'Come with us, then. Perhaps I thought to spare myself your whining, Menon. Proxenus, you should stay.'

'Not me,' Proxenus said immediately. 'I will be at your side.' His tone allowed no disagreement, but Menon spoke over them both.

'Whatever you two have planned together, I will discover. What is it, then? Is Proxenus to move the camp away while we are distracted? No, I would like to see Proxenus at my side as well.'

Clearchus found he had closed his right fist and was silently measuring the distance it would take for two quick steps and a blow to knock the Thessalian cold. It was a satisfying prospect, but he strangled the urge to lose his temper, as he had been doing since he was seven years old. The lessons of Sparta had been harsh, but they had given him a will like bands of iron. Instead, he smiled at Menon and bowed his head.

'As you say, then. We'll walk together into the lion's cave. And if it swallows us up, I will have your name on my lips, Menon.'

'You make a fine speech,' Menon said with a shrug. 'But you will not leave me behind. That I can promise you.'

Tissaphernes returned as the desert evening came, the sun drawn from a clear sky to the underworld beneath. He found all twelve Greek generals waiting, looking fresh and rested. They carried no spears or shields under the protection of a truce, but each man had decided to keep his short sword and, in the case of Clearchus, a kopis blade that rested across the small of his back.

Thousands came to watch them leave, standing in silence. Tissaphernes looked back at so many and scowled to himself. They did not look beaten or afraid. He could not understand such strange people, who did not even seem to know when they had lost.

'It is the king's order that your followers remain here while you are gone,' the Persian said with a sniff. 'My lord Artaxerxes will guarantee a truce while they are in this spot, but not if they move forward or back. Is that understood?'

Clearchus did not reply for a time. His eyes seemed unnaturally bright in the gloom.

'It is understood,' he said at last. 'Truce if we stay, war if we move.'

He spoke in a way that made it seem more a threat than a reassurance. It was Tissaphernes who looked away and nudged his horse to movement.

When they had walked some thirty stades, or the passage of an hour, the darkness had come.

'How much further is it, do you think?' Proxenus asked in Greek. 'My legs are stiff.'

'How would I know?' Clearchus replied. 'If they are stiff, I am willing to run for a while.'

'Where would we run? Do not forget I am wounded,' Netus said, indicating his bound arm.

'How could we forget it? You mention it all the time,' Menon replied, glaring at him.

'It's barely a wound, anyway. I've had worse from my wife,' Proxenus added.

Netus pushed past him suddenly, his bound arm flapping up and down.

Tissaphernes looked on in astonishment as a dozen Greek generals broke into a run, shoving each other like boys in a race. For a while, they surged ahead, then settled into a training lope. Tissaphernes could hear their laughter and curses as they went.

The Persian raised his eyes to heaven and urged his horse to a trot to keep up. The fires of the king's camp came into view in a hollow between the hills ahead and, of course, the Greeks called out the sight to one another. They no longer needed to be guided in. If anything, the pace increased, so that the Persians were left behind.

Tissaphernes could feel the eyes of his companions on him, two serious young men who had not known Greeks before. They looked to him for some explanation, but he could only shrug.

'They are mad,' he said, stung by their staring. 'Who can understand such men?'

The three Persians caught up to the Greeks and passed them before they reached the outskirts of the camp. To his irritation, Tissaphernes found he was sweating in the warm air. The Greek generals were grinning as servants came to take the horses. Tissaphernes wondered if he should change his robes before heading to the king's side, but his orders had been to return promptly. He wondered if Artaxerxes had expected him quite so soon, however.

'Follow me,' he said in court Persian. Tissaphernes gestured. He knew some of them spoke the tongue, but it suited his sense of superiority to wave them along like children or the simple-minded.

For their part, the Greeks walked in a tight group, their good humour vanishing at the sight of Persian soldiers watching them. Tight ranks stood to attention on both sides of the path into the camp, making an avenue of Imperials. To his confusion, Tissaphernes saw Clearchus drift to one side and stop by a great bull of a man, staring glassily at nothing. Tissaphernes watched in astonishment as the Greek straightened the man's tunic and said a few words into his ear that brought a twitch of humour to the gash of his mouth, hidden deep in a black beard.

The action seemed to amuse the others and they called to the Spartan in their liquid language. The progression along the path became an inspection, as if the Imperials had been assembled for Greek approval. Tissaphernes set his jaw. They were barbarians and, more importantly, the king's guests that evening. He could only smile tightly and wave them on, waiting for them.

'Does the fat one speak Greek, do you think?' Menon said.

'There will be someone who will,' Clearchus replied. 'Say nothing you would not like overheard.'

'You are a wise man, Spartan. In many ways, you remind me of my mother.'

'I think I met her once . . .' Clearchus began. Whatever he was going to add was lost as trumpets blared ahead. The opening to a great pavilion was pulled apart, so that light spilled into the darkness around them.

It was hard not to stare as the Greeks entered a royal tent that had been constructed on the desert floor only that day. Far from sand or mere rugs laid on bare earth, the floor appeared to be made of polished stone. Above them, the roof rose to multiple peaks and the air was thick with strong fragrances and flavours. Dancers moved languidly in time to some stringed instrument, women wearing just a simple kilt, boys with rouge and kohl painted on their skin. There must have been hundreds of Persian soldiers lining the walls like black or white beetles, their faces bright with heat and narcotics to fire the blood. The air itself was thick, though whether it was the warmth of the desert or the scent of oils rubbed on bare skin was hard to say.

The twelve Greeks entered in pairs, with Clearchus and Menon in the lead, Proxenus and Netus behind them. Menon had not chosen to stand on the Spartan's right hand, but found himself there as he gaped and blinked in the light of a thousand tongues of flame. The lamps rested on bronze spikes sitting in holes in the stone, or held in the hands of slaves whose only task was to provide light as needed.

The centre of the pavilion was a feast table set with knives and seats and bowls, all on a blood-red cloth. A great lamp turned slowly above the table's length, dragging the flames of white candles round and round. The table stretched left and right in front of the Greek generals, with Persian officers watching them from behind its bulk. Clearchus felt a strange mixture of emotion as he saw Ariaeus among their number. His first thought was relief to see him alive. Beyond that, the man's tight smile and guarded expression were clear enough. Clearchus should not have been surprised to see a man like Ariaeus restored to the king's graces. The Persian was a survivor, above all else.

Clearchus nodded to Ariaeus. He owed the man no more courtesy than that, though the Persian dipped his gaze to the floor in reply. Clearchus looked then to the one who dominated that scene, King Artaxerxes. The god-emperor of Persia bore some resemblance to Cyrus, so that there was no mistaking him, even if he had not been surrounded by slaves and so richly dressed and painted, he resembled a golden carpet. The king was also heavier of frame than Cyrus had described, a warrior rather than a bookkeeper. Artaxerxes wore loose robes of some light cloth, so that he appeared cool despite the heat of the tent. His beard had been oiled and drawn to a point. Clearchus saw the king wore an Egyptian breastplate in golden bronze under the sweep of cloth and a dagger through his sash. Yet Artaxerxes was smiling almost dreamily and there was no immediate threat.

'Good evening, gentlemen,' a man said, dragging their attention to him. The fellow bowed and Clearchus thought he had the look of a high-ranking servant.

It should not have been a surprise to hear Greek spoken. Yet Clearchus still blinked at being addressed in the language of home, so far away from all he knew and loved. He tried not to see voluptuous figures writhing together out of the corner of his eye, though the musicians and their plucking did not completely drown the hiss of skin. There was, in that place, a dangerous emotion on the air, a smell of blood perhaps, overlaid by strong perfume. It was a place of heat and desire, rather than coolness and safety.

Clearchus reached the huge table, surprised by the size of it as he approached. He went down on one knee, bowing his head. He and the others had discussed the best way to greet the king, from what they knew of Cyrus. They'd all agreed Artaxerxes would expect them to lie flat on the ground, but at the same time Proxenus had argued it would show weakness – and that such men as the king would only be inflamed to violence by such a display. Clearchus knew it was a risk, especially in front of the king's court followers and his whores. He dipped down and heard a hissing susurration go around the pavilion, though whether it was a murmur of astonishment or amusement he could not tell.

'Well, I told you,' Menon whispered in reaction at his shoulder. 'You have killed us all.'

Without raising his head, Clearchus replied in a low voice, '*You* lie flat then, Menon, if you think it will save you. Seriously.'

'Not me. I am a Greek as good as you, Spartan. Better than you.'

Clearchus rose to his feet and smiled at the king. He spoke in fluent Persian.

'Your Majesty, we come under truce to your pavilion. I see you have spared General Ariaeus and I give thanks for your mercy. My name is Clearchus of Sparta. It has been my honour to lead these men in peace and war.' One by one, he introduced the others standing behind him. Those who did not speak the tongue still knelt as they were named.

The king remained silent for the entire performance. Clearchus saw he was glassy of eye and flushed, as if Artaxerxes had already been drinking hard that evening. The general waited to be given leave to sit. He knew from his association with Cyrus that the Persians took the customs of hospitality very seriously. If he and his companions were welcomed to the king's table, they would be his guests. After that, any small breach of manners or custom could be forgiven. Clearchus waited, though he could feel fresh lines of sweat run from his scalp to darken his tunic.

Tissaphernes swept past the generals he had brought to that tent, prostrating himself and then taking a place at the far end of the table. Clearchus saw he did not dare to sit down without permission, but his arrival had broken the tension. The Great King of Persia blinked slowly, as if his gaze returned from the infinite to that place of heat and sweetness.

'You are welcome, Clearchus of Sparta. Please have your followers sit. You are all guests at my table this evening.'

A subtle tension went out of the room, as every soldier of Persia heard the words and knew they would not be called upon to strike the impudent Greeks down. Clearchus let out a long breath, though he made little of it. He had felt the gaze of many men who would have been happy to see him killed. The Spartans were the most famous enemy Persia had ever faced, the unconquered foe. Clearchus hoped he had added a few lines to that legend at Cunaxa, when he had shown he could go wherever he wanted on the battlefield. It was his private belief that if Cyrus had not fallen so quickly, they would have smashed the Persian army, though it would have taken a month to kill the last of them. He did not think that would be an opinion he shared at table that evening, however.

The Greeks took seats as they were guided to them, hiding their discomfort at having so many strangers and enemies at their backs.

Clearchus looked up into the eyes of the king. He could not help gauging the width of the table, finding it just too far to lunge with his kopis. It was the sort of detail Cyrus had loved, he recalled. No doubt there was a story of the thing's construction, though how it had come to a plain in the middle of a desert was beyond him. The Greek general could only marvel at the numbers of slaves around the Persian king. It made sense that the royal camp would have been ten times as great as their own – a Sardis or even an Athens on the march. Great tables, taverns, a royal mint, jewellers and weavers, carvers in ivory and stone. In a single night, they had raised a civilisation in the desert, and yet he still wondered if he would see the sun rise again. Clearchus took a deep breath and smiled. He laid his hands on the table in front of him and was pleased to see they were steady.

'Do you toast the fallen, man of Greece?' Artaxerxes asked.

Clearchus nodded.

'We do, Your Majesty, to give them honour and speed them on their way.'

The king gestured in the air and servants filled goblets in front of each man. Menon looked at his with a dark expression, but he knew better than to insult their host by refusing. The king rose to his feet and all twelve generals copied him, holding their cups high. The tension returned to the room as the Persian soldiers touched swords and made ready to draw at the first sharp movement.

'My brother Cyrus was a traitor and . . . a fool. But he was my father's son. May God find him a place in eternity. My brother Cyrus, gentlemen.'

'Prince Cyrus,' Clearchus said.

He heard Ariaeus' voice join the rest as they said the words and then sat, all too aware of the sudden threat of violence they had felt. Artaxerxes appeared not to have noticed. He smiled as the first steaming dishes were wafted in, addressing his attention to the particular way the food was presented. Clearchus waved the first few morsels onto his plate and refused anything else. He had no appetite and he could see

Proxenus too had chosen a bowl of soup and something in fried flour that could be dipped. Menon was heaping his plate full of everything on offer and only shrugged when he sensed the gaze of the others.

They ate until each man there had refused the servants many times, until Clearchus was fed up being asked. The king belched into his fist and emptied his wine yet again. The Spartan had kept count and knew it was the eighth time the king had seen the bottom of his cup.

'What am I to do with you Greeks?' Artaxerxes said suddenly.

Clearchus saw Tissaphernes look up from his own plate as he wiped it clean with some sort of flatbread.

'Majesty, we are mercenaries,' Clearchus replied. 'Hired men. We wish nothing more than to be allowed to withdraw back to the Royal Road.'

'Yet you came into Persia as an invading force,' Artaxerxes said.

The sense of danger had crept back into the room and Clearchus was glad he had not eaten too much and made himself slow. He could feel the threat rising in the stiff movements of armed men who thought they were unobserved. It was all the more dangerous for that and he felt a sense of resignation. They were surrounded. If the king meant to harm them, there was no chance at all that they would walk out, not from that place.

'We came for gold and silver, Your Majesty. Your brother Cyrus paid us to march. We are the same as saddlers or carpenters, though our trade is the sword. When our employer is killed, we hope to withdraw. In victory or disaster, we seek no grudges.'

Artaxerxes grunted a laugh.

'You may be disappointed here. In Persia, we have long

305

memories, general. You came into my lands seeking my head, my throne. You came to destroy everything ordained in me. And yet you expect to just walk away at the end, to take my hand in friendship! General Ariaeus has told me the truth of it, how he was forced into service by my brother. As he is a Persian, it was enough to break him back to the ranks, to be used by my guards for their entertainment.'

Clearchus glanced at Ariaeus, seeing the grief and humiliation in his eyes. No longer a favoured man, it seemed. Ariaeus shook his head a fraction back and forth, warning him. There was pity in his expression and Clearchus felt his stomach clench.

'But you . . .' the king went on. 'Truly, it is as Lord Tissaphernes has said. You Greeks, you are all barbarians . . . savages. Now, the meal has finished. Do you understand? Have you eaten your fill, each one of you? Can you complain to the gods that I treated you with disdain, or broke my oath of hospitality to you, my guests?'

There was a perfect stillness in the pavilion. Even the writhing women stood as statues and the last notes of music faded, seeming to hang in the air for a long time. Clearchus felt a powerful arm curl round his neck from behind. He drew his kopis and dug it into the elbow joint, making his assailant scream in his ear. Yet there were dozens of soldiers willing to grapple the seated Greeks. Proxenus broke the arm of one over the edge of the table, making the man shriek and fall away. Menon came to his feet and punched another Persian cold before he was brought down, swearing and cursing with every breath. The table rocked and almost went over in the struggle. Yet there could be only one end to it. In that small place, the Greeks were stabbed and overwhelmed in moments.

Artaxerxes rose to his feet once more, looking down at his

fallen enemies. One or two still writhed in the grip of those strangling or knifing them. He saw awareness remained in the eyes of the Spartan, though the man's face was as red as the cloaks of his people.

'How will your Greeks fare now, general? Without their leaders? I tell you, they will not leave my lands alive. Take that knowledge with you as you die.'

He thought Clearchus was trying to say something. The king frowned in surprise when he saw the man was laughing, but the Spartan's blood ran down his chest in a great slick and Clearchus was dead before Artaxerxes could ask him to explain.

23

The guards roused the camp with horns when they heard horsemen approaching. With the Persian king just a few miles away, the response was instant. The horns had Spartans and Thessalians stumbling up from their blankets, swords bare as they came to answer the threat.

Torches were brought in the deep of the night, to see the riders. Behind them, lines of men formed with spear and shield. They did not stand down when they saw only a few dozen men had approached the camp. Clearchus and the generals were absent and there was no one to order them back to their blankets. Nor would they have gone if there had been.

Two captains of Proxenus stood deliberately ahead of the rest as the riders drew up and halted. Slaves ran alongside the Persians, holding torches out to the side where the oil could not drip down onto bare skin.

Pallakis stood beyond the light, not daring to come any closer. She recognised Tissaphernes once more, with Ariaeus looking grim and grief-stricken at his side. She did not know if the Persian general was a prisoner, though Ariaeus seemed to ride unbound. It was Tissaphernes who addressed himself to the captains standing in his path – and then raised his voice to anyone who could hear him in the darkness beyond.

'In truce, I approach this camp. I have grave news for you all, with a decision to make before dawn. Your generals are dead. They displeased King Artaxerxes and they have been beheaded. You are ordered to surrender. If you do so, you may expect some form of mercy. You will be made slaves, but most of you will be allowed to live. If you do not give up your arms as the sun rises, you will be hunted down like dogs and killed, one by one, as an example to all those who choose silver over honour. The Great King does not approve of mercenaries. You have until dawn to make your choice. Do you understand your position?'

He addressed the last to a pair of captains, who spoke not a word of Persian. Sensing his gaze and tone meant they had been asked a question, they both shook their heads. Tissaphernes raised his eyes in frustration, waving a hand to Ariaeus, who moved his mount a step further and translated his fellow Persian's speech into Greek for all those who listened.

Pallakis bit her lip between her teeth, feeling tears come. Clearchus had gone trustingly into the nest of vipers that was the king's pavilion. His loss, so soon after Cyrus, made her want to fold into a child's posture, with her hands about her knees to hug them close. She could not go on. She considered becoming the slave of some Persian soldier or lord and despaired. She would never see Greece again. She wept, though she made no sound. She watched as Ariaeus repeated the message once more and saw how he flinched as Tissaphernes raised a hand to gesture. Ariaeus may not have been a prisoner, but he was no longer the golden general she had known.

Pallakis watched them turn their horses, the light of their torches visible in the night for a long way as they rode back. She wiped her tears then, feeling trails of them hot on the back of her hand. No doubt the kohl of her eyes had smeared. The night air was cold and though she knew she trembled, it helped to be hidden in the darkness. A thousand whispered conversations began around her and she was no part of any of them. Yet little by little, the camp fell quiet once more. They had suffered too many shocks and reverses in too short a time. The last blow had stunned them all, to see their generals go out so full of confidence and hope, only to vanish for ever. It was too much to bear. The stars turned overhead and Pallakis thought she would not sleep. It was her last night of freedom, after all. She tried not to think of what would come with the sun.

Xenophon watched Ariaeus and Tissaphernes leave. He stood in the shadows a few paces from the torches, invisible to them. He thought half the camp had turned out to hear what was happening – Greeks were curious enough when their lives weren't at stake. The news that Clearchus would not be returning was like being struck in the chest. Xenophon cursed softly. The idea that anyone could have overcome the Spartan seemed impossible. Yet there was no mistaking the poisonous triumph on the face of Tissaphernes. The man was a snake, but such men often prosper, as Socrates always said.

Xenophon walked to where he had laid a sheet on the sandy ground, sleeping on his back with his hands folded across his chest. He considered lying down, but knew sleep would not return. He had eaten a little earlier, the remains of some poor pack animal that was more bone than meat. He picked a piece of it from his teeth as he stood, looking up at the clear sky and the stars overhead in a great band that stretched across like mist.

He started violently when Hephaestus spoke at his shoulder.

'What are you going to do?'

'Zeus! Did you have to creep up on me in the dark?'

Hephaestus shrugged, barely visible under the moonlight. Xenophon glared at him. He had taught the Athenian gang leader to ride a horse and ever since the man seemed to look to him for guidance, as if he would have all the answers. Xenophon gnawed a piece of skin on his thumb. It was hard to admit he had no idea. He was still reeling from the news that Clearchus and Proxenus and Netus and Menon were gone with all the rest. Some he had admired, while others were strangers to him. To have them all suddenly swept from the board shook him badly.

A thought struck him and he lurched into movement. Hephaestus hesitated only an instant before following and catching him up.

'What is it? Have you heard something? What are we doing?'

Xenophon stopped, finding himself breathing hard. He turned to the younger man beside him, nineteen years old and hardened by a life of violence and unreliable meals from his earliest years. It was still a mystery why Socrates had suggested he accompany Xenophon. Hephaestus responded to most challenges with his fists, or sometimes with a stone held in his fists. He had proved a difficult companion, though he did have a surprising way with horses, Xenophon had to admit.

'I need to speak to the captains of Proxenus. There were two of them standing close to the Persians.'

He said nothing more, closing his mouth on a need to babble out the wild plan that had sprung fully formed into his head. To a man like Hephaestus, it would have seemed madness. Xenophon walked back to where Tissaphernes and Ariaeus had sat their mounts. One torch still burned there, the stick pressed deeply into the sand. He saw the two captains were close by, their heads bowed in worried conversation.

Xenophon approached them, keeping his voice steady, though it came out first as a croak.

'Gentlemen, if I had wine, I'd raise a cup to our last night.'

The two men scowled in his direction.

'You think so?'

'The king killed our generals, captain. He will do the same to us. The night is passing. When the sun rises, we will see them coming, I do not doubt. I am just surprised . . . but no, it is too late.'

'Too late for what?' the younger of the two asked him immediately, clutching at anything that might give him hope.

'If we go meekly to the king's hands, it is all over for us. This is the man who cut the head off his own brother. What can we expect from such a king? Most of us will be killed, the rest made slaves. None of us will ever see home again. Yet half the camp has gone back to sleep! I thought there would be more fight left in them. We were not beaten on the field, after all. No, we endure heat and cold and exhaustion better than any Persian, yet they expect us to just hand over our swords and shields and show our necks for the blade?'

More men wandered over to hear Xenophon speak. The two captains turned sharply to see who it was, suspicious of everyone.

'You think we can fight that great Persian host on our own?' the older captain said. 'With ten thousand camp followers to protect? With food for no more than a few days?'

His tone was not one of scorn, Xenophon realised. The man spoke without anger, but almost with need in his voice. He truly wanted Xenophon to have an answer and waited for him to reply. Xenophon responded as Socrates had taught him to, thinking it through aloud, so that his voice remained calm and reassuring.

'They could not break our formation on the field,' he

began. 'Not once. Numbers seemed to mean little. Yet we have only six horses, too few. So if they attack, it will not matter if we win: we won't be able to chase them down, where the real damage is done. And if we lose, they can send in horsemen to butcher our people. Yes, cavalry will be the greatest threat.'

He paused to look around at the dozen captains who had come to listen. He needed them to understand what he was about. He would not just talk to hear the sound of his voice or to while away the hours. He had once asked Socrates how a man should live, and the philosopher had replied, 'Thoughtfully,' saying it was what separated us from dumb animals.

'Each of you was raised by Proxenus or Netus to have authority over others. When we have made a plan, I would be willing to follow you. I know you will not just remain here, like lambs and goats, waiting for an enemy to still our voices. We are Greeks. We talk – but then we move. So . . .'

He smiled at their attention, at the way his confidence was beginning to affect them so that they stood straighter. It did not matter that his stomach churned with fear if he did not show it.

'Before we march, we must seek out those within our number who hunt with a sling or a bow. We need some way to hold off Persian horsemen, or they will ride rings around us and send arrows in all day to pierce our square. They could not do it in the battle, but if we are to march on open ground, they will whittle us down to a stub. Nod then, gentlemen! Let me know you agree, that you understand! It cannot be many hours to the sun's rise and we have to be moving by then. Why make it easy for those who murdered better men at their table? Why give them anything they want? No, we need slingers at the edges. After that, in the words of Clearchus, we'll need food and shelter . . .'

'This is madness. You'll see us all destroyed.'

Xenophon broke off at the voice of a man he didn't know. Others around him grumbled at the interruption, giving him the fellow's name. Xenophon raised his hand for silence and was pleased when it came.

'Apollonides, is it? Perhaps it is you who will lead us tomorrow. What do you suggest?'

The man blushed in the torchlight, looking uncomfortable.

'I'm not asking to lead, but I would ask the Persian king for mercy for us all. There's no chance of safety without his permission. We are in a desert, just about, surrounded by his cities and his regiments. We won't be going anywhere without his seal on it.'

The captain raised his chin as he stopped talking, almost in challenge. Hephaestus was watching them both with an astonished expression. They wanted someone to lead them out of an impossible situation. They needed one man to at least look as if he knew what he was doing. It was like a draught of wine in Xenophon's blood, to have them wait for him to reply. He could almost hear Socrates laughing at him, but he shook his head to clear it of all old voices. Perhaps Captain Apollonides spoke the fears of them all, but he could not be allowed his point. Xenophon could see the path they had to take. In the instant of speaking, that man had become his obstacle. Xenophon made himself breathe out all his anger. He wondered if this was how Clearchus had felt every day.

'You were here when we agreed a truce with the king, Apollonides. When Clearchus and Proxenus and all the rest went out in good faith, without their shields and spears, trusting the word of Artaxerxes. I pray now that they are truly dead and not being tortured and insulted by our enemies.

You would have us trust the word of one already proven in his deceit? Should we bend our knees to Tissaphernes, who betrayed the prince?'

Xenophon read the stances of the group of captains and realised they were not supporting the man who had spoken. They glared at Apollonides. It made his own anger surge back without restraint. Xenophon stepped closer and made himself a threat.

'If that is your wish, I say you are not one of us, Apollonides. I say your weakness will cost the lives of all those we have brought to this place. That makes you my enemy, Apollonides – and no Greek.'

As the man spluttered, Xenophon turned to the others.

'The choice is yours, gentlemen. My view is that this man should be stripped of his position and made to bear baggage as we move into the desert.'

'How dare you speak so to me!' Apollonides replied. He began to draw the short sword on his hip, but his wrist was gripped by another, so that he gaped and struggled but could not move.

A Spartan captain named Chrisophus reached up and tugged at an earlobe, though Apollonides jerked away.

'His ears are pierced like a Lydian,' Chrisophus said. 'I have wondered about him before.'

'Lydian? I am a Greek!' Apollonides replied hoarsely. He fought as his sword belt was removed, but he could not prevent it and stood panting.

'Walk into the desert,' one of the other captains said. 'I will not watch my back for spies and traitors.'

Apollonides turned in mute appeal to the others, but there was only implacable anger on their faces. He had become the focus of all the despair and betrayal in that group and there was no mercy to be had from them. With a poisonous glance at Xenophon, he turned on his heel and walked away into the darkness.

As they raised the torches to watch him go, more soldiers were revealed, their eyes reflecting the light. Every captain and pentekoster in the Greek force had come to hear the conversation. They looked for leaders and Xenophon felt once more as if he had drained a cup of wine. He was in the right place at the right moment, he could feel it. There were many voices whispering, but when he raised his own, they fell silent to hear.

'All we know is that our generals have been betrayed. Twelve good men will not return from the grasp of the Persian king – a man without honour. But that is not the end. Our first responsibility is to those who look to us: the soldiers and the camp followers. It is our task to meet the enemy with laughter and violence. Let them see we are not downhearted! You are officers, after all. Let them see the courage that brought you better pay!'

He paused a beat for them to chuckle and murmur that it was not so much. If there was one thing soldiers enjoyed it was to complain about not being paid well enough.

'The Persians took our officers because they thought we would be unable to act without them,' Xenophon went on. 'They do not understand Greeks, gentlemen! Before the sun rises, we must choose new generals from amongst those who have the respect of the men. They are dispirited in the darkness, their paths at an end. It will be our task to raise hopes once again, so that instead of saying, "What will happen to me?" they ask, "What action will I take?" Our task is to restore that animating force that makes us the terror of nations.'

A grumble went around the group, spreading further in the darkness. There were thousands outside the ring of torches, with more still coming in to hear their fate. Yet Xenophon realised he could not speak directly to those men and women. He had pushed a stone down a hill and he had to run alongside it for a time.

'I have seen before,' he said, 'that those who seek to save their own lives are more likely to lose them. Those who seek only to fight with honour are most likely to remain alive when the battle is past. Indeed, I have known them reach old age and spend their years in philosophy, the violence just a memory.'

He knew he spoke as a man who had seen a lifetime of military service, whereas the truth was he had only ever known Cunaxa. Yet it had been a cataclysm and he thought it true enough that all those who stood there in the deserts were veterans. They had seen the oracle and washed themselves in blood.

'That is what you must bear in mind, if we are to survive the day to come.' He pointed east, taking the direction from the North Star. 'When we see the light again, we must once more be regiments, with generals, with officers, with order. Do not mistake me, we will need greater discipline than before. Orders cannot be challenged when the whole world stands against us. We must be ten thousand Greeks, ten thousand Spartan generals. The Persians can never understand such a thing, nor copy it. If we can do that, we will see home again. We will march out of Persia and we will see Greece.'

The silence was as thick as heat in the air when he stopped. Xenophon could hear men breathing and shifting where they stood, but no one else spoke up to have them beg the king for mercy. It seemed he had found the words to reach them.

The red cloak Chrisophus wore set him apart from the

captains of Proxenus. More, he had twenty years of service under his belt and he was not one to wait on ceremony or manners. Instead, he cleared his throat loudly and deliberately.

'Until this moment, Xenophon, I knew you only as an Athenian and a horseman. I knew Prince Cyrus and General Clearchus trusted you, however. You've spoken well. Thank you. I think now the captains should elect new generals, so we are ready for the Persian approach when the sun rises.'

Xenophon bowed his head in reply. They moved away from him and he felt his heart sink. For just a few precious moments, he had seen them looking to him to lead. He knew he could, though whether it was something born in him or something he had learned in his discussions with Socrates, he did not know. Yet they would choose new generals from among their own. He was thirsty and sore, with bruises he could not remember picking up in the battle. For just a while, he had been lifted high by their trust and faith, if he had not imagined it. To be left behind while the real soldiers went to pick leaders was as if he carried a weight that bowed him down.

He started when he felt a light touch on his shoulder. Xenophon turned sharply and his eyes widened at the young woman who stood there, her fingertips still pressed against his skin.

'I think you spoke well,' Pallakis said. Her voice was barely a whisper, as if they could still be overheard. 'You gave them hope. I could see it in the way they stood.'

He clenched his jaw and dipped his head. She took her hand away and he realised he could still feel where she had touched him.

'Thank you. I must admit, I thought for a moment that . . .'

Approaching footsteps interrupted what he was going to

say, so that he turned, his hand reaching for a knife in case it was the man he had helped to banish. Instead, he saw Chrisophus as he came back. The other captains were behind him and they strode in with new purpose.

'We have discussed it, Xenophon,' Chrisophus said. 'We have a Spartan, an Arcadian, a Stymphalian and a Boeotian. We've found men willing to lead in place of those who were killed.'

The man paused and Xenophon looked at him in confusion.

'And we've elected you as leader, sir. As general. You'll be our strategos.'

Xenophon felt a smile spread slowly across his face, beyond his control, though he sensed he should be serious and determined. Chrisophus chuckled at the sight.

'I am glad to see it meets with your approval, General Xenophon.' He dropped his voice slightly, glancing at Pallakis who stood open-mouthed at Xenophon's side. She was a striking woman, Chrisophus thought.

'I – I'm . . . er . . .' Xenophon said.

'Take a moment, sir. You seem to know what to do – and no one else stood up before you. That matters. We await your orders. I'll make sure they're carried out when you're ready.'

In the distance, a line of palest rose could be seen on the horizon. Xenophon saw it and felt his heart thump faster.

'The day is upon us, captain. Rouse the camp. We stand or fall on how we greet this dawn.'

Chrisophus went to clap him on the shoulder and thought better of it. Instead, he bowed.

'Yes, general.'

'Chrisophus . . . do you think that man was truly a Lydian spy?'

'Apollonides? Perhaps. But he would have argued until the sun came up. That much I do know.'

The Spartan grinned and tapped his fist on his breastplate in salute before jogging away, raising his hands to his lips, to bellow the camp awake.

24

'Burn the rest of the carts. We must learn to march, and the carts and wagons are the slowest part.'

Xenophon gave the order and was pleased to find the protests were little more than a rumble through the crowd, a sigh rather than a voiced objection. Everyone there had heard the fate of Clearchus, Proxenus and the others. As they had not before, they understood that their lives were at stake, that the rising sun could set on their bodies. The Greek soldiers made a point of moving among them, looking for bulky items they tried to conceal. Everything went on the fires and they sacrificed the last of the rams to give as many as possible a good meal.

As the sun cleared the eastern hills, they stood ready and determined. Very few had known Xenophon before that day, but he had been accepted by the Spartans and the captains under Proxenus. There was no vagueness in his orders and most of them were content to shuffle into lines and watch their life's belongings burn, though they wiped tears away in the licking heat of the flames.

Before they were able to move off, a force of thirty horsemen appeared, with an unknown officer at their head. Xenophon and Chrisophus went out to meet him, enjoying his evident confusion.

'My name is Mithridates, gentlemen. Lord Tissaphernes sent me to accept your surrender.'

'From your speech, you are a Greek?' Chrisophus asked. 'One of us? You share the same blood, the same gods? And yet you sit with Persians. You serve a king who murdered our generals. It is very odd, Mithridates.'

A stain of colour crept into the man's cheeks, but despite the light tone of his words, the Spartan watched him unblinking, a sense of stillness in him like a snake about to strike.

'Will you surrender, Spartan?' Mithridates said. He looked nervously at the blank-faced Persians on either side of him. Tissaphernes was a subtle man. No doubt a few of them spoke Greek well enough to report every word.

'We have considered your offer,' Chrisophus said, 'and we have decided our answer is no. Instead, we have a counter-offer for you. We will leave the king's territory, doing as little damage as possible. If we are attacked, we will fight. Do you understand me, traitor? Can you take those words back to your masters over the hill? I imagine they are not far away.'

Though his colour deepened, Mithridates made an effort to shrug, trying to be more casual than he was.

'You talk to me, but it is a dead man talking. You . . .'

'Go on, Mithridates,' Xenophon said, suddenly. 'We have a long march ahead of us. I will not waste any more time on you.'

He and Chrisophus walked away from the gaping Greek. With a curse, Mithridates wrenched his reins around and headed back the way he had come. Only then did Xenophon and Chrisophus turn to watch him go.

'We need to move quickly,' Xenophon said. 'Give the order.'

'I was not one of the generals we elected,' Chrisophus said.

'Well, that was your choice, Spartan. Tell the men to move in my name, then.'

Chrisophus bowed his head and jogged away. Bonfires still spat and flickered across the camp, sending greasy black smoke into the clear sky. The square of hoplites formed around the camp followers, all standing in ragged ranks. Some of them had placed young children on their backs and shoulders. They seemed a parody of soldiers in their lines, but they looked determined enough. Xenophon turned his back on all that lay behind. He saw Hephaestus had brought his horse and nodded.

'Thank you, Hephaestus,' he said. The young man who had led a dozen robberies in the markets of Athens was not much in evidence in that moment. Hephaestus had learned to ride and march and stand in line while the world went to hell around him. He had left a great deal of his youth on the battlefield of Cunaxa. When he leaned in, he was utterly serious.

'Can you lead?' Hephaestus said, his voice a murmur. 'Truly? Tell me you know what you are doing, Xenophon. Tell me this is not some game to you.'

Xenophon considered. He had known Socrates, Clearchus and a prince of Persia, learning from them all. He put his foot into the clasped hands Hephaestus held out and settled himself on the saddle. He had witnessed despair the night before. In the face of utter defeat, Xenophon had simply spoken to them. He'd asked the questions that revealed what they already knew – and they had accepted him. He knew he had to keep them moving, so they never had a chance to consider the odds against their survival. In that moment, he understood he could not share his own fears with anyone.

'You know me, Hephaestus,' he said. 'Of course I can lead.'

In his brown eyes, Hephaestus seemed to weigh the man who had taught him so much, desperate to believe. Xenophon looked steadily down at him. After an age, Hephaestus patted the horse on its shoulder and stood back.

Xenophon saw Chrisophus watching the exchange and so Xenophon raised his arm almost in a salute and dropped it, sending them on. Behind them, both Tissaphernes and the king of Persia would be hearing of their refusal to surrender. Xenophon recalled an army that had been like a dark sea. He did not doubt the response would be savage, but he was still proud they had not gone meekly into captivity. They were a long way from home, but at least they would not vanish from the earth without a fight.

They had marched all morning and part of the afternoon when the four scouts rode back to report a village some eight miles ahead. It was just a walled compound by a stream, with a few fields of barley and wheat, some trees and half a dozen skinny cattle. Such places clung to the land by the tips of their fingers, barely holding on to life. Yet it meant food they needed desperately. Xenophon reminded his officers not to take slaves or kill the people they encountered. They wished only to be left alone by the Persian army and had no need to antagonise them. Food was vital, of course – any cattle or sheep would be driven along with the few animals they still had.

As they pushed on, intent on reaching that place before the sun set, word spread that the enemy were closing on their rear. Xenophon turned his horse and rode back, with Chrisophus peeling off to run alongside him. Together, they stared south, shading their eyes.

'Not as many as I expected,' Chrisophus said. 'How many do they have there, two hundred horse? Those men on foot can't have much armour, not at that pace. My eyes are not as sharp as they once were. Do they carry javelins?'

'Bows,' Xenophon said darkly. 'Mithridates has returned with archers and cavalry, to strike at us from a distance. Two hundred cavalry . . . no more than four hundred archers.'

'There must be more marching to intercept us,' Chriso-phus said. 'Such a small force can only seek to slow us down.'

'We are *already* slow,' Xenophon replied. He shook his head. 'We need to reach the village ahead of us. Pass word to increase the pace. Bring our shields to the rear. Your Spartans, Chrisophus. We cannot outrun this many cavalry, nor men who can hold the tails of those horses and run almost as fast. Yet we can make them work to reach us. It won't make their aim any better, at least.'

Chrisophus raced off, giving orders that brought a line of shield-bearers to the rear. It was barely soon enough as the Persian horsemen came on fast as soon as they spotted the Greek ranks in the wilderness. Some of them cantered, pulling men behind them. Others galloped in alone and threw javelins in swooping arcs. They struck with great force, but the shields held.

Xenophon remained at the rear, watching and thinking, cursing softly when one of the men was hit and had to be carried forward by his mates, dazed and bloody. More javelins flew. Some of the ones on the ground were snatched up by Greek warriors and thrown back with savage accuracy.

Far worse were the archers, once they got into range. The Persians seemed to know there were only a few Cretan bowmen left after the battle. Persian archers walked in a wide rank almost at a stroll, fitting their bowstrings and shafts as they went and sending out the first shots. They could advance at the same speed as the retreating square and they could hardly miss the lumbering beast that tried to stay ahead of them.

Xenophon felt Hephaestus flinch at his side and turned sharply on him.

'Would you stop that? You will embarrass me in front of the men.'

'Right. Sorry,' Hephaestus said.

He held himself rigid as four hundred archers jogged after them like wolves, sending shaft after shaft into the air. The range was not far off their maximum, for which Xenophon was thankful. If he'd been in command of the Persians, he'd have made them close up to a hundred paces, to pick their shots. At over two hundred, his men had time to see shafts coming. The shield-bearers in the rear were almost enjoying themselves, raising the bronze discs to pluck arrows out of the air as if it was a competition. They were cheering each other on until one of them was struck cleanly through the neck. There was no chance to stop and recover the body. The rest of them fell quiet as they watched him left behind, step by step. The Persian archers cheered as they bore down on the corpse. The Greeks watched as they picked up the dead man and hacked him to pieces.

'Pass the word for the last three ranks to charge on my order,' Xenophon said to Hephaestus. He needed a formal aide to carry his instructions, but Hephaestus was all he had. He had made the Athenian gang leader a horseman. He wondered if he could make him a soldier.

Hephaestus gaped at him.

'Pass . . . ? How do I?'

'You go to a general, or Chrisophus, the Spartan who leads but accepts no title – and you repeat my order. They pass it on to the captains and pentekosters, who organise the men.'

'What if they refuse?' Hephaestus said. He watched Xenophon's expression tighten in surprise.

'We are at war, Hephaestus, facing the enemy. If they refuse my orders at such a time, their lives are forfeit. However, they will not refuse. They elected me with the understanding that discipline, above all else, is the key to our survival. We need to be ten thousand Spartans, Hephaestus, do you see? Or we will not make it home.'

'I see,' Hephaestus said.

'Then pass on my order! And ride fast. The village cannot be far away now.'

Xenophon sat his mount and stared back over his shoulder for what seemed like an age, the ache in his neck eased only when he turned the horse in a full circle to survey the enemy. They seemed to have brought a good supply of arrows, he thought with ill temper. His first hope had been that they would run short, but the cavalry seemed to hold spare quivers. If anything, the rate of shots intensified rather than slackened off.

Xenophon saw the last three ranks were watching him, ready for his command. They were part of the Spartan contingent and he was grateful for that, knowing that they would carry out his order without any bickering or discussion.

Some of the rearmost hoplites walked backwards with their shields held out, while others had strapped them to their shoulders to walk on as if they were not beset by enemies. The Spartans all wore bronze helmets, so that they stood tall and scorned the threat from behind. They looked fresh enough. Xenophon hoped that was so. Still, he ignored the stares until one of his scouts came back to warn him the village lay only a mile further.

Xenophon pointed twice at the enemy archers, his hand moving sharply. In response, the rearmost ranks suddenly turned and charged, nine hundred men detaching and covering the ground with astonishing speed. The Persian archers were two hundred yards behind and they knew they had no chance at all against armoured hoplites in a hand-to-hand fight. They sprinted away like hares as soon as they saw what was happening.

Xenophon watched in rising anger as the archers who had stung them for hours raced clear. He saw the distance between his charging ranks and the rest of the square increase from a hundred paces to three, then four, so that they appeared smaller to his eye, with dust clouds still rising. He shook his head.

'Horns,' he called, cursing under his breath. He'd hoped for a sudden slaughter. 'Bring them back.'

He waited grim-faced while the Spartans halted their charge, visibly reluctant. Xenophon imagined they might be able to run the men down over a long enough distance, but he could not expose the rear of the square. They came back in good order, but before they rejoined the main force, arrows returned thick and fast, injuring three who had to be carried forward by others into the safety of the square. Xenophon growled in frustration. He could see exactly where to send a cavalry charge to break up the hornets that stung them – but they had no horses.

The village wall of mud brick was barely higher than a man, but still worked to provide shelter and shade. More importantly, it meant that neither the Persian archers nor the horsemen could continue their attack. If they came close enough to threaten, they would be in range of javelins or another sudden rush. On the dusty ground outside the village, the Persians halted in silence, their ranks dropping to one knee to rest. They remained there for an age, but at the first sign of twilight, their officers gave new orders and marched them away.

In the village square, Greek soldiers sat and panted. They would have welcomed a direct assault, but it did not come. The sun began to dip towards the west and the shadows of villagers could be seen running away across the fields in the distance.

Those few who remained were treated kindly on Xenophon's order, though it was in part because they amounted to half a dozen old ladies and a crippled Persian boy who could not run. As far as Xenophon was concerned, the attack gave them the right to take slaves and loot, whatever they wished, though the village was a poor place to begin. There was food and wine, with enough barley for the horses, so they posted guards and settled down to rest.

As shades of purple and rose touched the sky, Xenophon sent an order to summon the captains and generals. He knew Chrisophus, but not any of the others. As they settled themselves in the village square, he realised he would have to learn the strengths and weaknesses of each of them, to use them well. They nodded to him as they gathered and it was clear they did not blame him for the pointless charge that day. It had accomplished nothing, but it had demonstrated the priority, if they were to go on. He took a deep breath and leaned forward slightly, wanting them all to hear and understand.

'Gentlemen, our greatest weakness is the lack of cavalry and archers. I had the men charge today, but they could not close with a lightly armed enemy supported by horsemen. We found shelter tonight, but every day to come there will be an attack – and we have no defence on the march.'

'What then is your answer?' Chrisophus said.

Xenophon glanced at him, but the man was smiling. The Spartan could be infuriating. He was so clearly a natural leader that Xenophon wondered why he had chosen to follow him. He hoped it was because Chrisophus saw the same ability in him, but when the man grinned like that, it seemed that he simply amused himself.

'I said before we need slingers. That need is urgent now. I've seen men of Rhodes among us. They are famous for their skill with the sling. Some of them must have the ability and they can train the rest. Before we leave tomorrow, I want leather slings cut for four hundred men and as many hours of practice as they can get. They have range as good as a Persian bow, just about, but they do not need to be accurate. We are not going to attack, after all. Their task is to make the enemy think twice about sitting in our shadows and picking us off one by one. We can mask the good slingers in the stones of the rest.'

There was an olive tree in that square, wide and ancient, with a trunk so twisted and gnarled it might have stood for a thousand years. A man Xenophon did not know leaned on it with an outstretched right arm. He was a rangy fellow, sunburned and fit-looking, with a thick brown beard that needed to be trimmed. He came forward, taking a position to face the rest. Xenophon knew him then for one of those who had been chosen to replace the murdered generals. He did not step back, though he waited for the man to speak.

'I am Philesius of Thessaly. Nephew to Menon. I stand for him.'

Xenophon felt tension creep over him, as if his skin had been varnished. He had not agreed to lead with a council of generals. While an enemy was literally prowling around them, they could not afford to debate each order. Such a course would mean their destruction.

'Some of you know my uncle was a difficult man at times, though I think he was in the right more than most. Still, there are one or two who have come to me in the night to say I should lead. I speak today because I will not be silent. We can survive this, if we make fewer mistakes than the Persians who wish to see us left for carrion. Xenophon was chosen first by the captains of Proxenus, but I accept him. If I did not, I would keep my peace even so – for the one thing that will bring us down is petty argument and the bickering of factions. We are one blood, one culture. So I say to those who whisper and complain, that I am deaf to you. That is all I have to say.'

The man strolled back to the tree and leaned once more. His chest moved as if he breathed hard, but there was no other sign of strain. Xenophon inclined his head in astonishment and relief.

'Thank you, Philesius. The . . . er . . .' He paused for a moment to collect his thoughts. 'The old women of the village say there is a wide river, half a day from here. I would think it was eight miles, some sixty or seventy stades. They say there is a shallow ford by a copse of ancient olive trees. I will send two men this evening to ride out and find it. There will not be time tomorrow to wander the banks. Our slingers might hold the Persian forces back for a time, but we need a way across. For now, I say eat what you can and sleep well. We are as safe here as anywhere – and those few men we saw today will fear an attack from us in the night. They have pulled back in their cowardice, but we will wake before them and be on our way to the river.'

'And after that?' one of the captains asked.

The officers of Proxenus seemed to take a proprietary interest in him, as they had helped to raise him up. Xenophon let a beat pass before he answered, though he stared at the man, watching him flush.

'After that, I will see what lies ahead,' he replied. 'And I will do what needs to be done.'

Xenophon turned away rather than invite a discussion. He saw Hephaestus and in that moment the Athenian seemed a friendly face in that square. Xenophon headed over to him just to have somewhere to walk. It was only when he drew close that he saw the woman he had noticed before standing behind him.

'My lady,' Xenophon said, bowing his head.

Pallakis dipped to one knee in reply, showing the nape of her neck where she had bound her hair high.

'General,' she replied. 'I wished to ask . . .'

She closed a fist and he raised his eyebrows, intrigued. The fact that she was beautiful was part of it, of course. He had known for a long time that beautiful women are more interesting to men in all ways. The truth was that beauty can always ask for help and be certain of an answer. In a brief moment of relief, he thought how pleasant it was that men judged one another by different standards. Violence, skill and tactics could all be learned, after all. Beauty was rare and harder.

'I wished to ask . . . Some of the men see I have no protection. They are pressing me to visit them. More than one. I am not a whore, general. And I have no wish to be forced. If you are responsible for us, it is to you that I make my appeal.'

Xenophon glanced at Hephaestus, seeing infatuation. A quick answer suggested itself. He had more difficult problems.

'Tell them the Athenian, Hephaestus, is your protector. I am sure he will twist arms and break heads to your satisfaction – and he will demand *nothing* in exchange.'

Xenophon said the last with a certain emphasis to Hephaestus, who blushed a deep pink. Pallakis knelt to him again. He thought there was disappointment in her expression, though he might have imagined it.

'Thank you, general,' she said as he passed by.

In darkness, they were ready to move. The village had been stripped of its stores, with dried meat and bread given out amongst the children and the wounded. It was not enough, not nearly enough. Most of them were starving, but the

Spartans did not complain, so the rest remained silent, though their stomachs ached and murmured.

Before the light came, they set off in the direction of the river, relying on the stars to keep the right direction. The scout had confirmed it was no more than two or three hours of hard marching and the sun rose as they went.

Behind them, a warning shout went up from the outer square. Xenophon cursed and cantered his horse around the edge. He saw Chrisophus coming out to meet him. To his irritation, the man Philesius came as well. Xenophon rather admired him for the stand he had made the previous day. In that single speech, Philesius had almost certainly averted a rebellion and for the most noble of reasons. Xenophon bowed his head and greeted him by name, though all their gazes were on the force coming up behind their square.

Mithridates had ridden far and fast the night before, it seemed. Xenophon could not escape the sense that a vast Persian army shadowed him still, to be able to provide so many men. His only relief was that they kept underestimating the numbers they would need. He saw a thousand cavalry and four thousand archers, presumably all the Persian king had been able to gather in a single night. No doubt they were weary too from a long march, whereas his Greeks had rested well.

More galling was the fact that the Persians had learned a tactic and decided to raise it an order of magnitude. They feared the Greeks still, but they were willing to trail behind like a group of street urchins, throwing stones and spears. It reminded Xenophon of the gangs that had tormented him in Athens and he showed his teeth, wanting to see them destroyed.

Still, he had no cavalry. His six scouts could not run down an enemy of that sort. It was like bitter acid in him, but the

Persians were not wrong. His square was vulnerable to just that sort of attack.

'We'll have to endure this,' Philesius said, staring into the distance.

Without a screen of cavalry, they faced being whittled away, man by man. Alone, the hoplites could have stayed ahead of any pursuing force on foot. Yet the camp followers had slowed, if anything. They were simply not used to marching at that pace. When the heat built, they staggered, or crashed down in a faint, crying for water. It halved the speed of the Greek square.

'Menon wished to abandon the camp followers,' Xenophon said, watching Philesius closely. The man was about his own age, but seemed no green hand, no boy pretending to be a man. He too had endured the battle of Cunaxa and was as much a veteran as Xenophon, or more.

'Then he was mistaken,' Philesius said softly. 'I would not leave an enemy to be set upon by these jackals, never mind those who look to us. I will disobey that order, general, if you give it.'

Xenophon grunted as if displeased. He needed no friends, he reminded himself. He needed men who would follow without question. He went on as if Philesius had not spoken.

'Bring the slingers to the rear. The Spartans will protect them with shields. They might gain us a little time.'

The thought of asking village-quality slingers to walk backwards and whirl their stones around their heads was on the verge of hopeless, but he needed to try anything that might keep the Persians from pressing too closely. They would have to slow down for the ford crossing, he was certain. At that point, the enemy could pick them off at will. He clenched his jaw, thinking a way through. Socrates had taught him to look for the heart of a question – to peel back all the vanities and all the lies men told themselves. In the end, when the truth lay naked, a man could act on what he had learned. Lives would still be lost, of course, perhaps his own. Yet they had chosen him to lead because they believed he could. Because he believed he could.

'Gentlemen,' Xenophon said suddenly. 'Here are my orders.'

25

With the river in sight, the Persian archers came close enough to pick their shots. Shields and chestplates saved many of the Greeks they tormented, like flies biting at a horse. Yet shafts still struck home in the ranks. Wounded men were drawn forward, over the heads of those who still marched, then placed on stretchers to be carried. Few of them cried out in pain, and those who winced at the wounds only put their heads down and marched on.

The ford was barely twenty paces across, a bed of ancient shingle that was churned to brown mud in moments as the first ranks plunged in. Behind them, the Persians grew bold. The enemy archers surged forward and Xenophon felt the air hiss with shafts. He saw Philesius give the order and the slingers responded at last, with everything they had. Unlike the Persians, those men needed only smooth stones. They lay by the thousand along the river and the Greeks set the slings whirring at astonishing speed, each man holding a blur until he released and immediately reached for another.

The archers scattered in panic. Not more than a dozen of them were hit by the first strike, but they had known slingers before and they ducked and threw themselves down. It was true stones continued to rattle across them even then, but in the panic, the Persians assumed a greater force than actually faced them. Their officers bellowed at them to get up and shoot, but they were reluctant. One by one, the archers rose and saw how few stones there were, how few of their fellows actually had been wounded. They took on grim expressions then and reached for their bows once more.

In those precious beats of time, the Greeks had roared across the river. As the last of them reached the other side, the weary slingers moved back into the ranks. The rearmost hoplites gave up holding shields aloft and turned away, breaking into a jog. Hundreds looked back in fear as the Persian cavalrymen saw their enemy running away. Those men called in high-pitched voices to one another, pointing with their swords and jabbing spears in the air. The archers may have failed, but the horsemen saw a fleeing enemy, the backs of men. The ford was unguarded. There would never be a better time.

In an instant, they were digging in their heels and galloping across, scattering spray. Ahead of them, the retreating ranks suddenly stopped and turned. The Persian horsemen whooped and hollered, but they found themselves facing a steady line of red-cloaked warriors, with no sign of the panic they had sensed before. They bore down on Spartans as those men raised shields and lowered their helmets, presenting the unbroken bronze of the elite soldiers of Greece. The cavalrymen began to pull up, though the ones behind urged them on with wild cries.

Three ranks of Spartans charged the enemy horsemen, advancing at a lope, with shields ready and spears at waist height. The ford was the perfect pinch point and Xenophon had judged it well. His best men enveloped the Persian cavalry as they clambered out of the river, denying them the space to move. Even their archers could not support them from the other side, not with their own people fighting in the crush. Arrows still buzzed and struck, but fully half the Persian cavalry had to pull back, leaving horses in the bloody water and hundreds of their compatriots to be hacked down.

It was not long before the Greeks withdrew for real at a good pace. They had lost men but made a mess of their pursuers. Persians littered the ground behind them. Many of them had been butchered with deliberate savagery, to frighten those behind.

In exchange for that risk, they had won horses. Xenophon was delighted as he inspected every new mount and assigned them to volunteers, anyone who claimed to be able to ride. He appointed Hephaestus as their officer and took back a horse from an Athenian who objected, making the man apologise.

'That was a triumph – no small victory,' Xenophon called to them all. 'We will never be so vulnerable again.' He looked back to the bodies by the river and then ahead, to where hills lay in the distance. Persia stretched for half the world, but they would march out, he swore it.

With an enraged enemy still swarming on the other bank, Xenophon ordered the square onward. There was no opportunity to fill their waterskins, not with archers waiting, furious and humiliated at the way they had been fooled. Instead, the Greeks strode on dry-mouthed, across ground that showed a trace of green. They trudged all day and when the remaining Persian horsemen showed themselves at last on the rear trail, they had horses and javelins to keep them back.

By the time the sun was setting once again, they had lost the sense of excitement from the morning. Hunger and thirst were the greatest problems, though it seemed there would be shelter that night. The scouts had reported an abandoned city, at the edge of their range. They saw the walls growing before them for hours, until they marched right through an ancient breach in the wall, over a spill of broken stones.

The streets were dusty and there was no sign of life. It was a vast place to be so quiet, though long-tailed lizards skittered across every wall, leaping in fear at the presence of men where there had been silence for so long. All those who could hunt went out in bands around the city, trapping anything alive they could find. One such group encountered a leopard and saw a man badly mauled before they speared it. Others brought pigeons down and the rattle of stones sounded across the city as the slingers continued to practise, determined to be the threat they had only pretended before.

Xenophon found a great pyramid in a square in the city, some sixty paces high. He could see no entrance and had no explanation for its existence there. One of his captains handed him what seemed to be a glass lens, shaped like the rounded eye of a fish, just lying in the dust of the road. There were bones preserved inside some of the buildings and pieces of bronze armour lying there that had once protected a warrior. The city had known disaster at some point in the past, unimaginably far back.

The Greeks had captured prisoners at the river, keeping a dozen men alive to be interrogated. Xenophon ordered the first one killed as an example to the rest, then questioned them all evening, while his soldiers handed over food to the women of the camp. Fires were kindled with ancient wood, so dry it roared to life with just a spark of flint and iron. The smell of frying meat filled their mouths with saliva, and though there was no wine, they found clay jugs that had once contained it and a well of clear water. Mixing the two made a drink that was not completely unpleasant and had at least a memory of the grape.

One of the prisoners claimed the city was named Larisa, while another said it was Nimrud, which had once been a capital for the Medes. It all had to be translated by those who knew both languages and it was a slow business. Xenophon walked along the crest of the city walls while the prisoners babbled about the king's forces below. He had promised them their lives in exchange for all they knew. The stakes were survival and he felt no pang of guilt over ordering life or death. He told them so, quietly and clearly. With one of their number already lying on the dusty stones, they believed him and sang like birds.

He heard a whistle and looked up to see Hephaestus and Pallakis, man and woman rising to the level of the wall's crown by way of stone steps set into the side. Xenophon sighed to himself, though he smiled at them. Clearchus had never mentioned that leading people meant so little time alone, but that seemed to be the way of it. Xenophon knew Socrates enjoyed the company of others, the old man seeming to grow brighter and more alive in a crowd. For his part, Xenophon found simple conversation a strain. He preferred to have a serious purpose, to use his wits and his strength to solve each problem as it came. He wondered briefly if he should send the pair away. Once again, the beauty of a woman changed his mind. The city was a place of death and silence for the most part, eerie in all the centuries it had seen. Pallakis had a mass of black curls that she wore in a halo that day, so that she seemed almost a Medusa in the breeze.

'I asked to see you, Xenophon,' Pallakis said.

'Really,' Xenophon replied, glancing at Hephaestus. The young Athenian looked as infatuated as any puppy. Xenophon surprised himself with a twinge of envy as Pallakis touched the younger man's arm. He thought he showed them nothing, but had a suspicion Pallakis was probably good at reading men.

Xenophon sighed.

'My lady, I need . . .' He caught himself before he caused offence, remembering the discipline he saw in the Spartans.

He had to lead. If that meant the end of privacy, he would accept it. 'My lady, what would you have of me?'

'Merely your company, general,' she said. 'The people are afraid – and fearful men and women make poor companions. I wished to talk about our chances.'

Xenophon chuckled and shook his head.

'I would be a poor general if I said they were low, would I not? Yet I can't tell the future, not even as well as the humblest oracle.'

His smile faded as he saw the strain in her. He spoke more seriously.

'I will not fail for want of effort. I swear to you, I will be responsible for every man, woman and child who came to this place. They are my people, Pallakis. Clearchus would not abandon them in a foreign field, to be slaughtered or made slaves. Neither will I, while I have breath in me.' He waited until she nodded, accepting his oath. 'I will ask all they can give. I ask the same of myself. Beyond that . . .' Xenophon looked into the distance and stiffened, so that both Hephaestus and Pallakis turned to where he shaded his eyes.

A force of Persian infantry could be seen far away. It seemed King Artaxerxes had given up expecting their surrender, or relying on a small force of archers to bring them down. A huge number of regiments marched towards the abandoned city as a stain on the land, a summer storm.

'How many men?' Pallakis said, with awe in her voice.

'Who can say? Eighty, ninety thousand? Even then, it is not all. Which is strange.'

'Perhaps the king has returned to his palaces,' Hephaestus said. 'He won the battle, after all. He'll go home to parades and feasts.'

Xenophon was surprised to find he agreed with the sentiment.

'I hope so. If he has, it is to our benefit.' A thought struck him and he winced. 'Unless he leads another army as large on the other side of the city. Would you run and see, Hephaestus, please?'

The man who had once jeered at him in an Athenian market raced back to the steps and vanished without another word. Xenophon smiled slightly in satisfaction. Nothing moulded a man more than war, for good or ill.

In that instant, he realised he was alone with the prince's mistress for the first time. She seemed to know his thoughts had turned to the personal, even while he was watching the enemy trudge towards the city.

'Are you married, general?' she asked.

Xenophon coughed and went red. 'Ah, no, sorry. No, I am not married. I devoted my life to politics, in support of Sparta. It was not . . . a popular decision in Athens. Somehow, all opportunities passed me by during that time.' He squinted again at the enemy, reassuring himself they would not arrive at the city before darkness. 'I have tried . . . to find the best way to live, the best way to spend these few years we are given by the gods. To that end, I dedicated myself to great teachers and to crafts like horsemanship and managing an estate. I have been a student of Socrates, for four years now.'

'I do not know the name,' she said, deflating him. 'But this study of how best to live – you did not see a wife as part of that?'

She seemed genuinely surprised. He blushed further and cleared his throat into his closed hand.

'No, I did not. I will give some thought to it, my lady.' He shook off the strange mood and spoke with more certainty. 'For now, we must prepare either to move on or to defend a dead city.'

He took her hand and she let him guide her to the top of the steps. Pallakis was smiling when he looked at her, intrigued by a man far more interesting than she had expected. She had decided to encourage his obvious interest in her, as one who could keep her safe and protect her status. She had not expected to feel a flutter as he took her hand. It was odd. She admired men like Cyrus or Clearchus. They seemed to suffer no doubt in their own strength. Yet it was men who struggled that made her fall in love. Pallakis knew herself very well and as she stepped down to the city square, she urged caution to her inner voice. She wished to be needed, was the truth of it. She sensed Xenophon was desperately lonely and needed her very much indeed. The idea was intoxicating.

Xenophon slept on the wall. His stomach had shrunk and his head throbbed, but he was determined not to complain while so many others were going hungry. The last of the hunters' haul was shared out that evening. He could smell meat roasting on fires made from ancient furniture, dry as the desert winds that howled around the city. From where he rested, he could see Persian campfires like sparks spread across the blackness.

He pressed a fist into his stomach when it groaned and murmured, sounding for all the world like a little voice. The first share of the meat had to go to the soldiers, of course, then the children who did not have their reserves and could not survive on air and water for very long. In theory, the others would get their share after that, but it was barely a broth by then, though they did their best to eke it out to fill as many stomachs as possible.

As he had the thought, footsteps sounded and he saw a light growing as someone came up the steps. Xenophon rose to his feet, irritated to be disturbed even in the small hours. He felt obscurely disappointed when he recognised the Spartan, Chrisophus. The man bore a bowl of something that steamed in one hand and a flask in the other.

'You have not eaten, general,' he said.

'Have you?' Xenophon countered.

Chrisophus shrugged. 'I am a Spartan,' he said, as if that was answer enough.

Xenophon raised an eyebrow and waited, ignoring the bowl and flask held out to him. Chrisophus sighed and relented.

'We never had enough food when I was a boy. I can remember feeling full perhaps twice in my life, both times at a royal feast. We were encouraged to steal bread, of course, but I was never very good at that. I think . . .'

'You were encouraged to steal?' Xenophon asked in surprise.

'As I say, we were not well fed. If we managed to outwit the cooks and snatch a little extra, that was never punished. Unless we were caught – though we were punished then for being caught. We believe hunger makes a boy quick, where being full makes him slow and stupid. I think that is probably true.'

'But you are hungry now?'

'Of course. We resist the flesh, general. The flesh is a fat and foolish thing that seeks to control us. It is a slow horse, if you understand me – a horse that doesn't understand why it is slow. But do not mistake me. You must eat, because you need to be sharp tomorrow. Beyond a certain point, hunger is life.'

'I have no appetite, Chrisophus. However, share the bowl with me and I will eat. That is an order.'

The Spartan looked down at the bowl he was holding out.

He ran the tip of his tongue over his lips, allowing himself to enjoy the odour of whatever beans and flesh had gone into the thick stew. He gestured with it and Xenophon took the bowl and the flask from him, sitting cross-legged to eat. Chrisophus produced a small loaf from under his arm and broke it in two, handing over one half. Each man scooped up the stew with a piece of bread and ate it slowly, refusing to rush or reveal the desperate urge to speed up. Xenophon slowed right down, determined not to be outdone by the Spartan, though his body cried out for sustenance.

'We cannot stay in this place,' Xenophon said at last. 'If they surround us, we will have lost. Pass the word as you go down, would you? An hour, perhaps two, no more than that. We need to stay ahead of our pursuers.'

'That will not be easy,' Chrisophus said softly. 'There are no pack animals now, not after tonight. The children will have to walk or be carried.'

'Have the labour shared, then, a dozen men and women to bear each child in turn. If they slow us down, we will be eaten up from behind. We cannot hope to protect the camp followers and take the war to the Persians.'

'No?' Chrisophus asked. He had watched a Greek square roam almost at will on the battlefield.

'No,' Xenophon said. 'You wanted me to lead, Spartan. Do not question my orders now. Our aim is to leave the lands under the control of King Artaxerxes. Not to challenge him again where he is strongest. All we have to do is stay ahead of them.'

'They have cavalry now, in great numbers. We have, what, two hundred horse? It is not enough, I think.'

'It is enough to screen the rear . . .' Xenophon said. He knew the Spartan was an experienced soldier. For all he did not enjoy being pushed and prodded, he understood there was a point to it, just as when Socrates asked him a dozen times to say what love was.

'We are slow,' Chrisophus said, counting off one finger. 'We have too few slingers, so we are vulnerable over distance. We are intent on retreating at a steady pace . . .'

'They will become bold,' Xenophon admitted. 'When they see they cannot make us stop. They will harry us and nip our heels. What I wouldn't give for the prince's personal guard! Those six hundred horsemen could hunt and hold them back for a month. Without them . . .'

He trailed off, staring at the points of light in the distance.

'These Persians prefer not to camp too closely to us. I do not know why that is.'

'Even so many fear a night attack,' Chrisophus said. 'We are famous amongst them for our tricks. They do not trust us when we are close.'

'If that is true, it means that we will begin each day ahead of them,' Xenophon said. 'And if they camp closer, we might risk a raid and scatter their horses.'

'That's the spirit,' Chrisophus replied. Yet the Spartan looked grim and Xenophon caught his mood.

'You think we can get away?'

There was no answer for a long time, until Xenophon thought the man would not reply or had dozed off.

'It does not matter what I think,' Chrisophus said. 'We march, river to river. Four or six hundred miles – it is not too far. Yet they will try to bring us down, like dogs after a deer. Whether we succeed or die, it does not change what we must do. So I will set off with a glad heart. My people are all around me and my enemies are all behind. It will be a good day.'

To Xenophon's surprise, Chrisophus patted him on the shoulder as he rose up and stretched his back.

'Try to sleep, general. We'll need you up early tomorrow.'

'I'll come and wake you,' Xenophon said. He felt rather than saw the Spartan smile in the darkness as he went back down.

The Spartans in the square all knew one another as they gathered to march once more. They greeted friends and murmured comments about the long day ahead, or the strange city around them. The night had been warm enough to sleep in the open, rather than risk scorpions in long-abandoned houses. They emptied bladders and sipped waterskins, though thirst remained acute in all of them.

With the moon still in the sky and no sign of dawn in the east, the entire force set off, the camp followers contained in their own ranks within the square, making a rolling, restless heart with soldiers on all sides. They left the city behind and marched with goosebumps of morning chill on their skin. Some looked back, fearing a great howl or the sound of hooves rushing down upon them, but there was nothing but stillness and the night's silence.

By the time the sun finally rose, they were a dozen miles from the city and still going. Xenophon sent orders to Hephaestus to keep scouts out behind as well as ahead. Having horses brought them eyes and range, where before they had been almost blind. Yet there was no sign of the Persians and it was hunger that forced them to halt by two villages. They found penned goats on scrub earth and a winter store that was full of pistachios and almonds, ready to be sold. The villagers made no protest as they watched the cellars emptied, but nor were they killed or taken as slaves. Xenophon had to give orders on the last. They could barely look after the camp followers they had, never mind if they added to their number.

The scouts came cantering in before they had spent a half-day in the village, but it was enough time to refill every vessel and even to put the youngest children on two small carts drawn by mules once more. The owners watched disconsolately as the Greeks moved on.

They saw the Persian cavalry before evening came. A line of them rode up to observe the marching square, all large and powerful warriors who held out sabres and scimitars with unmistakable threat. There was no sign of the king himself, nor any of his lords. Xenophon was pleased not to see foot regiments alongside them. Cavalry alone could not break their formation, not against spears. He dared to hope the king might have given orders simply to escort them from his lands.

That night, they were kept awake by horsemen riding close to the camp. They had found a small stream and waded through it to rest on the far side, but any chance at sleep was hard when howls and shrieks sounded in the darkness. Hephaestus wanted to ride out and draw blood, but Xenophon refused. They needed to keep safe the few horses they had. Sleep was less vital than that protection, at least for a time.

The stars had circled their camp when warning horns sounded. Scouts came barrelling in, roaring incoherently, stirring those around to gather arms. Xenophon roused himself, itching one armpit where sweat had grown into a rash. Exhaustion had dragged him into a deeper sleep than he had known, but his yawns died stillborn as he looked up. The light was grey in the pre-dawn, but he could see an ocean of dark soldiers approaching in silent ranks, barely four hundred paces from where he stood. They had marched closer, advancing in the last breath of darkness. As the light grew to gold, Xenophon saw Tissaphernes sat his mount in front of that mass of men, the man resplendent in white.

Xenophon felt his heart thump in panic. The Persian tapped his breast in mock salute. The enemy ranks roared as one and charged.

26

Xenophon cursed as sweat stung a gash on his cheek. It had been a glancing blow from an arrow, but it just kept bleeding. Every time he wiped perspiration, his fingers opened the wound again.

Tissaphernes had thrown his entire force at the Greek square, trying to bring an end to the chase in one strike. He had come close. Xenophon tried not to think of the first moments of savagery. He'd seen a woman running after her screaming daughter, right across the Persian charge as it came in. They'd run her down, so that both woman and child vanished underfoot.

Perhaps a hundred had been left behind as the square formed and lurched forward, still open. Persian cavalry had darted in like wolves cutting out the old and sick. They took women, men, anyone they could reach. Some over-eager Persians were cut down by hoplites scrambling to close the formation, but that was no comfort to those who were caught. Most of them were killed on the spot, while others were kept alive to scream and hold out their hands in pitiful appeal, pressed across the saddles of laughing men.

The square closed and the Greeks marched on, stung and furious at the attack. Xenophon felt angry gazes on him, while he wanted to string Hephaestus up for not giving enough warning. He called the Athenian over and saw the man looked as mulish and dark as he had ever done on the streets of the city.

'Where were you?' Xenophon asked. He kept his voice

quiet, in part because the responsibility was his, regardless of how Hephaestus saw it. He could not blame the inexperienced gang leader for not keeping a proper watch.

'I left the scouts an hour out from camp,' Hephaestus said.

He hung his head as he spoke and for a moment he looked about ready to burst into tears. Instead, he steadied himself with an effort of will that impressed Xenophon.

'I went out with them, but then . . . I rode back to camp. I'm sorry.'

Xenophon looked at the young man. Hephaestus could neither read nor write his own name. He had learned to ride on the trek east into Persia. If there was a fault, it lay with the one who had left him alone, without anyone to advise him.

'Tell me what happened,' he said.

Hephaestus looked away, unable to meet his gaze.

'They must have had horsemen waiting – with archers.' He gestured sharply, cutting the air. 'A few of the lads got clear, but we lost a lot of men. They came on fast, Xenophon. I was still on my way back. By the time I was able to shout an alarm, they were almost on us. I'm sorry.'

He fell silent, ready for whatever judgement awaited him.

'I should not have left you without more experienced officers,' Xenophon said. 'The error is mine, do you understand? I do not blame you for my own mistake.' He made his voice brisk, as if the matter was already forgotten. 'Now, for tomorrow night, you'll need to place scouts in pairs, but always in range of one another. If one rider or a pair is brought down, the others hare back to camp. Always in sight, Hephaestus. That is the lesson to learn from this.'

'I am sorry,' Hephaestus said again.

Xenophon looked blankly at him.

'You have no need to be. Learn from this. They have won a minor skirmish, raised their spirits. It doesn't change

351

anything! How far have we come already? All we have to do is stay ahead.'

As he spoke, fresh shouts went up from those who watched the Persians in their wake. A moan of fear sounded from the open centre of the square, the first time Xenophon had heard such a sound from them. He clenched his jaw, angry at himself but also at an enemy who would not just let them go.

As he headed back along the flank of the marching square, Xenophon saw a mass of cavalry riding at an easy canter, as if on parade. They passed the Greeks at a distance of six or eight hundred paces, too far for spear or arrow. The Persian horsemen turned to watch the enemy they were leaving behind, of course, but they were riding ahead of the marching Greeks, using the advantage of speed and mobility.

Xenophon watched as Chrisophus came alongside. The Spartan looked healthy, barely breathing hard, despite the bronze and leather breastplate he wore.

'Any new orders, general?' Chrisophus called.

Xenophon was beginning to know how the man thought. The Spartan was more comfortable with subtlety than Clearchus had been.

'None for now,' Xenophon said. 'Any thoughts on those horsemen?'

'I imagine they will set an ambush ahead of us,' Chrisophus said. He had made his way to the flank to make sure Xenophon understood that exact point. 'They'll find a place where the road narrows, perhaps in the hills. They'll fell trees or roll stones, whatever they can find to hold us in one spot. Those behind will attack at the same time. It is what I would do.'

'I cannot stop them going ahead,' Xenophon said. 'Nor can we scatter the ones still trailing us. If we stop and offer battle, they can withdraw at the same pace. And if they accept

352

our challenge, our camp followers will be left vulnerable. That is the heart of our position.'

He blinked at having said it, feeling suddenly hopeless. Aware of the eyes of those around him, he shook his head slightly, putting such fears aside. A commander had to appear confident, even to experienced men like Chrisophus. He had to be beyond doubt and weakness.

'Still, we do not want to engage with these Persians. We have shown they are no match for us on the field. There is no glory in tormenting them further. No, our task is to walk out of their territory. I intend to do that, Chrisophus. If they take the high ground, we will march through with shields held overhead. If they attack us on foot, we will cut them down until they desist. We'll fight if we must, but our victory will be when we reach the Black Sea. There are Greek cities on the coast in the north. When we reach those, we'll be in range of home.'

Chrisophus bowed his head as he walked.

'Press on in good order, general. Understood.'

He grinned like a boy then and Xenophon felt his mask crack as he smiled. He had given voice to the problems ahead, but just by saying them aloud, he saw they were not insurmountable. He felt cheerful, for the first time that day.

'Carry on,' he said.

They marched a dozen miles to a river, where a wooden bridge had been built over the torrent. Xenophon gave orders to halt on both sides of that point, controlling the crossing long enough to take on water. Spartans stood with shields and spears ready for any sudden charge while the camp followers refilled every waterskin and flask. Though the deserts were behind, life still existed between rivers in that place.

All the while, Tissaphernes sat his horse some way off,

leaning over his saddlehorn in the centre of a line of bearded Persian warriors. They stared at their enemies, as if they were the wolves and the Greeks were fawns come to drink. Xenophon smiled at the thought. His men were warriors without equal, as they had proved at Cunaxa. That bitter draught for Persian sensibilities was all that was keeping them alive.

Tissaphernes let his men edge close and threaten those who waited to cross, but they offered no charging line, no advance of spears and swords. Not against the red-cloaked Spartans who sat talking or stared idly back. Some of the Greeks splashed and washed themselves in the shallows, throwing up spray and laughing. Others sang or recited poems to one another, declaiming to small groups. They knew such scenes would infuriate the watching enemy, but Xenophon found his own spirits raised by the insouciance of his people. Why should they dip their gaze in fear, even from so many? The Spartans were arrogant, of course, but it was an arrogance that had been earned.

Even without the cavalry, the Persian regiments stretched across the land – tens of thousands of them. Tissaphernes seemed to sense when the Greeks had filled their last gourds and skins and were making ready. The movement amongst the Persian lines became agitated, soldiers whipping themselves to rage with chanting and exhortation, driving each other on. Some of them came close enough to throw spears and Xenophon cursed under his breath at the sight of dark thorns arcing over. He gave the order to complete the crossing, passing the word quietly through the captains.

The Persians grew more frenzied and two groups ran forward with no warning. The first stopped short at the spears, a forest they could not pass. They sensed the Spartans would not break rank and so stood just beyond the points, roaring and jabbing the air.

Along the other flank, a pair of horsemen broke out of the Persian regiments and galloped in, low over their saddles, then rising to throw javelins with huge force. Both of them struck men from their feet, the spears finding spaces between shields. The riders howled in triumph, raising their arms to their comrades behind.

One of the Corinthians stepped out of rank in three quick strides, launching a long spear. It passed right through one of the riders, so that he fell from his horse and lay suddenly still, all life and noise gone from him in an instant.

It was the turn of the Greeks to laugh and jeer, while the rest pushed on across the bridge. Every new step brought Persians pressing closer, forcing them on. Xenophon rode onto the bridge with the final lines of his men, showing his back to archers and warriors in panelled coats, who snarled and closed the whole way. He reached the other side as the crossing became a wild rush.

The Persian officers lost whatever control they'd had. Their front ranks sprinted onto the bridge with swords drawn, while the last Greeks retreated backwards, holding spears out and shields up. They had to bear hundreds of blows, iron swords scarring and gashing the golden bronze, all unanswered as they went clear.

Xenophon raised his fist high as the bridge filled with Persian marching ranks. He brought it back to his side and the entire span cracked and fell, crashing into the racing waters. In the hours they'd held the crossing, the original supports had been cut through, replaced by single logs. At his order, a few sharp blows had been all it took to knock them out. The bridge broke under its own weight and tumbled right over, crushing the host still crossing in full armour.

Xenophon turned from their horror and panic to stare at Tissaphernes, still watching from the other bank. The Persian lord answered him with a flight of arrows by the thousand. He had brought archers up in secret, but losing the bridge blunted the effect. Even so, arrows soared into the air and every Greek ducked down under a shield in a great clatter of iron on bronze and wood.

Xenophon held himself still, trusting to the good fortune that had protected him to that point. Tissaphernes had not risked being amongst the first to cross. That would have made the day complete. Instead, the Persian and his men would have to find another ford, ranging up and down the river.

Xenophon squinted at the rising ground and the hills that lay ahead. The land was greener to the north, less hostile to life. He knew there would be an ambush waiting, but that was a problem for another day.

'Make good time!' he shouted to the Greeks, over and over, until he was sure everyone had heard. 'We'll leave them all behind . . .'

He forced himself to smile, showing a confidence he did not feel. He saw how many of the camp followers limped and stumbled along. Many of them had worn through boots and sandals, so that they had to wrap their feet in cloth. They had water, for which he thanked Poseidon, but very little food. He looked ahead, as if to brighter prospects. They could not see his dismay, nor his fears for whatever Tissaphernes had planned for him in the hills.

They walked steadily through the afternoon and a landscape that showed greater signs of life. The mouths of twenty thousand could never be satisfied, but those who could use a bow or a sling went out on all sides and brought back anything they could kill for food. They roamed far around the marching square, becoming the eyes of the Greek force as the land began to rise. Xenophon had ignored the fact that he was starving until he saw a dozen deer carried in, a herd of small bucks and does his men had managed to surprise in a crease in the land, trapping forty of the animals. More had leaped clear with prodigious bounds, springing high into the air to avoid the trap. It meant little more than a single meal for some of them that evening, but it brought hope as well.

Every hour on the march revealed new ridges and canyons, while the sun cast long shadows on a wide path through cliffs. Xenophon sent Hephaestus out with the remaining horsemen to look for other routes, but there were a thousand culverts that ended in sheer rock and only one great pass through the mountains. It was not too hard to guess where the ambush would come, but even so it could not be avoided. Their destination was to the north.

They made camp in an orchard of ancient apple trees clinging to life in a shallow valley. The road stretched before them, shrouded in darkness. None of them wanted to go on before they saw sunlight once more. The camp followers broke branches from dead trees and gathered as much dry wood as they could find. The hunters handed over the precious deer to women who knew how to gralloch and prepare the carcasses. Dozens of others sought out fresh greens in the hills around, picking herbs and grasses they knew could keep body and soul together. More importantly, they knew that playing a part in the preparation gave them a better chance of getting a taste. The hunters added pheasant, partridge and one skinny old goat who had run blindly from them until a boy wrestled it to the ground. Their need was greater than whoever had owned it before, though it still wore a halter around its neck. It was cut into pieces by a Spartan kopis and roasted on a shield across a cooking fire, watched by children with starving eyes as it sizzled and spat.

Though there was no wine, the water they had was clear and cold and the mood in the camp was light. Xenophon spoke to the officers about the day to come but they could only make vague plans until they knew what form the next attack would take. In some ways, that lay at the heart of Xenophon's good mood as he settled himself for sleep, staring up at stars. He had come to believe in the ingenuity of his people. They would not be rushed, it was true. They had a terrible tendency to argue through a crisis, but when they moved, it was with certainty and intelligence. He was proud of them all.

He only knew he had been asleep when he was startled awake, sensing a pressure against his side. His eyes opened to see Pallakis on the ground beside him, wrapped in her own blanket. He sat up in the darkness, aware that the camp slept around them, thousands of people depending on him for their lives.

'My lady,' he murmured. 'You do not need another protector. Is Hephaestus not keeping you safe?'

He heard her turn towards him in the dark, so close that he could feel her breath on his face.

'There is more to life than safety,' she said.

'Yes. Of course, you were the mistress of Prince Cyrus,' he replied. He sensed her stiffen in the darkness. 'And I saw you were at least a companion to Clearchus after that. And now you are here, at my side, though I gave Hephaestus the task of looking after you.'

'And then sent him away,' she said, her voice suddenly unsure.

He winced to himself, feeling the awkwardness of the moment.

'Because he is my master of horse, Pallakis. He commands the scouts and I send him away almost every night . . . Wait, have you been threatened?'

She sat up suddenly, kneeling to fold her blanket.

'No. Hephaestus is respected amongst the men. They know I am under his protection. I thought . . . I am sorry.'

Xenophon felt his face aflame, but he spoke before she could vanish into the night.

'Stay now, at least, as you are here. It cannot be long until dawn.'

The dark figure at his side was very still, staring at him. Then she settled down once more. He lay there, alert and awake for quite some time.

In the morning, Xenophon opened his eyes to find Pallakis gone. He wondered briefly if she had come to him in a dream, but put the thought aside when Hephaestus appeared with his usual mount, having checked the bridle and watered the animal. All the horses were looking thin, though they could at least crop grasses in the mountains, denied to them before. Unlike the men, they could not go long without being well fed, something that made both Hephaestus and Xenophon concerned. Without cavalry and scouts they could not survive, that was the truth of it.

Hephaestus seemed sullen as he handed over the reins and helped him to mount. The Athenian passed up a sword and Xenophon belted it on as he considered whether he should mention his night visitor. He had not promised Pallakis to Hephaestus, nor was it in his power to do so. Yet he had seen the young man was smitten with her and he needed no trouble between them. Xenophon chose to say nothing. He would keep his distance from Pallakis and the problem would solve itself.

The Persians were sighted behind them before they'd cleared the camp and were ready to move. Xenophon felt like thanking Tissaphernes for helping the lazier camp followers to spring to their positions and make ready for another day of marching. They could not form the square within a square that he preferred – the pass through the mountains was too narrow for twenty thousand to go in formation. Despite his misgivings, Xenophon agreed a column order with Chrisophus. The Spartan persisted in acting as if he was the formal second in command, and no one challenged his right to do so. The other generals who had been chosen seemed content to command their own and leave the overall strategy to him. Xenophon wondered how many more mistakes he could make before that changed.

The Spartan contingent insisted on leading the column through the cliffs. Xenophon ordered every shield ready all along the line in case the Persians had gained the heights above. He fretted as he rode to the front, trying to think of everything that could possibly go wrong and worrying that he would miss something vital. They looked to him and he felt the weight of it, while enjoying the exercise of authority he had not known before. Holding minor political power in Athens did not quite compare to taking an army through mountains.

The Persians pressed in behind, riding close as the Greeks moved off. The Stymphalians held the rear that morning, with slingers and most of the horses back where they would be best placed to hold off an enemy blow. Those men marched with aching necks from looking over their shoulders, but there was no help for that.

Ahead, Xenophon heard a yell and he trotted along the flank, forcing soldiers and camp followers aside to let him pass. The road was barely sixty paces across, a great causeway to anyone but an army. Ahead, the cliffs were split so that they rose sharply on either side of the road – and there on the flanks of a green mountain was a Persian force, waiting for him. He understood then why Tissaphernes was pressing in at the rear. The Persians knew their men were close and they were trying to force the Greeks deeper into the pass.

Xenophon was the only horseman at the front. He squinted into the distance, then smiled slowly to himself. The Spartans marched stolidly on, ready to endure the barrage that had no doubt been prepared for them. At that point, it could have been almost anything, from rocks and heated oil, to arrows dipped in filth. The Spartans began to ready their shields, but Xenophon shook his head.

'Chrisophus. The Persian position is overlooked. They chose that spot where it is wide and flat, but look higher — there is ground above them. Ground we could reach.'

'They'll see us coming,' Chrisophus called back, though it was not in argument, more in dawning delight.

'We'll have to run, then,' Xenophon said. 'Six hundred with me — your fittest men. We'll race up that hill and fall on them from above, just as they intended to do to us.'

He turned his horse's head off the road and onto the mossy flank of the cliff that led upwards. Behind him, Chrisophus shouted quick orders. Six hundred men broke away and came to join the two leaders. They looked pleased to be given a challenge.

'Soldiers!' Xenophon called to them. 'Remember this. You endure for those you will save, but also to see Greece. You fight for your honour — and to see your wives and children once again. Keep up and you will throw these Persians off this hill!'

'It's all right for you, you're on a horse,' one of the men replied. 'I'm wearing myself out carrying this shield.'

Xenophon stared, his good mood evaporating. With deliberate care, he dismounted and stalked over. His horse dipped its head to snatch at clumps of grass and Xenophon stood before the one who had spoken.

'Stay here, then,' Xenophon said.

He wrenched away the man's shield and sprinted up the hill. The rest lurched into motion to go after him. They went full pelt up the slope, while at the bottom, the man's companions picked up stones and threw them at him, making their displeasure clear.

Xenophon ran and leaped until he was red in the face and blowing hard, though he reached the crest of the mountain with all the others. He held up the shield like a trophy and those below cheered the sight. The Persians who had hoped to ambush them had already abandoned their position, making their way down by another path, as soon as they'd understood their advantage had been lost. The cheers of Greeks echoed through the mountains all around, reaching the ears of Tissaphernes as his regiments crept through the valley. He halted his men, unwilling to pursue in a place where the land stole the advantage of great numbers. Xenophon climbed down and rejoined the main force as they continued along the pass, through to the plains beyond.

27

The flat lands on the other side of the mountains were sheltered, showing more than a few marks of man. A wide river glimmered in the distance as the Greeks looked out over villages and stone farms. They could see woodsmoke and a herd of goats being driven. Many of them cried out in relief at a landscape that meant food and water, with no sign of the enemy encroaching upon them.

Xenophon called Hephaestus in to organise the scouts. He found the young Athenian tight-lipped and silent, though he rode clear smartly enough when he understood the orders. Xenophon watched him go with a trace of anger himself, but if that was the way it had to be, he could accept it. They had not been friends in Athens and he had greater concerns. Hephaestus was barely out of sight before Chrisophus brought the new general, Philesius, to walk at his side.

'Thank you for coming, gentlemen,' Xenophon said as they trudged down onto the plain. 'I've been thinking about making a small force of our better warriors. If we are to be harried through passes and across bridges, we need a rearguard, armed with the longest spears and accompanied by the best of our slingers and a few Cretan archers.'

'That is a fine idea,' Chrisophus said. 'I will select six companies of a hundred and appoint captains to oversee them. It will be work without reward, for the most part. I doubt there will be many volunteers for such a thankless task. May I suggest . . .'

'You may not suggest the Spartans, if that is what you are

about to say,' Xenophon interrupted. 'Impressive as they are, they are better in the front ranks, as you have told me any number of times.'

'Very well, general,' Chrisophus said, bowing his head. 'Though I came to you because General Philesius wished for a word.'

Xenophon glanced at the other man and nodded, grudgingly. He had heard Philesius address the camp precisely once, when he'd shown support. Even so, Xenophon did not trust his sudden reappearance.

'I see. While we talk, Chrisophus, you are in charge of opening up these villages. Take what food you find, along with all pack animals, flocks and any carts we can put to use. We need cauldrons and new waterskins to replace the ones that have split. More, we need shoes – let these people go barefoot for a season. They are not having to walk across an empire with a Persian army breathing down their neck. Understood?'

Chrisophus dropped to one knee, so that Xenophon left him behind as his horse walked on. He looked back at the Spartan, but Chrisophus was already jogging away, calling in the captains and pentekosters he would need.

Philesius watched the Spartan go for a moment, then cleared his throat. He was not happy to have to address Xenophon from the level of the man's calves, but there was no sign of the Athenian dismounting.

'You wanted to speak to me?' Xenophon prompted him.

'Yes . . . I did. I wished to point out that we have crossed a range of hills and there is no sign of Tissaphernes and the Persians, never mind the king himself. It struck me that while I had no business interfering before, perhaps now is the time to discuss how best to lead the soldiers clear.'

'And the camp followers,' Xenophon prompted airily.

'Yes, of course, the camp followers also. I meant that the immediate threat has been reduced, at least for now. You know Menon was my uncle. I have known service for fourteen years in his shadow, while as I understand it, you are –' he clenched his jaw, revealing muscles under the skin – 'less experienced than that.'

'Oh, considerably,' Xenophon replied. 'Though I notice your uncle did not appoint you his second in command. Still, you seized the opportunity when it came, and his men accepted you. That was a daring move – and I have not had the chance to thank you for your support. I am grateful, Philesius. Without men such as you, we would not have survived even to reach this plain. Without your courage and discipline, we will not see home. I am certain of that. Without the absolute obedience, *at all times*, of both the men you command and those who command them, we will *perish* in the empire of Persia and never taste the wine and olives of Greece again. We will not enjoy the plays of Euripides, nor listen to conversations in the agora of Athens. Worse, if we fail here, we will be forgotten by our people.'

He spoke almost in a daze, spinning words into a dream that surprised them both with the intensity of emotion it aroused. Philesius blinked as he gathered his thoughts.

'I saw his *Medea* in Athens. Euripides himself was present and the entire crowd rose to honour him. It was . . . astonishing. As I left, I felt as if a weight had been lifted from my shoulders, for the first time in years.'

Philesius considered forcing the conversation back to practical matters, but decided against it. He had never wanted to lead, not really. His uncle had understood that, though his captains had pressed him forward. Philesius smiled tightly and bowed his head.

'Very well, strategos. I pray you bring us all safely home.'

'That is all I ask,' Xenophon replied.

He nudged his horse into a trot and rode ahead. The sun was setting behind the hills, casting shadows across the fields. Xenophon found himself shivering as he went on. The crops had been gathered in, he noticed. That was all the better for his men, as they would be able to collect precious grain from the stores. Yet it meant the year was moving on and the seasons were turning. A cold wind seemed to answer his thoughts and he shook his head. Whatever happened, whatever came, they had to keep going. He owed that much to Clearchus.

'When we meet again, Spartan,' he murmured aloud, in prayer, 'when you ask me what we did after your death, I will not be ashamed. I promise you that. I will bring them back.'

He knew Philesius had been angling for more authority, or more of a say in the orders. Xenophon shook his head a fraction. They were his people. He was a noble of Athens and he had found his true purpose. He would not give it up, to anyone.

In the morning, Chrisophus sent foraging parties to strip orchards of fruit and to seek out the more remote farms away from the villages. They were not prepared for the thousands of Persians spilling out from another path through the mountains, on foot and on horseback, all racing to cut the foragers off from the rest of the Greek forces. Men and women pitched blankets full of fruit to the ground and withdrew at their best speed, while Chrisophus brought out the closest sixty Spartans at a sprint in the opposite direction.

They had been caught out of position and a running battle developed that was like a street riot in Athens, with both sides trying to score blows on weaker opponents than themselves. The delighted Persians hacked at anyone they could reach, armed or unarmed, then raced on rather than standing to fight. It was a mess, and dozens of Greeks were killed before Xenophon brought up the main square in support. The sight of that advancing line steadied the nerve of those who ran before the enemy, so that they allowed themselves to be taken back amidst the ranks. Bodies lay behind them in the fields, with plums and figs scattered in trampled slicks of fruit.

Faced with the main force, the Persians withdrew once more, using a vast number of horses to manoeuvre. Xenophon's eyes were drawn to a watching figure in white, though he could only curse Tissaphernes. Xenophon's revenge, if he were ever to enjoy it, would be to walk as a free man and leave that fat Persian lord behind to wonder what might have been.

The stripping of the villages went much faster now that they knew they were overlooked. Xenophon blamed himself for not setting better guards, but he was not alone in that. Chrisophus walked the camp for hours, snarling at anyone who dared approach him. They had let down their guard in a hostile place, with an enemy still prowling around and watching for the slightest weakness.

Worse news was that a great river blocked their path. The pass through the mountains had taken them east and north, but they could go no further without crossing a torrent too deep for the spears they thrust into it. Xenophon questioned prisoners from the villages and the news was not as good as he'd hoped. An edge of nervousness settled on the Greek forces as they understood they were bounded on one side by mountains and on the other by a river they could not cross. One of the Greeks suggested using sheep bladders to float over, but the idea of trying such an enterprise while Tissaphernes and his cavalry looked on was impossible.

South was Babylon and a return to the heart of Persia, west took them back through the mountains. The river blocked east and the villagers told Xenophon that Ecbatana lay in that direction, the summer residence of Persian kings and a place as well defended as anywhere on earth.

Xenophon gathered all his officers in a village square, while lines of hoplites formed around the camp.

'According to the villagers, there is a range of mountains to the north that stretches for months of travel east and west. If we can get through, our path will take us to Armenia. From there, we can continue north and west until we strike the Greek settlements on the Black Sea. I do not know how far that is from the mountains, but we cannot go round them. They must be passed.' He paused, choosing his words. 'The tribes in those crags are said to be unspeakably savage and great in number. The headman of this village talks of them like vengeful spirits. He says we would not survive the attempt.'

'This speech is not as inspiring as you think, general,' Chrisophus said, to a chuckle from the men. 'That fellow sought to frighten us, but what choice is there but to face these "Carduchi" in the mountains? We have done well to reach so far, but perhaps . . . we cannot endure for ever.'

Xenophon raised a hand and Chrisophus subsided immediately. One thing the Spartan did well was take orders.

'The river is too deep and too wide. With Persian cavalry to threaten us, we'd be slaughtered trying to get across. No, I agree our best way is still north – out of Persia by the fastest route.'

He looked at them and there was a part of him that rejoiced. For all the beards and corded muscle, for all some of them were older than him, they were not just his flock, they were his brothers and sisters, his sons and daughters.

'The Persians are said to be afraid of these Carduchi tribesmen. There is every chance they will not dare to dog our steps through the passes. We could leave them behind at last.'

Xenophon paused then, aware that an enemy who terrified the Persians might not be a welcome alternative.

'If anyone has a better idea, speak now. Otherwise, I will take us north across the plain and through the highest peaks. Gather what blankets and coats you can find here. We will need them all.'

He sat quietly while they discussed it, knowing that they would come to the same conclusion he had. Xenophon had not mentioned the tale the village headman had told of a Persian army that had passed through eight years before. One hundred and twenty thousand men were said to have gone into the Carduchi fastnesses. Not a single man had made it back alive. Xenophon hoped the wrinkled old headman was just spinning tales to frighten foreign invaders. The fellow had one white eye and long brown teeth in a face like a walnut shell. If he was telling the truth, or any part of the truth, it was possible Xenophon was making the mistake of his life – and still the only choice he could see to take.

Beyond that village square, the rest of the Greeks formed up. Twenty thousand men, women and children seemed a vast number when they crowded around, but in square, the ranks were dwarfed by the distances they had to cross. Xenophon had arranged columns forty men wide on three sides, with eight hundred Spartans at the fore. They enclosed almost the same number within, though the camp followers looked more and more like ragged pilgrims come to an oracle or a shrine to be healed.

At least eating well for two days had improved their mood and their health. Chrisophus had overseen the stripping of the villages and he had been thorough. Those left behind

369

would starve that winter, but Xenophon felt that was a problem for Tissaphernes, rather than his own concern. Had his people been allowed to leave in peace after Cunaxa, he would have been less harsh on the villages they passed. He paused in his thoughts, realising he had described the twenty thousand as his people. They looked to him to keep them alive, and he knew in that moment that he would die trying. He'd searched for purpose in Athens and never found it. He shook his head and chuckled, wondering if he'd ever have the chance to describe the revelation to Socrates.

By the time the officers had finished discussing the way forward, those in the square were waiting with some impatience and the sun had risen almost to noon. When the horns blew, they all found their positions from habit, by the faces of those around them. The strongest carried meat wrapped in cloth, or nets of chickens and a waterskin on their shoulders. Many more bore bundles of winter coats and woollen blankets, all they could find. Small boys drove a herd of goats along with them, clicking in their throats and whipping them with long sticks.

Xenophon rode to the front as soon as Hephaestus and the scouts cantered ahead. As he did, the Persian army spilled out of the passes behind them like oil from a cracked pot, watching balefully, but making no move to attack. The Greeks were safe enough while they marched between the villages. Houses and streets stole the advantage of those who chased them. Xenophon knew the plain would be a different story. The village headman said it was a march of many days, a hundred parasangs or more. Xenophon still hoped the man sought to undermine their morale.

'We head north,' Xenophon called to those he led, feeling his heart swell with pride. His people. His family.

*

The Persian regiments pressed closely as they left the villages behind, but the truth was that everyone in the Greek square was getting fitter with each daily trek. Skin and muscles hardened with use, so that those in the centre had begun to take on the lupine look of those who marched around them. Certainly there was no softness in the Greeks. That had been burned out of them in the deserts.

Tissaphernes sent smaller groups running alongside, catching up to the marching square and sending barbed shafts into the mass. Yet when they came close enough to strike, they were threatened in turn with the slingstones, launched by men who were getting better each day.

The Persian horsemen were a greater threat. They rode up fast in thick groups, throwing spears or javelins while the rearguard struggled to raise shields and keep moving. The Greeks lost a trail of men that first day, in pairs or threes, so that sixty were missing from the tally when they came to camp. It was hard not to imagine the same slow bleed all the way to the mountains, until they were too few to defend themselves and the last of them were hacked down. The mood was dour as they halted, panting and sore.

Xenophon watched as the sun touched the horizon and the Persians drew up in their regiments, reining in. He still wondered at such a fear of a night attack that they put a great distance between the camps. According to Hephaestus, who had trailed them back on foot, they withdrew for miles before they felt safe enough to hobble their horses.

Xenophon saw Tissaphernes raise a hand almost in salute before turning his horse away. The light was beginning to fade. He thanked the gods for the good fortune in the enemy he had been given. A more determined Persian might have pressed the attacks with twice the vigour and never relented or fallen back until they had been pared down to nothing.

Xenophon thought of the sixty men he had lost that day and bared his teeth in sudden rage. It was too many. He knew some of the soldiers wanted him to stop and fight. Persian pride would force Tissaphernes to stand and the Greeks might slaughter half his army before driving the rest off.

It was tempting, though Xenophon knew nothing was certain. If he lost even a quarter of the hoplites, those who remained would be too few to protect the others. They would lose all. He made the argument to his generals and they had accepted it, though grudgingly. He was the strategos they had raised to command them. Until he failed, his orders were as iron.

Each morning for a dozen days, they set off when the turning stars showed dawn was close. They butchered the animals and devoured every last scrap of food they had looted. There was never enough and hunger returned quickly as a beast prowling amongst them. After a time, the food was gone and they had to rise and start into movement with just cold water.

They left behind mounds of their own faeces for the Persians to track through, which was the only consolation for being bearded and stinking. Dirt had become ingrained on that march, and if they emptied their bladders in peace in the morning, they had to do so while marching for the rest of the day. Women suffered worst, but there was no place there for modesty. The men around them turned away at first, giving them what privacy they could. After a while, the emptying of bladders became so commonplace it went unremarked.

The nights grew bitterly cold as they approached the mountains. To their astonishment, snow fell one night, so that they woke covered by it, shivering and numb. Some of them came to blows over a hard word or nothing at all. Hunger brought a constant, simmering anger into the camp.

They groaned each morning as they set off, muscles loosening and complaining. Only the Spartans swung into movement as if they could do it for ever. They had grown long beards and their braids hung right down their backs over the cloaks. Yet they smiled and washed their mouths with a bare sip of water, grinning over cracked lips.

Behind them each day, the Persians appeared in the distance, pressing on at a cruel pace to make up whatever ground they had lost. It meant the morning was a respite, until the enemy came close enough to shoot and throw. The Greeks waited for that moment and it was almost a relief when it began. They settled then into the trudge across the plain, with the mountains growing slowly before and men dying in their tracks behind. They drew lots in the evenings for the honour of the rearguard, but those who survived a day under constant, needling attack were too weary to speak by the end, worn down by fear and rage.

On the eighteenth day, they were marching like ghosts through the wilderness. The hunters went out with sling and spear, but most had only water to keep them alive. They were red-eyed from staring into the distance. The mountains had tormented them for an eternity, seeming to float on the horizon. Yet on that morning they were noticeably closer, though no more welcoming than they had seemed before. The crags were brutally sharp, rising from the ground like daggers rather than gentle slopes. A mantle of snow rested on the highest peaks and they seemed to go back and back for ever.

Tissaphernes called down an attack while they were in the foothills, when their destination was clear. In the front ranks, Xenophon could actually see right into the first valley, to where Hephaestus had scouted a pass as far as he dared. It seemed the Persians would not let them out of sight without spilling more blood. The regiments behind them were looking ragged themselves, having had to march four hundred miles after an enemy they could not bring to heel.

As the Persians formed up in a wide line, their officers were close enough for their exhortations to be heard. Xenophon gestured to Chrisophus, and the Spartans came through the square to form the rearguard. They had lost some of the gleaming muscle they'd enjoyed before. Their beards were wild and they were wiry, savage-looking men, but still better trained than any Persian regiment. Their confidence showed, though the breeze from the mountains was chill and their teeth chattered as they stood there. Red cloaks swirled as the Persians pressed in. With the mountains at their backs, the camp followers had gone into the pass, leaving only the hoplites. White teeth flashed as they drew swords and raised spears.

Chrisophus carried no shield that day. In his right hand he held a short sword, the blade no longer than his forearm. In his left, he carried the shorter kopis. He hefted the weight of them both and grinned at the advancing enemy.

'Advance Lacedaemon,' he roared across the ranks. 'Advance all! This is the only chance you'll get, you whoresons. One glorious moment of play, before we withdraw from this empire for ever more. Choose what you tell your children now.'

The Persians had begun to falter in their approach as soon as they saw the red cloaks of the ancient enemy. Their officers ordered them on and some used short sticks to batter them forward when they hesitated.

Ahead of them, they saw golden discs of bronze, as well as shining helmets and greaves in the same battered metal. The Spartans looked like men of gold and red, and for the first time in an age, they were not retreating but coming forward in a great rush.

The lines met and the Spartans crashed into an enemy

who had stung them. Despite the pain and exhaustion, they were like boys finally able to stamp on a wasp nest. In delight, they endured cuts to hack and stab, using the spear, then the shield and sword, and finally the kopis, which took fingers and lives in quick, chopping blows.

The Persians fell back from the onslaught, but Tissaphernes saw a chance and sent regiments spilling around the Spartan flanks, crashing into wearier men, some of them barely able to stand. They cried out in warning and the sound reached Chrisophus as he killed at the front. He cursed, straining to see. He would wager his Spartans against a force ten times their number, but Tissaphernes had brought eighty or ninety thousand across the empire in their wake. The Greeks could not win. They could only leave them bloody.

'Fall back now, Spartans, in good order. Hold the flanks and withdraw. Take up our dead. See how many of their families will wail and weep when they think of us.'

He grinned at the laughter in the men around him as they began to pull away, raising shields once more and taking up fallen spears so that they bristled and could not be charged by horsemen, though enraged Persians yelled curses down upon their heads and promised vengeance.

Tissaphernes feared his men would be drawn too far into the mountains. He had heard of the tribes that infested those peaks. The empire of Persia had taken entire kingdoms under its wing, from Babylon to the Medes. Yet those crags remained, isolated and untamed. He watched the Greeks withdraw and the sprawled bodies they left behind, like rags or scraps of flesh on the ground. The retreating square seemed to vomit them up as they slid into the mountains.

On impulse, he raised his hand in farewell to them. A Greek officer on a horse turned to watch him, not one Tissaphernes knew. The stranger raised his hand in answer, then trotted away into the crags. Tissaphernes shook his head. He'd thought they would surrender when he killed the generals at the feast. He'd promised King Artaxerxes that they would be helpless without leaders. Instead, they had chosen others and survived, somehow. They were a strange people, he thought. He wondered what the Carduchi would make of them.

He turned to his second in command, Mithridates.

'Would you like to go with them?' he said.

The Greek shook his head.

'Not for a crown, my lord. We will not see them again.'

'That is my thought. When I return to the king, I will report them destroyed. Is that an accurate description, do you think?'

The Greek bowed his head.

'It is, Lord Tissaphernes. They do not know it, but they are all dead. You drove them into the Carduchi, so it must be your success. Congratulations, my lord.'

Tissaphernes smiled and put away the little blade he held in his palm. The last of the Greeks had gone into the pass and vanished, as if they had never existed. The peaks had swallowed them all.

He thought suddenly of the resourcefulness of the Greeks. He had believed them helpless more than once, yet they had survived.

'Do we have pigeons, still?' he asked.

Mithridates nodded.

'Of course, my lord.'

28

The cold increased with every step as the path narrowed and led upwards. Lines of hoplites marched together with shields ready and spears acting more like staffs as they climbed over broken stone. Cliffs soared high above them, with mists preventing anyone from seeing the peaks. Xenophon left Hephaestus at the rear to watch for any sort of last stab at their back from Tissaphernes, but there had been something final about the way the Persian raised his hand before passing from sight.

It was not long before the plains were a memory. They helped one another over boulders, shivering all the while as the cold seemed to reach into their bones. Xenophon understood quickly that he would not be able to take his horse into the mountains of the Carduchi. With a sigh, he dismounted. The animal had served him well and it was hard for him to call for a hammer. Killing a horse is not an easy thing, but their need was great. One of the Corinthians said he had been a butcher in a previous life. Xenophon held the reins and refused to look away as the man brought a mallet down hard and the horse sagged and collapsed, its tongue showing. Men and women clustered around as if they could claim a bit of the meat for themselves by laying hands on it.

'Get back, all of you,' Xenophon snapped at them. 'Hunger makes you fools. We have a dozen mounts. We'll stop here and eat . . .' He looked around, but there was little in the way of firewood in that place. A few stunted trees clung to cracks in stones higher up, not enough to roast meat for a starving multitude. He shook his head. 'We'll carry the meat further in, until we have firewood and a place to defend.'

The promise seemed to satisfy them, though they watched like wolves as the butcher cut great strips and chops out of the animal's ribs.

What path there was led deeper, until they came to a great fork. One side must have been a goat path for its thinness, little more than a white line disappearing around a bend. The other was more rockfall than path; the grey stones were tinged with moss and it did not look as if anything had moved there for a thousand years. Xenophon came forward, though the truth was he was no better able to guess the path than the grubby child who walked at his side for a time. Even so, they expected him to make the decision, so he gave the order, without hesitation. They would climb the rockfall, to make their way higher. As soon as he had spoken, the boy smiled at him, wide-eyed.

'What's your name, son?'

'Adrios, sir.'

'You approve, do you, Adrios?' Xenophon said to him.

The child nodded, making Xenophon smile and ruffle his hair. After a time, the boy's mother tracked him down and lifted him onto her hip.

'I'm sorry, strategos. His father was lost in the battle. He keeps looking for him, amongst the men. He's always off somewhere, tugging on sleeves and asking if they've seen him. I hope he wasn't a nuisance.'

'Not at all. Adrios agreed with me about the way we should go, didn't you? He is a good lad.' She blinked in surprise at that, but Xenophon found his mood had lightened.

An hour of solid effort followed, an extraordinary process. Men and women clambered up, offering their hands to one another. Some made hard going of it, while others leaped from stone to stone like mountain goats. All the time, they tried to be wary of attack, but it was simply impossible to hold a spear ready to strike and yet scramble across loose shale as it scattered and trembled beneath. Xenophon glimpsed Hephaestus as he worked his way closer. He knew by the man's pinched expression how hard it had been to give up the other mounts.

'You gave the order to kill my horse?' Hephaestus said, when he was near enough. It felt like a challenge and Xenophon responded quickly.

'I did. They cannot climb.'

For a moment, the other man glared, but then a shadow passed across his face. Hephaestus was a long way from the streets of the city and the realities there. He had seen enough to know Xenophon had made the only possible choice.

'The Spartans are butchering them like sheep,' he said, bitterly. 'They have no souls, those men.'

'They have no sentiment,' Xenophon replied. 'It is not the same.'

'How did you know the path to take?'

'I chose the one that led upwards. We'll have to climb high to get over these mountains, Hephaestus. If there is a pass through, it will be near the peaks, as high as we can go.'

Hephaestus paused, panting, to stare down the slope. Every time they did so, they were amazed how far they had come. They had learned quickly to rest often, but for short amounts of time. In that way, they made faster progress than forcing themselves to exhaustion and collapse.

The whole trail behind was crammed with people labouring over the loose and broken rocks. They were worn down, but they had not yet come close to giving up. Xenophon looked on them with pride and Hephaestus saw the expression.

'They will not thank you, you know,' he said. 'I see the

way you look at them, as if you are their father. I think they will break your heart in the end.'

It was a surprising thing to hear from a man who had once robbed theatre-goers. Xenophon leaned back as if to take a better look at the Athenian, squinting at him.

'You are a thoughtful man, Hephaestus, though you hide it well. The truth is, we will be lucky to see home again. If we do survive, I doubt any of us will be the same. And you do not expect enough of your people. They will surprise you yet, I am certain of it. As you have surprised me.'

He saw Hephaestus flush in pleasure at the compliment as they turned to continue on.

High above them, in the mists, a strange hooting began, more like the raucous cries of gulls or apes than something that might have come from the throats of men. The sound echoed back and forth across the crags until it filled the air and every one of the Greeks had frozen. Thousands of them stood staring upwards, almost like children in their fear of the unknown. Hephaestus and Xenophon looked at each other in grim surmise.

'They know we are here,' Xenophon said softly.

The first hill led down into a sheltered valley, where there were some thirty houses. All were abandoned, but there was food and, best of all, wine in clay vats set into the ground. The hooting continued in the darkness and prevented many of the men from drinking too much and making themselves useless. All they wanted was to get through those mountains and back to the plains beyond as fast as they could. They lit torches and moved about the village as night came, but quickly found the lights invited arrows and slingstones from somewhere above them, without warning – and that the Carduchi were skilled. Three men died before they learned not to carry the torches and make themselves a target. Those who slept outside remained awake and two more hoplites were killed before the sun rose again. Worse somehow were the bonfires lit in the distance, high overhead so that they burned like yellow stars. Xenophon had no doubt they were to summon all the tribes and families of the Carduchi. He could not shake the dull fear that pressed into his gut like hunger, or the cold. In the shelter of one of the houses, his shivering died away by a warm fire. He ate better food than he had known since setting out and he felt tears come to his eyes at the fresh bread and salt butter that was not rancid. It was a small pleasure, but when he added a cup of red wine that was young and near sour, it was almost too much.

In the morning, Xenophon walked to the end of the valley with a few of the men. The mountains opened out beyond and they could see tiny figures moving on the highest slopes, though whether they were coming down to attack or waiting in ambush was hard to say. Xenophon slapped his hand on the base of a rock spire stretching up into mists, wondering if someone was sitting above him at that moment, their hearts full of rage for the invader. The whistling sounds had begun again, all around that valley, though it was hard to tell distance in the echoes.

'We'll need to capture guides as soon as we encounter them,' Xenophon said evenly. 'There are too many dead ends in these mountains – we could wander for a year.'

'Very well,' Chrisophus said. 'Will you take the vanguard or the rear? I believe my Spartans are the ones to lead in this sort of terrain. It is not unlike the mountains of home, here. I am almost nostalgic for the playgrounds of my youth.'

Xenophon blinked, uncertain if the man was joking or not. He had learned to trust Chrisophus, however.

'I will command the rear. I'll keep our scouts out as

runners between us – they'll be panting today, after so long on horseback. Do not go so far ahead that we are separated.'

Chrisophus bowed his head in reply, untroubled at getting such advice from a less experienced man. He had come to like the Athenian and accepted that Xenophon was an officer of the sort who tried to keep soldiers alive. Chrisophus approved of such men, much more than those who rushed at every challenge without a moment of reflection.

'I think this pinch point will serve another purpose this morning,' Xenophon went on, running his hand over the rock. 'Two or three can pass through here at once. I think we should check the men for weight and looted goods, Chriso-phus. We need to be light and fast, not burdened down.'

The Spartan grinned at that idea and set about summoning the camp to pass through a single narrow space, all under Xenophon's eye. It was not long before the first ones were marching past the general – and just moments later when the first looted goods were taken from them, forming a pile by the side of the path.

It was astonishing, Xenophon thought. He had not realised quite how many things the soldiers and camp followers had simply picked up as they travelled. As well as unwieldy saddles and strange weapons too ancient to be useful, they had sacks of salt and herbs, rolls of cloth and great cured skins. One man carried a door, though when he claimed it served as well as any shield, Xenophon let him keep it. Somehow, his Greeks had hung on to a thousand heavy items, including tools and reins for horses they no longer had. Xenophon was ruthless with those, ignoring complaints and counter-arguments. They had begun to resemble a market in Athens more than a lean army fighting their way across the mountains. Though it caused immense bad feeling, the pile grew and grew until it would make an astonishing find for the Carduchi who stumbled across it. Xenophon considered setting it on fire, but he thought it would serve them better as an offering to the gods.

He also allowed the soldiers to keep the slaves they had somehow managed to collect over the journey. Many of the men had taken lovers and it would have been cruel to abandon them to the tribes of the mountains. Still, there were more foreign slaves than Xenophon would have believed possible. No wonder they had known hunger. He seemed to be feeding half of Persia. He was in a simmering temper about it by the time the last of them passed through.

Hephaestus was one of the rearguard and he walked alongside Pallakis, somehow making a claim on her by their closeness. Xenophon felt her gaze drift across him and his own mood soured further. Xenophon had rejected her, but he'd hoped even so that she would be pining for him. That did not seem to be the case. As if to prove his suspicion, Pallakis reached to the young man's neck and brushed at something, a gesture of intimacy that made Xenophon clench his teeth together. It did not occur to him that she had made sure he saw how she touched Hephaestus, or that any part of the display might have been for his benefit.

By the time the entire Greek force was through the pinch and out onto a wider slope, they truly were less burdened. A few looked longingly behind to the pile of valuables, but Xenophon had made his point. He sat in higher favour than he knew as he went to the rear in a temper, waving the column into movement.

All along the path, hoplites raised shields and readied spears, ramming helmets down over hair grown overlong and thick. Above them, the hooting suddenly ceased. Everyone looked up sharply into the mists above. They had grown used to the sound, so that its absence was almost more frightening, as if the hills themselves were staring down. Xenophon shivered.

Up ahead, Chrisophus came under attack almost immediately, with stones rattling down onto his men as the Carduchi crept along narrow paths above their heads. Arrows came in bursts and the tribesmen were good shots. Chrisophus responded smartly, sending the youngest and fittest Spartans up to the hills around them. Whenever they encountered a path that led upwards, a hundred would break off and pelt up it at full speed. They discovered the primary tactic of the Carduchi was to run from an attack, to scatter light-footed over the crags like mountain goats, so that the Greeks were left to pant and stare down over sheer drops.

It became a savage game, but the Carduchi were having the best of it. Groups of six or twelve of them would appear on some ledge and shoot down in a rattle of arrows against shields and armour. If they were lucky, they would score a wound or take a man down. Before Chrisophus could mount a challenge, or when they sighted the Spartans pursuing them across the peaks, they were off once again, hooting and leaping.

It was infuriating, but the actual losses were few, as long as the Greeks kept formation and used the shields. Being in column was helpful as a single shield could shelter two or three of those marching along, overlapping to frustrate the enemy. Without those shields and the discipline to hold them steady, it would have been a slaughter.

At the rear, Xenophon saw a larger force come into view as he trudged past the opening of a valley to the side. Perhaps a hundred Carduchi bobbed and threatened there, their faces marked in soot or blood. They were tantalisingly close and about as ready to run as to attack, but his task was to support Chrisophus and he could not break away. Xenophon ordered shields pressed together in an unbroken line on that side, while stones and arrows shattered against them. Philesius was there to bear the brunt, with the Thessalians and the Stymphalians just ahead in column. They were solid, experienced soldiers and they did not falter. Xenophon was settling into the routine and accepting it, when the rhythm changed ahead.

Without warning, Chrisophus and the entire front end of the column broke away from the camp followers and raced clear, charging an unseen threat. Xenophon was left bringing up the rear with no idea what was happening or where he needed to be. He swore, calling Philesius over to him.

The Thessalian looked pale but determined. He saluted with one arm across his chest.

'We need to capture a few of these people,' Xenophon shouted over the noise of marching and the rattle of stones and shafts still coming from his left. As Philesius opened his mouth to reply, a hoplite in the rearmost rank took an arrow through his head as he peered over a shield. He fell without even a cry and both Xenophon and Philesius stared as his body was left behind.

'We can't stop here,' Xenophon said. 'Get me a guide, Philesius. These people know every part of their hills. They will run rings around us until we have eyes. Create an ambush for them. Tempt them in – with women, or a wounded man.'

Philesius chuckled as he set about bringing two reluctant young women to the fore. One of them was accompanied by the hoplite who was her lover, complaining loudly until he saw it was Xenophon who had ordered it. Even then, the young soldier watched with jealous eyes as the two women were made to run from the line of shields, as if they had escaped.

The rattle of shafts stopped immediately. Women who might bear children were never overlooked. With no hesitation, eight of the Carduchi ran forward with arms outstretched to grab the shrieking women before they could be taken back. In turn, they were enveloped as the Greek line erupted before their eyes.

All eight of the Carduchi who had come forward were grabbed and hauled back into the ranks. Four of them were killed as they struggled, their bodies thrown down to be left behind. The remaining four were bound and taken into the column where they could not be rescued or killed. The shafts and stones rattled once more, but the column marched on. Ahead of them, the camp followers increased their pace, trying to rejoin the force under Chrisophus that had vanished ahead in a great charge.

Xenophon turned sharply to Philesius.

'Have someone who knows Persian speak to those Carduchi. The sooner we know where we are, the better.'

He saw the camp followers trudging miserably ahead as the path curved. They were desperately vulnerable and he had no doubt the Carduchi were creeping in on all sides by then. Without anyone to keep them moving, his people were coming to a halt on their own, terrified. Xenophon could only curse Chrisophus for chasing ghosts and abandoning them. He made a decision, though his heart felt like it would beat out of his chest.

'Press on. Double speed. Form up around the camp followers as best you can. Hostile terrain! Shields up and spears ready to repel attack. No one stops until we see our vanguard. No one!'

Above them, he could see slender lines of archers sidling

out, on ledges barely able to hold them on sheer cliffs. Arrows and stones came whistling through the air and it was enough to keep them all going faster, with the shields protecting them. As they pressed on, climbing over stones and pushing through narrow places, cries of pain could be heard whenever the Carduchi found flesh instead of bronze.

Xenophon forced them on for a mile, though everyone was panting by then, as if the air had grown too thin to breathe. They climbed with every step and yet it was never high enough to stop the hail from above.

Ahead, they caught sight of the rear ranks of the five thousand with Chrisophus, hunched up like a beetle or a tortoise, with shields protecting the men. Xenophon felt his temper surge, but he controlled it like a Spartan, telling himself Chrisophus would not have left him unprotected without good reason.

The man himself came back to meet him as the rear half of the Greeks joined once more with the front. The relief was indescribable. Apart, they knew they had faced destruction.

Chrisophus dropped to one knee to apologise, the gesture as good as words.

'Where did you get to?' Xenophon said, hoping he had not misjudged the man, or given him too much authority.

'I am sorry. There was no time to send word. Look there and you will see what made me run.'

He pointed and Xenophon stared into the distance. He had reached the point by then where Chrisophus had lurched into a charge. He could see the pass through the hills that shrank to a narrow cleft – and the swarming mass of tribesmen that waited for them there.

Chrisophus had not risen from his knee.

'I saw them coming down the hillsides and I understood they were trying to reach that point before us. I did not – I do not know why it is important, only that they were racing to get there. I broke the chain of command to stop them, general. I apologise.'

'Rise up, Chrisophus. I am relieved. I thought you had lost your mind. Have you captured guides? I have four, so I can lend you a couple. Perhaps there is a way around this pass. I would not like to drive through it.'

As Chrisophus stood up, the Spartan put out his hand and Xenophon took it on impulse. No more needed to be said between them.

'I captured a few myself, strategos,' Chrisophus said. 'I will question them. There is often a small path over the hills, good enough for goats and shepherds. That is how the Persians overcame us at Thermopylae. It would give me pleasure to find such a path here.'

Xenophon called to Philesius nearby. 'Bring me those damned Carduchi – and someone who speaks Persian.' He could only hope the tribesmen understood the imperial tongue, or they would be useless to him.

Philesius found one of the Greeks who spoke enough Persian to ask simple questions. To demonstrate the urgency of the situation, Philesius had some of his Thessalians batter two of the Carduchi to unconsciousness with steady blows, before turning to the remaining pair and asking if there was another path.

One of the remaining two was a man in his forties, weathered and yet pale, as if he never saw the sun in that place. He swore the pass was the only way through that part of the mountains. He made vows by Zoroaster and Ahura Mazda, promising them he spoke only the truth. Xenophon saw the eyes of the other turn to him, widening at the awful oaths he was hearing.

'Take the older one away,' Xenophon said. 'Release him unharmed with the other two. I have no more use for them.'

He smiled at the last man, not far from his own age, watching him warily.

'Tell him we know his friend was lying, but do not understand why. Tell him we can be merciful, or cruel. The choice is his.'

The Greek soldier translated his words into the simplest Persian he knew and the young man bit his lower lip, thinking. After a time, a sudden torrent of words spilled out, much faster than their translator could echo in Greek.

'He says . . . the other man did not want to tell you of a path . . . over the hills, because his daughter has a home in that direction, but it . . . does exist, there is a narrow route that takes you around the pass ahead of us. He asks that the older man be killed if he has not been released, or he will tell the elders . . . he will say this young man helped an enemy and his life will be over.'

Xenophon gave a quick order and the man they had been about to release was killed instead. The younger one grinned when he saw that, visibly relaxing.

'He says the old one was a friend of his father and he is pleased . . . to see him dead.'

Xenophon blinked to have been used in such a way.

'Show us where this path begins,' he said.

29

Xenophon called for a force of volunteers, the fittest and fastest. He accepted four captains and two thousand of the men, explaining their task and the speed it required. They grinned to hear it, preferring to go racing up hills than plodding along in line with all the rest.

'This pass has to be important, or they would not have gathered in such numbers to defend it,' Xenophon said. 'You cannot fail in this, gentlemen. Go now . . .'

As he spoke, rain came down from the mists like a curtain drawn across the valley. They were all drenched in an instant, bowing their heads against drops as it settled into a steady downpour. Xenophon cursed under his breath. Rain would make all things harder. The mists seemed to creep down with every passing moment, so that none of the peaks were visible overhead and even the pass was just a vague outline against a brighter sky.

'Heed the guide. We will be ready,' Xenophon said.

He watched as two thousand of his youngest and best men went jogging away. They left the floor of the valley and he watched the Carduchi guide run with his hands tied behind his back. The young man led them across a canyon to where an animal trail vanished into thick ferns. It did not look as if it went anywhere, seeming to die out in the rocks. Its true extent was hidden from below and Xenophon knew they would not have found it without him. It gave him some small satisfaction that the ones Chrisophus had captured had suggested nothing of use.

For a time, he could do nothing. The rain continued and his people were still shivering and miserable. Without a sighting of the sun, it was hard to tell how late it was, though he thought evening had to be close. He made a quick decision and ordered the column forward in good order – just far enough for those waiting at the pass to know they were advancing. At that point, Xenophon ordered them to rest. There was no sign of arrows or rocks coming from the crags above. He wondered if that was because those men too were drenched in the rain. Archers complained bitterly when they were forced to work with wet strings, he knew. Or perhaps they had heard the steps of two thousand Greeks up there and they sensed they were hunted. Either way, it helped to raise his mood despite the rain. It was getting dark, definitely. His men would spend a cold night up on the peaks. He only hoped the mists cleared by morning, so that he could see the Carduchi surprised by them.

The floor of the valley ran with rivulets and there was no dry place. Xenophon saw many of the camp followers settle in pairs or groups, back to back so that they could keep some part of themselves out of the damp. Even with that cooperation, it would be a miserable night.

Pallakis came to sit by him as the light faded. She wiped a hand across a wide, flat stone and perched on it, crossing her ankles and drawing her legs in close to keep some heat. She had a sleeping blanket that was already dark with moisture. Even so, her teeth chattered and he wished he had shelter for her. Greeks and the cold did not do well.

'You look like a half-drowned bird,' he said, though he smiled. The hair that massed in thick curls had become limp, clinging to her face in long tendrils. She drooped in the wet.

'I feel like one,' she replied. 'Are we to stay here then, for the night?'

'Until we can clear that pass, we must.'

'What if we can't?'

'Then there is a harder path to be climbed. One way or another, we will go on tomorrow.'

At that moment, the night ahead seemed to stretch for ever. He realised he was shivering as well. His teeth made a sound he could hear and his hands were white and shook visibly.

'You are freezing, Xenophon!' she said. 'Sit next to me. My blanket is damp, but it is better than nothing.'

'Where is Hephaestus?' Xenophon asked without moving.

She stiffened, a double line appearing on the smooth skin between her eyes.

'I am not his, Xenophon.'

'You are not mine, I know that,' he replied, quicker than thought or sense.

She said nothing for a long moment, staring at him.

'I . . . thought that was what you wanted, for a time. But I saw you were overwhelmed, with all you had to do to keep us alive. I understood, Xenophon. Are you saying now that you want me to come to you? That you want me in your bed? Play no games with me, Xenophon. Speak or be still. Ask, or go without.'

He swallowed, staring at her. It seemed he had to say it. Yet it was madness. They sat in hostile mountains with little food and enemies all around. He realised he wanted the appearance of love, but not perhaps the reality. He wanted to exchange looks of longing with a beautiful woman that did not take too much time. He had no place in his life for lingering conversations, for laughter or song. All he wanted could be had in instants – and though he ached for her, he understood that would not be enough.

Her days were not filled with events and decisions. He

could not be a distraction for Pallakis. And if she distracted him, they would all perish. He tried to remember the points as they spun in his thoughts. The silence enlarged around them both and he realised he had not replied for too long.

'There you are!' Hephaestus said, striding along the stones. The younger man held a warm blanket and draped it around Pallakis' shoulders without another word. Once again, it seemed he claimed her, to Xenophon's eye, in the way his arm remained.

Xenophon knew Hephaestus was very aware he had interrupted something. Each flashing glance took in the soft stain of her cheeks, or the intense stare that Xenophon had to blink to break. Hephaestus too became flushed, his movements awkward.

'There is a little food, further back,' he said. 'Dried meat, boiled with a few herbs. A cup of wine. It all tastes pretty foul, but it's better than starving. Will you come before it's gone?'

He addressed the question to Pallakis and she rose easily, busying herself with the sodden blanket and gripping the dry one close. She looked once more at Xenophon before she turned away. His gaze was on the ground between his feet. An expression of exasperation, almost of fury, crossed her face. Her bottom lip thinned to nothing and she took Hephaestus by the arm, surprising him. The darkness came down over the hills and the Greeks dozed and shivered under blankets, waking over and over with cold water trickling down their skin.

The rain had stopped as the mists lightened overhead, showing them more of the mountain crags than they had seen before. Xenophon roused the rearguard while Chrisophus gathered the Spartans at the fore, ready for whatever came.

They were all starved, but there was cold, clean water and though they were still wet, they stank a little less. Some of the men steamed as they limbered up, shedding heat in the morning.

The army of Carduchi began to move in the pass. They had no ranks and, to Greek eyes, looked for all the world like a hive roused to action. The sky brightened beyond them, so that they appeared as capering black figures, but so many that there was no way through. The Greeks formed before them, making them face the threat. Xenophon had the column ready with shields as he ordered them forward and then halted once more. The swarm had grown still as the Carduchi waited, but the Greeks stared back, not two hundred paces from the narrow point they had blocked.

Xenophon thanked the gods as horns sounded above. The note was muffled, but it echoed in joy for him. He'd been worried the two thousand he'd sent had lost themselves in the darkness up on the heights. They'd spent a night in silent shivering, enduring the rain with even less protection than those below. Yet they'd crept up on the enemy at first light and he could have blessed them.

He saw consternation in the Carduchi. They knew warfare in the peaks and they had a horror of being overlooked, that much was clear. As his men came roaring down the slope, Chrisophus sent the Spartans forward at double time. They began to sing the paean, the song of death. It tugged right into Xenophon's chest and he joined in with the words, filling his lungs with air. Some of the Greeks around him looked at him in astonishment.

The Carduchi gave up the blockade at the pass, fleeing like rats. Xenophon heard a great cheer go up from those still coming down the flanks. The secret path had led them right around the pass, so that they were already heading to a valley beyond. For his part, all he could do was march with the rearguard in good order, passing tree branches and spikes that had been knocked aside. The Carduchi were gone, and though he could hear hooting start up behind him, it was a sound of mourning rather than a challenge.

Sun broke through the low clouds as the Greeks came through, tracing beams like fingertips on green ground. Xenophon saw clusters of houses and herds of goats and sheep. His mouth twinged at the thought of roasted meat. The valley may have been narrow, but it had a green floor and it was clearly a rich part of the hills, a hidden heart. For all he knew, there was nowhere else like it in the entire range. He looked for Pallakis, to smile at her. She was lost to view, somewhere up ahead, with Hephaestus as her companion.

The following noon, one of the old men of the Carduchi came to the house Xenophon had taken. The stranger bore bruises he had endured just by approaching Greek sentries, though he held out his empty hands and kept his head down, accepting humiliation to be heard. Xenophon brought up the young warrior who had revealed the second route around the pass. He strolled up to the old tribesman and slapped him across the face, leering at him. Xenophon had to order the man back.

The old Carduchi spoke in their tongue and when prodded with a spear-butt, the warrior translated with bad grace.

'He asks you not to burn the houses here. He says his people wish to be left alone, but he is lying. They sent an old man because he has no value. Kill him if you wish, it does not matter.'

The scrawny old man began to struggle and kick at the younger long before the words had been translated into Greek.

'What's that? What are you saying?' Xenophon said.

The young man shrugged, muttering his own language, though the other hissed insults at him.

'We make war to win. There are no rules. If this old fool is here, I would check your guards and make sure no one is out there cutting throats. We have many warriors.'

The old man spoke once again as Xenophon was listening to the translator. He did not recognise Greek as true words and so chattered over the sound, still making his case. Xenophon held up a hand for silence and pinched the spot between his eyes. He had eaten well and taken delight in the stores these people had gathered for a long winter.

'Tell him this. All we want is to get through. I will not burn his houses if he returns the dead to me for burial and consecration to the gods. Tell him that and add nothing more.'

The Carduchi warrior did so mulishly. Though some parts defeated the translator, the old man took his hand and bowed at the end. Xenophon waved him away, weary of them all. As they were taken outside, he decided to tour the edge of the camp and check the guards were in place and still alive. He did not trust the Carduchi.

That night, the bodies of Greeks appeared on the edge of the Carduchi village. The guards gave an alarm when they saw shadows moving, but those who rushed up with torches found only the corpses of men they had known, laid out on the ground. They took them up with reverence, as brothers. No one slept that night, as they offered prayers over the dead. The bodies were cleaned and anointed by the women of the camp, then dressed once more. Wounds were sewn shut and beards oiled. No weapons had been returned with the dead men, or they would have been shared out among his friends and allies. All they could do was dig one great grave and lower the bodies in. It was a cruel thing to see by torchlight and Xenophon heard the women wailing. He wondered if the Carduchi would understand what they were doing, or whether they would open up the grave the moment the Greeks were past. He put the thought aside. They could only do so much. They laid the bodies in with dignity, with prayers and weeping, before gently tamping down the earth.

The sun rose on a determined group marching out of that valley. They left the homes unburned and there had been no slaves to take, but once again they had snatched up everything that could be eaten, including herds of goats and sheep they drove along in the midst of them. The column had reformed in fine style and their spirits were higher than they had been before.

The first stinging attacks began before the sun could be seen above the crags. Carduchi crept above them by the thousand and from that height even a thrown stone could knock a man out. Worse was when the tribesmen rolled great boulders down the hill, skipping and bounding and crushing anyone too slow to get out of the way. At least those could be seen. The mists lifted all day until the highest peaks sparkled in a winter sun. The temperature seemed to plummet, but the fighting kept them warm.

Xenophon and Chrisophus worked out a routine between them. If the Carduchi hit the front of the column, Xenophon would send men from the rear onto side paths, looking for height. The Carduchi disliked that above all things and abandoned positions as soon as they were flanked in such a way. If Xenophon came under attack, Chrisophus would do the same with his Spartans, sending men up and back in support.

It was hard and brutal work, so that the end of the winter's day found them exhausted and frustrated. The Carduchi had chosen to defend one peak, perhaps because they saw no way down. With snow crunching underfoot, they had offered battle to the Greeks. It was their bad luck it happened to be a group of fifty Spartans. They left the snow splashed red and threw Carduchi heads at the next group as they charged.

When darkness came again, the toll of bodies had increased. Xenophon wondered if he would be offered another deal to return his dead, but there were no more houses for him to spare. They wanted nothing from him and he did not see them as the sky cleared and terrible cold frosted the camp. He wondered how much longer they could endure – and how many miles he and his men had covered that long day. He closed his eyes on a prayer.

He dreamed of breaking chains, of iron fetters falling away. In the morning, he sought out Chrisophus to tell him. It had to be a good omen, a message from the gods. Xenophon found he'd woken in better spirits than he had known since entering the mountains. The dream was responsible.

He told it to the Spartan and saw the same old smile return to the man's face. Xenophon was pleased to see it. He missed the friendship that had sprung up between them, separated as they were by the column itself. Men needed moments of warmth and laughter, or they began to wither. Pallakis seemed to be avoiding him, which meant Hephaestus was no longer near to hand. Only Chrisophus remained – and he looked exhausted and thin. The Spartan's beard was matted and showed a great patch of white on the chin.

'That is a good dream,' Chrisophus said. 'I will tell the men. Perhaps we should sacrifice the goats we brought out.' He waited for permission, but Xenophon didn't hesitate.

'We'll bleed them as sacrifices, but take the meat with us. It will not be long now, Chrisophus.'

*

The attacks were sporadic over the next two days. Arrows flew from clefts in the hills around, arcing high and usually caught by a shield. A Spartan was killed by such a shaft on the second of those mornings, taken through the side so that he coughed red and sat down, unable to get up. There was no earth to bury him, nor tools to break ground, so they built a cairn of smooth stones and added to it until it stood as a hill.

The young Carduchi warrior Xenophon had captured escaped in the night, having either chewed or rubbed through the ropes that bound him while he slept. Xenophon remembered the dream about fetters falling away and hoped it had not meant his prisoner escaping.

On the third morning after the valley, the seventh since they had entered the mountains, they came to a cleft in the path that led down a steep slope of loose scree to a vast plain beyond. From that height, they could see a full day's march. A huge river ran not half a mile from the crags.

Beyond it, on a plain of green and gold, an army stood waiting for them. Cavalry regiments camped on the plain, smoke from their fires rising like threads of rain into the air. On low hills, squares of infantry gleamed. They had sought out high ground, though there was little of it to be had, so they clung to the crests of slopes like islands on an ocean. Chrisophus called Xenophon to the fore when he'd reached the final pass. Despite the enemies waiting over the river, they gripped one another by the hand and shoulder and laughed. The mountains were behind.

'I wonder at a satrap who waits for us in winter,' Chrisophus said, sheltering his gaze as he peered into the distance. 'He must owe the Persians a great favour to freeze out here.'

Xenophon hid his disappointment. He had cast fetters aside, but he'd hoped to leave battle and bloodshed behind him in the mountains. He'd endured enough, and the thought of fighting again was exhausting. Whoever the enemy were, whatever their loyalties or promises to Persia, they waited for him – and they stood in his path.

'We need to get across that river, to go home,' he said.

'You'll find a way,' Chrisophus replied. Xenophon looked to him, but there was neither mockery nor humour in his expression. 'You have before.'

30

In silence, the Greek column came skidding down the slopes, carving arcs with each long step. Some of the camp followers went tumbling, but the hoplites spread out in good order, placing each foot with care. Those at the rear went even more slowly in case of attack, until they too felt the delirium tugging at them. They were out. They were alive. They began to run in great bounding leaps, faster and faster. Even the air tasted sweeter than the dank mists of the mountains. They laughed and called in delight to one another as they reached warm earth below. The crags of the Carduchi were blades behind them, in all senses.

Xenophon marched up and down the flanks, exhorting them to collect themselves and move into proper formation. He missed his horse. All men had been boys once, looking up to their fathers. He wondered if the simple act of raising their heads made them more likely to obey, stirred by their earliest memories. It was not quite as easy to command large bodies of men at their own eye level.

They had space once more to form the square within a square. It was almost comforting to see old ranks around them, though too many faces were missing. Hundreds had been killed in the mountains, as well as a dozen women snatched away in the running battles, borne off screaming. Those who stood in that place had survived, but it was not without memories that would haunt them for a lifetime.

Xenophon felt he had aged by ten years. He looked on the army waking up to his presence on the other side of the river with a sort of dull rage. He didn't know who they were, nor why they had come to that plain. He was angry with them because they stood in his way – and he was weary of those who dared to stand in his way.

He found Chrisophus waiting patiently for orders, with the Spartans in neat blocks. They looked unkempt somehow, after all they had endured. It was not just the beards and braids, but a sense of being worn down, as if even these could not go on for ever. It was a disturbing thought to have, Xenophon realised. He had relied on their endurance above all the rest, using them first and hardest. Yet, they were only men. The long red cloaks showed light through them in rents and tears, or flapped ragged where cloth had been cut to bind a wound. Many of the Spartans wore red bands on their thighs or arms, darkened by blood. Helot slaves stood amongst them, bearing shields and spears in silence. Together, they were an elite and Xenophon knew he could not have reached that place without the blood they had shed.

They gazed on him without anger, waiting for orders. In turn, he met their eyes without flinching. They had played their part, but so had he. Xenophon looked across the river, to where tramping regiments of foot soldiers were still assembling, driven to excited madness by the presence of the enemy. There were perhaps three or four times as many as the Greek hoplites, some thirty thousand or so. It might have seemed a great army for anyone who had not stood at Cunaxa. As it was, Xenophon gestured across the water and shrugged.

'Who are these fools, to stand against us?' he said, making his voice carry and ring with his anger. 'We, who walked through the army of the Persian king without challenge. We, who crossed the Carduchi mountains and lived! So it seems Lord Tissaphernes had messenger birds in his dancing troupe. Those men over the river have never seen Greeks. They have *no idea* what they will encounter in us.' He grinned at them. 'Imagine their faces when they realise!'

Even the grim Spartans responded at that, picturing an enemy in disarray. They allowed themselves few pleasures, but that was certainly one of them.

Behind the ranks by Chrisophus, the great square of Greeks waited. They too looked battered and thin, worn down to sinew and will. There had been too little food for too long – and too many days spent fighting for their lives. The edges of their blades had been blunted and not one of them had washed in over a week. Yet he felt such pride in them it might have burst his chest.

Xenophon stared over the river. He had brought them to that place. It was a weight on him, but he would not have put it down for a chance to drink that night in Athens and sleep in his own bed.

'Walk with me to the river,' he called to Chrisophus. 'Bring your longest spears and a few shield-bearers to keep them safe. We'll find a ford and show these vassals of a Persian king who we are.'

A small party walked forward with him to the river's edge. Xenophon could see banners he did not know waving in the wind on the other side. The men there wore armoured coats like the Persians, though they decorated their flags with strange symbols and seemed smaller in stature. It was hard not to despair at the sight of so many, but Xenophon forced himself to stroll to the river bank as if he saw no threat at all.

The river was much wider than he had realised, stretching at least a hundred paces to the far side. It flowed too with a fast current, creasing the waters in shapes that resembled flights of geese. Xenophon watched as impudent enemy archers decided to test the range on the other side, coming as close as they could and bending their bows. There were around thirty of them and Xenophon had to stand behind two bronze shields raised by Spartans, trying not to react to the thump and hiss of iron arrows aimed to kill.

In between volleys, spears were dipped into the water all along the bank, but no fording place revealed itself. Time after time, the longest spears disappeared right to the hand holding them. When one of the men was struck by an arrow and taken back swearing and cursing, the Greeks retired out of range. Xenophon felt Chrisophus looking at him as they walked away. He raised his eyebrows in question, unsure how to go on. He'd assumed the enemy forces knew the river. It looked instead as if they'd come a long way to answer the summons of their Persian masters, no more familiar with the fording places than he was himself. Either way, without a place to get across, he could not answer their challenge.

He felt a little deflated as he walked back to the waiting Greeks. They would just have to search further. He'd seen from the heights that there were no bridges, as far as the eye could see. They had to find a spot where the river ran shallow, where some ancient shelf of stone or gravel still resisted the flood. Worse was the thought of spending a night on such a bare plain. The wind had grown stronger, tugging at cloth and hair. More importantly, the Greeks needed to eat.

'We could send hunting parties back into the foothills, for bird eggs, perhaps,' Chrisophus said, echoing his thoughts.

Xenophon was already looking beyond the square of his people, to the crags of grey and green that had vomited them forth. Movement in the high pass caught his eyes and he squinted before shaking his head.

'I don't think they will allow that,' he said, pointing.

Where the Greeks had come out of the mountains, the Carduchi had assembled in vast numbers – more than

Xenophon had known they could summon. Thousands of them jerked spears and bows into the air and hooted, though the sound was made weak by distance and the breeze.

'Ah. So we cannot go back and we cannot go on,' Chrisophus said. 'I think we should have a day to mend, sir. To use the last food and wine. To heal and restitch wounds as well. Some of the men are feverish and we have too many on litters. Let the Carduchi howl up in their peaks.' The Spartan shuddered as some memory flashed across his inner eye. 'While they do, we will rest and grow strong.'

'I will ask Athena to show us the way forward,' Xenophon said.

Chrisophus bowed his head at the name.

'We honour her. Shield-maiden, mistress of both war and wisdom. How can we not? She is a very Spartan goddess. Perhaps she sent you the dream of breaking chains.'

Xenophon smiled in memory.

'I think so. It gave me hope at a moment when I was close to despair.'

Chrisophus stopped, a look of surprise on his face.

'Close to despair? You showed no sign of that.'

Xenophon looked away.

'Let us say I am pleased to be out of those mountains. I feel as if we crossed the land of the dead and are once more in the world. Do you understand?'

'Of course,' Chrisophus said. 'But we did come through.'

There was no one close enough to hear them as they walked back. The other men had gone ahead as the two leaders strolled together, enjoying a moment of peace.

'I . . . It has been an honour to lead Spartans in war,' Xenophon said, awkwardly.

'Yes. It always is,' Chrisophus replied. After a beat, he grimaced and went on. 'I saw that young friend of yours,

Hephaestus. He had his head bent towards the mistress of Prince Cyrus . . . what was her name?'

'Pallakis,' Xenophon said softly. The sound was a breath on his lips and Chrisophus took note.

'Would you like me to have a couple of the lads warn him off? She's yours if she's anyone's.'

Xenophon shook his head, glaring at the ground as they walked.

'No. I won't force her. She'll come to my hand of her own will, or not at all.' He opened his mouth again to begin an argument with himself, but thought better of it.

'They seemed *very* friendly,' Chrisophus said.

Xenophon turned sharply on the Spartan, making him laugh.

'I'm sorry, I'm just teasing you.'

'I thought Spartans didn't laugh,' Xenophon replied, unwilling to see the humour.

'Who ever said that? If we didn't laugh, at least at love and war, it would be a sad old world. I saw a leopard drop on a man once. Ten years have passed and the memory of his expression still gives me joy.'

That night, Xenophon slept fitfully, waking half a dozen times, so that he believed he had not slept at all when he saw the sun again. After seven days in the high crags, he sat up to enjoy the dawn over the plain. The river was a ribbon of gold and even the Persian vassals summoned to obstruct them took on grandeur in that light. There was, in such moments, the very meaning of being alive, he thought. More than joy, it was a sense of beautiful awe. He tried to capture the thought, to be able to describe it again to Socrates. There were so many things to tell the old scoundrel! Chief among them all was the desire to thank the philosopher for the suggestion to leave. Athens had grown sour to Xenophon, though he had not been able to see it. After Cunaxa, after their long trek out of Persia, he could finally understand how small his old concerns had been. He could know peace again and put aside the corrosive anger that had eaten at him.

'Good morning, general,' Chrisophus said. 'I have two young men here. I think you'll want to hear what they have to say.'

Xenophon stifled a yawn, feeling unwashed and bristly in the morning as he rubbed his eyes. His birthday had passed weeks before, almost unnoticed. He was twenty-seven, but felt older at the sight of the young Spartans. They stood wearing almost nothing beyond their sandals. One had his cloak tossed in a thick rope over his shoulder and clasped at the throat. He wore a sword belt like a loincloth, while the other was nude and completely untroubled by it as he stood there. They looked extraordinarily healthy, Xenophon thought, rubbing his chin.

'Yes, gentlemen. I was enjoying the dawn. Tell me then, whatever it is.'

'My brother and I were looking for kindling, strategos. We walked for an hour or two last night, some thirty stades downriver. It was getting dark when we saw an old man and woman hiding clothes or cloth in the stones on the other side of the river. They had some bread and cheese. We thought it might be a place we could swim across, so . . .'

His brother interrupted him in their excitement.

'So we put our knives between our teeth and waded out, but the water never came higher than our waists the whole way. By the time we reached the other side, the old couple had gone and so we came back.'

'Were you seen? Did you disturb the clothing?' Xenophon asked, now fully alert.

He saw Chrisophus grin at his reaction, but ignored him.

407

Both brothers shook their heads in reply. Xenophon clenched his fist in delight.

'Then you have earned my thanks, both of you.'

'Well done, lads. Go back now and check the kit,' Chrisophus said. 'I don't think we'll be resting today.'

Xenophon smiled.

'I have a plan, Chrisophus.'

'Of course you have.'

With the last of the food a memory, delay only weakened the column. It took a little time to rouse the camp followers to their feet, but the sun was still climbing in the sky as Chrisophus led the entire force along the banks of the river, with the two brothers acting as scouts. The fording place was barely two miles away, but the moment of true danger lay in the crossing. Up to their waists in water and fighting a strong current, they would be horribly vulnerable. In the history of Greece, more than one army had been caught at a ford and utterly destroyed.

On the other bank, the enemy forces watched them break into movement. Indecision showed in their response to the move. Formations of cavalry began to shadow the Greeks along the bank, while thousands of foot soldiers remained on the outcroppings and plateaus of higher ground, preferring the classic positions of advantage to being drawn away.

On the mountains behind them, the Carduchi too were awake. They swarmed on the high ridges, observing everything. Xenophon kept an eye on them as he marched with the rearguard. He still had little understanding of those tribesmen. He could not plan for them.

As soon as Chrisophus moved clear, the Carduchi edged further down the loose slopes than they had dared before, skidding and leaping almost to the plain. They may not have intended to attack, but if a chance presented itself, it was clear they would fall on the Greeks like wolves on spring lambs. The Carduchi had taken a terrible mauling in their own mountains and their pride still stung.

'Steady, Hellenes,' Xenophon called over them.

The captains knew what he was about to do and had approved it. The crossing was just too narrow and too vulnerable a spot to try and force their way across against a well-armed host. More, the Greeks were weaker than they had been; there was no longer any point in denying that. They needed good food and rest for a month or more to be back in fighting trim.

On the opposite bank, thousands of horsemen milled. While messengers galloped back and forth, the rest barked orders at one another, clearly confused or afraid there was a crossing point nearby. Xenophon shaded his eyes, trying to see the rest of their forces far behind. Perhaps they thought it was a feint or a ruse. Perhaps Tissaphernes had warned them against Greek treachery. He showed his teeth.

'Rearguard! Captains and pentekosters ... on my mark ... Now!'

His voice cracked across them and the first ranks with Chrisophus stormed into the waters, sending spray that caught the sun like glittering wings.

At the rear, in the same instant, half the hoplites turned away and *ran* back along the river bank. They scrambled along as if they were in a race, pushing and yelling to one another, so that the effect was astonishing, a torrent of Greeks. Only the camp followers remained, as they had been ordered, waiting on the bank. Some of them carried swords and spears, in case they came under attack. That had been the hardest decision, but Xenophon had given the order. No army could manoeuvre on the field with ten thousand civilians to protect at the same time. Xenophon prayed to Athena to bring the camp followers to safety, while he ran like a boy and laughed for the strangeness of it in that place.

On the other bank, the sudden reverse and dashing away of five thousand Greek soldiers brought instant chaos. The commanders of cavalry saw a trick they could defeat only with speed, their single greatest advantage. Half the horsemen who had gathered to block the first crossing galloped back ahead of Xenophon's running men, shouting for those they had left behind to be ready. Marching regiments of archers who had been converging on the river ford were halted and drawn back at a jog, stringing their bows as they went.

The Greeks with Xenophon were clearly heading to another ford further upriver. If they made it across uncontested, they would be able to attack on two fronts. There was utter chaos in the dark ranks shadowing Xenophon. Regiments already moving encountered others who had been ordered to halt along the banks, so that men were knocked down and commanders bawled conflicting orders.

Xenophon breathed well. He was fit, but thin. Somehow, watching the complete disarray he had caused gave him the sense that he could run all day. His was the feint. There was no second crossing.

'Make a noise, then! Raise your swords and spears!' he called to his captains.

Five thousand Greeks could roar, he discovered. They could shake the heavens if they wanted. As he ran, Xenophon knew he had to judge it finely. He had come back as if to cross at another point. Yet he dared not exhaust his men over too long a distance. Sooner or later, he would have to give up and return in his own steps to the ford the two brothers had found. His task had been to draw the enemy away from Chrisophus. The Spartans had to be across by then. It was hard not to grin at the thought of the enemy meeting those warriors for the very first time.

'Make ready!' Xenophon bellowed to them. 'We have warmed ourselves up, gentlemen. See the result, over the water. Make ready now, to go back to the crossing place once more.'

There was some laughter in the ranks. They were in high spirits, enjoying the chaos they were causing on the other side.

Xenophon caught movement out of the corner of his eye and cursed softly. They'd needed the ruse to confound the enemy long enough to cross the river. The one part of the plan that could not have been predicted was what the Carduchi would do, watching from the heights. As he had feared, they saw he had split his forces. They saw weakness and so they came down in a great surge, driven mad by the need for vengeance. Xenophon drew in a lungful of air.

'Come to a halt on my mark! Hellenes . . . halt!'

They crashed to a stop and the laughter was gone as they watched the howling Carduchi streaming down from the mountains.

'Greeks! Men of Corinth and Stymphalia, of Thessaly and Arcadia, of Rhodes, of Crete and Thebes. Form up now, gentlemen. Listen to your captains – and remember this. We faced the Carduchi in their hills before. They face us now on a plain. They have never seen a fighting shield line, with spears and short swords! Let them come, with all their yelping and howling. We will treat them like the dogs they are – and cut them down!'

He shouted the last and they roared again in response. To his delight he could see some of the Carduchi faltering in their rush to attack. Away from the safety of their hills, they felt the great emptiness of the plain around them.

Facing that wild charge, the Greeks shuffled into formations they knew as well as breathing. They took comfort from reaching out and tapping those in front and to the side with their fingertips, finding the perfect distance.

'Where is my shield?' Xenophon said.

One of the Spartan helots came trotting up with a shield on his back, bowing deeply as he handed it over. He had remained behind to serve. In relief, Xenophon thanked him like a free man, then pushed his left arm through one leather loop and gripped hard on the other. It felt part of his arm and he swung it through the air with pleasurable anticipation.

'Steady, Hellenes!' he called over their heads. 'There is time yet. Advance sixty paces and halt. Spears to repel attack! Steady!'

The Carduchi must have seen a solid block of five thousand Greeks, more metal than flesh, with the river at their backs. Xenophon had made them lurch forward when he thought about archers gathering on the other bank. The movement seemed to steal some part of the howling savagery in those coming down at them. The Carduchi saw a great beast move, a tortoise of bronze and the promise of death. There were no camp followers to protect in their number. The Greeks were lean and filthy and worn down, but they *hated* the Carduchi.

Two or three thousand of the tribesmen crashed against the Greek formation like hail spattering against a stone wall. They were cut to pieces all along the line. They leaped and screamed, but against the discipline of a shield rank, they could not break through. Xenophon watched in awe and exultation as the survivors fell back. Those behind had slowed at the sight of that impregnable formation and the blood of their people shed in such numbers.

'Sixty paces forward! Now!' Xenophon ordered.

The ranks jerked into movement and the Carduchi circled and ducked away like wounded dogs, still savage, but afraid. More and more retreated up the slopes, and for a moment Xenophon wanted to rush after them. Instead, he watched as hundreds came to a halt on the slopes, resting on their spears and just watching the Greeks. There was no sign of them charging again. Xenophon shook his head, delighted.

'They know us now!' he roared suddenly. The Greeks answered him in wordless triumph, so that the sound echoed back from the mountains.

'They will not attack again, but if they do, we have their measure. Back then along the river. Back to the ford. Your best pace, gentlemen.'

Some of them groaned and he laughed at them.

'What? You've had your rest! You've enjoyed yourselves here, haven't you? It's time to run once more, or will you leave the Spartans to take all the glory for themselves?'

There was a rumble of assent from the men and they were off again. Behind them, the Carduchi were finally silent.

It was close to noon when Xenophon's five thousand returned to the ford, dusty and grinning at their success. They were greeted with cheering by the camp followers, with clusters forming around them and hands patting at backs and helmets. The relief was palpable in that place. The camp followers had watched their protectors racing away in two directions, leaving them alone on a hostile field for the first time since Cunaxa.

Xenophon learned the Spartans had made it across without real opposition, then cleared the bank of anyone foolish enough to stand against them. Banners littered the ground on the other side, where they had been thrown down. As he peered across the waters, Xenophon could see the path

Chrisophus had taken by the trail of bodies he had left. He set his jaw, wondering where the Spartan had gone. The plan had been to secure the crossing point and then wait for him to bring the camp followers safely over. The enemy had too many cavalry to be contained.

Xenophon shuddered as he walked into the torrent, reaching down to gather a handful of freezing water and rub it over his face. He was dismayed Chrisophus had not remained. He had to remind himself that he trusted the Spartan, even more after the mountains of the Carduchi than before. If Chrisophus had decided to leave the area of the ford, there would have been a good reason.

A dozen hoplites stood in the flow to mark the ford's course. With gestures and calls of encouragement, they shepherded the camp followers over, all the while keeping a close eye for any sudden appearance of horsemen or archers. Xenophon's five thousand had gone across first in a great rush, then secured the area while the rest stumbled and carried each other over.

Xenophon remained in the ford, though his legs grew numb. He had meant to stand there for just a short time, but hundreds of them thanked him as they drew abreast, calling blessings on his head until he was almost dazed with their praise for delivering them. It was not as if he'd had a choice.

When they were all safely across, he formed the hoplites around them once more. The sides of the square were thin without Chrisophus, but Xenophon marched them uphill away from the river, seeing the other side of the plain for the first time while standing on it.

Regiments of the Persian vassals stood motionless on the crests of low hills, not far from where Xenophon rested the square. He saw some of the foot soldiers he had marked from the other side, still in position. They had taken high ground and decided to hold it, regardless of any ruses or games the Greeks played on the other side. He watched as a small square moved up the hillside to where they stood. He knew those men instantly and his heart swelled with pride and concern.

As a crawling insect might show its carapace, the Spartans suddenly glittered gold. The entire force raised shields, overlapping against a black rain of spears and arrows from above. This was war as they knew it and Xenophon ordered a steady march towards that point. The enemy would not know how many of his square were untrained men and women. They would see only a massed advance. He smiled at the thought, feeling weariness lift away.

As he marched, Xenophon realised the plain was far emptier than before. Vast numbers of cavalry seemed to have vanished. Banners lay abandoned all along the river bank, too many for even Spartans to have cut down. The signs were of an enemy abandoning the field. He dared not hope.

Those who remained were in islands on ridges and hills. They had seemed well placed before, but with so many having fled, the positions looked isolated.

As he watched, the Spartans gained the plateau or ridge, forcing their way through the enemy as if they were eating a leaf, bite by bite. Xenophon saw black figures beginning to stream down the sides in every direction. He had seen a mass of baby spiders disturbed once, when a child poked it. This reminded him of that, with crawling soldiers scrambling to get away from the gold shields and the red cloaks.

The winter days were short and it was not long before the sun was a line of brass along the horizon. Chrisophus came down from the ridge he had won, his men carrying all the baggage of the army that had abandoned it in chaos. They learned from prisoners that the leader who had fled the field was the Armenian satrap, Tiribazus, a childhood friend of the Persian king. It was a friendship that had cost the man a fortune. Chrisophus brought Xenophon a chest, carried by the two brothers who had discovered the ford. It was full of silver coins, the pay for all the mercenaries Tiribazus had assembled.

'Most of them vanished, but those on the hill stayed in place,' Chrisophus said. 'I made a decision to see what could keep them there, while all the rest ran.'

'The right decision,' Xenophon confirmed, absolving the man.

Chrisophus bowed his head, relieved. He had been worried Xenophon would berate him for abandoning the camp followers.

That night, Xenophon gathered the captains and raised cups of looted wine. The camp of Satrap Tiribazus had been full of food and drink. The Greeks enjoyed a great feast, and on the plain, huge bonfires were made from spears and bows, crackling like laughter.

31

They marched away from the mountains for thirty miles over two days, a gentle pace that suited the camp followers. They rested by the source of the river Tigris and then went sixty miles further, to the banks of the flowing Teleboas. They saw no soldiers in that time and the land they passed through contained villages and towns, even a palace that belonged to the satrap. There was no sign of Tiribazus in the area, so they contented themselves looting his treasury. The Greeks picked up carts and mules and slaves once more wherever they came across them. The carts in particular were soon heavily laden. Xenophon made no attempt to restrain their acquisitions. They passed temples to strange foreign gods, where pilgrims had left offerings for centuries. Those offerings went with the Greeks as they moved on.

The winter deepened as they drifted north, settling into a routine as they walked day after day through landscapes that varied from dark tilled fields, to forest or vineyards in neat rows on the hillsides. Friendships were formed and broken on the long march, with a dozen marriages celebrated. Xenophon had his private doubts as to how many of those would last, but those who made the vows seemed happy enough and it gave them all a brief moment of happiness.

For the rest, the labour of moving their bodies across the face of the world wore them down. Every man hacked his beard away in clumps by then, if he bothered at all. They washed as often as they could, but when they shed the ragged clothes, it was to reveal bodies so thin they could tell every bone. They took all the food they found, but it was never enough.

Over a long stretch of sixty miles and four days through sand dunes, Xenophon found himself walking close to Pallakis and Hephaestus. They strolled side by side and he thought they looked like lovers. It was hard to be sure. He had felt her eyes on him a thousand times, burning away from the crowd. He'd wanted her to wait for him, to be ready for the day he did not have so many souls on his shoulders. It was he who had told Hephaestus to keep her safe! He had been stronger then, somehow, too distracted by all those who needed him. As he walked along, with the ground rising ahead, he could not help stealing glances at her, telling himself it was no more frequent than it might have been with any other woman. He had the sense that she knew he was doing it, however. Women often did know, when men were struck by their beauty and tried not to stare.

He shook himself, imagining how Socrates would laugh when he heard. All men are fools in love, he'd say. Wine existed for that very reason.

There was a commotion ahead, dragging Xenophon away from his musings. He squinted into a weak winter sun to where his scouts had gone further on, climbing a slope to look for the best way forward. At a distance of some twelve hundred paces, they were small figures, though the sight of them was a cold hand in Xenophon's chest. He watched as they jumped and waved their arms. Was it an attack? He looked round, seeing afresh how ragged his people had become. They had been marching so long they no longer looked like an army, so much as an exodus of some nomadic people. He began to prepare orders, looking for Chrisophus, yet as he did so he saw a number further up had run forward, called by the scouts to see. They too began to shout

and wave and he could hear their voices, crying, '*Thalassa!*
Thalassa!' – the sea. The sea.

Xenophon dropped the pack from his shoulders and ran
to the crest of the hill with hundreds more, as the shouts
grew and grew before him. The sea. They had dreamed it
from the deserts. Ahead of them were Greek settlements,
Greek cities, above all, Greek ships to carry them anywhere
they wanted to go. Xenophon saw men and women fall to
their knees and just weep, covering their faces in the crooks
of their arms as they sobbed in relief. He stood, stunned, as
men and women pressed him into embraces, thanking him
for all he had done, for saving them. He felt tears streaming
down his face and he wiped at his eyes, trying to recover his
composure.

'Here! Bring him to the general!' Xenophon heard, so that
he turned his head to see a shepherd boy being ushered to
his presence. The boy looked Greek, but when he spoke in
that language, Xenophon gave a great cry of joy that spread
through all those crowding around that place.

'I am a free Greek,' the boy said. 'Oldest son of Lycus. You
may not take me prisoner.'

Xenophon shook his head.

'You are safe, with all your goats, I promise you. But tell
me of Greece. What news of Athens? We have been away for
over a year, boy. Does she stand?'

The boy stared around at the wild-looking men and
women, all watching him in something like wonder.

'She stands, sir. The orator Polyemis was put to death, as
was Socrates. The council has rebuilt the city wall the Spartans pulled down – and repaired the temples on the Acropolis.
Do not think we are some backwater here, sir! We are Greeks
as good as you, one of the thousand cities, as if we had our
walls in Arcadia or Thessaly.'

The boy beamed as he proved his knowledge, though the expression faded as he took in Xenophon's wide eyes and sick pallor.

'Sir? Have I given some offence?'

'No, boy. You said Socrates has been put to death?'

'Oh, did you know of him, sir? It was a famous trial. They said he did not believe in the gods – and that the young of Athens preferred to hear him speak than to work. They offered him banishment or silence, and the old fool chose death instead! He was allowed to take poison, sir. Now, Polyemis was a different matter, so my father said. He . . .'

Xenophon turned away from the garrulous boy and pushed through the crowd. For a time, he felt completely blank with sorrow, as if no thoughts could reach him. He had come such a long way and learned so many things. If Socrates was not there to hear them . . . He found himself weeping and this time made no attempt to hide the tears. He sat on his own, away from the joyous crowd, apart from them in all ways.

After a time, he heard footsteps and opened his eyes, raising his head from where it rested on his arms. He had expected Chrisophus, but it was Pallakis who had come. He looked up at her with eyes made red and sore, his cheeks pale.

'I wish you could have known him,' Xenophon said. 'He was a great man, truly, a rare man. Yet I don't think he ever wrote anything down! Can you believe that? What are words? In a century, he will be forgotten. There are no statues to Socrates. Men will never even know he lived.'

'Perhaps you could write what you remember,' she said. 'I imagine he would trust you to do it. It's clear enough you loved him.'

She sat down at his side and Xenophon struggled with a wave of grief that made him want to turn to her and bury his face in her shoulder. He resisted that urge, feeling his will return. She was not his, though he considered that she had come to his side. Perhaps his cause was not hopeless after all.

'What will you do now?' she asked. 'We have silver and gold. Will you share it out with the men? Or . . .'

He blinked as an idea came to him. In a moment, he had put his grief somewhere deeper down, to be examined later. He would toast Socrates in wine and the written word, he swore it, but there was a chance in that moment for something even greater.

Xenophon rubbed his hands over his face and returned to the group. He saw Chrisophus wore an expression of honest pity, but he rejected it, calling the man away from the rest.

'Officers to me!' Xenophon called across their heads. 'Captains, pentekosters, generals. Hephaestus, you too, if you would.'

They gathered quickly enough and he led them apart along the hillside, until he came to an olive tree clinging to the sand, grown from a seed that might have blown halfway across the world. He patted the trunk, his thoughts aflight.

'Gentlemen, this tree came from far away – and put down roots here. Like the Greeks on the shore of the sea before us, we have the seed of a city here. Look at all those we have brought to this place! We have soldiers and women, children and slaves. We have gold and silver and men of skills and craft. We have everything we need to begin a city of Greece in this land. Here. Would you see us scattered to the four winds, after everything we have been through? I tell you I feel a greater sense of brotherhood with you – and with those others – than anything I knew before. Is there one of you who can't say exactly the same? Yet if we return, it will be to old lives and old concerns. Why not be the seed of a state instead? A new nation. Our children might inherit an empire from what we decide here. Why not? Our whole concern has been to survive and to reach this place. Now we are here, now we know it can be done, why not build? We are enough to raise walls and homes in a valley by a river.'

He looked at Chrisophus, watching him intently.

'We can be another Sparta, another Thebes. If we choose a river running to the coast, we can be another Athens. Perhaps we'll sail there in ships we have made ourselves.'

'Would you lead us, if we choose to stay?' Chrisophus said, gently.

Xenophon returned his gaze without wavering.

'If you wish it, if you would have me, yes, I would. It would be the honour and the greater purpose of my life. I thought it was to bring you safe to this place, but perhaps this is just the beginning.'

Chrisophus nodded.

'We will have to ask the others,' he said. 'You understand a decision like this cannot be made without a discussion.'

'Yes . . . of course . . .'

Xenophon trailed off, looking over the sand to where the sea shimmered. He felt it as an ache, but in Athens, who would he be? Not the man who had saved them. No, he would once more be unknown, no more popular than he had been before. Without Socrates to visit, the city of his birth was no longer his home.

'Choose carefully, Chrisophus, please. This is the only chance we will ever have to do this. We are all Greeks, my friend. Only we could even consider it.'

They remained in that place, with the sea glittering in the distance, for three days. Xenophon waited for them to reach a conclusion. He answered any questions they had for him, as honestly as he could. In the end, they sent Chrisophus himself to deliver the verdict and Xenophon did not know if that was good or bad.

His stomach felt light and nervous as he stood to greet the Spartan. Chrisophus came right up to him and rested a hand on the shoulder of the Athenian nobleman who had brought them safe across an empire.

'I'm sorry, Xenophon. We just want to go home.'

Xenophon felt it as a knife between his ribs, a sudden pain that brought tears to his eyes. He dipped his head, clearing his throat and realising he was trembling.

'Of course, I . . . Very well, my friend. You'll have to share out the gold and silver between them. It should be enough to make a good settlement, enough at least not to starve until they can find work.'

'Will you not be with us?' Chrisophus said.

His eyes were dark with grief and Xenophon knew it was an ending between them. He shook his head.

'No, I don't think so. I inherited a little land in the Peloponnesus, not far outside Sparta. There is an estate manager who breeds horses for me. I'm sure he thinks he owns the place, after so long. No, Chrisophus, I will not stay. I am not good at farewells, my friend. I will make my own way back there. Perhaps in time, you will seek me out and bring a flask of wine with you. I would . . . like that.'

Chrisophus took his hand and gripped it.

'I give you my word, strategos,' he said. 'And my thanks. I will see you again, I promise. We will raise a cup then, to all we did here – and to absent friends.'

'We did it, Spartan,' Xenophon said, smiling through eyes that gleamed with tears. It was enough. Without another word, he clapped Chrisophus on the shoulder and set off down the hill with a light step, heading towards the sea.

Historical Note

Xenophon's book *Anabasis*, published as *The Persian Exped-ition* in Penguin Classics, is roughly translated as 'the way up'. It is the story of Prince Cyrus' rebellion against his brother, the army he raised, the battle of Cunaxa he fought and lost – and then the appalling situation in which the Greek mercenaries found themselves. They were far from home, surrounded by enemies, but still such an elite fighting force that they could not easily be destroyed. It takes place eighty years after Thermopylae and some seventy years before Alexander the Great.

Persian historical context: King Darius of Persia invaded Greece in 490 BC – and was beaten at Marathon. He was gathering another army to try again when he died, so it was his son Xerxes who came by land and sea. Xerxes is the king the Spartans fought at Thermopylae. He actually reached and burned Athens, but the Athenian navy won an extraordinary battle against his fleet, reducing his ability to manoeuvre. Xerxes ran for home, leaving his general Mardonius to face a Spartan-led army on land. Despite being hugely outnumbered, the Greeks slaughtered the enemy – and Xerxes was killed by his own bodyguard in 465 BC. His son Artaxerxes became king and had the sense to leave the Greeks alone, enjoying a peaceful reign until his death around 424 BC.

That King Artaxerxes had three sons. The oldest became king for a few weeks before he was murdered by a second – who was then killed by the third: Darius II. Darius II had two sons – Artaxerxes and Cyrus, which is where this story begins.

In Greece, Sparta came to dominate the thousand cities, defeating Athens and imposing a Spartan council to rule there, known as the Thirty. Young Xenophon was an Athenian nobleman who admired the Spartans more than his own argumentative Athenians, who could find a dozen opposing views in a decision to eat dinner or see a play. Xenophon was a student of Socrates, it is true, but unlike the more famous student, Plato, his interest was less in existential concepts, or the perfect society, than in the practical application of philosophy. Xenophon was one of those Athenians who tried to create a good life through sheer will, who wanted to know how to live. He found Spartan discipline and self-sacrifice admirable, so that he was always a man torn between two cultures.

Note on distance. Persians of the period tended to use 'parasang' as a unit of time, which was often somewhat confusingly used as a measure of distance as well, in Greek texts. A modern equivalent would be 'It's an hour away'. Herodotus estimated the parasang as roughly thirty 'stades' or 3.5–3.75 miles. I have left some mentions of miles in the text, to give readers who do not think in parasangs and stades a clearer idea of the distances involved. A 'stathmos' was also not a precise distance, but roughly the length of road between stopping places, so around eighteen or twenty miles. On his way east, Cyrus is recorded as marching his men between twenty-two and twenty-four miles a day – some seven hours on the road, including stops. That is a pace equivalent to that of the later Roman legions, and good going in great heat. It

426

is interesting to compare the distances recorded by Xeno-phon later on, when they have camp followers. Then, fifteen miles a day was more usual. The effect of the need to stop at every river to replenish water becomes obvious.

The events in Cilicia with Queen Epyaxa – where she brought funds to Cyrus after he was cut off, and then stayed the night with him – is a fascinating incident. I wish we knew more, but Xenophon is the only source. He described a mock charge put on to impress the queen, a charge that acciden-tally routed a part of Cyrus' own native forces, when they saw it coming. He also describes a longer meeting, involving her husband King Syennesis in Tarsus, chiefly interesting as the birthplace of Saul of Tarsus in a later century, who would become St Paul.

The difficulty with such detailed historical accounts is that they are impossible to fit into a novel. Xenophon might describe a skirmish on a hill in three lines; I could not do it in less than a chapter. For the details I could not fit in here, I recommend *The Persian Expedition*, particularly to any reader interested in how the Greeks thought and acted. It deserves to have survived over two thousand years. Sometimes, as I found with *The Secret History of the Mongols*, one key book can be the doorway to a world.

Xenophon gives the army of Cyrus as a hundred thousand, but the army of Artaxerxes as 1.2 million, with two hundred scythed chariots and six thousand cavalry. It is impossible to know if those numbers were exaggerated, though I've gone with a lesser estimate of around six hundred thousand men – still a vast number that made the hordes of Genghis Khan look small.

Four commanders led the Persian army: Abrocomas, Tissaphernes, Gobrias and Arbaces. Apart from Tissaphernes, I have not made much of these, for fear of losing the reader with too many unfamiliar names. My aim is to tell the story. As E. L. Doctorow said, 'The historian will tell you what happened. The novelist will tell you what it felt like.' My intention here, of course, was to do both.

On that subject, the mutiny that General Clearchus handled was described by Xenophon in some detail. It was around the time the column discovered who they were really facing – something that might have been known to the generals, but not the common soldiers. Clearchus wept in front of them and indulged in some interesting theatrics. He said they forced him to betray the prince, but that he would never abandon them.

In historical fiction, the writer looks for key relationships, so to read that Clearchus sent a messenger back to Cyrus, telling him not to worry, indicates a true friendship. The Spartan argued and persuaded to bring them back on side, appealing to emotion and duty – and finally arranging a 50 per cent pay increase for each man, which did the trick.

The battle of Cunaxa comes from one source – the description by Xenophon as an eye witness. His personal account comes with one mention of himself, in the third person, where he exchanges a few words with Prince Cyrus before the battle is joined. We cannot know if that scene took place, or was a device to place Xenophon in the narrative.

Prince Cyrus sent the Greeks in, but they were bogged down by the sheer number of soldiers they faced. Tissaphernes had convinced King Artaxerxes to gather a host – so perhaps the entire enterprise was always doomed. It is hard to say. It is always possible for a prince or a king to stop an arrow, of course. Perhaps the wonder of leaders who took part in battles, like Caesar and Genghis, is that they survived so many brushes with death.

Cyrus saw the battle could be won with a single blow. He and his personal guard rode across the face of the approaching armies in what seems now to be a wild gamble. He reached his brother and injured him, but was struck down by a thrown javelin. It is tempting to think his was a great life unlived – that this was one of those moments in history when a dynasty might have reached greatness but was cut down. It would not be too many years before Alexander the Great's army looted those Achaemenid tombs. The Greek king might have treated the land of Cyrus with more respect, perhaps.

Xenophon described the prince having his head raised on a spear and paraded as proof he was dead. The great size of the battlefield is demonstrated in what followed. King Artaxerxes rode for some way with his grisly trophy. Meanwhile, Clearchus and the Greeks still had no idea Cyrus had fallen. They continued to cut a swathe through the enemy and believed they had won. News of the true situation came slowly to both sides – and the Greeks suddenly realised they were in a lot of trouble. The native army brought to Cunaxa by Prince Cyrus was pulled away by General Ariaeus. This seems to have been a reasonable attempt to remain alive, though it left the ten thousand Greek allies completely exposed. Only the extraordinary superiority of those soldiers kept them alive. In scenes reminiscent of Leonidas at Thermopylae, they could march through enemy formations and come out unscathed. The Persians were simply not their match, in tactics or armour or discipline. It led to the oddest scenes, where the Greeks were vastly outnumbered, but could still go wherever they wanted to.

Part Two begins with an extraordinary situation. The Greeks gathered in their camp, so in all were roughly ten thousand soldiers and as many camp followers. They were over a thousand miles from Greece and without support, food or water. I omitted the argument when the Persians ordered the Greeks to surrender their arms. The Greeks pointed out that either they were allies, in which case they were more valuable with weapons – or they were enemies, in which case they would need their weapons even more. Either way, they would not be giving them up. It is just one example of Greek logic and stubbornness that is a hallmark of the society of the time.

I did include an exchange where the Greeks were told it would be war if they moved, truce if they stayed in one place. In reply, they said they understood, but they repeated the terms in such a way that they seemed a threat: 'Truce if we remain, war if we go forward or backward.' The confidence of elite soldiers shines through twenty-five centuries.

I have compressed the last month for Clearchus before his death, aged around fifty. The truce he negotiated with Tissaphernes involved days of nothing happening at all. Other Greeks urged Clearchus to make a break for it, but he refused. He was acutely aware that he had no cavalry to speak of – and that the Persian king had vast numbers of horsemen and chariots to run them down.

Rather than an immediate betrayal, as I have written it here, Tissaphernes escorted the Greeks away from Cunaxa for many days, allowing them to take food but not slaves as they found villages. The Greeks even passed a Persian army still on its way to the battle, having missed all of it. Suspicion grew between the two sides, but Clearchus was revealed as a wonderful leader of men at this last stage. I could not give more than a flavour of it here.

Tissaphernes persuaded Clearchus to attend a supper with five generals and some twenty captains as well as a couple of hundred other soldiers to gather provisions. Inside the tent, they were all seized and killed. One dying man made it back to the main camp and the treachery was revealed.

The Greeks ran to arms and Ariaeus and others approached to tell them the news and demand surrender. The immediate danger of bloodshed dwindled as the night wore on. After all, the Greeks had been made leaderless. Who was left who could command?

I changed the name of the Spartan who helped Xenophon at a crucial juncture – he is recorded as Chirisophus, but 'Chrisophus' looked better to my eye. Trivial, but a choice rather than an error. He must have been an interesting man, as Chirisophus guided the crowd in their acceptance of Xenophon. Perhaps Chirisophus might have taken overall command himself, but Xenophon had spoken first. It was Xenophon's idea to make a square within a square, Xenophon who saw that the lack of cavalry was the biggest tactical problem. In short, Xenophon was the one who knew how to lead in a crisis. It is a testament to them all that the murder of the Greek generals did not destroy morale. They elected new leaders as soon as they heard – and they did not trust the Persians ever again.

The story of Xenophon chasing up a hill with his men to overlook an ambush is from the original account. As Xenophon urged them on in heroic terms, a man named Soteridas said, 'We are not equal. You are on horseback! I am exhausting myself carrying a shield.' In a temper, Xenophon took the shield from him and ran with it, while others pelted the man with stones.

The embattled Greeks shed their Persian pursuers only when they entered the mountains of the Carduchi – or Kardoukhoi. The story of a vast Persian army entering those mountains and being slaughtered is from Xenophon's account, though there is no way to confirm it. This is the first mention of the Carduchi anywhere. It is possible that they are the ancestors of modern Kurds in northern Iraq, Iran and Syria. Xenophon described villages, animal husbandry and agriculture – as well as a ruthless and implacable enemy who was the master of difficult terrain. It took seven days to cross those mountains. Xenophon's account of fighting hilltop to hilltop and how the Greeks countered their advantages is extraordinary.

After the fight to get across the river, the journey through western Armenia in winter is brutal. They experience heavy snowfall, with frostbite, loss of toes and snow-blindness. Men died every night and the entire enterprise was on its last legs, defeated not by an enemy, but by worse cold than they had ever encountered. Xenophon's advice to prevent snow-blindness by keeping something black in front of the eyes is fascinating. He describes soldiers who sat down in the snow and would not go on, so were left to die. Some asked to be killed. Only the threat of an enemy force behind roused them to action.

They travelled fifteen miles a day for around two hundred miles further. It is then that the most famous scene of

Xenophon's account occurs, when the forward scouts sight a coast they know contains Greek settlements and shout '*Thalatta! Thalatta!*' – the sea, the sea. The emphasis is on the first syllable and though Xenophon recorded it in Athenian Greek as *Thalatta*, I prefer the alternative dialect version of *Thalassa*. The Greeks embraced each other with tears in their eyes. They had found the way home at last.

In Xenophon's account, the journey does not actually end at that point, but continues the travelogue through the country of the Macronians, where they see off some local warriors. After that, they walked to Trapezus – a Greek city where they rested for about thirty days and held sporting events – wrestling and boxing, sprints and long-distance running. It would have been there that Xenophon heard Socrates had been executed, a man who chose death over banishment, saying, 'The unexamined life is not worth knowing.' It is true Socrates wrote nothing down – all we know of him comes from Xenophon and Plato, his students.

The Greeks took warships at Trapezus and went on plundering expeditions, determined to leave the coast with as much as they could carry. Xenophon's share allowed him to buy an estate on the road from Sparta to Olympia, where he wrote most of this story.

I have cut out the aftermath of seeing the sea, as it was essentially an anti-climax. However, I had to include Xenophon's idea of founding a city – and the fact that after all they had gone through together, the Greeks turned his offer down. It seemed the natural end to this extraordinary event – the march of ten thousand out of Persia.

Conn Iggulden, 2017